EMBRACING
MIDNIGHT

EMBRACING MIDNIGHT

DEVYN QUINN

APHRODISIA
KENSINGTON BOOKS
http://www.kensingtonbooks.com

APHRODISIA BOOKS are published by

Kensington Publishing Corp.
850 Third Avenue
New York, NY 10022

All Kensington titles, imprints and distributed lines are available at special quantity discounts for bulk purchases for sales promotions, premiums, fund-raising, and educational or institutional use.

Special book excerpts or customized printings can also be created to fit specific needs. For details, write or phone the office of the Kensington Special Sales Manager: Kensington Publishing Corp., 850 Third Avenue, New York, NY 10022. Attn: Special Sales Department. Phone: 1-800-221-2647.

Aphrodisia and the A logo Reg. U.S. Pat & TM Off.

ISBN-13: 978-0-7582-1654-0
ISBN-10: 0-7582-1654-8

First Kensington Trade Paperback Printing: December 2008

10 9 8 7 6 5 4 3 2 1

Printed in the United States of America

To Tammy Batchelor, who taught me the meaning of
"applying self to chair."*

*Translation: Who wouldn't let me rent movies unless
I finished the damn book.

1

Literally and figuratively, Iollan Drake had given feds the finger. And that was pissing Callie Whitten off. Time and time again the outlaw she was supposed to be tracking had turned the tables, dodging the night's stakeout. Despite her team's best efforts, Drake always seemed to be one step ahead.

"Maybe tomorrow." Muttering under her breath, Callie reached out and punched the call button for the elevator. Bone tired, she checked the clock in the lobby. Three thirty in the morning. Too late to be out, and too early to get up. A little groan escaped her lips. Goddamn. Another day gone and agents still weren't any closer to cornering their quarry. Drake's talent for appearing and disappearing seemingly at will was puzzling—and enviable.

Gaze dropping, Callie caught a brief glimpse of her face in the shiny doors. A thatch of messy blond hair ruled over bloodshot, kohl-lined eyes, painted cheeks, and a mouth slashed with crimson. A figure-shaping bustier, leather miniskirt, laced leather wrist cuffs, and Victorian-style boots completed her outfit.

The image didn't match the woman inside, which was part of the reason the bureau had picked her for this assignment. Her ability to change from grunge to glam in the blink of an eye meant she was able to work most any type of undercover operation. Her lack of a husband and children was another. Callie was one of the few female agents ready to pack and leave on ten minutes' notice.

Where the hell was the elevator? The only thing she wanted right now was a hot shower and cool sheets, and that was taking far too long in arriving.

Losing patience, Callie burrowed inside her purse for a cigarette. With her nerves on the edge of frayed, quitting was not an option. A shot of nicotine would help her relax. Extracting a cigarette from a crumpled pack, she put it between her lips.

A man stepped up, his shoulder lightly brushing hers. Engrossed in her search, she hadn't even noticed his arrival.

"Allow me, please."

His voice snapped her flagging senses to attention. Touched with an Irish brogue, his voice was familiar. Dangerously familiar.

Callie gasped. The man beside her was so drop-dead gorgeous her heart skipped a beat. His presence, so riskily close, heated her skin as heavy awareness pulsed through her veins.

Iollan Drake. In the flesh. Right here. Right now.

All lean muscle and sinew, the outlaw was stunning. Thick hair brushed his brow. An unusual shade best described as pearlescent smoke, it settled in tousled layers around his chiseled face. Deep-set eyes, wide strong nose, and an absolutely sensual mouth ruled over a jaw brushed with stubble. Narrow hips and long legs were hugged by a tight pair of boot-cut Levi's. A calf-length denim duster and polished black boots finished his sleek but casual style.

Drake looked devastating, much more appealing in person

than the blurry photos she'd studied before joining the investigation. Solid, lean, and muscular, he was handsome in an unusual, edgy sort of way. His features weren't perfect, but were arranged in such a way as to make him striking enough to countenance a second—and third—look. The top button of his creamy silk shirt was undone, and below his beltline was a suggestive bulge she couldn't possibly miss even if she'd wanted to.

Swallowing the lump in her throat, Callie tugged the cigarette from her mouth. Numb fingers curled around the fragile paper cylinder, crushing it. "No thanks. I changed my mind." She dumped the remnants into the nearby receptacle, dusting off bits of lingering tobacco. "I'm trying to quit. That oral thing, you know—"

Pocketing his lighter, the outlaw smiled. The lithe way he moved compelled attention. "I understand. It's a difficult habit to break." Eyes a woman could drown in raked her body. Easily his most striking feature, the irises were a brilliant shade of copper, the pupils not quite round but slightly oval. Odd, but strangely attractive. "I'm glad I caught you, though. I was afraid you'd gotten away from me."

Gotten away?

Blindsided, Callie made a grab for her wits. She gave her head a shake to clear it. "I didn't know you were looking for me." *Holy shit.* Had the criminal pegged her as a federal agent? Self-preservation conflicted with the need to remain cool. Whatever move he might make, she needed to be ready to counter without hesitation. Her mind sidetracked to the fact that she was unarmed and had no backup whatsoever. Being caught alone with a sex trafficker and suspected killer wasn't exactly an appealing thought.

He visually explored her, eyes lingering on her breasts pushed high and plump by her form-shaping bustier, then moving back up to her face. "I'm always looking, Calista."

She resisted the urge to fidget. He didn't act the least bit hostile, dangerous, or savage. Loose and relaxed, his face reflected nothing more than friendly interest. "How do you know my name?"

His eyes skimmed over her again. "The tag you're wearing," he said in the accent sprinkled with a dusting of leprechauns and blarney. "That's your name, I assume."

His brash attitude shot through Callie like a bolt of electricity and her cheeks heated. Her ability for thinking fast on her feet seemed to have vanished. Calista wasn't her real name, but close enough that she remembered to answer to it. Her cover as a waitress at Hell-Bound Train, the Goth club Drake frequented, gave her access to all areas of the club.

"Um, yes, it is. I usually don't have men following me home from work just to ask about it though."

"When I notice a beautiful woman, I want to know more about her." His comeback was smooth, a heart-stopping flash of charm.

Callie tried to detour around the remark. "I didn't even think you'd glanced twice at me."

He smiled. "Oh, I glanced. More than once, I assure you." He stepped closer, holding out his hand. "And in case you want to know whom your stalker is this evening, my name is Iollan Drake."

As if she didn't already know.

To be polite, Callie accepted his offering. Long graceful fingers curled around hers. His grip was sure, strong, and firm. Much to her surprise he hadn't pronounced his name the way it was spelled, *ill-an,* but had used a soft "y" instead, *you-lan.* She liked the sound of it better. Suddenly, coming from the lips of its owner, it was personal—belonging to more than the ink on a dry dossier.

"Unusual name." Feeling his skin against hers, a thrill wove its way through her veins and her body temperature inched

EMBRACING MIDNIGHT / 5

higher. If she let him, he'd easily seduce her with his laid-back manner and obvious charm. That was his goal, no doubt. She hoped he didn't feel the tremble in her hand.

"Around here, yes. But I've had it all my life, so I'm used to it."

She grasped for an intelligent rejoinder and came up dry. "I guess you already know my name."

"I do." His grip tightened subtly. "And the pleasure is entirely mine."

Flustered, Callie drew back her hand. She'd bet dollars to donuts this man didn't have a problem charming women. His leading-man good looks and easy manner made him seem too good to be true. Were she not aiming to put him behind bars, she'd have been more than happy to be the object of his attention.

"Thanks."

He let her hand go with seeming reluctance. "You're most welcome." The flash of white teeth revealed an alluring dimple.

Callie inwardly groaned. She loved dimples, would love to plant a soft kiss right at the corner of his fine mouth.

Swallowing over the lump in her throat, she took a step back. Widening the distance. She didn't know what his motives were, but she suspected he was looking for something more than a late-night diversion.

"Well," she said. "I guess I should get going."

His eyes clouded, then just as quickly cleared. "I don't suppose there's any chance I might get you to join me for a cup of coffee. It's late, I know, and I probably haven't got any right to ask."

She forced a casual shrug. "No harm in asking."

"Any chance I'll get an answer?"

Callie stared into his expressive face. Her training as an agent had taught her to delve past words and study body language. His unexpected appearance notwithstanding, nothing in

Drake's manner hinted of intimidation. Trying to pick up a woman he'd seen in a bar was typical male behavior, partly opportunistic and partly sincere.

Except picking up women wasn't his hobby. Flesh peddling was his profession. Then it dawned on her. He didn't see her as a threat but as a potential victim. Callie wasn't one to flinch from the demands her job placed on her, but the idea of being alone with this man made her stomach clench. Not from fear. *Desire.*

The minefield she'd unexpectedly walked into was getting tricky. One false step and the situation could blow up in her face. She considered brushing him off, then quickly realized that wasn't an option. She had to continue to play her role.

Backed into a corner, she made a play for a little more time to think. "I, ah, I'm not sure."

Amused, his eyes crinkled at the edges, a hint of mischief woven with longing. "Perhaps you could use some help making up your mind."

Giving no warning, Drake bridged the brief distance separating them. The air sizzled as his strong hands slid over her hips.

A strong sensual tug filled her. "What—" Callie started to protest, but he gave her no chance to continue. His mouth descended, forcible and warm, branding her in a way promising pleasure if only she'd submit. She was surprised at the sense of strength emanating from him. Arousal—unexpected, potent, and definitely forbidden—reared its head, delivering a thrilling hum that stretched all the way to her toes. Physical tension ratcheted up. He was good. Better than good. Superb.

A shudder ran through her. Instead of pulling back, Callie opened her mouth, allowing him to deepen the kiss. He stroked her tongue with his in a manner making it clear he'd also like to claim her.

A soft moan escaped her. Ropes of desire tangled around her

whole body as the heat from his palms seeped through her tight leather skirt. Her skin crackled with the electricity of his touch. Heart pounding, she felt her nipples harden. She'd played scenes with Drake in her mind a thousand times, and not once had she ever imagined herself as a target of his seduction.

Without warning, the elevator clamored open, expelling a couple of early-morning joggers. Disconcerted, Callie took a hasty step back, breaking their passionate embrace. The pair bustled by, heads turned and eyebrows notched in disapproval.

She ducked her head, swiping at her tingling lips in embarrassment. She'd lost her head, briefly succumbing to the excitement his kiss stirred inside her. No telling what would have happened if they hadn't been interrupted. "I guess they didn't approve."

"Seems like." Amusement danced in his eyes. "What about you? Not convincing enough?"

Think criminal, she reminded herself as a guard against his colossal appeal. "One kiss isn't anything special."

She started to reach for the elevator's call button, but his light touch on her arm stopped her hand in midair. "I'd like it to be."

As her scalp prickled deliciously, her inner mercury shot up another notch, into the red zone. She'd have to tread carefully to stay one step ahead. "This is moving a little fast. I wasn't expecting you to walk into my life tonight."

A touch of wryness brushed his expression. "This wasn't quite how I'd planned to ask you to spend a little time with me." His hand slid down her arm, his fingers finding hers. "Or maybe it was."

His words stroked the hunger deep inside her. "Sounds like you know exactly what you want."

"I do." He leaned in, an inch or two closer. "Say you will."

She hesitated. "I— I'm not sure. . . ."

His hand squeezed hers. His intimate touch reminded her all

over again of carnal hungers too long unfed. Desire became a palpable thing, creating a sheen of perspiration across her forehead and down her spine.

"It'll be good." He spoke intimately, his accented voice and entrancing copper eyes almost hypnotic. "I promise."

Of that she had no doubt. The thought of his hands exploring her naked skin sent a fresh pulse of moisture straight to her core. Callie felt as if she were burning up. His body heat seemed to enter through her lips and spread through her veins like molten lava.

Mind reeling, she pursed dry lips. The more she resisted, the harder he was going to try. "The least I can do is offer you a cup of coffee."

Drake's smile didn't ease her tension. "That's a start."

Thoughts tumbling through her mind, Callie eyed him like one would a cobra; beautiful, mesmerizing, and absolutely lethal. Iollan Drake was suspected of kidnapping women with cold-blooded regularity, then selling them into the sex trade. Two far more experienced agents pursuing the human trafficking ring Drake operated had lost their lives.

She shivered. She'd been instructed to take whatever steps were necessary to gain his trust, be it by hook or crook. Her superiors hadn't suggested using her own shapely ass. Dedicated to catching the bad guys, she'd never in her wildest fantasies thought of having sex with one. How far she intended to go, she didn't dare to imagine. At the moment only one thing was for sure.

The night was about to heat up.

2

They rode up the elevator to Callie's apartment in silence. As she eased open the door and snapped on a nearby lamp, apprehension warred with lust. She couldn't help but look forward to the few hours they might share, though she knew she was walking a thin line. Shivering, she let out a slow breath. *You're getting in deep.*

Stepping inside the narrow foyer, Iollan Drake squeezed past her. His body brushed hers, his hands lingering a second longer than necessary on her hips. "Excuse me."

"No problem." Though it only lasted a moment, it was enough to set Callie afire. Her heart raced, and her sexual senses were attuned to his masculine strength. Every beat inside her chest made her that much more aware this was a man she deeply desired.

She almost sighed with relief when he stepped back and slid off his coat. His tall frame seemed to fill every inch around her, hammering home his very presence. Did he know how aroused she was? Six months had passed since a man had touched her in an intimate way.

Oblivious to her thoughts, he glanced around for a place to hang his duster.

"Let me." She hung his coat on the rack beside the door.

"Thanks."

"You're welcome." Callie debated whether or not to lock them in. After a moment's hesitation, she slid the dead bolt into place. There'd be no going back, no changing her mind.

"I'll make coffee," she said, leading the way into the living room. The apartment was miniscule. An open kitchen/living room arrangement branched off into a small bedroom with adjoining bathroom. The furniture was well used in a shabby chic sort of way: serviceable, but scarcely more. The next stop would be the junkyard instead of the Salvation Army. Nothing was amiss except the ashtray full of cigarette butts on the coffee table—and the dozen peach roses arranged in an exquisite crystal vase.

Seeing the flowers, Callie felt her gut spasm around the meager snack of peanuts and coffee she'd earlier consumed at the bar. They hadn't been there when she'd left this morning. Bile rose, burning the back of her throat. She didn't have to read the card tucked into the middle of the arrangement to know who'd sent them. Roger Reinke. Her current boss. And her ex-lover.

Her impromptu guest also noticed the flowers. "Special occasion?"

Callie cleared her throat. "My birthday."

An eyebrow rose. "Oh?"

"Yeah, today's my big three-oh."

He touched the delicate petals of one bloom. "From anyone special?"

"Not by a long shot." Dropping her purse, Callie plucked the small envelope from the roses. *To my best girl*, it read. There was no name. She rolled her eyes. Roger Reinke knew how to cover his tracks. The handwriting wasn't even his, but that of some female florist fulfilling the order.

She crumpled the card. She shouldn't let the gift disturb her, but it did. Now wasn't the time for Roger to try and make nice. She'd just convinced herself ending their affair was the right thing to do. Her life—and work—was much less complicated without a jealous lover.

But emptier, an inner voice pointed out.

Her sigh sounded defeated. "They're from an old boyfriend." A hairline crack opened up in her heart when she said the words. Apparently the mending was easier said than done.

Iollan raised an inquiring eyebrow. "Someone you still care about?"

Her jaw tightened. "Someone who doesn't realize it's time to let go." Knowing their breakup was necessary didn't ease her longing one bit. It only served to make her a brooding, bitter woman.

He nodded. "I see."

"No, you don't," she snapped. "You don't know anything about me or my life, so don't think what you have to say is going to help one bit."

He held up his hands as if to ward off blows. "Hey, I'm just an innocent bystander."

Callie's desire for company vanished. She'd rather be alone. If he had any grace about him, he'd take note of her sour mood and leave. Investigation or not, she had half a mind to cuff the asshole and beat him senseless. One less criminal wouldn't be missed in this world.

Come to think of it, one less man wouldn't be missed, either.

Make that *two* men.

Needing to steady herself, Callie sat down on the futon and reached for the pack of cigarettes on the coffee table. Digging a cheap plastic lighter out of her purse, she cocked her head toward the rear of the room. "There's the door. Don't let it hit you on the ass on the way out, okay?" Hand trembling, she lit her cigarette.

Goddamn men, she silently cursed. So much for remaining detached. Her composed, aloof control was crumbling with each passing second. She took a deep drag, welcoming the pacifying rush of smoke filling her lungs. The cigarette's tip glowed red before dying into ashes.

"I think the door can wait a bit longer." Instead of leaving, Iollan crossed the living room and sat down. "Something you need to talk about?"

Callie scowled her nastiest frown. Didn't this man know how to take a hint and haul ass? "No." Warning of her impatience, she flicked her cigarette toward the ashtray. She missed, and the ashes scattered to the floor. She brushed the ashes away with the tip of her shoe.

He snagged her cigarette with a deft hand. "You're getting a little irresponsible with that thing."

Callie protested. "Hey! What do you think you're doing?"

Snuffing it out, he shook his head. "You're quitting. Remember?"

Annoyance gritted her teeth. "I've decided to start again. Since I haven't got a bottle of whiskey, nicotine will have to do."

Iollan Drake leaned close, so close she could kiss him if she wanted. "This asshole ex of yours—he really broke your heart, didn't he?"

Hands clenching into fists, Callie dug her nails deeply into her palms. "It's none of your concern."

He took hold of her hand, working her fingers open until he had access to her inner palm. She tried to pull free, but he held her tighter. Not enough to hurt or threaten. Just enough to let her know he wasn't letting go. "You're wrong, love. Anything that hurts you concerns me."

She speared him with a cold emotionless glare. "As if you'd care." She twisted her wrist and he let her go. He could have restrained her, and for a moment Callie wished he would. She enjoyed that sort of thing.

"I can," he said softly. "If you'll give me a chance."

"I'll be just fine—" she started to say, but got no further. The cracks in her composure widened. Giving into the pressure building inside, she felt a tear spill down her cheek, and then a second.

Iollan's hand rose, swiping away the moist trail. "Whoever your ex-boyfriend is, he's a bloody bastard."

Callie turned her head away, blinking to clear her vision. She wiped her damp eyes, smearing her mascara. She didn't care. Right about now she was sure she looked as attractive as a puffy-eyed raccoon.

Squaring her shoulders, she tried for cool and unemotional. "I'm being stupid about it, too. He's married, and he didn't make any promises. I thought it wouldn't hurt if we didn't get involved too deeply—just enjoyed the pleasure of each other's company."

And they had, for three years, sneaking around for clandestine meetings. All to sate the hunger for the forbidden desires no other lover fulfilled. What hurt most was that Roger had dropped her without a word. No indication of trouble. No reason. Suddenly he was too busy, unavailable. Never answered his cell when her number popped up. Callie suspected the bureau had a hand in their breakup, such as it was. Roger never would say.

Iollan's gently probing eyes met hers. "It doesn't happen that way, lass. There's more to sex than a collision of body parts. When you make love to a person, there's always a connection that'll never be broken. He'll always be a part of you because his body joined with yours. That's nothing you can easily forget."

She shook her head. "I'm trying to." Her words came out

bitter, laced with poison. She'd been vulnerable and was punishing herself for her lapse in judgment. Not because she'd slept with a married man—but because she still wanted to.

He glanced at the roses. "He obviously hasn't."

As the mistress of sex without commitment, Callie forced a shrug. "He needs to. I did." She glanced over at him, anger and frustration pulsing through her. "I made a mistake and fell in love, but I won't let that happen again."

"It still hurts," he said softly. "I can see in your eyes something's missing inside."

He spoke as if he'd opened her up and peered inside the dark secret recesses of her mind. A tremor wound through her and her body visibly quivered in reaction. She hadn't been prepared to face all the unpleasant memories of an affair she was struggling to forget.

She glanced at the roses, hating the sight of them. They were a mockery, a blatant slap in the face. What the fuck was Roger trying to do, messing with her head like this? Six months ago he'd kicked her to the curb without a word of explanation, not even a good-bye kiss-off fuck to ease the transition.

Burying her face in her hands, Callie closed her eyes and leaned back into the cushions. Emotions were more exhausting than the long night spent on her feet. Her head ached, her feet hurt, and she was just plain tired.

"Sorry." As if that moment of weakness was all she allowed herself, she parted her fingers, peeking between them. "Sorry. You seem to have caught me in the middle of a nervous breakdown."

Fingers curling around her wrists, he lowered her hands. "It's okay. I know how it feels. Been there, done that."

His unexpected touch reignited her inner fires. Sexual awareness hummed through her, tantalizing and seductive. "I'm being stupid, unloading my problems on a complete stranger."

He was watching her watch him. "I'm glad to be here for you." A pause. "I'm glad to be here with you."

The lump in her throat lessened. A comfortable warmth settled in the pit of her churning stomach. "You're too damn good to be true."

And he was a puzzle, one Callie couldn't quite piece together. Exactly how one of the bureau's most wanted gave the impression of being a seriously nice guy was a mystery. Either the intelligence was seriously fucked, or he deserved an Oscar for a full-on performance of genuine sympathy. If he intended to take advantage of her with concern, well, he was giving a realistically convincing performance.

She looked at him, so up close and personal. She'd read the man's dossier, for God's sake. His criminal history was chilling, describing him as almost sociopathic. Yet here he sat, calm, graceful, boyishly charming. That's what makes most criminals so successful, she reminded herself.

The notion of equating Drake with a murdering fiend somehow didn't sit right in her mind. True, physical attraction blinded a person to qualities they'd rather not see, but Callie seriously doubted that was the case. This man didn't act dangerous. More important, he didn't *feel* dangerous.

He did feel right, though, and that unsettled her. With little effort she easily pictured herself in his arms, tonight, tomorrow, and the next day after. She didn't believe in soul mates or anything of the like, but she had a strange feeling Iollan Drake was inextricably bound to her future from this moment forward.

A self-deprecating grin tugged at his lips. "Does that earn me any points for being a sensitive guy?"

She gave a wry grimace. "Humor's the last defense of a guilty man."

Her companion moved closer, his thigh brushing hers. "Maybe I'm just a good listener who can help you sort out a few things."

Callie recognized his words for the come-on they were. The door to her trust was open. Whether or not she let him inside was her choice. "What kind of things?"

A grin tugged at his lips. "You'll never know until you let me try, love." Unmistakable innuendo laced his accented words.

She cocked her head cynically, regarding him through narrow eyes. He'd segued neatly back around to sex without missing a step in the dance. No doubting the intention behind his calculated manner. Having been around that block so many times she could've paved the path, Callie had to admire his tenacity.

"Oh, you're definitely a smooth talker," she said, arching a mocking eyebrow. If he had an act, now was the time to drop it. "I suppose a man will say anything to get a woman to spread her legs."

To her surprise, he didn't seem to receive her words as an offense. Instead he leaned forward, focusing on her face. A sensual combination of musky spice and hot male skin tickled her nostrils. Up close he smelled of heat, a lure as tempting as it was troubling.

"I don't play head games, Calista." He cupped her cheek in one large hand. Warmth and tenderness suffused his intimate touch. Compelling eyes engulfed her, in an all-consuming wave. "The first time I saw you, I knew you were special."

In danger of sensual overload, Callie drew a breath against the tremor of awareness suffusing her body. Any doubts she'd entertained about him fled, scattered like morning dew under the rising sun. "Meaning?"

Iollan glanced over his shoulder, toward the bedroom. "Meaning you invited me in, but I won't take advantage."

Her stomach curled into tight knots, and a strange buzzing filled her ears. His closeness prickled her skin as liquid heat pooled between her thighs. Desire surged, the urge of raw lust achingly transparent. Without doubt, she wanted him, naked and inside of her. A wait of more than one more minute would be torture.

"I wouldn't have let you in if I weren't considering it."

Iollan looked her over, anticipation sharp, as if he were dissecting her piece by piece. "I'm not after just any woman I can talk into bed." An edge of possessiveness deepening his voice, one of his hands covered hers. "There's a reason I chose you."

Silence followed, an uneasy lull in which no sound but that of their breathing came between them.

Callie stared back at the man sitting so uncomfortably close, wondering if he was truly sincere or if he took some perverse pleasure in playing games with emotionally needy women. If so, she was playing right into his hands. Judging by her rapid heartbeat and the curling heat in her groin, her body had certainly chosen him—even if her mind hadn't quite settled on the decision.

Emotion waged war with sexual need. Not because she didn't desire his touch. She did, more than anything. But the tenderness his presence ushered in went far beyond the physical.

This attraction was getting personal.

Callie sneaked a glance his way, then averted her eyes. He sat quietly, waiting. The move had to be hers.

She pursed her lips. Maybe every damn word he said was a fucking lie. But her heart had been wounded and needed a salve. Maybe Iollan Drake wasn't the answer. She'd been without hope for so long, she wasn't sure.

The silence stretched on, uncomfortably long.

Feeling more alone and lonely than she'd ever dreamed possible, she swallowed the lump building at the back of her throat. "What makes me so different?"

Mouth curving into a smile, he leaned close. The tension in the air was thick enough to slice when he traced a finger above one mound of flesh pushed taut against its prison of leather and form-shaping wire. "This mark you wear is very meaningful to my kind." His voice was a low sultry rumble, sexy and oh so enticing.

Pleased he'd noticed it, Callie's hand automatically settled on her left breast. Upon turning eighteen, she'd had a tattoo of the Tree of Life etched on the soft curve. The fit of her bustier only served to enhance its presence.

"It's Celtic," she explained of the unusual design.

"I know, lass. Do you know its meaning?"

Callie didn't move, content to concentrate only on his nearness, on his body so seductively close. The glow in her belly grew hotter, more intense. "I've never been able to explain why it appealed to me."

He traced the design with the tip of his index finger. "It symbolizes the connection to spiritual entities and doorways into other worlds. When I saw it, I knew we belonged together."

She let out the breath she'd been holding. The heat of pure animalistic desire pulsed through her, sending a delicious twinge straight to her clit. "That's a come-on, if I've ever heard one."

Finger still moving across the swell of her breast, he grinned. "I'm doing my best."

She stared back at him. "At least you're honest."

His laughter was warm and unexpected. "If I tell a lie, I have to remember it. It's easier just to tell the truth."

She grabbed the chance to turn the conversation back on him. "So, any tattoos of your own?"

"A couple."

"Going to show me?"

A sly look. "Maybe." A pause. "Maybe not."

She snorted in pretend disdain. "Going to be a tease, huh? In that case"—she lightly swatted his hands away from her breast—"hands off."

A look of mock horror crossed his face. "You wound me."

"I'm just being fair."

A sly smile. "So it's a matter of if I show you mine, you'll show me yours?"

She pretended innocence. "Depends on what you've got to show."

He eyed her, making a point to go from head to toe and back again. "It's nothing like you've got, love. But I'll do my damnedest to make up for any shortcomings you might find."

The compliment pleased her, more than she should have expected. She realized then how much she missed having a man in her life, the comfort of spending a lazy weekend in bed, eating takeout, and watching stupid movies.

She *really* missed sex.

She eyed him back. If he had any shortcomings, they weren't apparent. In fact, she couldn't think of a thing he might be lacking. If the theory had to be tested ... That damn prickle down her spine came again. Shivering, her fingers knotted in her lap. Might be better to keep her hands to herself.

Catching her, he moved a little closer. Any closer and he'd be sitting in her lap. Or vice versa. "Nervous?"

Her heart skipped a beat. "I'm a little cold," she said, uncertain whether or not she was warning him or encouraging him.

His fingers brushed along her jaw. "Maybe I can do something about that." He lowered his head, brushing his mouth across her bare shoulder. "Think that might help warm you up?"

She smelled the scent of his hair, perfumed with the scent of some exotic pomade used to arrange the tousle just so. She smelled the soap he'd bathed in, the silk of his shirt, warm from his body. She smelled her own arousal, the heady and intoxicating odor of a female in heat.

She didn't pull away as he reached for her, didn't stifle her moan when he buried his face in the valley between her neck and shoulder. Her moan grew louder as his tongue traced the sensitive pulse at the base of her neck.

"Calista . . . I've looked for you so long." Suddenly his mouth was on hers, giving her no chance to question. A low grown escaped his throat as his tongue slipped inside to conquer and claim. His unique taste filled her. His mouth was like steel, immovable and overpowering. His hands pulled her tight, giving no escape.

Callie surrendered helplessly, caught up in the feverish passion she'd too long denied. Her resistance dissolved like a sand castle under an ocean wave. Want ignited with need. She was on fire. No matter how wrong or right sex between them might be, she needed him to the very core of her soul.

A moment later their lips parted, breathless. Their gazes locked, ravenous. A yearning needy sound escaped her as Iollan's hand slid up her side, under her arm, then over her breast. His touch was light, sensual. Limbs turning liquid, she felt a fresh rush of sexual warmth fill her. Her nipples tightened anew, the tips peaking.

Close to losing her breath from delight, Callie gasped. "I can't do this." She put her hands on his chest, trying to push him away. All at once she was scared witless. "It won't work."

He didn't budge. "Why not?"

"I don't usually do this," she stammered.

He flashed a lazy grin. "What?"

A blush reddened her skin. "Make love to strange men."

His smile was boyishly charming. "Me either. So maybe we should quit being strangers." Adept at manipulating women's clothing, he briefly fingered the leather before inserting a finger into one cup and peeling it down. He teased the erect nub, thumb circling her pink areola.

Squeezing her eyes shut, she moaned in protest. Not very convincing at all. "I invited you for coffee . . . not Callie."

"I didn't come up for coffee." His mouth covered her nipple, swirling around the little nub.

She almost exploded from the pleasure, her voice trailing

off. His lips felt like warm satin, sucking gently, then with more pressure. He flicked and teased with his tongue and teeth until she trembled.

Her moans were her acceptance. Trouble didn't begin to describe what she was getting herself into.

At the moment, she didn't care.

3

Body trembling, Callie tangled her fingers in his thick hair, backing away and looking into his eyes. The intimacy of the moment thickened, jelling into something dynamic, explosive. The tension between them ratcheted up another notch.

"I've needed this." Biting her lower lip, her attention edged toward the cock straining inside his tight jeans. His penis was rigid, hot, and definitely huge.

"Think it's something you might like for your birthday?"

Callie didn't hesitate. "Thinking and knowing are two different things." She reached for his zipper. "I know what I want."

He caught her roaming hands. Linking her fingers with his, he took a deep breath. "Not like this."

She looked at him, stunned. Staring into his serious face, she wondered what had gone awry. She was ready, willing, and able. Why had he suddenly stopped?

Callie barely endured the strain. Panic fluttering in her belly, she fought to control the raging hormones that hadn't yet gotten the stop sign. "I want to—" she started to say.

His grip tightened, reassuring and warm. "I do, too." He

reached out, tracing the soft lines of her neck and jaw. "But slowly. I want to know every inch of you, touch every inch."

She sucked in a steadying breath. "Say that again, please."

He smiled. "I want you, love. All of you."

"Then take me."

"I intend to." He eyed her extreme Goth gear. "How you got yourself into this bloody outfit, I don't know." He fingered the tight lacings and grinned. The look was far from innocent and definitely provocative. "But I'm dying to get you out of it."

Callie glanced down at the breasts he'd somehow worked out of the leather prison. A weak laugh escaped her throat. "You're doing a pretty good job."

"I'd like to do better. Stand up, love. Let me see if I can work my way through this maze you've got going here."

Callie stood. Sitting up straight, he guided her to stand between his legs. Examining the ties, he began unweaving the complicated lacings between her breasts, all the way down to her belly button.

As he worked on the tight silk bindings, Callie cast a glance to the mirror hanging across the room. Her lips were parted, her skin flushed, and a hungry wanton expression colored her features. She looked like a woman ready to be fucked. No, a woman who needed to be fucked.

Now.

The last of the laces undone, Iollan let the bustier drop. Angry red lines were imprinted on her skin. He ran his palm across her sensitive skin. "As good as you look in it, you look better out of it."

"Feels better, too." She stretched, smiling in relief. "I can breathe."

He fingered the zipper on her left hip. "Now let's see what we can do about this." A tug and her skirt fell to her feet. That left only a pair of thigh-high sheer hose, heels, and the leather wrist bindings covering her arms from elbow to wrist.

"Nice." Iollan gave her near-naked body a friendly smile, taking in every last inch. If he saw anything he didn't like, he wasn't showing it.

Basking in his appreciation, Callie glanced down. Full breasts and shapely hips flared out from her tiny waist. Her legs were long and lean, her belly flat and solid as a brick. All those extra days working out in the gym had paid off. Her body was in top shape, a necessity of the job she followed with near-religious fervor. Roger had reminded her many times during her training—in and out of bed—that an out-of-shape agent was a sloppy agent.

"You're perfect in every way." Pulling her closer, he leaned forward, nibbling the bare skin just below her breasts.

Callie's breath caught. His lips were soft and warm, moist as he licked the sensitive area. The heated sensation of his mouth on her bare abused skin felt wonderful. A lusty moan slipped out.

"You like that?"

"Oh, yes." She purred in rapture. "More, please, sir."

He pulled back, taking away the wonderful torture. "Good girl. You catch on fast." He reached for her left wrist. "But not yet. Still have to finish the unveiling."

Callie stiffened. Oh, shit. She'd totally forgotten the reason she wore those cuffs in the first place.

Undoing the ties, Iollan peeled away the leather cuff. Pale and white, dozens of white scars were stark against her abused inner wrists. The veins wove pale greenish-blue paths beneath the obvious damage.

His face darkened. She saw him swallow, fighting the urge to question their presence.

She tried to pull her arm away. "Don't."

He persisted. "I want to see." He unbound her right wrist, visually probing more scars.

"Seen enough?" Her words were an unpleasant snarl.

He shook his head, tracing one with a single finger. "Tell me why?"

So warm only moments ago, Callie felt ice cold inside as the blood drained from her face. She'd always explained the irregular scars away as a childhood accident.

Trust. Treacherous, but necessary. He had to believe everything about her, down to the last detail. Shifting uneasily, she gave him a level look. In for a penny, in for a pound.

"I'm a cutter." Her voice quavered, but she quickly gained control. "Or rather, I was. When I was a teenager."

Warm hands touched her hips, holding her still and steady. Beneath his touch, her skin raised into goose bumps. "What happened to make you do that?"

Callie shivered. Her stomach felt as if thousands of snakes writhed inside and her palms felt clammy. Her life hadn't been easy or pleasant. What do you do when the state sends you to a foster home, and your foster father finds you more attractive than his wife sleeping down the hall?

You close your eyes and endure.

Racked by insomnia, fearing the man who would come and use her body in ways she didn't then understand, Callie had turned to the only solution she knew to vent her fear and frustration.

"What can I say? I was a fucked-up kid." She struggled to get the words out. Shuffled in through the foster care system since her third birthday, Callie had never known the security of a stable home, much less a family who loved her—or wanted her.

A muscle at the corner of his lower jaw jumped. "I'm sorry."

"Don't be." Her hands were shaking cold. The past was the past. Her intensity was out of place, leaving her too exposed. "When I was a teenager, I cut a little, drank a little, and fucked a lot. It was a fetish. I'm over it now."

"Let's see if you are." He reached for her hand.

Dismayed, Callie resisted. She felt nauseated. "Don't take me there." Muscles tense, she stood, waiting.

"I know the darkness inside you." Succeeding in the capture, he raised her inner wrist to his mouth. Moist warmth spread across her chilled skin.

She closed her eyes, heart skipping at the sheer primitive power of his lips on her skin. Her brain was totally paralyzed, trapped by his utterly sensual acceptance.

Another warm, slow, wet stroke went straight to the center of her pulsing clit. The delicious skim of his tongue was followed by the scrape of his teeth. His move—sexy, amazing, enticing—gripped her fractured senses.

"Harder," she gasped.

He obliged. More scraping. More sucking. More bliss.

Dimly aware of the sensations pooling between her legs, a fierce shudder knotted her muscles. Body aching and straining with a need too long unfulfilled, she imagined his cock sinking inside her, stretching her until the last inch filled her.

Another long stroke of his lips on her wrist sent her over the edge. Body going rigid, Callie climaxed. A groan vibrated through her as her inner muscles clenched tighter and tighter. Her legs trembled. Unable to support her weight any longer, she collapsed.

Iollan caught her before she fell. Only dimly aware of what he was doing, Callie felt herself swept up into his arms as he carried her somewhere . . . toward the bedroom? As shadows closed in, Callie felt the softness of a mattress beneath her back.

Forcing heavy eyelids open, Callie raised her head. Silhouetted by the light emanating from the living room, he looked ethereal and mysterious. Only the sound of ragged breathing betrayed his presence. He stood by the bed, unmoving. Though she couldn't see his face, she felt his gaze through the darkness.

She smiled, patting the empty space beside her. "Little lonely here."

"You won't be for long." Unbuttoning his shirt, he slid it off his broad shoulders and tossed it aside. The mattress sank under his weight as he stretched out beside her. Body to body, she felt the swell of his cock pressed against her thigh. His erection strained to escape its cruel prison, and he was so close she smelled the heated vibrations emanating off his body.

Aware of her own nakedness, she hinted. "You're still a little overdressed." Having him so near, yet still inaccessible, set her nerve endings on fire. Her heart beat rapidly in her chest. She didn't want to wait another second, but apparently he had other things in mind. She closed her eyes and pictured his cock in action. The thought sent a little tingle of excitement down her spine.

Propped on one elbow, he stroked a hand down her cheek. "All in good time. It's not nice to rush a man when there's so much to taste."

Heavy eyelids opened. "That's a good thing, I hope."

"The best." His free hand trailed lower, finding the swell of her right breast.

Callie pulled him down, closing the gap between them. Their kiss started out slow, gentle, but that didn't last. Their appetites were too voracious, too fierce, to contain. His tongue swept in, arriving and conquering with an intensity that left her breathless.

Giving a helpless whimper, she rose into the kiss, pressing her body into his. She slid an arm under his body, bringing her hand up across his back. Her fingers flexed, long nails scraping deliciously across his bare skin with gentle but insistent pressure.

A satisfied moan passed from his mouth to hers. "Mmm, I love the feel of that."

She dug her nails a little deeper. "I think I can oblige, provided I have proper . . . motivation . . . from you."

His exploring hand slid lower, over the flat planes of her belly, then lower, down one bare thigh. "I think I can give you that." His hand slipped between her legs, urging her thighs to part. With a kiss and caress, his fingers investigated the moist, warm nest.

Pulse zinging, Callie spread wider. She knew she shouldn't be doing this, but couldn't help herself. With her vision going dark, her heart skipped a few beats. Limbs turned to liquid, a yearning sound breaking from her throat. "I've needed this . . ." Her moan was frantic, raw with lust.

"I know." Giving her a lazy smile, he slid his fingers along her honey-slick labia.

She lifted her hips to a better angle. "I can't wait," she said, gasping for breath. "I'm so hot I can barely take it."

A single thick finger caressed her silk before sliding past creamy lips. Rippling inner muscles grasped and closed around him. "You'll take it all right." His head dipped, mouth nuzzling an extended nipple. His lips were warm, like melted chocolate. Soft, sensual, and insinuating.

Her shivers began in small waves, growing and spreading until they swamped her in intense tremors. Every stroke of his finger was perfect. Fiercely aroused, she hovered on the brink of shattering into a thousand flaming shards.

"You really shouldn't be this good," she gasped.

His tongue flicked an erect nipple. "Don't you like a little spoiling?" Another flick, then a light nip at the sensitive nub.

The tug went straight to her already sensitive clit and she moaned. She laughed. "I—right now I can barely think. It feels so good."

"Don't think, love. Just enjoy."

Before she caught her breath, he was on the move, sliding down between her legs. Fingering the edge of her lacy stockings, he traced his tongue along the line they formed over the top of her leg.

She caught her breath. "I guess it's too late to change my mind."

Gazing at her neatly trimmed bush, he gave a low, sexy laugh. "Now's not the time to do that to a hungry man." His hands parted her thighs. Wider.

"Haven't eaten today?" The hint of what he could do with his mouth and fingers made her mouth run dry.

"No." A single finger glided along softness.

"Me either." She licked her lips in anticipation. "Shouldn't it be ladies first?"

"And indeed you are." He lifted a leg, hooking it over his shoulder. His hands moved under her ass, bracing her body and tilting her hips upward. Closing the distance, he dipped his head low.

The first pass of his tongue snapped Callie's fragile grasp on sanity. Shivering uncontrollably, she moaned a long moan that caught her breath. Seeking the tip of her pleasure center, he nipped, just enough to give her a start. A jolt went straight up her spine.

Arms shooting up to clench the headboard, Callie arched her back. "Holy hell!"

He grinned up at her. "You like?"

Barely able to breathe, she puffed out her answer. "Fantastic."

"You knew it would be." Disappearing again, his tongue moved up and down her swollen labia, teasing with endless flicks delivering ideal sensations in just the right places.

Callie groaned, lost in the wonder of exquisite oral sex. His mouth was on her, working her most responsive center. All she had to do was feel, and enjoy. She wriggled her hips, pressing into his mouth, urging him to explore her deeper.

So much for my self-control.

Iollan Drake was a suspected murderer, a man with a hidden past and a life even more so. Having sex with him hadn't exactly been part of her plan. It just happened. And now that she'd crossed the line, there was no backing out.

Not that she wanted to.

Further thought took a kick to the curb when he circled the tip of her clit. Letting out a rush of air, Callie tightened her thighs against his head. Sensing she was ready for the free fall, he tongued her violently, stabbing deep.

Pleasure caught hold, grabbing and lifting her into the abyss of rapture that was his mouth and lips. Her body was a hot coil of anticipation, and her final shred of control slipped away as the electrifying pleasure of climax went on and on, swamping her in a pool of indescribable bliss.

Trembling uncontrollably, Callie felt her nerve endings hum. Stress, exhaustion, and tension drained away. An eternity passed. Finally her universe stopped spinning.

As the sensation faded to bearable levels, she pursed dry lips. She felt good. Better than good. Fucking incredible.

Iollan Drake definitely had *the* touch.

"Oh, God. It's never felt like that before."

He stretched over her, hands coming down on either side of her shoulders as he cloaked her body with his. Arms bracketing her shoulders, he eased her lower until their faces were just inches apart.

Callie's arms instinctively circled his body. Under her searching palms his back was sleek, muscular, ridged with the tension consuming him from inside. A shudder ripped through her as his hips sank between hers. They fit together perfectly. The press of his cock against the nest of her belly was as long and inflexible as an iron bar, and just as hot.

"It's not supposed to, love." His accented voice was gentler than any physical caress. His hips rubbed against hers. "What other men have done to you and what I can do to you are two different things."

A foolish grin turned up the corners of her mouth. God, this man was incredible. Amazing. Too good to be true.

"Keep doing it, then." The overwhelming need to rip off his jeans had her sparking with frustration. She'd gotten a sample of his wares. Now she wanted the entire package. Skin tingling, her stomach felt as if a thousand butterflies had taken flight. Arousal ached for completion. She was hot, wet, and definitely ready.

"Gladly." Softly grinding his hips against hers, his mouth crushed hers. Steering with the same sizzling need that scorched her soul, he wanted her to share in the feast.

She accepted his kiss greedily, inhaling his taste, mingled so deliciously with her own unique juices. The wanting, the needing, drove her wild—yet he was holding back, making her wait.

Another second and Callie felt as if she'd spontaneously combust. "You're still a little overdressed for this party," she hinted.

He held his body up from hers, creating a space between them. "Do something about it, then."

Eager hands went to work. Her shaking fingers found and opened the buttons. His cock jutted free, magnificent. To feel more skin against hers, she slid her hands into his jeans, pushing them down his hips and over his fine ass. He wore no underwear. As tight as those jeans were there wasn't room for underclothing.

His erection pulsed in her hand, thick and long, like steel wrapped in velvet. Callie stroked, bringing her fist up to the flaring crown, then back down.

Iollan's lips moved from hers to her cheek, then her jaw, to her ear. "I've only just started."

A soft gasp escaped her. "What?" she asked in a husky voice. Her need was so raw, so deep that it threatened to consume her.

His hips shifted between her legs, the tip of him pressing, but not entering. "To make you mine."

Callie gazed into his face, half in shadow, half in light. "I don't believe in fairy tales."

"Anything's possible," he said, and glided into her molten depth with a vigorous and demanding thrust.

Callie couldn't think. He filled her to the brim, until it felt that she would overflow with the glorious joy of having him inside her. They weren't just joined, they were one, as if her body had been created for this man only, and forever.

A bittersweet ache filled her heart. Tonight, she'd be his, utterly and completely. Tomorrow, that wouldn't be possible. Paradise gained wasn't destined to last, no matter how badly she wished it.

The descent of his lips chased away her negative thoughts. For now there was only the moment. To be savored. Seized. Guided by the grind of his hips into hers, they came together and parted, a joining almost holy in its purity. If she'd had other men before him, they were soon forgotten, erased by penetration. His thrust inside her was his brand, marking her as his.

Just as Callie neared her third peak, he captured her wrists, pinning her arms above her head with a force that took her breath away.

Iollan groaned, pumping his body into hers. His hips moved faster, grinding her down into the mattress. The bedsprings grated under the savage motion of two bodies in action.

Panting to counter his savage thrusts, she filled the air with her moans. Gritting her teeth, Callie came up under him, not to break his hold but to enhance the feel of him inside her. Her move created an exquisite agony begging for deeper entry.

Sensing her silent plea, he increased his tempo, bone-jarringly fast and furious. He was in control, would give her no leeway, no mercy until he'd sapped every last ounce of her strength.

Climax built at the base of Callie's spine, the explosion preparing to come from the inside out.

Iollan separated them long enough to reach into the back pocket of his jeans. He pulled out a condom. Ripping the foil open with his teeth, he expertly sheathed himself with the protection.

Surprised, Callie opened her eyes. She hadn't expected him to be that thoughtful.

He glided back into her slick heat with a hard, demanding thrust. His head was thrown back, his body rippled, and his chest rose and fell each time his cock penetrated her. With his tousled hair, pale skin, and rippling muscles, he looked predatory, the hunter in fierce pursuit of his prey. He'd won the chase. His possession of her was complete.

It's the heat of the moment.

Regaining control of himself, Iollan stared down at her. He smiled. "You're so damn tight it's difficult to hold back."

"Any time you're ready," she invited.

"Getting there." He lowered his hand between their bodies and his thumb worked her clit as he glided inside her slick depth one excruciating inch at a time.

The feel of him inside her seemed to stretch on forever, again filling the emptiness. The blood rushed from her brain, making her body uncomfortably hot, her arousal more painful as he stroked her sensitive inner flesh. A flaming arrow shot from Callie's slick channel straight to the center of her heart. Her breathing grew shallow, a dark whorl of pleasure threatening to grab and asphyxiate her.

Just when she believed he'd surprise her no more, he slid his arms under the small of her back, lifting her into his lap. Legs closing around his waist, her arms automatically lifted to circle his neck. He was so deep inside that her sex gripped and held him fast. Bodies joined, he could go no deeper.

He met her gaze and held it, watching her reactions to his touch. Face-to-face, she noticed his eyes change. Lit by an illumination seeming to emanate from inside, they glowed—dazzling, brilliant, and electric.

The sight was entrancing. "Beautiful," she murmured. His eyes wove an unspoken spell, mesmerizing her with an awesome and pure beauty.

Iollan unexpectedly stabbed deep, one fast stunning thrust. "Come for me, love. Show me what I do to you."

Callie's hands convulsed, fingers digging trenches in his skin as his body undulated against hers. Arriving from nowhere, an extraordinary surge of energy pulsed through her, jolting her nerve endings into extreme sensitivity. She didn't just feel him inside her, she felt he *was* inside her. Their minds connected. A pathway into an endless eternity opened up and stretched out before her. Her heart hammered, threatening to tear itself from the confines of her ribs. Spasms built from the center of her core, spiraling outward.

Surrendering, she climaxed with the speed of a bottle rocket, whizzing and exploding into a million sparks of pure energy. The aftershocks seemed to go on forever. She gulped, struggling to take in fresh air.

He gave her no time to catch her breath. "We're not done yet." Nuzzling her damp mouth, he kissed her with the longing of a man desperate not to lose contact. His tongue penetrated her lips, opening a fresh surge of passion. Cock engorged, his own excitement was at the boiling point, ready to erupt.

Drawing back from their kiss, his mouth sought and found the vulnerable flesh between breast and shoulder. He licked. A second later he bit, sharp teeth razoring through her skin. Blood welled to the surface.

Callie pulled in a quick breath as erotic delight blazed straight down. Sanity seeping away, she trembled beneath the sensual blitz of pain. The heated, moist sensation of his mouth sucking at her blazing skin sent white-hot darts of fire up and down her spine.

Craving—half-anxious, half-repulsed—knotted her body. Her own attraction to the darker side of her sexual appetite felt stronger than ever. The crimson-robed beast rose in the back of her mind, glorious and magnificent in scope and breadth. Her master was sleek. Controlled. Hard.

Mouth going bone dry, she yearned for another caress as the room spun around her. The intoxicating mix of wanton need rose with her body temperature. Erotic quivers nudged her toward the edge. Core going molten, she felt moisture trickle between her clenched thighs. There was no mistake. She *craved* his domination. With all the skill of the seducer he'd deftly reawakened the senses she'd fought to dull and deny.

Heavens, yes.

Hungry lips suckled. Iollan consumed her, controlled her, taking his pleasure. The manipulations of his talented mouth and cock made her gasp.

Hands grasping her ass, he redoubled his thrusts, taking her with unrelenting force. With each swallow, he stroked her hips down against his. Stress knotted and pressure rose to the point of eruption. Biting deep into her flesh, he plunged with a final, brutal intensity. Body vibrating fiercely, he ended in a long groan.

Callie screamed as climax claimed her a fourth magnificent time. Orgasm struck like a red-hot poker up the ass, simultaneously delivering a liquefying release that snatched what few brain cells she had left.

4

Callie woke in her least favorite way, feeling like she'd been hit by a tractor trailer. Not only had the Goddamn thing smashed her flat, it had apparently backed up and run over her. She felt the pressure of a headache threaten from the safety behind her temples. The twinge prompted a groan. She heard her blood drum against the walls of her skull.

Pushing aside the thick patchwork comforter covering her, she tried to rise. Not a good idea. An inky veil settled over her eyes, blotting out her vision. She felt her body go numb, the room sway around her. Her stomach turned over.

She swallowed, clenching her jaw, trying to fight off the sickness threatening to overtake her. She pressed the heels of her hands to her forehead, as if she feared her skull would crack and her brains would spill out.

"Damn, damn, damn."

Callie tried to concentrate through her suffering. She heard her heart beating in her ears; felt the reverberating thuds in her chest.

Head feeling heavy as an anvil, she lay back against her pillow. She lowered her hand and took several fortifying breaths. That helped clear her vision, steady her shaking body.

"What the hell happened?"

And then she remembered the night's dream lingering in her head, flashes of great ecstasy mingling with the sensations of intense pleasure. *And pain.* Images of the midnight demon soothing her loneliness drifted to the forefront of her memory. Their encounter, veiled in the mists of her memory, seemed so unreal she was half-inclined to believe it hadn't really happened.

Her body told another story. Usually she slept in a sports bra, T-shirt, and panties. She was naked, wearing not a stitch. Surprise tightened her throat when she remembered she hadn't gone to bed alone.

Keeping her eyes shut, Callie let her hands drift over her skin. The tips of her nipples came to pebble-hard attention when her palms brushed over them. Bits and pieces of the previous night floated across her mind's screen. Acutely aware of her actions, she cupped her breasts, rubbing them. As she did, her lover's form appeared out of the miasma, taking form.

She smiled, welcoming him.

He was all eyes and all cock, and both burned through the pain in her mind. The haze began to fade, details of the previous hours seeping back in a lovely kaleidoscope of color, sounds, and sensations. He leaned over her, kissing her parted lips, his tongue invading her mouth.

Responding, she tugged her nipples, twisting them between thumb and forefinger until a little twinge of delight shimmied down her spine. Everything was so clear, so intense that Callie believed she smelled the heat of his sex. She gasped, skin flushing as she remembered how he'd taken her.

Not content with nipple play, she passed a hand down the flat plane of her stomach, slipping it between her legs. She shivered as her inquisitive fingers probed her softness, still damp from the night's lovemaking. Beneath her touch her clit was swollen and pulsing.

She pressed deeper, one finger, and then two. She spread her legs, seeking fuller and deeper access. Pleasure peaking, she began to make a sound down in her throat, which worked its way up as she slipped two fingers inside her depth.

Come hard, love, she imagined him urging in her ear.

Rapturous crescendo arrived without warning. A lusty moan broke from her lips, loosening a cry that melted her senses into a mass as pliable as Silly Putty.

A moment later her hand slipped out of her depth, fingers sticky with her own cream. She took a deep breath to control the wild beat of her heart. The organ hammered in her chest like a mustang battling the ropes of unwanted captors.

Callie breathed in, and then out. Comfortable warmth radiated through her, helping shed the last grasping talons of her headache. Amazing. She'd learned long ago that a quick climax really helped lessen a body's stress.

She was close to floating off in a dreamy haze when a familiar voice sounded in her ears.

"There's nothing I love to see more than a woman getting herself off." The words flooded her mind and set her stomach to rolling. What the fuck?

Bowels cramping with unease, Callie forced her eyes open. She blinked to clear her blurry vision. It took a moment for her eyes to focus in the direction of the bedroom door. Recognizing the intruder, she groped for something to cover her nudity. Astonishment was huge, but quickly absorbed. She glared at the skinny little snitch leaning against the frame.

"Jesus Christ, you little punk. How the hell did you get in here?"

Short and boxy, with shoulder-length dirty blond hair and

an even scragglier beard, Paul Norton's smile stretched across his face in an obscene grin. "Duh. I picked your lock."

She eyed him. "What for, you little creep."

Norton snuffled and wiped his nose with one grimy sleeve of a jacket most likely dug from a Dumpster. Dressed in baggy cargo pants at least two sizes too big and a shirt that had more holes than intact material, he looked every bit like a shabby junkie on crack. "I'm a thief. It's what thieves do."

In reality Paul Norton was her partner of two years and the closest friend she had, a fellow agent working the Drake investigation. Where Callie's job was to identify Drake's associates for agents, Norton's was to photograph and run down their identities. A whiz with a knack for breaking and entering, he could breach any lock on earth.

Sighing at the imposition, Callie peered around for her robe. Of course it hung on the peg behind the door. She pointed. "Could you hand me that?"

Norton retrieved the robe. "You want this?" A shit-eating grin of pornographic mischief crossed his face.

She held out her hand. "Please. If you don't mind."

He waggled it like a tempting morsel. "Why don't you come and get it?"

Callie rolled her eyes. "I'm naked, asshole." Despite his best attempts to get her into bed, Norton had failed. He seemed to enjoy paying her back for the many times she'd brushed off his sexual advances. He'd wanted to be more than friends for years.

He made an exasperated gesture with his hands. "I know." He chuckled in a most unappealing manner. "And from what I saw, it's glorious."

Callie's eyebrows came together in an ugly scowl. "Stop it, Paul. You're giving me a headache."

Grin set like concrete, Norton shook his head. "Didn't look

like you had a headache a few minutes ago. God, you looked so hot getting yourself off. I hope you were thinking of me."

She eyed his short, chunky frame. She barely imagined their bodies entwined in a naked clinch, his lips brushing hers. It just didn't compute. The physical attraction wasn't there and wouldn't be even if they were stranded on a desert island and were the only male and only female. Her partner was single and probably the safer choice. But Callie never took the safer path when it came to men. "Christ, Paul. You're a nice guy, but—"

He interrupted her. "I know." He pushed crooked wire-rim glasses up on his beaky nose, which gave him the look of a bemused owl. "You want tall, dark bastards. Short, blond, and dumpy just doesn't turn you on. Hell, it doesn't turn me on either."

She made a derisive sound. "That's not it at all."

He grimaced, giving a self-deprecating smile. "Sure it is. But, please, don't penalize me for worshipping beauty. I'm a man. We can't help being attracted to naked goddesses."

Callie rolled her eyes. "Don't start. I don't need a lecture on what men want, or what I want in a man." She held out her hand for the robe. "You think you could hand that over?"

His perky grin returned. "Nah." He began to breathe heavily, imitating an obscene caller. "I still want to see you naked."

"Fuck you."

He grinned. "Please do."

"You're a maggot, Paulie. A horny little maggot."

Norton spread his arms in his defense. "What do you expect? I walk in on a gorgeous undressed woman doing things to her body I can only dream about and you expect me to just turn around and walk out."

"That would have been decent of you," she muttered under her breath.

He eyed her, sitting in a crumpled mass of patchwork quilt

and nothing else. "How can you expect me not to get a woody the size of Texas when you're so damn close and so damn naked?"

Callie pulled her cover tighter to her body, wishing she could hide every last inch. "Rhode Island is more like it," she bit off dryly.

Hand flying to his heart, Paul winced. "You wound me."

"Get over it." Tired of playing games, Callie bunched the comforter around her body and slid off the bed. Her legs shook but held her weight. "I need a shower." The garments she'd worn the night before—skirt, bustier, panties, and hose—had been neatly placed on the nearby bureau. Her shoes sat directly below, on the floor.

Grabbing them, she fled into the bathroom and shut the door behind her. Stopping to catch her breath, she leaned against it for support. Teasing aside, Paul wouldn't be here unless something had gone down, or was about to. She had no computer, cell phone, or any other high-tech gadgets one would expect a government agent to carry—not even a gun. For this assignment she'd been forced to strip down to the barest essentials. Paul was her go-between with the rest of the team.

"No time to stand around," she muttered. She needed to get moving.

5

Turning on the cold tap, Callie stepped into the shower. A blitz of icy water needled her skin. Any desire she felt for Iollan Drake vanished, just what she needed to get her mind out of her crotch and back into her work.

Adjusting the water to a more comfortable temperature, she washed her hair. Soaping not once but twice, she washed the feel of Drake's hands off her skin. To her chagrin, the memory stayed in place. Every move of her muscles reminded her of his vigorous lovemaking. Even now her skin tingled in the places he'd caressed and kissed. One thing was for sure. She'd been thoroughly fucked, and fucked well.

As she washed, she turned Iollan Drake over in her mind, mentally exploring every angle. Definitely like no man she'd ever slept with before, seemingly sincere and totally without guile.

To keep reminding herself he was a vicious criminal was almost impossible every time she thought about his muscular body and sexy accent. If he were really tied up in a sex cult, then he was responsible for the horrible fates that had befallen countless missing women and men. No matter what her personal feelings toward him might be, the bottom line was solidly drawn.

Imagine a cockroach, she thought, a defense to guard against his immense charisma. Her feminine instincts warned their paths would cross again.

Finished with her wash, she stepped out of the shower and reached for a towel. Her hand stopped in midair. A glance in the mirror revealed something she hadn't been expecting—or was even aware of.

Water dripping from her skin, Callie stepped closer to the vanity. She planted both hands on either side of the sink, leaning closer to the mirror. Her gaze flicked across her reflection, settling on her left breast. The punctures were shallow, too uneven to be a human bite. A purplish bruise surrounded them, as though the skin had been vigorously sucked.

She probed the small patch with curious fingers. It hurt. And, oddly, she didn't remember when he'd inflicted it. Pity. She would have enjoyed it. Still, she'd been marked. Branded by his passion. She found the idea strangely erotic.

Then reality set in.

Drake knew she liked pain. And he'd promised the night would be exquisite. Indeed, it had been. The thought that he knew her fetish heated her cheeks. Yes, she'd certainly opened up, in a way she hadn't intended. Confessing her secret had been utterly out of character. She had a weakness, an Achilles' heel, and had exposed it without thinking through the consequences. Not a wise move, but nothing in her training had prepared her for last night. *I thought I'd slain that demon.*

Apparently not.

Callie's mind snapped back to the present. Her mind had leapt off track, and she needed to focus. She reminded herself Drake was a criminal, a stone-cold killer suspected of taking down two of the agency's own. She shivered when it occurred to her that had she not played the game correctly, she might've been number three. Keeping cover and staying alive was worth forking over a little pussy.

Not that she regretted her decision. She didn't. She was a grown woman and hardly a virgin. Aware of her sexuality at a very early age, she'd come to terms with the fact that men wanted to fuck her. Sometimes she enjoyed it. Sometimes she didn't. Iollan Drake, she'd enjoyed.

But she'd never admit it aloud. In fact, she'd rather not admit that at all.

Sleeping with Iollan had put her in bed with the enemy. Roger would have to be informed. The thought made her cringe. As special agent in charge, Roger Reinke not only directed the investigation against Drake, he had an almost fanatical desire to bring his quarry down.

She knew without question Roger would push her to take Drake to the edge. Winning the criminal's trust was exactly the move he'd consider a master stroke. Truth be told, being the agent responsible for getting the cuffs on Drake's wrists would go a long way toward erasing the unflattering marks in her employee file. She needed the coup.

Her debriefing was going to be uncomfortable but unavoidable. Roger was frustrated by their recent lack of progress. Slippery as eels, Drake and his associates seemed to know they were being watched. Being led around by the nose like amateurs wasn't pleasant.

Brooding about it would accomplish nothing.

Callie finished toweling off and dropped her gaze toward the clothing she'd grabbed in haste. Dressing in a bustier and miniskirt this time of day was out of the question.

She glanced toward the closed door. Norton? Surely he wasn't waiting for her to come out. He wasn't that dumb. He'd probably taken the hint to scram.

She peeked out the door. The clink of utensils in motion

sounded. She smiled. Good old Paulie. He knew she'd be jonesing for her coffee. Caffeine and sugar first thing in the morning were needed to jump-start her system. Without it, she'd wilt like a daisy. Food was a negotiable thing; coffee, never!

Ten minutes later, she emerged from the bedroom. She walked into the living room. In the harsh morning light filtering through the open windows, there was no evidence she'd ever had company. She pressed her lips together, unsure if she was disappointed or relieved. Maybe even a little of both. Everything was where it was supposed to be. Almost. She cringed as her eyes reluctantly settled on the roses Roger had sent, still in their place.

She frowned. The crumpled card still lay beside them. Only it was no longer crumpled. It had been smoothed and laid out neatly. Bitter bile rose in the back of her throat. Her tongue suddenly felt like a piece of grit under her teeth.

She glanced at Paul Norton. He, in turn, was studying her intently with cat-green eyes. "Did Roger have you deliver these?" Her tone was cool, emotionless, detached. She wanted information, nothing more.

"Of course," Norton said. "Last night when no one was around."

Her throat tightened. "Did he say anything?"

Norton shrugged. "Happy birthday."

She gave him a dry look. "I guess it's good someone remembered."

"He's still a bastard, Callie," he said softly.

Pain speared her heart, starting in her chest and working its way outward. Tears misted her eyes. She quickly blinked them away. Paul had helped her through the breakup, keeping the flak from Roger at a minimum while she struggled to make the adjustment from lover back into employee.

"A fucking jerk," she agreed. Her affair with Roger was the

kind that left a woman breathless and quivering. An inventive and demanding lover, he'd found ways to use her body that left them both panting with exhaustion. For three years, everything had been perfect. Too perfect.

Working under the man she'd spent so many nights with was tough, but not impossible. Callie was used to things in her life ending without warning. Until she'd graduated high school and gone out on her own, she'd never known stability or permanence of any sort.

She'd never belonged to anyone or anybody for more than a few years. In the midst of agony, only one thing remained constant. At the end of the day when the door was shut and the lights turned off, she was alone.

It would, she felt, always be that way. Men might drift through, use her, abuse her, but they'd never stay. No one wanted damaged goods, no matter how prettily the package was wrapped.

Norton leaned over the counter separating living room and kitchen. Unspoken but hanging in the air between them was his support. He was letting her know he'd be there.

"Well," she said, struggling to say words that didn't quite come out. She wished she found him attractive. As a friend he was great. As a lover, she had the feeling kissing him would be like kissing a sibling. Unnatural and entirely wrong.

Norton scrubbed his scruffy beard as if fleas lived in the mass on his cheeks. "The fucking cupboards are bare," he informed her. In the process of making coffee, he'd set out a couple of mismatched mugs and spoons. A small jar of instant coffee sat nearby. "How the hell do you live here?"

She shrugged. "I don't." The bureau had rented the apartment as part of her undercover identity. She inhabited it as she did any other, simply as a place to lay her head until the time came to move on. Being shuffled through the foster care system had taught her never to get attached to anyone or any place.

She sighed. *Always living in, but never at home.*

Norton's gaze ranged over her well-worn leather jacket, T-shirt, faded denim jeans, and boots. "Still riding that Goddamn motorcycle without a helmet?"

Busted.

Callie ran her fingers through her hair to straighten the damp mess. Cut in a short, easy-to-style shag, blonde locks fell into place to frame her face. A half-assed grin tugged up one corner of her mouth. "Guess so."

He frowned. "You got a helmet?"

She shrugged. "Didn't have room to pack it."

"One of these days you'll hit asphalt and bust that skull of yours, brains leaking everywhere. Not a pretty ending for a pretty girl like you."

Callie rubbed the scar under her chin. She'd already kissed asphalt, not once but twice. Both times an asshole driving a car had caused the wreck. "I can walk away from a crash-and-burn. It's my specialty, you know."

He scowled. "Walking away?" he asked sourly, spooning instant into both mugs. Her brush-off obviously bothered him.

She shook her head. An emotional knot wedged in her throat. "Crashing and burning."

He stirred the coffee in both mugs, watching it dissolve. "I think you should be more careful."

Recognizing genuine concern beneath his frustration, Callie sighed. Damn. As an agent, Paul was top notch. As a man in lust, he wore his heart on his sleeve.

Norton slid a cup her way. "Coffee's ready."

Callie sat down on a stool in front of the counter, the equivalent of a dining room table in such a small space. She added a ton of sugar and a touch of cinnamon vanilla creamer Norton had dug out of the fridge. Aside from the creamer and a quart of skim milk, there was nothing else inside.

Ignoring his own coffee, Paul lit a cigarette.

Callie snagged it. Blessed nicotine filled her lungs. She welcomed the burn at the back of her throat. It reminded her she had a bit of life inside her. Her heart might be crushed, but her lungs were alive and well.

"Thought you were quitting." Paul lit a second for himself.

"I was, but I changed my mind." She took a deep drag; a pacifying rush of smoke filled her lungs. Nicotine was the only drug she indulged in. Already she was a pack-a-day smoker, and that number was increasing. "Just trying to keep myself together since Roger brought me in on this case."

Callie hadn't been one of the original agents assigned to the hunt. After her breakup with Roger, she'd been shuffled from field investigation to desk work, as nothing more than a glorified secretary. The cases she worked ranged from the mundane to just plain boring, not even a challenge. Her penance for being a bad girl. She'd been close to asking for a transfer when Roger had called her into his office and informed her she was on his team.

Callie had taken it as a sign that things were thawing between them, that they'd proceed with their relationship as professionals and nothing more. The arrival of the roses had thrown her. Surely he was just being kind; surely it hadn't been an overture toward taking up where they'd left off.

She wouldn't know until she saw him. And she wasn't sure she wanted to see him. Keeping her panties up while being around a man like Roger was a tough order for any woman.

Sighing, she smoothed a few stray wisps of hair behind her ears, then wrapped her hands around her coffee cup. Its warm surface was soothing. She lifted it to her lips and drank. Her hands, she noticed, trembled. A gurgle reminded her she'd soon need some breakfast. As usual, she'd have to eat out. There wasn't a morsel of food in the place.

Norton agreed. "This one's been a real bitch. I swear to

God, I've never seen people who can disappear so damn fast. I no more than get an ID on them, and they're gone."

Another long draw on the cigarette. Its tip glowed red before dying into ashes. "You think they're feeling the heat?"

Mouth drawing down in a vexed frown, Callie crinkled her brow in thought. Thinking back on her time with Drake, she couldn't recall a moment when he'd seemed uncomfortable or ill at ease in her company. She wasn't sure what it felt like to be a wanted criminal, but she knew if she'd been the fox in the henhouse that she'd be nervous as hell about the farmer toting the shotgun. Drake hadn't acted a bit out of the ordinary. Either he was a very good actor, or he didn't know. Or he did know and was setting a trap.

"I just don't know," she finally admitted. "Which is probably why I'm not the brains behind the investigation."

Norton nodded. "Yeah. This one's always been Roger's baby."

Callie leaned forward, placing her elbows on the counter and massaging her temples with her fingers. No one blamed Roger for wanting to get Drake into custody. If Drake weren't the murderer, perhaps enough leverage could be applied to find out who was.

A tremor shimmied down her spine at the thought of the two men in the same room. *That* would not be pleasant to witness at all. Had Roger not been an agent of the law, his pursuit of Drake would have bordered on vigilantism. In the back of her mind, Callie wasn't quite sure one of his agents wouldn't pull the trigger if given the chance and a clear shot. Several had volunteered to do the job. Roger would probably reserve the honor for himself.

Very probable and very possible. Such an incident could probably be swept under the rug without much fuss or bother. She doubted any of their superiors would care much.

Callie took a sip of her coffee and grimaced. Yuck. Cold. She found herself wishing for a tall double mocha latte with extra whipped cream and a warm croissant with sausage, egg, and cheese to appear. Instant was fine to get your eyes open, but she needed a real cup of coffee.

Norton took the hint. "You want me to skip out for something? There's a bakery down the street. I can grab some donuts and better coffee."

Callie considered his scruffy vagabond look. Few would suspect a well-educated, well-spoken man existed under the layers of grime and shabby clothing. "Sure. Donuts would be great."

Inwardly she winced. Junk food wasn't her normal choice, but with her schedule so whacked, she'd been eating catch-as-catch-can, and none of her choices had been healthful in the least. Add in the fact she'd been scrimping on her exercise, frequently missing her regular routine of a thousand sit-ups and equal number of push-ups. It was a mistake to get soft, lazy. She silently resolved she'd catch up as soon as possible.

Norton gave a thumbs-up. "Cool." He checked his watch, one of four cheap bands decorating his hairy wrist, just like a dime bag–buying junkie would have stolen. "Give me twenty minutes."

"Don't let anyone see you," she cautioned as if it were necessary.

Norton started to say something but a muddled beep interrupted his reply. He fished through a pocket, digging it out. "Christ," he muttered. "Such timing."

"What?"

He showed her the digital readout. The hair raised at the back of her neck. Jaw hardening, Callie's gut took an unpleasant jolt.

911.

6

Receiving the same message on her own pager, Callie set into action. Splitting up from Norton, she took off on her motorcycle, heading toward the nearby bus station. Once there, she claimed the large duffel bag she'd stashed in one of the coin-operated luggage lockers.

Bag in hand, she headed for the ladies' room and locked herself in a stall. Identification, badge, and gun were squirreled away inside the bag, along with a handheld computer, credit and gas cards, five thousand dollars in cash, a cell phone, and a change of clothes. The message on the pager meant one thing, and one thing alone.

Someone was dead.

She checked her cell. Two messages waited on voice mail.

Opening the phone, Callie called the service, punching in her code to pick up her messages. Both were terse, from Roger: County morgue, ASAP.

Jesus.

Slipping out of her jeans, she pulled on a pair of slacks before buttoning a black jacket over her T-shirt. She filled her pockets, arming up as a member of law enforcement. She drew a steadying breath. Catching a brief glimpse of her face in the mirror, she saw lines of worry puckering her forehead. Shadows lingered behind her gaze, the ghosts of disappointment and disillusionment. For all her apparent success in the field of law enforcement, her personal life was a washout. Work was the only thing keeping her sane. She wondered how long that would last working with Roger Reinke again.

"We are over." She slipped on a pair of sunglasses, happy to hide behind the impenetrable shield of plastic.

Callie returned her bag to the locker, slipping more coins into the slot. The woman walking out of the bus station looked and acted nothing like the woman who'd walked in. Not so much in the disguise, but in the attitude. She hailed a cab, heading downtown.

Thirty minutes later the cabbie dropped her off in the parking lot surrounding the offices of the county.

Paying the driver, Callie pocketed her change. The cab didn't have a good air conditioner, and recent rains had made the moist air even balmier than normal. A layer of sweat clung to her skin, something it seemed no amount of cold showers and soap washed away. She felt wet patches under her arms, trickles of sweat making their way down her spine to her underwear.

She pulled in a deep breath, taking in the scents of the city: a mixture of carbon monoxide and damp concrete tinged with the smell of pure human waste from a sewer system that threatened to overflow under the continual torrent of rain. Such were the familiar smells of Belmonde, Virginia.

She looked past the sidewalks, farther out onto the acres of beautifully manicured lawns. The grass was still green, reluctant to give in to the end of the cycle that would have it wither away to autumn's drab brown cloak. Stately old oak trees lined the northern perimeter of the grounds, perfectly in sync with the manicured hedges acting as a fence in lieu of man-made materials. Beyond the hedges lay the rest of the world, blissfully unaware death had struck down a fellow human being.

Callie hurried inside. The maze of halls confused most outsiders. Getting directions, she followed a narrow hallway to examination room number three. Her guts roiled. God, she hated looking at dead people.

Through the glass, she spotted Roger Reinke standing with three other agents. Agent Norton wasn't present. Roger, Charlie Grayson, and Mitch Reeve, she knew. The third man was Assistant Director in Charge Samuel Faber, their boss. So far he'd distanced himself from the investigation. Apparently that was about to change.

All agents present were dressed identically: black suit, white shirt, black tie, and shoes polished to a mirror-bright sheen. No wonder bureau agents were frequently identified as the *men in black*.

Brad Jackson, the county coroner, worked over the body. His skin was pallid from a life spent under fluorescent lighting, drinking too much coffee, and exercising too little. Dark circles drooped under his eyes, the result of many late nights laboring over the dead.

Callie tapped on the glass.

Reinke glanced up. There wasn't a sign of familiarity or warmth in his eyes in his acknowledgment of her arrival. He was in his work mode: stone cold, formal, and absolutely focused. Seeing her, he beckoned her inside. His gesture seemed to say, "hurry up and get your ass over here." The day was going to be a long one and these guys wanted to get on with business.

She walked to the door, braced herself, then opened it. Though outwardly calm, her nerves were on edge. "Death waits for no one," she murmured under her breath.

Set to a chilly sixty-five degrees, the air-conditioned room was like a salve on her flushed skin. All shiny metal and cool white tile, the autopsy room was immaculate, close to germless. The cleaning solutions used to sterilize and sanitize scorched her nostrils. Death, however, still lingered. Not exactly an actual smell, but more a psychological one. In Callie's mind each person's passing seemed to have a different odor—some not so bad, others reeking.

This one reeked.

Reinke broke away from the group examining the body. A strapping, no-nonsense veteran of the streets, he was all sharp edges and razor creases. Standing well over six feet, he not only entered a room, but filled it. Not only with his size, but with his commanding personality. Raw energy radiated around him.

Roger's intense gaze studied her a moment. "Agent Whitten. Glad you made it. We've been waiting." He didn't allow his expression or tone to give away his thoughts.

Her heart rate sped up. Roger had fifteen years on her age-wise, but that meant nothing. At forty-five he was vital and vigorous, having twice the energy of a much younger man.

Figuratively speaking, seeing Roger was like having shards of glass ground into her eyes. It hurt. "I came as soon as I got the messages." There was nothing else to say that would be appropriate, so she said nothing. Callie could only look at her ex-lover.

And remember.

Seeing him so close, a fierce urge to beg him to take her back shot through her mind. How in the name of God had she gotten along without him for six months? If she closed her eyes, she easily pictured him naked, palming her hips in his huge hands, fingers digging tightly, almost painfully, into her skin, pushing the tip of his cock against her clit, teasing but not entering. Roger enjoyed making her beg for it.

She'd begged.

Remembering his possessive touch, her skin responded with

fire. The air in the cramped room seemed to evaporate. She was suddenly burning up despite the chill. She unzipped her jacket.

Roger's eyes caught the move. A secret knowing smile crossed his lips. He knew exactly what lay under her clothes. She might as well have stripped down to her skin by the hungry look lurking in his eyes.

She turned away. Damn, that man's gaze was an *eyefuck* almost as satisfying as sex itself. She'd believed she was ready to work with Roger again, despite the ugly end of their affair. She was mistaken. She was far from ready. She had no business accepting this assignment.

The rhythm of her heart sped up. She cursed herself for allowing her emotions to simmer. In the back of her mind, she measured the man she'd have to stand up against. If he wanted to play it that way, she'd have to brush him off and give him the cold shoulder. Indulging herself with him had almost ruined her personally. Letting it destroy her professionally would be the last nail in her coffin. That couldn't happen. It would be a test of her mettle to go on as if nothing had ever happened between them.

Nothing at all, would be her mantra.

She swallowed, attempting to banish her fear and discomfort. The morning's coffee curdled in her stomach. Fear was an emotion for the weak. Fear would make her too afraid to go on with her life. Fear would destroy her, shred her like a small animal under the claws of a larger, hungrier beast. She had to be intense, focused, relentless.

Clearing her mind of thoughts related to their affair, Callie refocused her attention. "What happened?"

Without missing a beat, Reinke answered. "We've got another victim." In the span of a few seconds his gaze had changed, to cold, flat, and impersonal. "Take a look for yourself."

Callie looked. Tension returned. Damn. She hated looking at dead people, especially murder victims.

Under the glare of probing lights, the naked victim was female, young, and, once, very pretty. Hair the color of pure corn silk straggled around her face and shoulders, strangely bright against the unhealthy pallor of her skin. A simple gold cross on a chain circled her neck.

The jolt of recognition struck powerfully.

Callie felt the blood drain from her face. Just a day before, the girl had been alive and, seemingly, well. Though not a particularly religious person, Callie hoped the cross offered a comfort to the woman before she died. In the back of her mind she doubted the thought.

Squelching her rising emotion, she clenched a hand at her side. If she cried, it would ruin the illusion she was desperate to create, one of control and distance.

Callie blinked.

The victim didn't. Brown eyes stared up with an opaque gaze. Her complexion was pale, as if God had cast her in wax instead of flesh. Dried blood crusted both nostrils. The trail had rounded her mouth to track down her chin and neck. Colorless lips were drawn back in a rictal grimace. She'd resisted death.

And lost.

The medical examiner caught the look on her face. "First one you've seen like this?"

Callie nodded. "Yes."

Reinke watched her every reaction like a hawk. "Know who she is?"

Mouth all of a sudden desert dry, Callie swallowed, reminding herself to breathe. Still, the invisible fingers refused to lessen their grip. Trying to clear her mind, she felt both sick and shaky, like someone suffering a nerve-shattering shock. Her head felt as though it had been squeezed in a vise.

She swayed slightly, then shook her head as if to regain her inner balance. The twinge in her shoulders was turning into relentless knots. "I don't know her name, but I saw her at the bar last night with Drake. They seemed on good terms."

Reinke's lips formed a cruel line across his face. "Apparently things changed." His voice was barely restrained fury.

Stay calm. "So it seems."

Leveling an unflinching gaze, Reinke angrily pointed to the body. His expression was so intense it seemed the pressure from his clenched jaw would shatter his face. "That's what Drake does when he tosses them back."

His words flooded her mind. Fighting the clench of nerves, Callie drew in a breath, striving to keep her own expression neutral. "How long has she been dead?"

The coroner raised his head. "Not long. From the liver temperature, I'd guess it was sometime late last night."

Feeling a sudden pressure behind her eyes, Callie lifted a hand to massage her temple. A queasy sensation was slithering into her bowels. This case had taken a turn down a complicated path. She knew for a fact Drake had slipped out of Hell-Bound Train around two AM—taking the woman with him. It seemed inconceivable he could commit murder, and then chase Callie down a few hours later.

Inconceivable, maybe. Impossible? Not entirely. Especially if he had help.

"Where was she found?"

Agent Charlie Grayson consulted his notebook. "Down in the NoLo, an alley behind one of the abandoned hotels. Sanitation workers found her this morning around seven." *NoLo* was local slang for Belmonde's lower north side. Part of the city's red-light district, the sin and skin trade was alive and well. Along the strip of back streets hosting the city's sex trade, the sultry town sizzled with blazing hot adult entertainment.

The time was presently ten after one in the afternoon. It hadn't taken long for the feds to swoop in and claim the victim from local law enforcement.

"Go ahead and fill her in," Reinke said.

The ME nodded. A balding gnome, nature had put tiny eyes over a large nose and an even larger mouth, none of which matched. Fingers stained with nicotine, he continually dressed the same way: wrinkled khakis, and a lab coat stained with blood, food, and God knew what else.

"We know this one belongs to our suspect, as he rarely deviates from his chosen methods." Brad Jackson lifted one of the victim's hands. A series of gouges, like a perfect dotted line, ringed the girl's wrist. The gouges weren't deep, just enough to penetrate the surface of the skin. The other wrist bore identical damages, as did her neck.

Callie gave a tight grimace. "What did that?"

Jackson peered over the rim of heavy plastic frames. "My guess is some kind of restraint, very tight and most likely very uncomfortable to endure. Only the most sadistic mind could've conceived something like this to assert control."

An emotional knot wedged in Callie's throat. Her hand clenched tighter, as if to squeeze away any influences his words might have transferred to her. The prickle rising at the back of her neck kicked up a notch. Being bound with something that invasive must have been terrifying.

"Go on." Not that she wanted to hear any more.

With the help of an aide, the body was lifted and turned. A shallow hole gaped at the base of the victim's skull. "Of the five victims we know of," Jackson continued, "all have this same injury—the death blow. Savage, cold, and downright barbaric."

An understatement.

Jackson commenced to fill her in for the next fifteen minutes. The rest of the girl's body bore intense bruises and other cuts. By the bruising between her gently spread legs, there was no doubt that she'd been sexually assaulted. Their best hope at this point was for semen or saliva to provide them with a DNA profile of the offender—or offenders. The possibility existed that more than one man was involved.

Though Callie heard Jackson's words, they registered as little more than a drone in her ears. Too many thoughts were tumbling through her head to pay attention. Less than twelve hours ago the corpse was a living, breathing human being.

Now the unknown girl was dead, no more than an empty shell soon to rot away into little more than a pile of bones. Who she was, what she was, the sins she'd committed didn't matter anymore. Death had wiped away her identity, her joy and sorrows. Only her pain remained, stark and brutal. Because she'd passed from life in such a tragic way, those who survived would be responsible for seeking justice, speaking for one no longer able.

By the time Jackson finished, Callie was too drained to think. Fighting the clench of nerves, she scrubbed her numb face, disbelieving. "Shit." The victim's injuries exactly matched those in autopsy photos she'd viewed of other victims.

Small scars flicked across the victim's neck, shoulders, breasts, and abdomen. Well healed, these were obviously inflicted before death.

Callie thought about her own scars, and wondered. The impulse died before she gave it further consideration, vanishing like ashes in the wind. Something else took its place, more important than a few old scars on a corpse.

As much as she hated the idea, it was entirely possible she'd just slept with the man who'd carried out the vicious rape and execution. The location of the body was too near the previous three victims to be a coincidence. This one, like the others, wouldn't be going into the papers. As an ongoing federal investigation, a press blackout would be declared.

Callie turned away from the body. She needed a moment to think, gather her thoughts. Not an easy thing. Her mind was a jumble, personal knowledge warring with duty, doing the right thing versus doing the wrong thing. Without really considering the consequences, she'd put herself between a rock and a hard place. Sleeping with her had given Drake something she hadn't remotely considered.

An alibi.

Science could only guesstimate when the girl had died. Eye witnesses might place Drake in the bar with the victim, but leaving a bar with a woman and killing her were two different things. His best bet toward a plea of innocence would be to have another person verify his whereabouts.

Preferably someone he was intimate with at the time. The strategy was brilliant. A master stroke.

She leveled an unflinching gaze at the image reflected in the window. Head tilted slightly, her pale face was taut with uncertainty. She didn't want to look at herself more than she had to, but some inner compulsion drove her to stare down the face the glass presented.

She swallowed a gasp. The woman in the glass looked guilty. *If it's true it's him,* she silently fretted, *how do I confront this?*

Her heart beat wildly, pulse racing with anxiety. Oh, God, why didn't she think things through before letting Drake into her apartment? Unfortunately, regret, like hindsight, was always more easily examined in retrospect.

Callie closed her eyes, leaning forward to press her burning forehead into the glass. The cool surface was soothing, like a balm to her soul. She felt as if someone had led her to the top of a cliff and then, without warning, pushed her off. Somehow, she'd managed to catch the edge, but she was still left to dangle helplessly high above the ground.

I fucked up.

Roger's voice broke into her thoughts, sharp and more than a bit annoyed. "Something wrong, Agent Whitten?"

No answer.

Snapping out of the trance she'd fallen into, Callie considered her options for a few seconds. Drawing in a deep fortifying breath, she made a decision.

Time to confess.

7

"And you're sure of the time frame Drake was with you?" Roger Reinke asked.

Callie nodded. "Yes," she answered crisply. "After leaving the bar, I made contact with Norton to debrief, then proceeded along my normal route."

Roger scowled. "No side trips anywhere?"

Ignoring his apparent dissatisfaction, Callie shook her head. "None. I've been careful to keep the same schedule and habits."

"And your contact with Drake has been . . ." He let the question trail off. An hour had passed since the agents pulled together a hasty meeting in the morgue's conference room, but no one seemed satisfied with her answers.

Callie sighed. The grilling was uncomfortable, but unavoidable. She'd already covered these details, twice. Her superiors had expected progress, were hungry for the break that had thus far eluded them. She understood she had to be precise, give agents all the information they needed to establish Drake's patterns.

Ignoring the edgy tone in Roger's voice, she broke eye contact and reached for her cigarettes. Her fifth so far. The idea of quitting had long passed. Charlie Grayson asked to bum a smoke, his third. She quietly passed him one, mentally noting the morning's freshly opened pack was nearing empty as the afternoon progressed.

Wasting no time, Grayson lit up and took a long drag before returning the lighter. "Thanks. Now a cup of coffee would make my day."

She briefly nodded. "No problem."

Reinke cleared his throat in disapproval. "If you don't mind, please proceed."

Callie exhaled a lungful of smoke. "My contact with Drake has been exactly as instructed. I've been friendly, making small talk, eyeing him up and expressing my interest." She flicked the ashes into a nearby ashtray. "I suppose he got the message."

Having let Roger Reinke conduct the majority of the interview, Assistant Director in Charge Samuel Faber looked up from his notes, which he'd jotted on a yellow legal pad.

An ex-military man still sporting a crew cut, Faber was fanatical about bending no rule. He was one rung up in the chain of command, the man calling all the shots. "Is it possible you and Norton were seen together?"

Callie glanced up at Faber. Through the last hour, his laser beam stare hadn't left her once. Probing, dissecting, visually slicing her to pieces. She wondered if he simply disapproved of her less formal style, or if he was sizing her up and finding her performance inadequate.

Or maybe he knew she was lying. It occurred to her Norton was able to slip into her apartment any time he wanted—easy enough to plant a listening or recording device.

Paranoid.

Reining in her wild theories, Callie concentrated on focusing on the task at hand. She had information. These men needed it. Simple. She shouldn't be taking it personally. Faber wasn't being a bastard for putting her feet to the fire. He had a job to do, as did she. "More than possible," she finally concurred. "Same street corner, same time, every night. I buy a couple of joints and slip him a twenty-dollar bill."

The marijuana Paul Norton sold was, in fact, nothing more noxious than parsley, better eaten than smoked. Buying from her dealer gave a plausible reason for the two to be seen together. Local law enforcement had the heads-up that both were federal agents. Norton had been hassled by the street cops as part of his cover. Callie had been busted once, taken in, but quickly cut loose and hustled out the back door—a vital move allowing her street credibility to remain intact.

Faber nodded. "Any chance Drake's made you out to be an agent?"

Callie briefly focused her attention on her cigarette, watching the smoke rise from its tip. "I doubt it. We've been too damn careful. My professional judgment is he believes he's found an easy snatch."

Mitch Reeve snickered, giving her the eye. "And was it easy?"

Callie glanced across the table. Her eyes narrowed. Asshole. "Was what easy?"

"For him to pick you up?" Innuendo laced Reeve's broadside. He'd struck a nerve, and not in a pleasant way.

A quicksilver cutting remark jumped to the end of her tongue. Close to letting loose a verbal bitch slap, Callie thought better of it. Men were pigs. Why did they turn into immature jerks the minute sex was mentioned?

Sitting among these men, Callie felt every bit the outsider, an interloper in their all-male club. Every damn one of them had degrees out the ass. She had two, a bachelor's degree in computer science, as well as an associate's degree in criminal justice. She'd served her country and earned her qualifications and the right to sit among their rarefied number. Yet something would always be a barrier between them.

They had balls. She didn't.

She had a twat, and her sex would always be a strike against her in a man's profession. *As long as you can do the job, it's not about being male or female*, she reminded herself. *It's all in the details.*

Fighting to maintain her composure, Callie clasped her hands together until her knuckles whitened from the pressure. She hated the games, but she knew how to play them. "Sure. I'm cheap and I'm easy." She intended the statement to sound blithe. Instead, her tone was tinged with a longing and loneliness betraying the hollow void in her soul.

Reeve's tongue went into his cheek in a manner leaving no doubt what he was thinking about. "And you did what?"

So hot a moment ago, a chilly perspiration soaked her, dotting her forehead. "I almost had a fucking panic attack," she snapped. "What would you do if the man you had under surveillance followed you home at three in the morning?"

A cunning glint sidled into the depths of Reeve's eyes. "I'd invite him in."

The rest of the men laughed.

Barely hanging on to her composure, Callie tried to ignore them. Impossible. The tension in the room still felt like a noose around her neck. At any moment someone was bound to kick the chair out from under her feet. "That's exactly what I did," she shot back coolly. "I felt contact should be maintained as long as possible."

Charlie Grayson clapped her on the shoulder. "You did the right thing. You are one cool chick." He pointed to his partner. "Now Mitch here, he'd have screamed like a little girl. God forbid some sexual predator got hold of his precious virgin ass."

Sitting on the other side of the narrow table, Mitch Reeves tossed his middle finger. "Fuck you, Grayson. You've been trying to get in my pants since we partnered. That 'don't ask, don't tell' policy is totally bogus."

Grayson flicked his butt toward his partner. "No, it just covers perverts like you." He pretended to think a moment. "Maybe I should tell them about the stakeout of that gunrunner's farm. . . ."

A service weapon was drawn, safety flicked off. "If you say one Goddamn word, Charlie, I swear to God, I'll blow you away." Reeve's eyes were crazed, almost fanatically so. "I'll fucking sit in prison, man."

Charlie Grayson raised his arms in surrender. "Chill, dude. Chill. I'll never tell."

The gun was put away. "I'm warning you, asshole."

Charlie Grayson flicked a shit-eating grin. "I want your house, your car, and your wife in return for my silence."

A set of keys flipped across the table. "The tank's almost empty, so fill it up on the way home, please. And good luck with getting the fat bitch off the couch."

Grayson considered the keys. "I'm a fag, remember?" He tossed the keys back. "And I've seen your wife. No wonder you prefer sheep."

The two agents collapsed into snickers and giggles. Charlie Grayson wasn't gay and Mitch Reeve, as far as anyone knew, didn't screw farm animals. Partnered long enough to practically be Siamese twins, they loved nothing better than to keep the jokes flying.

Callie rolled her eyes and blew out an exasperated breath. If the taxpayers who signed their paychecks saw them in action, Grayson and Reeve would be fired as idiots.

Roger Reinke cleared his throat in a severe manner, leaving no room for argument or further high jinks. A certain amount of joking was necessary to keep the pressure down. However, enough was enough. His frown was deadly, silencing the guilty. "Up the hall we have a dead body, yet another victim of a man we can't seem to lay our hands on. I am sure that poor girl's family wouldn't find your jokes hilarious. Put a cap on it. We have work to do."

Grayson and Reeve sobered.

Roger nodded approval. "Now, back to Agent Whitten." He addressed Callie directly. "You said you believed Drake might try to use you as an alibi. How long, exactly, was he with you?"

As if she hadn't given this answer already. "An hour." She paused. "Maybe a little more. I can't really remember."

A hint of irritation drew down the corners of Faber's mouth. A ridge of muscle tightened in his jaw. "You can't remember?" He spoke precisely, watching her in a way that scraped along her exposed nerves. Focused gray eyes never wavered. He watched her like a hawk, ready to swoop in and snatch its prey.

Callie rubbed her eyes with a trembling hand. Her head hurt, her body burned and she didn't want to tell the whole truth. "With all due respect, sir, I was tired. It was a long night. I fell asleep."

Samuel Faber sent her a look that nailed her protests into the ground. "Ah. I see." A smirk played around the corners of his mouth. "Before Drake left, or after?"

That one caught her by the short hairs. Shit. Must he keep circling back to what she and Drake had done? In a roundabout way, she'd already revealed all she cared to. "After, sir." Her first lie. So far she'd managed to wriggle around admitting she'd slept with Drake. The fire under the frying pan was getting hotter. Her ass was starting to sizzle.

"I see."

No, you don't. The throbbing building behind her eyes threatened to knock her eyeballs out of her skull. She pressed a hand to her forehead. Mistake. Anyone able to read body language could tell she was lying.

Realizing her error, Callie let her hand drop. The pain receded, but the slivers stabbing her psyche did not. Heaven help her, she was about to have a nervous breakdown. At the critical moment something she'd misidentified as desire had turned her into a liar. She neither liked the bitter feeling in the pit of her soul, nor the bile rising in the back of her throat.

Faber leaned back in his chair. Lacing his fingers together, he studied her carefully. "Now, when Drake was in your apartment, what exactly did you do?"

Hearing his question, Callie suddenly lost her breath. The room had fallen deathly silent. A painful sensation began to work its way up her spine. Traveling her shoulders, it snaked through the back of her neck and straight into her skull. She felt the air around her shift, the pressure on her lungs almost robbing her of breath. "I offered him a cup of coffee and we talked."

"About?"

"About the same thing I told you last time." A hint of exasperation colored her tone. "He wanted to know if I was single, had a boyfriend, all the things a man tries to find out about a woman he wants to fuck."

Faber didn't blink. "And did he?"

She didn't flinch. "Did he what?"

"Did you, Agent Whitten, have sex with the suspect?" Faber asked.

Callie met Faber's gaze with her own wary one. He looked at her like he knew she'd committed the unforgivable sin. A prickle of fear needled under her skin as she turned her answer over in her mind, examining it from every angle, dissecting, poking, and probing. Faber, she felt, was going to hammer away at the point until he got the answer he seemed to want. Down to the wire, concealing her actions from a superior to shield a criminal would be a stupid move. There was little time to debate her answer.

She lied.

"No. I did not." In the back of her mind, she wished another female agent had drawn this one. Her attraction to Drake wasn't good at all. In a room full of her peers, she'd just perjured herself in the investigation of a federal case. If asked the same question by a grand jury, the consequences of her falsehood would probably inflict more than a guilty conscience.

As it was, her lie was threatening to eat through her guts. She considered excusing herself, asking to use the ladies' room. No, if she went she'd be sick. Totally wiped out, she hung onto her composure by the thinnest of threads.

One bound to snap at any moment.

Faber folded his arms across his chest. "Good. You know, that would have been a violation of bureau policy."

Callie drew a deep breath, trying to organize her thoughts. She felt nauseated. "Yes, sir." Her throat worked painfully. "I am aware of that."

Roger Reinke leaned forward. "So what's our next move?"

Faber shifted his gaze to his second in command. "We've been working this case how long, Roger?"

"Almost a year, sir. A lot of time, money, and manpower have gone into bringing Drake and his people in. We have five known civilian victims, and we've lost two agents."

Faber frowned. "There's no doubt in my mind we need to catch Drake. "However it's clear that our methods to this point haven't proved successful. We're going to have to rethink the mousetrap."

"We're open to suggestions," Reinke said.

Faber thought a moment. "So far as I have ascertained, Agent Whitten is the one who's gotten closest to Drake. I think we should encourage this connection." His unblinking gaze settled on Callie. "I am going to assume you were given no way to contact this man, that the meeting was entirely of his time and choosing."

Callie wiggled a little. "He seems to be working on his own timetable, sir."

Faber continued. "You stated earlier you were somewhat intimate with Drake. Did you find this disagreeable?"

The men around her had fallen deathly silent. Surely Faber wasn't going to suggest . . . No! It seemed too outrageous that he'd even consider the idea.

She decided to hedge. "Considering I was faced with a man known to be dangerous, I found myself a bit uncomfortable in his company."

"Yet you were able to make small talk, and share in some level of intimacy?" Faber asked.

Callie nodded.

"Please speak up for the tape recorder, Agent Whitten."

She cleared her throat. "During the time we spent together, the suspect conducted himself in a pleasant and appealing manner. As a woman, I found him attractive in a curious sort of way."

Roger Reinke's face brewed a sudden thundercloud of jealousy. By the look on his face he clearly wasn't happy with the direction Faber's line of questioning was taking.

Callie gave a quick shake of her head. *No, not now.* He quelled his anger before the rest of the agents noticed it.

Faber's thick fingers tapped the tabletop. "Good. Then you had no objection becoming intimate with him?"

Callie's cheeks heated more. She inhaled a breath. "No, sir. I had no objection when he kissed me." She didn't elaborate on what else they'd done.

Samuel Faber leaned forward in his chair, pinning her down under his heavy gaze. "I'm going to ask you a question, Agent Whitten."

Tingling anticipation tightened Callie's chest. She hadn't meant to get in this deep. Yet with one indiscretion she'd put herself in a situation she couldn't back out of. She certainly couldn't argue unfamiliarity with illicit sex. "Go ahead, sir."

Faber went on. "Before you answer, please think about it. This investigation is at a point where we can't afford to make any mistakes. What I am going to ask of you will require something that will take you above and beyond the call of duty."

Callie's hands clenched into tight balls in her lap. "I understand."

Faber rubbed one droopy cheek, considering his next words. "Good. Because as of this hour I am giving you sanctioned clearance to pursue a sexual relationship with Iollan Drake."

Profound disbelief caused all male jaws to drop. Silence followed, as if everyone in the room had ceased to breathe. The lull lasted only a second, then the conference room exploded into a series of protests.

"Sir, I must remind you that an agent having sex with a suspect to gain information toward prosecution is a gray area where the law is concerned," Roger Reinke pointed out.

"The bureau has never exactly enforced the rule against exploiting sex in an investigation," Faber countered. He glanced over the rim of his glasses to emphasize his next words. "And as far as I know, it isn't illegal for two consenting adults to have relations."

Reinke's brow furrowed. "This one's tricky, sir, as we're dealing with a man who acquires and manipulates females for sexual purposes."

Faber spread his hands. "Seems a little hypocritical to balk, Roger. What is she supposed to do? Play patty-cake with him? If Drake thinks she's someone he can manipulate, he'll take her. Once we know his base of operations, we can move in and shut him down. Until we have that location, we're dead in the water."

Charlie Grayson broke in. "If the agent agrees, I say it's worth the risk."

Callie wasn't sure whether to hug the man or slap him. "I'm willing to do this."

"We've lost Kelso and Parker already," Reeve reminded, shaking his head. "A third agent would be unconscionable."

"I second that," Reinke said. "Putting a female agent directly in the line of fire is irresponsible."

The argument consumed fifteen minutes, with the pros and cons all listed and checked off one by one. Everyone was clearly tired and frustrated with the progress of the investigation, or lack thereof. A break was vital and needed. Soon.

Faber listened to both sides, then rapped the table with his knuckles. "Don't think I haven't considered all those options. I'm also considering the fact Agent Whitten is the only—and I repeat, the only—operative who has gotten one-on-one with Drake. The rest of you have seen him, tailed him, and lost him time and time again. If you've been made as the heat, he'll continue to give you guys the slip. As she is new to the investigation, I believe Agent Whitten is the best one to continue contact."

"I'll accept that," Roger Reinke said. "As long as my objection to the plan is recognized and documented."

"So noted," Faber said toward the small recorder taping the entire meeting. He turned back to Callie. "It's going to be your call, Whitten. Do you think you can do this if we send you in deeper? I won't lie to you, and you obviously know the risks."

The fact that she was being sanctioned to do what she'd already done immediately helped clear Callie's conscience. It also took her butt out of a sling.

"I can handle this," she assured them.

8

Donna's Diner looked like it hadn't been cleaned since the day it opened, at least thirty years ago, maybe more. More antiquated than antique, it was little more than a hole-in-the-wall, somehow surviving on an avenue ending in a cul-de-sac.

At Donna's, none of the questionable clientele had either eyes or ears. In such an area it was better to be blind and dumb. At least half the people had outstanding warrants on their heads. Not even free donuts enticed law enforcement to step through the door.

Blinds covered the front windows, darkening the booths inside. Easy to disappear, take a load off. Eat some bad food, drink coffee stout enough to curl hair. More than that, Donna's was a free zone. Come inside and the world outside didn't dare intrude.

Usually.

Callie sat in the rear of the diner, back to the wall so the entrance would always be in plain view. Hands curled around a hot cup of coffee, she waited for the meal she'd just ordered from the waitress. A dive stinking of lard and backed-up sewer, it was not the best place in town to get decent food. Operating twenty-four hours a day, the place mostly served the drug dealers, pimps, and hookers working the north side strip. Shootings were as common as the roaches skittering across the linoleum.

She sipped. The chipped cup wasn't exactly clean, but the coffee was strong and hot. With enough cream and sugar added it even tasted good. At half past four in the afternoon, if she didn't get some food in her soon, she'd faint from hunger.

Her gaze traveled to the front of the diner. The door opened. A man came in.

Callie winced, sliding down on the torn vinyl seat. She closed her eyes, muttering a silent curse. Shit. What was he doing here? She'd hoped she'd given Roger the dodge after the meeting. She didn't want to see him, didn't want to talk to him right now.

Go away, Roger.

He didn't.

Picking her out of the half-empty diner, he walked up to her table. "I need to talk to you."

A frown wrinkled her forehead, punctuating the headache that had been building behind her eyes for the last hour. Sharp suit and with an air of getting down to brass tacks, he was clearly out of his element, standing out like a sore thumb among the riffraff. He didn't fit in; he didn't want to.

"No, you don't."

Ignoring her, he slid into the seat across the table. He was breaking the rules tracking her down in public. If he wanted to trash his career and hers, he was getting off to a fine start. If word of their meeting got around, they would both be sunk with a capital *S*.

Roger didn't look happy. "Don't do it," he said flatly.

She tensed. "What?"

His burning gaze settled on her face. "Don't play dumb, Caroline," he said, using her real name. "I want you to go to Faber and tell him you changed your mind."

Callie bristled at the possessive tone in his voice. "Why should I do that?" she returned coolly. "It could be the break we've been waiting for."

Roger shook his head, swearing lightly under his breath. "You've only been on this case a couple of weeks. You don't know all the details. Drake's dangerous."

The look she gave him showed no amusement.

He smiled thinly. "I'm not calling you a fool, but you don't have to be so blindly stupid either. I'm not willing to let you put yourself in danger just because you think you need to prove yourself."

Anger knotted through her. She felt a certain hollowness in her gut that had nothing to do with hunger and everything to do with resentment. "Your concern for my safety is touching, but I was under the impression Faber put me on this case because I have the ability to do the job."

He ignored her. "If you're doing this to get even with me, fine. We're even."

Callie leaned into the table, bridging the gap between them. There were a lot of ears in this place. Anyone could hear anything. "This isn't about you, or whatever we might have been in past times, Roger. I'm a federal agent, just like you. Trained to do whatever it takes to do my job."

Gaze colliding with hers, he smiled thinly. His eyes narrowed, skimming over her in blatant disapproval. "Spreading your legs for Drake isn't the way to do your job," he hissed in an accusatory tone.

His words hit like a slap, the force literally taking her breath away. Insides going cold, Callie swallowed against the wave of mortification rising in her gut. She gave herself a mental shake, forcing herself not to take it personally.

Dangerously close to losing her temper, Callie reminded herself that he'd worked the case a lot longer than she had.

She'd gotten closer to Drake in three short weeks than he had in months. She couldn't afford to make any mistakes now.

Seething, she propped her elbow on the table. *He's just being a prick.* If he thought he was going to get her tossed, he had another think coming. Let him needle. She was a big girl. She'd survive.

"That was low," she said quietly. "I didn't deserve that at all." Emotion tightening her throat, frustration lent a bite to her voice.

Roger started to say something, but the waitress interrupted. Callie's order had arrived, giving a welcome break to the tension, almost a physical barrier between them. The waitress deposited a greasy cheeseburger and greasier fries on the table in front of her. "Here you go. Need anything else?"

Sitting like a stone, Callie shook her head. "The food looks fine." It didn't, but she wasn't about to argue. She was so damn hungry she'd eat a shoe.

The waitress looked at her new customer expectantly. "Anything for you?"

He nodded. "Just coffee, please."

The waitress sashayed off, returning a moment later with the coffeepot. She plunked down a cup and filled it to the brim. The gum in her mouth snapped. "There you go, honey." For good measure, she refilled Callie's coffee cup.

"Thanks."

"Yeah." The waitress sauntered over to another table, leaving them alone.

Roger sipped his coffee and grimaced. "Pure shit."

Callie fiddled with her food, dousing the fries with a load of watery ketchup and picking the tomatoes and pickles off her burger. "It's cheap." She nodded toward a pack of garishly outfitted women, obviously hookers. "Just the kind of place a whore would hang out."

Roger's brows drew together. "I'm sorry." His apology

was more automatic than sincere. "When I said that, I didn't mean it."

She shrugged. "Uh-huh." She bit into a French fry. It crunched like grit under her teeth. She forced herself to swallow it anyway. "Whatever."

He leaned forward, rubbing his face with his hands. "You don't know how damn difficult this is for me." He glanced up, his gaze seeking hers. Tightly restrained passion simmered in the depths of his eyes. "Seeing you, not being able to be with you, is driving me crazy."

Appetite vanishing, Callie pushed her food away. A cold damp sweat had risen on her skin. She wasn't prepared to deal with the raw wound their breakup had inflicted on her heart. Just when she thought she'd mended, he had to come along and rip the fucking bandage off. She bled all over again. "Don't go there, Roger."

He shook his head. "I can't stop myself." He reached across the table. His fingers brushed hers. "I still love you, baby."

Callie glanced down at the hand that covered hers. Surprisingly, his touch didn't heat her blood the way Iollan Drake's had. She started a bit, cheeks flushing. Her body didn't yearn to press close to his.

Nothing.

She felt a twinge of guilt at the realization, but only the slightest of twinges. His wants and desires were irrelevant. She simply didn't care how he felt, and resented that he'd tried to manipulate her.

An awkward and uncomfortable silence throbbed between them.

Struggling to hold on to her calm, Callie slowly moved her hand out from under his. She picked up her coffee cup, taking a long drink of the fortifying caffeine. It was cold, tasted terrible, but she forced herself to swallow it anyway.

Ignoring his own coffee, Roger watched her. The pressure to

say something hung between them, but he refused to be the first to speak.

Lowering her cup, Callie exhaled a heavy breath. She was tired of collecting memories she'd only regret later. "I don't love you." She cleared her throat and forced herself to say the rest. "Not anymore."

Surprised by her words, he abruptly drew back. Lines of frustration creased his brow. "You really mean that?"

Hands clenched around her cup, Callie refused to drop her gaze. She studied him a long moment, considering. "Yes, I do. I really do. I've moved on. I suggest you do the same." The words came out easier the second time, stronger and more confident. A curious lightness filled her. She felt better. A whole hell of a lot better.

A ridge of muscle tightened in his jaw as a hint of irritation drew down the corners of his mouth. "I just don't want you to get hurt."

Callie wondered if that was supposed to give her any comfort. How ironic, she mused. He was the last damn man on earth who should be able to say that.

She leaned back in her seat and tried to relax. "Spare me your concern, please. You made your choice and I've had to make mine. What happened between us is in the past. We have to work together, so let's just keep it professional."

Roger's lips pulled into a thin, tight line. He leaned back to put some space between them. "I suppose that's the only way we can play it now."

Callie shrugged stiffly. "The only way," she agreed. "Let's not make this any harder than it has to be."

Uncomfortable now, he cleared his throat. "Do you have anything else to add?"

She considered her options for a few seconds, then made her decision. No reason to further the antagonism between them. She sucked in a deep breath, clearing her mind of thoughts related to their affair, and refocused her attention on the assignment she had yet to fulfill.

"I'm a good agent, Roger. You know that." As an emphasis to her words, she pinned him under an unblinking gaze. "You trained me."

He flinched, but didn't waver as she'd thought he would. Hand rising to stroke his chin, he appeared to give her words due consideration. "Personal considerations aside, you are one of my best. Faber knows it, too. He believes you have what it takes to put the heat on Drake. Truthfully, when we considered a female agent, you were the only one we thought of."

A feather would have knocked Callie on her ass. "Thank you. I appreciate your confidence."

He frowned. "I'll be frank when I tell you that what we're asking you to do isn't something agents haven't done before to get necessary evidence. You know as well as I do that undercover work sometimes takes agents outside their comfort zone. If you can handle the assignment, then let's proceed."

She had to give him credit. When it came to putting on the stiff upper lip, Roger Reinke could do just that. The bureau claimed his loyalty, first and foremost. Wife, mistress, family. Everything else came second.

A smile tugged at her lips. She suppressed it. She'd had her taste of Drake and liked it well enough to take another. No matter the risk. Because of the danger or simply because being with a man dulled the ache of going without sex for six months she wasn't sure. "It's just sex."

His intense gaze studied hers for a long moment. He considered her words before responding. "For which you are expected to take all precaution."

She nodded. "That would be reasonable. I think I can handle it."

A really long pause followed.

The silence got to her.

"What?"

He drilled her down under stormy gray eyes. "I'm not going to lie to you. This assignment will seriously change your status as an agent."

His words sent tiny little shivers all over her skin. A volatile mix of emotions writhed in her gut. She forced herself to sit still. Damn it, she was stronger than this. "What do you mean?"

Expression stern, he shook his head. "Just that your career is about to move into an entirely new level," he said for clarification. "I'll give you fair warning and one last chance to back out. After that, you're in, come hell or high water. Understood?"

She took a minute to absorb that tidbit of information. Curiosity took hold. She'd expected Roger to somehow find a way to railroad her out of the investigation. Roger was a spiteful, vengeful bastard when he wanted to be.

Waiting for a response, he sipped his own cold coffee, grimaced, sipped some more. "It's your call. Are you in or out?"

Callie sucked it up and did what she had to do. "I'm in," she said crisply.

9

Stripped down to a sports bra and shorts, Callie concentrated on her push-ups. Her arm muscles were burning, and she was nearing exhaustion. Whenever her thoughts threatened to take her into the "bad place," that dark box inside her mind, she had the urge to cut. Fortunately time and training had taught her to channel her self-destructive impulses into other outlets.

A lot of things were packed inside her skull. Memories, the graves littering the ground inside her brain. Some memories were well covered, grown over, barely leaving any impression. She'd made peace with them and refused to look back. Others refused to rest. Buried alive, they struggled to return to the forefront, exhuming themselves to point accusing fingers.

Her father's ghost was one.

The first important man in her life. Daddy. A long shiver ripped through her, and she felt a chill creep into her bones. Her heart beat heavily; she had difficulty breathing. Clayton Whitten had been the first to teach her not to trust the male sex. Nobody could fail to be unnerved by the concentration of sheer hatred her father projected for the women in his life.

Clayton subscribed to one inflexible and fast rule when he came to dealing with his womenfolk: beat them, fuck them, repeat process liberally.

Whether going after his wife or his daughter, Clayton wasn't particularly concerned whom he destroyed in the process of his drunken rages. He beat and belittled until he made people hate him, the humiliations and physical blows he dealt like cards were simply the by-products of his own wretched childhood. Instead of breaking the cycle of abuse, he perpetuated what he'd learned from his own father.

Jaw tightening, Callie fought the gripping squeeze of icy fingers around her heart. Thinking of her father never failed to unnerve her. She'd hated being a little girl, hated being smaller and weaker than a full-grown man.

Her whole miserable childhood had come to an abrupt end with her father's murder. A bullet to the brain—delivered by the hand of his bitter wife—had ended Clayton Whitten's life.

No one blamed her mother for pulling the trigger. Except that she hadn't pulled it once. She'd pulled it twice. The second shot had made Callie an orphan and ward of the state.

She pressed on, forcing all her nervous energy into her efforts. Too much. It sometimes felt like her head would explode. She grimaced between breaths. She needed to focus. Concentrate. She'd hoped a good workout would drive her parents from her mind. Fat chance.

She pumped her body harder, forcing fifty more push-ups out of her tired arms. Thank God she'd discovered exercise as an outlet for her frustrations. Getting into top shape had been a focus and a goal, one leading down her future career path. Education had been the second key to help lift her out of despair. Early on she'd discovered schoolwork remained constant, even as the foster homes she occupied changed with frequent regularity. Maintaining straight A's was a goal she never let waver.

She went straight into the army at eighteen years of age to help pay for college.

Ending her push-ups, Callie rolled over onto her back for a set of crunches. She liked a nice flat belly and trim waist. Men certainly seemed to like it, too. Once she'd gotten out of the gawky stage of being too tall and too skinny, her body had filled out in ways that men found pleasing. Very pleasing. One of her foster fathers had claimed her virginity when she was fifteen. She'd cut a lot after the bastard had returned to his wife's bed. Forced sex didn't feel good or right.

She stopped her exercise routine, going dead still.

For a long time, she'd avoided sex, putting her energy into her studies. The military had discovered and honed her talent with computers. Thanks to her training, cracking and hacking any system in the world was a piece of cake. Graduating at the top of her class had put her squarely in the sights of the bureau.

Roger had been the lover to teach her that sex was to be enjoyed, was more than a physical act. For a long time she didn't invest any emotions into their affair, simply learning to enjoy the pleasure of a man's body. Time had passed, and her resistance dropped. Just when she'd come to view the act as one of deep love, she'd gotten burned. Badly.

Their affair had ended, but her need for sex hadn't lessened. She enjoyed the intimacy of intercourse. She'd simply have to learn to keep head and heart separate. Given the tenets of her assignment, she didn't see why she shouldn't enjoy making love to Iollan Drake. Last night had felt good. Excellent, in fact.

Callie drew a breath to fortify herself. Another twenty-five sit-ups and she'd quit. She attempted to keep her focus on her workout, but every time she closed her eyes or let her thoughts stray for a moment, she daydreamed about the outlaw. Iollan fluttered around her skull like an elusive butterfly, tantalizing, teasing, always out of her reach. He wouldn't leave, no matter how she tried to shove his image out.

Feeling exhaustion nibble, she sighed and flopped back on the carpet. "You're attracted because Drake's forbidden," she puffed. "He's a criminal, nobody to be attracted to." But she *was* attracted, damn it. More than she had a right to be.

Shut down brain, please quit working.

Callie tried frowning him away. Didn't work. Something about him reached out to her. Her intense attraction had caught her totally by surprise, opening up her mind to a world of possibilities. More than a rebound, more than an infatuation with the forbidden, Iollan Drake tantalized. His look, his accent, everything about him felt right when she was in his arms. He felt familiar. How or why, she didn't know. It was a foolish idea.

Thinking about him sent a slow ribbon of desire through her insides. The tingle of current passing between them when they'd connected was all too enticing. His touch, like his strange mark on her skin, was hot, sweet, and intoxicating. If she didn't take care, she'd soon be giving her heart away to the man.

Callie felt a lump rise in the back of her throat. She swallowed, forcing it down. "Silly idiot," she muttered. "He's work, not play."

A burning iron stabbed through her stomach when she remembered how Drake had taken her. His experience wasn't to be believed. He knew how to touch a woman's body, where, and with the perfect pressure guaranteed to induce furious orgasm.

Callie closed her eyes. Her palm spread over one breast. She felt the tight bud under her hand. Using a single finger, she traced slow circles around her distended nipple. Warmth trailed a path to the center of her belly, then lower. Her breathing grew shallow. Anticipation building inside, she sucked in a breath, moaning softly. Currents of desire rippled through her as she guided her hand lower. Her hand slipped under the elastic band of her sweatpants. Wet heat between her thighs, the throbbing ache.

She brushed her fingertips over her pulsing clit. Pressure built, fast and furious. She moaned and shifted her hips, sinking two fingers inside her tight channel. Inner muscles gripped and rippled. Unable to endure the torturous tease, she thrust. Tension coiled, then exploded in a blast of heat and dazzling light.

Violent shudders wracked her body. Splayed out on the carpet, she took a deep breath, forcing her heartbeat back to normal. Slowly her breathing evened out. She didn't feel any better, though. She still felt empty. Masturbation had only whetted her appetite for a man's touch. She wasn't prepared for the rush of emotions she felt when she realized Iollan Drake was the man she wanted.

No other man had ever touched her the way he had. With every brush of his lips, every caress of his fingertips, she'd felt cherished. He understood her darkness, the devouring emptiness that had once driven her to mutilate herself. He'd accepted that, and in doing so had embraced her.

She traced her lips with the tip of one creamy finger. Drake's mouth had ravished hers, devoured her, his actions completely focused on nothing but possessing her in every way possible. Goose bumps tripped over her skin when she remembered his tall, well-muscled frame. Their bodies had fit perfectly together, and when he sank within her depths it was as though he was doing more than entering. He'd claimed her, marking her in an animalistic way. He'd taken her to the edge, only to draw back at the last second, leaving her hanging, wanting, needing more. Hot and wild, their lovemaking had gone on and on. She'd lost count of the times orgasm had claimed her.

Don't think about that.

Curling into a ball, Callie drew her knees to her chest. Her hands were locked around her legs, a parody of a woman expecting a high-speed collision. There were too many things in her mind right now.

How could she *not* think about sex with Drake? The bureau

had just given her sanction to seduce the man! What would her bosses think if they were to find out she'd already bedded their suspect once, and thoroughly enjoyed it?

Careful, she warned herself. Seducing Iollan Drake was supposed to be nothing more than a part of her job for the bureau, most certainly not for her pleasure. Entertaining personal feelings about him would be stepping over the line. It would also be a mistake.

A tic of frustration tugged at the corner of her mouth. She lifted herself with a jerky heave. Her entire body trembled with the effort. Nevertheless, she drew back her shoulders and called on all her willpower to appear calm. Her stomach was churning acid. Her job was to get close—closer—to him. Moreover, her superiors expected results.

Unspoken but hanging in her mind was the fact that Drake was a target. Because of her attraction the thought bothered her. The idea that she'd be setting him up for the fall wasn't exactly appealing.

A frown wrinkled her forehead. She didn't want him to be an outlaw. She wanted him to be . . . "innocent *until proven guilty*." Totally stupid, but she couldn't stop the thought, or the hope. If only.

Struggling to maintain objectivity, Callie ran her fingers through her damp, sweaty hair. She was smart enough to know the agents' belief in Drake's innocence was a myth. More than likely Drake was guilty and his hide deserved to be nailed to the wall. Her job was to prove his guilt. A tall order. But someone had to do it.

She needed to focus on her objective. Now wasn't the time to get emotional over any man, past or present. No man would ever hurt her again. She'd taken too many strikes to the heart. Never again. Sex with Drake would be strictly to scratch her carnal itch.

Nothing more, nothing less.

Workout over, she walked into the kitchen and retrieved a bottle of water from the refrigerator. "Be better if it were vodka." She lifted it to her lips and drank deeply. The water was like a balm on her soul. She'd forgotten how refreshing cold water was to a feverish body.

A whiff of armpit odor wrinkled her nose. Yuck. She stank like a boar. She also needed to run the razor over her stubbly legs. Limbs aching, she decided a bath would be just the thing to soothe her. She wanted heat, a total, all-over body soak. Her apartment's tub wasn't large, but if she bent her knees, everything fit just fine.

Heading toward the bathroom, she reached in and turned on both taps, adjusting the temperature to a comfortable level. Steam filled the air as she stripped off her workout clothes, tossing them into the hamper.

A tap on the glass behind her caused her to turn her head. Since her bathroom window looked onto the solid brick wall of the building next door, she never bothered closing the blind. She hadn't considered the fire escape outside the window. Anyone who wanted to could climb up and peek inside.

Snatching a towel to cover her nudity, Callie gaped at the man outside. He smiled back, tapping the glass a second time. He wanted in.

Think of the devil and here he comes.

Recognizing her quarry, Callie gasped and her heartbeat jumped into a double-time dance. She hesitated, caught between surprise and relief. When she'd gone to work at the bar earlier in the evening, Drake hadn't shown up. Considering the body cooling in the morgue, that wasn't a surprise. If she were suspected of murder, especially if she'd actually committed one, she'd be inclined to lay low, too. The fact that Drake had chosen an alternate route to her apartment solidified her suspicions of guilt. An innocent man didn't try to conceal his actions.

Gaining his trust meant she had to play along.

Callie threw on a cloak of composure to make up for her lack of clothing. It would have to suffice. Fortunately she was fairly comfortable with her own nudity, scars and all. Tucking the towel around her breasts, she turned off the faucets before the tub overflowed. She unlatched the window, tugging it up. The screen had fallen off a long time ago, never to be replaced. "What the hell are you doing here?"

Iollan Drake grinned. "I wanted to see you again, love."

"I have a front door, in case you've forgotten."

His grin widened. "This route's much more interesting."

She blushed, glancing down at her towel. "If I'd known you were coming, I would have put on something more appropriate."

He ducked and guided his lanky frame over the waist-level sill with the ease of an experienced burglar. Getting in and out of places unseen didn't seem to present a problem. He straightened, his full height dwarfing hers by at least six inches. "What you are wearing is more than appropriate, love. In fact, it's perfect."

Feeling her towel start to slip, Callie quickly crossed her arms over her breasts. He seemed not to have changed clothes, dressed in the same outfit of the night before. He looked a little rumpled, a little tired, but no less worse for wear. She, on the other hand, felt like a sweating, stinking piggy. "Why? You think you're going to get me in bed again?"

His gaze snapped with interest. "I'd hoped to do that, yes."

She tried to look offended. "Do I look that easy?" She visually scanned his length, enjoying every damn inch. In truth, a woman would have to be blind or pushing up daisies to not get turned on by this gorgeous hunk.

His brows shot up. "Not for just any man, I hope," he answered with a wry twist of his lips.

Callie relaxed slightly, her inner tension easing to a manageable level. Her tongue worried the inside of her cheek. "But you're not just any man, right?" Her voice was a breathy whisper.

Stepping closer, he cocked his head, meeting her gaze directly. His hand came up, stroking her cheek in a familiar way. "No," he whispered, the cadence of his voice laced with sincerity. "I'm not just any man."

His touch was pure delight. A tingling current filled her. His presence, so near and so desired, was altogether too enticing. She was going to have to fight to keep from falling in love with this man. That would take a lot of energy and a cool head. She hoped she was strong enough to do her job without letting her emotions rule her. Drake was different than any man she'd ever known.

Callie's breath shuddered out. She shifted on her bare feet, uncomfortable. "Then who are you, really?"

His gaze suddenly broke from hers. He stepped back, sighing and sifting his fingers through his thick hair. "I wish I could tell you."

On paper, there was no record of his existence: No passport, driver's license, immigration record. Nothing. No one believed Drake was even his real name. He'd obviously taken great care to erase his past. Even the accent tailored to his speech could be a carefully practiced act. Until agents sat him down and questioned him, nobody knew where he'd come from.

Anxious, Callie leaned toward him. Damn, he knew how to intrigue a woman. "Tell me."

Iollan shook his head, brows knitting together in thought. "I can do better than that," he said slowly.

"How?" She raised her gaze to his, waiting for his answer.

His eyes met hers again. He offered a smile and a shrug. "I'm going to show you."

10

Callie dressed in haste, throwing on a pair of jeans, T-shirt, and her leather jacket. Waiting patiently, Drake watched her pull on a pair of socks, then her boots. It felt odd dressing in front of a strange man, but what the hell. He'd already seen her naked. Slipping her keys, cell, and billfold into a pocket, she looked at him. "I'm ready."

He nodded. "Good."

She started to head for the living room.

Iollan shook his head, indicating the bathroom. "Let's go out the back."

Callie played dumb. "Why?"

"Eyes I don't quite trust are watching. It's safer if we go out the back way."

"Okay."

A few minutes later they were making their way down the fire escape. Their steps took them down into an alley, a forbidding narrow chute of Dumpsters, gloom, and decay. Nobody had any business hanging around back here in the middle of the night.

Callie looked around and saw only murk. "Where are we going?" Belatedly, it occurred to her that Drake could turn around and pump her full of lead and no one would be wiser. That's how the other two agents had taken the fall. A bullet to the head, execution style.

Mouth all of a sudden desert-dry, she swallowed, reminding herself to breathe, but invisible fingers refused to lessen their grip around her heart. Trying to clear her mind, she felt both sick and shaky, like someone suffering a nerve-shattering shock. Her head felt squeezed, as though caught in a vise. Perhaps she shouldn't have nixed the bureau's suggestion she wear a wire, hardly feasible when you're naked and locked in a sweaty clinch. She'd opted to go commando in every way. If she had nothing to find, there'd be nothing to explain if his suspicions were aroused.

Iollan's hand slipped into hers through the darkness. His fingers curled around hers in a warm grip of reassurance. He seemed to know where he was going, leading her to the motorcycle parked beside a Dumpster. "I hope you don't mind the ride."

A bit relieved not to be pumped full of lead, Callie shook her head. "Motorcycle's fine with me."

He straddled the bike. Lifting it off its stand, he flicked out the kick-starter with one booted foot, then came down on it with a stomp to bring the big machine to life. The engine purred with a steady hum. Doubtful anyone had even noticed the sound. "Get on and hold on tight."

Though she preferred to be the one doing the driving, Callie clambered onto the back of the motorcycle. She kicked down the passenger footrests, giving her a place to put her feet.

Settling onto the narrow leather seat, she felt her crotch make a direct connection with his ass. A wave of desire suffused her body, the sudden pulse of heat throbbing all the way down in her clit. Tension grew, a strange sexual fierceness filling her as sure as the moist heat between her spread thighs. The massive machine vibrated, sending a heady, almost wanton pleasure straight to her core. Legs locked around his delicious ass, she almost climaxed.

Iollan turned. "Hang on, love."

Callie nodded, passing her arms under his and locking her hands across his chest. He tensed, chest rock-solid under her grip. His casual move redirected her attention, making her gut-wrenchingly aware of his body, his almost primitive maleness. Her skin felt red hot. The memory of his touch made her clit twitch. All she wanted to think about was this man, aroused and wanting to make love to her. A fine thrill pierced her heart. She felt positively fragile, and all female.

A soft sound of appreciation escaped her throat, thankfully muffled by the engine. "I'm ready."

"We're off, then." Giving the engine a shot of gas, he simultaneously released the clutch and shifted down into first gear. In one smooth motion, the motorcycle roared down the deserted street, passing darkened windows and parked cars. Everything familiar receded into the distance, left behind in the shadows.

Watching the streets whiz by and change faster than she could keep up, Callie tensed.

She didn't have to ask where they were going. The lower north side was Drake's preferred territory. Strip clubs, no-tell motels, and sex shops hosting titillating entertainment ran seven days a week. Drug dealers and prostitutes competed for the influx of dollars such forbidden goodies inevitably attracted.

The older parts of the area were poorly maintained and badly lit, a place where no sane man or woman would be caught walking alone after dark. Streets were paved in the original cobblestone, quaint and perilously narrow. Streetlights were few and far between, casting their dim glow on barred, boarded-up windows. The streets were a god-awful maze of cul-de-sacs and dead ends. Were she alone, Callie would have serious doubts about her safety—not that she wasn't already having a few.

Iollan chose one of the buildings, a multistoried sentinel guarding the economically ravaged area. Most honest businesses had shriveled up and died when the focus of the city turned away from the railroad and toward interstate highways. A masterpiece of urban blight, the lower north side was considered a lost cause. Graffiti, litter, gang wars, property squatting plagued the entire area.

Callie blinked at the behemoth meeting her eyes. She wasn't sure if anyone actually lived inside or not. The windows were boarded over and barred. Given the neighborhood, that wasn't entirely unexpected. No one, however, seemed to be in residence. Even the windows on the upper levels were unlit.

Guiding the motorcycle up on the sidewalk, Iollan parked under a low-slung canopy, killing the engine. "This is it."

The apparent lack of habitation pressed down on her. "Wow. Dark." She let her words trail off with a helpless shrug. Iollan had driven so fast she hadn't even had a chance to catch the name of the avenue. Most of them didn't seem to be marked anyway. She had no idea where they were. If you were a criminal, it was the perfect place to hide. The thought flashed through her mind that it was also the ideal place to commit a little torture.

No one would hear you scream.

That thought wasn't welcome at all. She wavered. "Are you sure people live here?"

Iollan's hand slipped into hers. He gave a reassuring squeeze. "Just hold on. In a moment, everything will change."

She hesitated, her instincts kicking in. The anxiety she felt was tangible. As a federal agent she'd known there'd be times when her job would cross into the danger zone. The line between knowing it was dangerous and knowingly walking into a dangerous situation was a thin one. Her cell phone served as her sole lifeline. Lose that and she'd be shit out of luck.

"Not the busiest part of town, is it?" She tried to sound unconcerned.

Iollan led the way up a set of narrow cement steps. "I like the quiet. Not a lot of traffic at night."

A pale, naked yellow lightbulb of questionable wattage cast its light on a huge gray metal door, one of the heavy kind meant to withstand fire or friendly neighborhood pillagers.

He dug in his pocket for a key, sliding it into the dead bolt. "Enter freely, and of your own will." The door swung open, hinges creaking more than a bit.

Callie shivered. What a fucking odd thing to say. Nobody had ever invited her into his apartment quoting a Dracula movie. She was outwardly calm, but her thoughts were raging like wild cats in a steel cage.

Allowing him to lead, Callie gazed around. They were in a narrow, uninteresting foyer. The linoleum on the floor was as yellowed and peeling as the paint on the walls. Not attractive. Slots of mailboxes claimed one wall, most unmarked. Her first impression wasn't a good one. Truthfully the place was a dump.

Iollan indicated a set of narrow stairs. "Third floor."

Great. A walkup. Probably a cold-water flat, too.

The third floor entryway greeting Callie's curious gaze looked a little bit nicer than the one below. Carpeting replaced the linoleum, that indoor/outdoor kind so popular in high-traffic areas. There were three doors—right, left, and middle—quite a large and spacious spread. Condos, she imagined.

Another key was produced. The second door opened. "Come in, please."

Callie followed Iollan under the threshold. Walking through the front door was like stepping into a time warp that captured the simpler pleasures of a bygone era. The reception area was huge, open, and inviting. The walls were covered with thick, rich wallpaper in a blue and cream toile print. Original artwork added to the charm, marvelously blending with the décor.

Though the shades were drawn against the prying eyes of outsiders, the reception area was intimately lit. Scented candles burned in sconces, their sweet fragrance winnowing gently through the air. The faint scent of dryness and dust tickled her nostrils.

Passing through the foyer, Iollan led her into a living room. The heels of his boots clicked on the hardwood floors as he walked. A T-shaped partition divided the rooms, and there was a large archway separating the kitchen, dining, and living rooms.

Slipping off his coat, he draped it over a nearby chair. "Welcome to my home." He held a hand out for her jacket.

Callie peeled it off and handed it over. "I can honestly say I wasn't expecting a place like this. Have you lived here long?"

He shrugged noncommittally. "Off and on through the years." He looked around, a fond smile parting his lips. "It's one of my favorite places. Maybe it's why I keep coming back even when I shouldn't."

"I can see why you can't stay away." Her words were honestly offered.

He looked around as if memorizing every nook and cranny. "Someday I shall have to leave it and never come back." His mouth turned down and his eyes looked sad. "That will be a terrible day indeed."

Good to know. If he was getting ready to make a run for it, agents would have to act fast before he skipped town. "I hope it won't be too soon."

His reply was vague. "Soon enough." He forced a smile. "But tonight is no night for sadness. I hope you don't mind, but I've arranged a little surprise for you in the bedroom."

Wondering what he had in mind, Callie found it difficult to breathe. She managed a tremulous smile. "Really?"

Iollan held out his hand, waiting for her to make the decision whether to accept or not. "Will you come?" His eyes, so bright and intense, caused her breath to catch in her throat.

Body wound up tightly, she didn't hesitate to slip her hand into his. "Yes, of course." Anticipation built inside her as strong warm fingers closed around her own, the way she hoped their limbs would soon tangle together.

Inside Callie was shivering. At the moment nothing mattered except feeling his touch on her naked skin. She wanted him so damn bad it scared her.

11

The suite Iollan led her into went beyond opulent. Lush would be a better word. Absolute sumptuousness beckoned, the décor so splendidly arranged that Callie's heart leapt at the sight of it all. Jaws agape and eyes wide, she stared at the chamber, mesmerized by its beauty.

A large open arrangement ruled under a low ceiling. Several large empire sofas were spread throughout, the burled walnut covered in warm red and green. Scads of fringed pillows were scattered on the floor covered with plush crème-shaded carpeting. Thick fabriclike wallpaper was a rich lustrous shade, deep ruby red. The color of lust—of the forbidden. Side chairs were covered in a muted gold fabric, a welcome break to the eye awash in the sanguine theme. A beautiful set of bay windows stretched across the rear wall, offering a breathtaking view of the city by night.

Hanging lamps with Victorian lace shades provided intimate lighting. An elaborate canopied bed dominated, its heart veiled by a fall of sheer curtains, strangely enthralling in a darkly seductive manner.

Drawn in as though sinking into a pit of warm honey, Callie felt the jolt of pure electric energy around her. Her senses were overwhelmed with the sights, the sounds, and sensations around her, caressing her, closing in with each breath she drew into her lungs. Heart hammering in her chest, she gazed around the rest of the chamber.

A huge Jacuzzi dominated the rear of the room, a buoyant and effulgent cerulean pool beneath the high arched ceiling. Two men were stretched out on towels beside the water, lolling like indolent tigers under the hot African sun. As naked as the day they were born, they left nothing to the imagination. Nothing. The musk of sexual heat mixed with the cloying scent of sandalwood incense, burned in such quantity that the air was hazy with smoke.

Seeing Iollan and Callie, the men waved.

One of them raised a glass. "At last you've come," he greeted warmly. "We've been waiting." His voice, like Iollan's, was tinged with an Irish lilt.

Iollan waved back. "I had to fetch my lady." He reached for Callie, sliding his arm around her waist in a reassuring manner. He bent toward her ear, whispering words only she heard. "Do you like it?"

Letting out the breath she'd been holding, Callie nodded. "My God. It's magnificent."

His potent gaze caught hers. "I thought you'd be pleased. I want you to feel completely at home here."

She pressed a hand to her stomach, trying to settle the butterflies. No such luck. She was nervous as hell. "Um, not that I'm a prude or anything . . . Who are the naked guys?"

Iollan laughed. "They are my brothers." Seeing her hesitate, he slipped a hand over her shoulder, caressing her nape. "I can ask them to leave if they make you uncomfortable."

Callie quickly shook her head. She'd come this far. Now she

had to see the night through, go wherever the coming events might take her. "No, it's fine. I'd like to meet them."

At that moment she knew there would be no turning back. She'd been the first to take her contact with Iollan to a sexual level, well before she'd been given official sanction to proceed in such a manner. Not exactly a stranger to sex with multiple partners, she found the idea of spending the night with three handsome men wasn't exactly unappealing.

"Excellent." His hand slipped into hers. An unexpected spark shot between them.

A rush of excitement flooded her veins, assuring her she'd made the right decision. No matter how much she tried, she couldn't quell her incredible attraction to Iollan Drake. Forbidden fruit was the sweetest, most satisfying. She had to take a bite of the apple, poison or not.

Both men stood as she and Iollan approached, comfortable and unself-conscious in their nudity. She tried not to stare at the muscular, fine-planed lengths of their bodies. Impossible. Neither modesty nor embarrassment moved them to reach for cover.

Twins, they were very fair with long blond hair and full mouths. Both were lithe, tall and lean with narrow waists and strong muscular legs. Both men had the same bright copper eyes as Iollan. But their physical resemblance to Iollan ended there. They looked nothing like brothers.

Without trying to seem obvious, Callie's gaze strayed lower. As for the rest of them . . . Both were well hung. Flaccid, their cocks were impressive. Magnificent, even. Her tongue found the inside of her cheek. She could do a lot with those, and she looked forward to trying.

Iollan made the introductions. "Calista," he said, nodding toward the twin on the left. "This is Toryn."

Looking at the two men, Callie knew she was in deep.

Though the twins shared a resemblance, each man appeared unique. In fact, the twins were stunning. If forced, she'd be pressed to make a choice as to which one she found more attractive.

Intense awareness throbbed through her, keeping perfect rhythm with her hammering heart. All three were yummy enough to eat up with a spoon. Not that she planned to use a spoon if given the chance to get a little taste of the twins.

Toryn's large hand claimed hers, offering a familiar squeeze. "A pleasure, my lady."

"And this," Iollan continued, "is Cadyn."

Cadyn, too, took her hand. "An honor," he said, bending and pressing his lips to her palm in a courtly kiss. "Our brother has told us much about his chosen."

Callie's brows rose. "Is that so?" She glanced to Iollan. "I had no idea."

Iollan's grin was shy. "You must forgive my bragging."

Toryn clapped his brother on the shoulder. "And brag he has. We've heard nothing but praise of your beauty and charm since he laid eyes upon you."

A bit embarrassed, Callie demurred. Hair in a tangle, cheeks reddened from the night's wind, and dressed in old jeans and a T-shirt, she didn't think she looked beautiful or even remotely attractive. "He flatters me in a most unjust manner."

A glimmer of mischief lit Cadyn's eyes. "I assure you, my brother offers no praise unless it is due." He gave a little wink. "Trust me when I say his words are more than true. I admire—and envy—his choice. If you are ever unhappy with his attention, I will be glad to make up for his grievous failings."

As if she needed reminding of Iollan Drake's potent lovemaking.

Callie's pulse unexpectedly shifted into high gear. Need throbbed between her legs. "I'll keep that in mind."

Iollan's hand slipped around her waist, giving a reassuring

squeeze. His touch was somehow comforting. Nervousness began to fade. "Don't listen to him. He's smug in his arrogance, perhaps the reason no woman will put up with him."

Cadyn laughed. "Not arrogance. Confidence."

Iollan held out a hand, shooing his hovering brothers away. "Easy, boys. Don't scare her on her first night."

"Of course," Toryn said agreeably. "What she needs is a drink to calm her nerves, then a good long soak. Sit, and I will do the honors." He headed to a low table. A crystal carafe and glasses were arranged on a beautiful, gold platter. Two glasses were filled and duly delivered. "The best batch I've brewed yet, if I do say so myself."

Callie sat down on the love seat he indicated, settling back on its cushions. She accepted a glass filled almost to the brim with a dark rich liquid. It didn't seem like anything she'd ever imbibed before. It looked strangely murky. "Thank you."

Though the others drank, she hesitated. "What is it?"

"Mead." Licking his lips after quaffing a healthy mouthful, Cadyn smiled. "Honey wine."

Callie lifted her glass, sniffing. "I've never had mead before."

Seeing her hesitation, Toryn rolled his eyes. "It's very popular, actually. Though you can buy it, I prefer to make my own. The ingredients are simple, little more than honey, yeast, and water. Truly the nectar of the gods."

"You're in for a treat," Iollan broke in. "Toryn makes it dark and sweet, with a hint of cinnamon and clove."

Callie sipped, rolling the rich sweet drink over her tongue before swallowing. It tasted wonderful. She took a larger drink, and then another. The next thing she knew her glass was empty. She didn't protest when Toryn offered a refill. Somehow time crept by and her glass had emptied again. Odd. She didn't remember drinking it. Her brain felt mired, as if her senses were suddenly wrapped in a layer of cotton.

Sitting beside her, Iollan laid a hand on her arm. "You'd better take it easy," he warned, shooting a wry glance at Toryn. "Mead is much stronger than it tastes."

Darkness bubbled around the edges of her mind, like gray angry storm clouds building on the horizon. She felt a little dizzy. Hitting her empty stomach and then her bloodstream, the mead had triple the effect. Her head started to spin, the room around her whirling deliciously. "I'm beginning to think so."

Helpful hands settled on her shoulders, strong fingers working the tense areas around her neck. "Perhaps you'd enjoy a little massage and a dip in the water," Cadyn suggested.

Slipping the glass from her hand, Toryn reached to help her stand. "Come on, girl. We'll take good care of you."

For an instant nothing existed except a vast dark void. Callie felt dazed, dizzied, weightless, floating in a pleasant haze. If Toryn let go of her now, she'd fall flat on her ass. "What are you going to do?"

"They're going to make you ready." Iollan settled back, obviously comfortable with the idea.

She giggled. "For what?"

He eyed her from head to foot. "For me."

Addled from the potent drink, Callie smiled agreeably. "Cool. Sounds good to me."

"I'm glad you agree." Swooping in from behind, Cadyn swept her up in his arms, depositing her on a nearby stool covered with crushed green velvet. "Steady now," he breathed in her ear. "We'll take good care of you."

Callie gazed up into his mesmerizing eyes. "Promise?"

Smiling, Toryn joined them. "You'll get only the gentlest of care. All the pleasure you can imagine lies within us. We only want to share that with you."

His words struck a chord deep in her core, unwittingly augmenting her already insatiable appetite for debauchery. The heavens above had just handed over the chance to fulfill her secret heart's desire: sex with these three gorgeous men. She had no doubt they were most skillful in intimate play. Her excitement built as she imagined their touch on her skin.

Caught in the snare of her most delicious fantasy, Callie made no protest when two sets of male hands reached for her, tugging at her in a familiar way.

"Take it easy," Cadyn breathed, moving behind her. His warm fingers worked at her T-shirt, easing the thin material out of her tight jeans. "Can't get into the water in your clothes."

Callie relaxed, content to go with the flow. She lifted her arms, allowing him to take her top off. His firm fingers grazed the skin on her back as her tight sports bra followed, leaving her nude from the waist up.

Toryn knelt in front of her. Seeing him so close, she noticed a series of small scars riddled his neck, shoulders, and abdomen. Untying her boot laces, he slid them off and set them aside. He smiled up at Callie. "Your jeans next, please."

Callie stood. Wobbling, she placed her hand on his shoulder to steady herself.

Toryn undid the top button and slid down the zipper, watching with eager eyes as they peeled away from her hips. He tugged them down, panties and all.

Naked, Callie tried not to tremble. She wasn't cold or nervous, but untapped desire had given her the shivers. Her breasts stood pert, her nipples pebbled with excitement. Her pubic mound was hairless, shaved as slick as a whistle.

Sandwiched between two men opened up hundreds of possibilities. Toryn took her breasts in his hands and squeezed as if testing their weight and size. "Nice," he murmured.

Callie blushed to the roots of her hair. "Thanks."

"May I?"

"Of course." The words escaped before she'd considered saying them.

"Thank you." Toryn's head dipped low, tongue swirling around one pink nipple.

Caught in the moment Callie ran her hands through Toryn's thick hair, pushing her nipple deeper. A lusty moan broke from her lips. "Don't stop," she gasped. "That feels so good."

"Looks like you'll have to work to satisfy her," Iollan chuckled.

Straightening up, Toryn placed a light kiss on her lips. Then, kissing the valley between Callie's breasts, his mouth moved to the other nipple. He suckled it slowly, exploring the soft ridge with his tongue.

"And we shall try." Cadyn's hands came into the action, parting her ass cheeks.

Callie stiffened when his tongue probed deep, making contact with her anus.

He chuckled, giving one round cheek a playful bite. "This ass isn't virgin." Diving in, he licked in long slow strokes, tasting and enjoying.

Trying to contain the wild impressions careening through her skull, Callie started to tremble, body shuddering as the twins pleasured her with their mouths. Each slow, wet sweep of two sets of tongues sent her higher into the stratosphere. The scent around them was wild, musky, and hot. Between her thighs, her clit was swollen and pulsing, ready for action.

Just as she was about to peak, she heard Iollan's amused laugh. "Slow down, brothers. Take it easy and let her get used to the idea there will be three men to serve her pleasure tonight."

"He just wants you to himself," Toryn whispered in a conspiratorial tone.

"I found her first," Iollan reminded with a laugh.

Caught up in having her clothes so delightfully shucked off, Callie hadn't even noticed Iollan had discarded his own.

Grin as saucy as his body was sleek, Iollan sauntered toward the Jacuzzi, giving a nice view of his delectable ass in motion while he descended into the water's depths.

With a twin escort on each side, Callie moved toward the water, making sure she kept her footing on the slick steps. As she descended, warm water bubbled around her. A long hot soak was just what she needed to ease the stiffness of her earlier exercise. The twins returned to their towels, stretching out to watch the love play commence.

Iollan's gaze grazed her with admiration. His lips curved into an appreciative smile. "You look beautiful."

Callie's heart beat furiously, driven by unbound desire. "I still can't believe you want me." Breath catching in her throat, she felt need warring inside her soul, so strong it both consumed and un-nerved her. She raked her bottom lip with her teeth.

"More than my life." He opened his arms, closing her in his strong embrace.

Callie nestled against his chest, the touch made all the sweeter by the steamy dampness of his skin. Her hand gripped his back, sliding sinuously over powerfully rippling muscle.

Iollan's lips pressed against her brow. "Sure about this, love?" He traced her slender body with warm palms, slipping them beneath the water that only half-covered her ass. Pulling her tightly against him, he barely managed to assuage the ache between her thighs.

The thrill of his caress went clear to her toes. Tipping her head back, her teeth grazed his chin. "Oh, yes," she murmured, voice sweet and thick as sun-warmed honey.

"An hour away from you was an hour too long." Hands sliding to her hips, his lips came down on hers. Their kiss didn't start out slowly. Seeking and demanding, his tongue swept past her lips in a silent message. He might share her with his broth-ers, but in the end Callie would belong to him and him alone.

A shiver of anticipation traveled through her, ushering in that familiar heat of desire. As the sensations of arousal spread, sheer undiluted pleasure rolled through her. Her clit ached with the need to experience the pleasing slide of his fingers, mouth, and cock. Her thighs were taut, the water between her legs sensuously mixing with the liquid warmth flowing from her hungry depth. The muscles deep inside her core contracted, anticipating penetration.

Using only the tips of his fingers, Iollan traced over her chin, down her neck, to her breasts. His touch was light, sensual. "Speak to me, Calista. Tell me what you want."

"Everything." Her voice was breathy, slow from the effects of the potent drink.

He held her tighter, giving a longer, slower kiss. "I promise I'll do that." Gripping her bare waist, he dipped his head and his tongue snaked out, circling one delicate bud. His voice grew playful. "But where to start. Here"—he suckled softly at the tip, teasing with soft nips, then drawing on it with all the sexually charged intent in his muscular body—"or perhaps here." His hand covered her other breast.

Skin flushing, feeling suddenly too tight to fit over her bones, she sighed beneath his touch. "Mmm. Touch me everywhere."

"Tonight we will please you in every way." Iollan's hand slid down her belly, urging her legs apart. His caressed her clit with slow, deliberate flicks.

Callie moaned her answer, biting her lip as he made circles around her clit with his wet finger before slowly penetrating her tight, slick pussy. Imagining three cocks in action caused her to shudder in delight. "Careful," she warned between gritted teeth. "I'll come right now."

Iollan lazily nuzzled the side of her neck. Her pulse beat frantically beneath her skin as he savored her softness. "And that would be bad because?" He nibbled at her lips as though enjoying a cherry Popsicle. "Tonight we will take you to a place you've never been before."

Slipping in another finger, Iollan slowly pumped into Callie's depths. He pressed deep inside her with a slowness and sureness of purpose. He gently pinched one nipple, rolling it between thumb and forefinger.

Callie whimpered. Her hips undulated faster, in time to his thrusts. The feel of his mouth and hands, of firm wet skin against wetter skin, was almost more than her senses could stand. She wouldn't last long against the vibrations building deep inside, igniting every nerve in her core.

Other deeper moans and sighs of gratification mingled with hers. She didn't have to look to know the twins were engaged in a little mutual masturbation. The idea that they were hitting their peaks watching her get off sent her mercury soaring. She'd never felt so desired, so female, and so powerful in her sexuality.

With a groan of surrender, she grasped his fingers with her taut inner muscles, beginning a climax so powerful she feared she might pass out. An eruption of pleasure turned her muscles into taut electrified cords, tightening with tension. Climax grabbed her clit and held on, every inch of her body clenching as hot fire traveled up her spine. In short order she was gasping for breath in the same rhythm as a stormy night's wind. Crying out, she began to shake, fingernails raking his shoulders. Savoring the exhilaration, she groaned, the last coherent sound she was capable of making.

Iollan held her, letting her tremble until every last ounce of strength had been wrung from her body. Still quivering with gratification, Callie drew a breath when his fingers slid from her sex. She wasn't ready to be empty.

He grinned. "That should get you started."

Callie struggled to find her sanity. "Not nearly enough," she gasped. "I want more. A *lot* more."

Iollan clucked his tongue. "I thought you would be insatiable."

12

Hovering at the edges of the Jacuzzi, the twins swooped into motion. Producing a thick towel, Cadyn grinned and held it open for her. "Better get you dry first."

Callie giggled as strong male hands claimed her, guiding her out of the water. "As if that's possible." Like a newly anointed goddess, she was rosy from the heat of the water and her delicious orgasm.

Cadyn knelt. Beginning at Callie's feet, he worked the towel over one calf, then the other, up her legs, between her thighs, over the soft curve of her rear, her waist, breasts, and shoulders.

A soft sigh escaped Callie's parted lips. A moment later every inch of her was dry. "Thank you." The timbre of her voice had changed slightly, into a smoky female purr of contentment. Pride in her taut firm body held her posed a moment longer than necessary. She felt no embarrassment whatsoever that they'd watched her take her pleasure.

Cadyn gave a courtly nod. "Only the beginning, my lady." He spread out a fresh towel. "Lie here and Toryn will give you a relaxing rubdown."

She dropped to her knees and stretched out on her stomach. Toryn swooped in with a fragrant body oil. His deft hands went into fabulous motion, working her shoulders and neck with skill.

Callie sighed, pillowing her head on her hands. Iollan lifted himself out of the water, sitting a couple of feet from her head. He reached out, stroking damp hair off her forehead.

"Feel good?"

She smiled. "God, yes. This is heaven."

He stroked over her cheek and jaw. "All for you and no other woman," he murmured.

Her body quivered as Toryn's hands slipped down her back, thumbs pressing against her spine inch by delicious inch. "You'd better stop it then."

A caress across her lips. "Why?"

She rolled over onto her back, opening her arms. "I might not want to leave."

Iollan studied the planes and contours of her curves, visually appreciating every inch. "Stay then." He touched his mouth to hers, teasing, tasting, then searching.

Callie arched up into him, tangling her fingers in his thick hair to deepen their kiss. Just as her eyelids fluttered shut, another mouth came into play, claiming one distended nipple. A third mouth joined in, trailing a path to her navel, then lower. Strong hands parted her thighs. A tongue flicked at her clitoris.

She gasped, the realization only heightening her need to continue this delicious exploration. Three at once? Dangerous, but, *oh!*, tempting.

Iollan broke their kiss. Hovering over her, his gaze captured her. "Shall we continue?"

Callie didn't hesitate. The primitiveness of their possession, three males on one female, only heightened her need. Body quivering and straining to experience every sensation, she would find stopping now to be unbearable.

She swallowed, eager to continue. "Yes."

Hands claimed her, lifting and carrying her toward the waiting bed. "All prepared for you, my lady."

A soft moan escaped her lips. The throb of blood through her veins sounded strongly in her ears, a muffled pulse seeming to entwine with those of the three men surrounding her. For a moment, she felt as though she were rising, expanding toward the ceiling above her head, passing through it to touch the far-flung moons. Her soul fluttered in an invisible breeze, a wraith of energy shimmering as lightly as a snowflake in chilly air.

Suddenly, her senses shifted and light and sound seemed to fuse, twisting and contorting into an indescribable blending of her pulse and the hot darkness of the heart of the universe. The men she was to embrace were powerful. Endless. Eternal. Wet with desire, hot with aching need, she nearly climaxed right then.

Her spirit slipped back into its shell, leaving her almost insensible, yet she held onto consciousness with what she was sure must be the last wisps of her strength. Though it seemed hours had passed, in reality only a few minutes had ticked by since her descent to the mattress beneath her back.

She lay as if blasted by an intense jolt of energy. She wasn't sure what had happened in that brief moment. It felt as though she'd lost all control of her mind and body.

Toryn and Cadyn stretched out on either side of her. Guiding her body into position, they stretched her arms up over her head. A series of leather straps circled the bed's posts. The men expertly bound her, drawing the tethers tight around her wrists and ankles. Spread-eagled across the mattress, she was a prisoner now, unable to escape what was about to happen to her.

Callie tried to speak, but her command of the language seemed to have deserted her. Her mouth worked soundlessly until a few words tumbled over her lips. "What's going on?"

Toryn stroked damp shreds of hair away from her forehead. "The ties will keep you from hurting yourself when we feed."

Confusion filled her. "I—I don't understand. Feed?"

Cadyn looked to Iollan, who had taken a position at the foot of the bed. "Did you not tell her yet?"

Iollan guiltily shook his head. "Not yet," he admitted. "I'm not ready for her to know."

Both brothers nodded as if his words were perfectly logical.

"When?" Toryn asked.

"Tonight. Tonight she will see the truth. She will know what we are."

Again, the twins nodded.

"She needs to know," Cadyn said. "Before more of us die."

Iollan sighed. "She will. I believe she can help us."

"No one has ever helped us," Cadyn cut in. He glanced at her with new suspicion. "What if she's like the rest of them?"

Iollan cut him off. "She's not. She's different. I know it."

Callie followed their words in bits and pieces. She lay newly tensed, tied between three men and totally unable to help herself. Having heard enough, she tugged against the leather cuffing her wrists. "Hey, guys, I'm still here. Talk to me."

Toryn hushed her with a single finger across her lips. "Tomorrow you will know the truth of us."

Cadyn stroked his palm across her flat belly. "For tonight, enjoy the pleasure."

Callie's skin rippled in anticipation, the way a cat's does when awakened from its sleep. A weak smile crossed her lips. Her gaze rolled up, toward her bound wrists. "Guess I don't have any choice, do I?"

Iollan climbed onto the bed, positioning himself on his knees between her spread legs. His palms traced the insides of her thighs with a light caress. "We won't hurt you, Calista," he reassured her in a husky voice. "Will you trust us?"

Callie couldn't look away from his deep, persuasive eyes. She experienced a sense of urgency, of compulsion throughout her body, the ache needing fulfillment at any cost. She shivered. She wanted the three men to lick, suck, and taste every inch of her.

She shuttered her eyes against the blaze erupting between her spread legs. "What do you want from me?"

He echoed her earlier answer. "Everything."

Body rigid with the tension that crackled through her, she forced herself to swallow the lump forming in her throat. "I'll try."

Iollan tipped his head to one side. His gaze met hers and his mouth lifted into a gentle smile. "Good."

Experienced male hands began to caress her arms, shoulders, and breasts. Heart beating, chest rising and falling with each breath, she smelled the clean smell of their skin, which tickled her nostrils.

Callie closed her eyes, determined to welcome every sensation. "Oh, my," she gasped through trembling lips when Toryn brushed the soft hollow of her throat with his lips.

Still dizzied by the lingering effects of the mead, her world started to spin in slow motion. She was barely conscious of Cadyn's mouth covering one nipple.

At the same time, Iollan slowly traced the folds of her labia, finger sinking into her softness to find her clit. Each time he flicked the small hooded organ, her insides tightened and a flash of pure heat surged. A flood of creamy juices prepared her all over again for the entry of his cock.

Whimpering, she squirmed in delighted agony. Her skin felt luminous, glowing and vibrant. With each beat of her heart, the blood pulsed through her veins and her passion grew heated, verging on the point of desperation. It was one thing to be caressed by one man, quite another to be touched by three men at the same time. The instinct of a female seeking—no, needing—

a male was never stronger in her than it was now. She luxuriated in their touch, in the rigid flesh pressed so intimately against her bare skin. The heated length of two shafts lay along her hips, searing her with the carnal nudges of molten steel.

A low, primordial groan rose up from her throat, creeping past her moist, parted lips. Carnal words spilled shamelessly from her mouth. A fervent need was beginning to flay her senses, plunging her into a spiraling abyss, then lifting her high on a sensual current from which she was sure she would never come down.

Back arching, Callie twisted her wrists against the cruel restraints holding her down. Her tender wrists rubbed against leather bindings bringing a strangely sensual pain that only added to her exquisite torment. Mouth cotton-dry from her rasping breath, she ran her tongue over papery lips. If only one of the men would enter her now, thrust his cock deep inside her waiting depth.

She growled fiercely. "Please." Her voice was an arid rasp. "I can't take much more." Thighs quivering with tension, she arched her hips toward the finger teasing her wet, swollen nubbin. The need to climax, to slake the desire burning in her soul, was unbearable, threatening to entirely consume her.

Toryn claimed her mouth. Their kiss was a whisper, a fervid dance of exploring tongues. He tasted sweet and yeasty, like the rich dark mead he'd consumed. She pressed her mouth against his, her tongue eagerly entering into the duel. The sensations were so intense, surging upward at an incredible rate of speed. She let out a loud moan. The thunder of her heartbeat was so strong she almost felt as if she would pass out from sheer pleasure.

Toryn's fingers found and teased a nipple. The nub immediately hardened under his touch. He nibbled her lower lip. Her pulse kicked into high gear, sending erotic signals to every part of her body. "I can't wait to taste you," he murmured. "My brother swears you are the sweetest he's had."

A thrill shimmied up her spine. Callie couldn't wait either. The yearning inside rushed over her with unbearable eagerness. She swallowed, growing hotter by the second. "I want all of you inside me." The tightening of muscles, the tensing of nerves were wonderful sensations.

Cadyn kissed the pink tip of her free breast. "And we shall be," he breathed, between teasing nips at her sensitive skin.

Moving her hips, Callie moaned when Iollan slipped his fingers inside her, stroking her with an easy slow motion. Increasing the friction, his head dipped and his mouth joined the fray. Kissing the insides of her thighs, his mouth claimed her.

Losing control, Callie shuddered and started to buck against her restraints. Her wild cries of pleasure bounced off the walls.

Moving to the head of the bed, Toryn guided his swollen erection toward her mouth. "Do you want this, Calista?" he asked, holding his cock just inches from her lips.

"God, yes." Callie opened wide and took him deep, sucking and licking, letting him set the tempo.

Iollan guided his swollen erection to her creamy sex. He began to tease her with the tip. His cock was long and thick, the plum-ripe crown engorged. He parted her slick labia with his fingers, then slipped inside her waiting sex.

Callie let out a deep whimper as he pressed past her gently yielding inner muscles. He started to pump, slowly at first, letting the tempo build. Driven by a passion both rhythmic and fierce, he grabbed her hips and slammed into her with full force.

Callie rocked with the motion, grinding herself against him. Iollan's fingers dug into her hips with a bruising force as he thrust up inside her, seating his thick shaft deeper inside.

"Fuck, yes," she moaned around Toryn's erection. "Give me the last inch." Creamy inner muscles tightened around Iollan's throbbing erection, pulling him in and holding him. The blazing coil of her approaching orgasm tightened her toes.

Toryn snatched his cock away from her clenching teeth, wrapping his hand tightly around his shaft and dragging it down to the base. His body tensed as his semen erupted from the tip, spurting over her naked breasts.

Cadyn rubbed it into her skin, scenting her with Toryn's seed. Bending over, he sucked a nipple into his mouth. "Tastes excellent," he assured her.

Callie responded with shivers and jerks. When Cadyn bit down on the tender tip she felt herself losing control and slipping over the edge. A low moan started in her throat. By the time it reached her lips it was a full cry of pure pleasure.

Iollan stretched out over her, supporting his weight on his outstretched arms. Corded from the effort, the veins stood out on his arms. On top of her, he had total control. He slowed his thrusts, giving her long slow strokes. His gaze burned with an arousing intensity that set her heart afire. "I need you, Calista." Eyes snapping with electricity, the depths around his irises whirling with a strange glimmering starburst pattern, he focused on her face. He was clearly enjoying watching her take her pleasure. Their lips met briefly, tasting each other.

Callie released a moan and arched up against him, urging him to drive his shaft deeper. Her inner muscles flexed around him, greedily drawing him in. "I won't break," she gasped. "Don't be gentle."

Obeying, Iollan began a circular motion, sheathing his cock as far as their bodies would allow. His balls slapped against her ass, ripe and full, ready to burst. "I can't hold it much longer."

As her desire grew, she became more demanding. "Just a little longer," she gasped, relishing every inch of his deep penetration. Her hands clenched into fists, fighting the straps around her wrists. God, she longed to tear free and rake her fingernails down his back.

Suddenly, their positions changed.

The bonds around Callie's wrists and ankles suddenly fell

away. Lifting her up, Cadyn slid behind her as he lifted her into Iollan's lap. She was close to climaxing when he parted her ass cheeks. Wet fingers probed her anus, then slipped inside. Callie's clit throbbed with carnal pleasure as he wiggled his fingers inside. She gasped, releasing a soft groan.

Toryn slipped behind Iollan, kissing his neck as he held his hips. Mouth gaping open, Callie realized their intent. She and Iollan would be taken by the twins. At the same time! Never in a million years had she dreamed she'd actually watch while three beautiful males of appealing, masculine sex appeal brought each other satisfaction—all at the same time.

Glancing up she saw Toryn's eyes narrow into two slits, while Iollan's closed in anticipation of penetration. Toryn moaned in pleasure and slanted a quick smile at Callie.

She gulped. The idea of the four of them locked together, sweaty flesh simultaneously gliding into sweatier flesh was absolutely mesmerizing, and she found herself panting all over again with fresh arousal. "Holy shit, this is incredible."

Cadyn's warm breath tickled the nape of her neck. "Easy, Calista," he whispered. "Giving pleasure to each other is one of the Niviane Idesha's greatest joys." His fingers pressed deeper, opening her narrow passage.

Callie cried out, not from pain but the total pleasure of the sensation. A moment later his finger slid away, replaced with the press of his cock. Her body tensed and she quivered.

"Relax." Cadyn pushed, easing his cock up her ass. He was huge. Not big. Not impressive. Huge.

Callie felt herself open, stretch around him. She gasped as he kept inching up inside. She closed her eyes, fighting not to cry out in protest of the burning sensation filling her. His cock was like a hot iron bar. The deeper he went, the more the pain blazed.

Thighs pressing against her buttocks, Cadyn stopped, his

erection buried to the hilt. His lips brushed the back of her neck. "Damn, that's deep."

Callie gasped out a few unintelligible words, helpless to do anything but surrender. The depth of her passion stunned her as her inner muscles involuntarily gripped his cock. She squirmed against the delicious torment. Now that she had him inside, it was more than pleasurable.

Cunt and ass completely filled, she could neither give nor take any more. She let out a loud moan, the sound starting from deep in her throat and working its way to her lips, becoming louder with every second. A long slow stream of molten heat coursed through her. Simmering on the edge of orgasm, she closed her eyes and simply enjoyed the sensations of pleasure. She was holding nothing back, demanding as much as she gave.

The sexes not only seemed to mingle, but merge. Though there was no music, they rocked together in rhythmic slow motion, as if moved by a fantasy orchestra only they heard. Their bodies moved in perfect synchronicity, forming the ideal gestalt of utter pleasure.

Deep inside her, Iollan slowed his thrusts. His hands slid under her arms, drawing her close. Pressing his mouth to the crux of her neck, he sucked gently at her skin. From behind, Cadyn claimed the other side of her neck. Two sets of teeth grazed her sensitive skin, sending a shiver down her spine. A tiny frisson of sensation coiled through her, an ache she welcomed.

"Come for us, love," Toryn coaxed in his slumberous voice.

She shuddered violently, her lips pressed together as she struggled to make the sensations last just a moment longer. Losing control to the needs of her body, a primeval growl of pleasure broke from her throat. She came with such force, she nearly blacked out from the pure gratification. Her grunts filled the air, her body trembling from the force of orgasm. At the same time, the two cocks inside her simultaneously surged. Hot semen jetted into her depths from both sides. The powerful explosion of sensations left her weak and dizzy.

Shaking with the aftermath of her second orgasm, she floated down slowly. Iollan and Cadyn still suckled at her neck like two kittens at the teat.

Callie opened sleep eyes, glancing at Toryn. He nuzzled at his brother's neck. Then, as if sensing her gaze, he slowly lifted his head. The low, undomesticated growl of an animal emanated from his throat. Before her eyes, his face grew contorted, shifting and rearranging in a glowing haze. Seconds later he smiled, baring his teeth. Only they were no longer human teeth. They'd changed.

Callie's heart lodged in her throat. Fangs. He had fangs. Two sets of canines on top, one set on the bottom. Six of the sharpest fucking teeth she'd seen in her entire life.

Toryn's face filled her vision. The power he radiated enveloped her, kept her silent as blood pumped through her veins, filling her with adrenaline. He gave a devilish grin. "All the better to taste you with, my dear."

Two sets of fangs penetrated and her world spun. A spark of pure electricity traveled straight down her spine as a swell of exquisite pain swamped her. Drawn into the heart of a luminescent corona of heat and light, images of the three men twisted in her mind, dizzying her with a series of swirling and sparking tides. She collided with their light, their heat. An exciting, wicked warmth filled her, penetrating her most secret places. Her blood thrummed through her veins, pressing furiously for release.

Oh, God, if only the ache would ease. . . .

13

Callie fought against the snare of sleep refusing to let go of her addled brain. No matter how many times her body shifted, she couldn't seem to get comfortable.

The pain, damn it.

Lost in the strange fog between waking and sleep, she rolled, trying to curl up into a more comfortable position. Some unbreakable object prevented the move. Muttering incoherently, she shifted again. A sharp edge scraped along her ribs. The unexpected sting of fresh pain propelled her back toward the waking world. The fragile mesh of consciousness reattached itself within her brain. Time sped up. The strange disturbing visions haunting her dreams slowly faded.

She woke with a start. Pain pummeled her head, and to a lesser extent throughout her body. Her world spun in dizzy circles.

She hurt. Bad.

Eyes little more than narrow slits, she grimaced, trying to swallow. Temples pounding double time, she felt her heart pump shards of ice through her veins. Deep inside, she felt chilled despite the fever raging through her. A curious numbness spread through her.

Half-conscious, weak to the bone, she shifted her head, trying to make out her surroundings. The effort of movement forced a gasp from her lips. She lay, panting, the chill creeping up her legs and spine. The pain in her skull danced a jig, throbbing in time to a lingering beat hovering on the edge of her hearing. Even her eyeballs ached, the sensation akin to a thousand tiny needles being driven into her nerves.

She blinked, staring dizzily around, trying to get a bearing on her whereabouts. As far as she could tell, she was alone, lying battered amid a great pile of charred wreckage. The sharp but not unpleasant pungency of burned wood tickled her nostrils.

How or why she'd arrived in such a place, she had no idea. A hazy gray veil of nothingness hung right in the center of her brain, cutting off all memory of her recent activities.

She struggled to rise. Sheer will and determination moved her. Managing to ease herself into an upright position, she discovered the source of some of her agony. She'd been lying on a pile of debris. Realizing what it was, she cast a wary glance toward the ceiling. The roof looked none too stable. Many of its sagging spots appeared to be nearing collapse at any second.

"Where am I?"

No answer. The silence took great delight in scoffing at her. In her dazed state it seemed to her this place had looked different once, yet she recognized nothing tangible in the ruins. Sunlight filtered in through gouged-out doors and windows. The skeletal remains of furniture were scattered throughout, little more than twisted metal frames. Gaping cracks were visible in the scorched walls, giving the impression the exterior was being torn apart by giant phantom hands.

The atmosphere of the place was stifled, quiet and eerie, as though a part of some alien world. She didn't know where she was or why, and that frightened her. Whether it was premonition or self-preserving instinct, all warning signs were pointing the same way. She was in deep trouble.

A fierce churning sensation caused her guts to clench in agony. She was going to be very ill. Barely able to get onto her hands and knees, she vomited, managing to catch her breath before another body-wrecking spasm struck. Nothing came up except putrid yellow strings of bile. She gagged until dry heaves set in and a raging thirst clawed at her throat. Mouth bone dry, she wished for a cool drink of water. Not that there was any chance of getting one now. By the looks of it, the facilities were definitely shut down, probably never to reopen.

Waking up without caffeine and sugar was a bitch. Wiping chapped lips, Callie sat back on her knees. The room around her bobbed and weaved in an alarming manner. Her skin was hot, burning with fever. Her hair hung in limp strands, plastered to her forehead by perspiration. Her limbs felt like noodles. She gulped, trying to keep from falling into a dead faint. Huge blurry spots rose up before her eyes, threatening to merge into one big ugly abyss.

A painful sensation began to work its way up her spine. Traveling her shoulders, it snaked through the back of her neck and straight into her skull. She felt the air around her shift, the pressure on her lungs robbing her of breath. A chilling sweat drenched her, giving rise to a foul odor that assailed her senses. *Fear.* Her little demon had grown into a giant, knocking at the doors of her mind with ferocious insistence.

Don't let it in.

Her training kicked in. Panic would weaken her to a potentially fatal degree. Keeping cool, keeping calm, would get her out of this place faster than blind fear.

She crouched, silent and motionless as a fresh wave of nausea rippled through her. The room was spinning. Body cold and soaked in sweat, she squeezed her eyes shut, fighting the surge of sickness. "I can't pass out," she gasped. Trying to jump-start her groggy self, she slapped at her cheeks. All she wanted to do was curl up in a tiny ball and die.

Not the way to think at all. Stubbornly, she shook her head. "I have to stay awake."

And then she noticed. She had no clothes on.

Oh, shit.

Something bad had happened. The specter of rape rose in her mind as she struggled to her feet. To her relief a pile of clothing lay a few feet away. She staggered over. Tears of relief stung her eyes when she recognized them as her own. Thank heavens.

Aching and barely erect, she struggled to dress. She'd never have thought such a simple act would become so difficult. Miserably frustrated, she tried to move her numb fingers, but they refused to cooperate. Getting into her jeans proved to be a task she almost didn't complete. She had to sit down to slip them on, then move up to her knees to finish pulling them up. Her socks were easy enough to pull on, but the laces of her motorcycle boots defied her. She left them undone, hoping she wouldn't trip and break her neck on the way out. Dying, alone in this deserted place, wasn't an appealing thought.

Heavy and suffocating, the silence surrounding her chewed ceaselessly at her imagination, stoking it at the same time. Her throat was dry, and her breath came in choking gasps. Her heart skipped a beat. She pricked up her ears, attuned to any sound. She had to make a decision, find a way to go.

Breath rasping over raw lips, she stood up. Her legs shook but held her weight. She took a step forward, then another. As her boots shuffled over the remnants of some tattered carpeting, she imagined she heard a whisper. She stopped dead, cocking her head. Listening.

All at once, the room wasn't so peaceful or calm. The temperature dropped significantly as a chilly breeze winnowed around her, whistling among the wreckage. A grating voice sounded around her. *Calista.*

It was an illusion, of course.

Unease gnawing at her guts, Callie shivered. "Knock it off," she muttered, chastising her imagination.

She started to walk again, closing the distance between herself and what she hoped was the nearest exit. She'd taken no more than ten steps when an unexpected force, invisible to her, gave her a push. Caught by surprise, she staggered, nearly knocked back on her ass. A shadow whizzed past her, no more than a blur to her eyes.

"Shit!"

The voice spoke again, this time clearly and much more audible. *Stay, Calista.*

She shook at the sound of her name on invisible lips. Fighting for composure, she closed her eyes and tried to suppress the tremor shimmying down her spine. As if gripped in the clutch of some invisible force, she stood rooted to her spot, not moving a muscle. Bruised, exhausted, surging with pain, her breath caught. Closing her eyes her awareness was stretched to the breaking point. She experienced again that strange tentative inreaching of contact, as if something was trying to directly enter her mind.

I'm here. Waiting. The drone of the words became an oddly echoing chant that seemed to sound not in her ears, but inside her own skull. Some inner instinct warned her she wasn't alone.

"Where? I don't see you," she called, wavering violently. Voice tight with emotion, she felt every nerve in her body scream with tension. "This isn't funny."

The strange breeze immediately vanished. The stillness surrounding her became a heavy, suffocating cloak, so weighty it took all her willpower not to sink to her knees. Something wasn't right. Something had wanted her, had brought her here, for a purpose.

Feeling as though she'd disintegrate, Callie bowed her head. She massaged the ache in her temples, feeling the pulse there under her fingertips. Was she losing her mind? Gritting her teeth, she shook her head. Control threatened to slip through her fingers.

Look, the voice said.

Callie froze. Her heart clogged her throat as a giant's hand squeezed her windpipe. A whimper escaped her lips, and she glanced around. A flicker of movement caught her attention out of the corner of her eye, little more than a wisp of shadow. She turned, but there was no one there.

A strangled cry of frustration and fear escaped her. Confused and frightened, she ran her hands through her disheveled hair, then clenched them into tight fists. The room seemed to be spinning in slow circles around her. Her lips trembled. "Look at what?" she groaned in frustration.

Something pushed past her from behind, streaking by so fast all she caught was a smudge of darkness. Maybe the size of a large rodent, though lacking such a discernable form, the shadowy thing darted toward a rear wall. It came to a rest, hovering perhaps three feet above the ground.

Callie's eyes narrowed, then widened in recognition. Her thoughts skittered away like a frightened kitten, but she knew she had to fight to overcome her fear and disbelief.

She forced herself to stay calm. Staying in control was strictly up to her. That was an agent's job, hanging on to self-discipline when everything else was falling apart. *Concentrate.*

Barely aware she was in motion, she walked toward the thing. The strange entity vanished as she approached, zipping out of sight before she was even sure it had gone.

She blinked, puzzled by the attraction. Though fire had earlier gutted most of the place, the flames had only licked at this wall. Remnants of wallpaper, patterned in red and green, still clung to the plaster. Recognizing it, her whole body started to shake. The silence around her felt charged with electricity. Hand trembling, she reached out. Her fingers trailed its pattern, sapped of its vibrancy but still recognizable.

Callie shivered. For an instant her mind merged with the past as the shackles holding her memory prisoner fell away. The gray veil parted a little, thinning. Bright lights and crawling colors wriggled through her brain, merging together to form a new picture. Accompanied by a slow prickle of wonder the decay around her seemed to fade, turning into something breathtakingly beautiful. She shut her eyes to better visualize the place. It came, the splendor of sight, sound, and colors slowly seeping back. The picture wasn't complete, but at least she knew why she was in this place now.

The grayness curling around her brain receded a bit. Her eyelids fluttered shut. A soft moan escaped her lips. For a moment her sense of reality vanished and she found herself in another place. Lying on a canopied bed, naked, awaiting the illuminated angels representing a magical realm existing everywhere around her . . .

Toryn and Cadyn. The twins.

And Iollan.

Her mouth filled with their taste, her nostrils with their scent. How could she forget their tease, their bite? The way they'd slipped inside a depth longing to be filled, then out again—only to return with a deeper plunge. Claiming. Binding. Nibbling.

A fit of unexpected quaking overtook her. Her spine turned to icy water. One hand rose to her neck, pressing her fingers against her skin. She remembered sharp fangs and a sharper bite.

Her forehead ridged, the folds growing deeper as her animosity toward her abductors intensified. Images filtered through her mind, tugging her back to the vicious events.

Clearer now.

She could see them.

Feel them.

Callie felt her blood pressure drop, the air in her lungs becoming a deep, heavy weight in her chest, a crushing sensation. She felt dazed and sick. Her mouth moved a little as she struggled with strong emotions.

"Blood," she murmured, for an instant feeling an inner surge of revulsion. A slew of images ravaged her feverish brain. Jesus Christ. Had they really drunk her blood?

Sick bastards.

An odor assailed her nostrils, one she too well recognized. The smell of fear. A palpable thing, more sour than the bile rising at the back of her throat. Her fear was a specter, mocking, laughing, a leering death mask.

The realization disturbed the precarious control she held over her mind and body; the surging disparity left her alarmed. Without knowing quite why, hysterical laughter bubbled up in her throat. She was almost physically sick with the knowledge that she'd been used and discarded like so much trash.

Dissenting voices began to echo in her brain, teasing and taunting. Against her will, an awful defilement had taken place, a hideous event nothing in life prepared her for. Gasping to catch her breath, she made a peculiar unfocused sound much like a sob. "I've been drugged." Her palm flattened to her forehead.

And raped, her mind filled in.

A fit of unexpected quaking overtook her. Fighting the mental quagmire of writhing snakes in her head, Callie concentrated her energies and struggled to center her thoughts. It *had* to be some sort of hallucinogen.

"It didn't happen." She ran her hands through her disheveled hair, then clenched them into tight fists. "It can't be real." Was she losing her mind? Gritting her teeth, she shook her head, struggling for control.

Feeling her disintegration, Callie bowed her head and massaged the ache in her temples. She swallowed, trying to breathe past the incredible lump in her throat. No other reasonable explanation made any sense.

Just when she believed she had a grasp on logical answers, everything changed.

Great clots of blackness rose before her eyes. She struggled to concentrate, forcing them back. More mysteries brooded beneath, behind that dark veil. Afraid her memory would falter into nothingness again, she shook her head, trying to orient herself. She was attacked from inside; her mouth flew open and her jaws gaped. The pictures in her mind wavered, began to dissolve. Through long, frightening minutes she saw naught; the wall in front of her faded into a dusky gray nothingness.

Something doesn't want me to remember.

The realization disturbed the precarious control she held over her mind and body; the surging disparity left her alarmed. Her hands rose to cover her eyes, shutting out all light, all sight, as if by blocking her vision she could keep the memories inside her brain her own.

Weary, weak beyond belief, Callie sank to the floor. Her body stiffened. Jerked. She writhed in anguish, convulsing, and her body arched with the agonies of the strange invasion. Her head thrashed and her arms beat the air, defending herself against an enemy snaking its way into her skull. There was a low throbbing throughout her body, but it was all far away, held at bay by the voices reverberating around her. A sluggish groan rose to her ears, feeble and without objective, extended by the wheeze emanating from her mouth. Invisible fingers clawed at her, threatening to drag her back into the abyss of insensibility. She resisted, struggling to remain aware.

Moaning, she twitched, the feeling of abject helplessness only adding to her panic as her senses reeled. A chill seized her brain. Limbs out of control, she couldn't rise to her feet. She became conscious of the beating of her own heart. The organ hammered inside her chest, a hollow, irregular rhythm. Her blood thrummed at a furious pace, pressing for release.

Her body went limp. She lay in a huddled mass, her strength all but gone. She swallowed, trying to breathe past the incredible pressure squeezing her throat.

Sick and tormented, she withdrew her mind into the deepest, darkest parts of her skull, where not even the soul dared to tread. Heavy with weariness, she surrendered to exhaustion. She was slipping away, almost insensible but holding on to awareness with what seemed to be her last wisps of strength.

Her eyes dropped shut, and she felt no emotion except muffled relief. She wanted to stay in this safe haven of darkness. Merging with the merciful womb of unconsciousness, she willingly gave herself to that sinister void where none could follow and cause her further distress.

14

Callie sat on the floor, waiting. Positioned across from one of the burned-out windows, she watched as the sun sank lower on the horizon. Half of the fiery orb had already vanished. Another few minutes and total darkness would envelope the city.

She shifted to ease some of the numbness in her butt. She'd been sitting almost an hour, simply waiting. She'd wanted to arrive early, be in place before sunset. Not sure what would happen, if anything.

After she'd awakened from her second bout of unconsciousness, she'd done what any reasonable person would. Gotten the hell out.

As she'd suspected, the building was abandoned, condemned, according to the sign outside. Third floor gutted by fire and water damage, the entire structure was well beyond salvage, one of many on the block slated for the wrecking ball. Depopulation, property abandonment, crime, and a desolate and unfriendly landscape all added up to the need for an urban renewal program. Good people wanted out, and bad people wanted in.

Certainly, no one would think to look for vampires in a condemned building. Great place to hide. Brilliant, even.

If you believed in vampires.

Callie wasn't sure she did. In fact, she still wasn't sure she
hadn't dreamed, or hallucinated, the entire episode. There were
plenty of powerful mind-altering drugs on the market, includ-
ing Rohypnol, a popular "date rape" drug. A very potent tran-
quilizer with a sedative effect, amnesia, muscle relaxation, and
slowing of psychomotor responses were just a few of the side
effects. Completely colorless, odorless, tasteless. She remembered drinking wine. That shit must have been seriously spiked.
Melting walls and fanged men seemed to belong more to a
wild-ass psychedelic trip.

Logical and made sense. She'd heard about people seriously
tripping on it. Blackouts, visual hallucinations—some people
even believed they were able to fly. Why couldn't she halluci-
nate vampires?

Except hallucinations didn't leave bites on your neck.

She had two fresh sets. That made three bites in all. Weren't
people supposed to turn into vampires after three bites? She
hoped not. That would mean she was dead. And she didn't
want to be dead. Even when she was cutting, death hadn't been
the goal. She'd just wanted to feel something other than numbness inside. Dead, she'd feel nothing. Dead, she'd be nothing.

Callie didn't want to be nothing.

Maybe she was having a nervous breakdown and none of
this existed at all. Maybe reality was really a padded cell and a
straitjacket. Possible. Very possible. Mental instability ran in
her bloodline. Would an insane person know or remember
when they crossed the line between reality and fantasy? She'd
inflicted damages on herself before. She'd thought she was past
needing the pain. Maybe she wasn't.

Trouble was, she wasn't sure. But what did an insane person

know? Nothing. Not a goddamned thing. Might as well start flicking at her lips with her fingers. Blub. Blub. Blub.

Okay. Stop it. Not funny. Not cute.

Shit. Now she had a headache. Her head hurt from thinking too much. Sometimes she couldn't see the point of it.

Today was one of those days. Definitely.

Had to have been drugs. But until she knew what was what, she wasn't budging.

Leaving would have been the sane thing to do. The logical thing to do.

Callie felt neither sane nor logical. She wasn't sure how she should feel, except that going was out of the question. Not yet. Her reality had somehow become blurred and something in her nature desperately needed to complete the connections between what she remembered and what she believed that she remembered.

She hadn't strayed far from the old building. With her memory strangely unreliable, she didn't want to leave the area. A tacky convenience store two blocks away had provided restroom breaks and she'd even talked the semicute clerk into a free cup of coffee and a candy bar. Not the best or most nutritious, but it filled her stomach. Casual questioning of the clerk revealed the building had burned at least a decade ago. Those brave or stupid enough to live in the area had been waiting at least that long for new construction to begin, but the city simply lacked the necessary funds. The decay continued and nobody cared anymore.

Armed with that little nugget, she'd spent the rest of her time exploring the building and napping. She'd found nothing indicating any sort of habitation. While not the best rest of her life, she'd found a quiet corner and dozed enough to take the edge off her fatigue.

She sipped from her coffee cup, swallowing down the last

few ounces. "Come on, already," she muttered in irritation. She tossed the empty container away. It landed with a hollow thunk, rolled a few inches, and stopped, joining her candy wrapper. A little more litter didn't matter. "Let's get this show on the road."

The sun sank lower.

Darkness advanced, skimming along a junk-ridden back lot. The sky was layered: bright yellows, dazzling pinks, and blazing blue hues. Each grew a little less brilliant by the second, slowly vanishing under a deepening purple hue. A sprinkling of stars would bejewel the crisp, clear, late-summer sky.

Callie yawned and stretched. Though she'd left a text message for Norton briefly detailing further contact with Drake, she hadn't given any clue of her whereabouts. She wasn't ready to share her information yet.

Maybe not at all.

Shadows crept into the wrecked apartment. As they invaded the place, something utterly unexpected began to happen. Accompanied by the lightest flicker of a breeze, a strange distortion commenced. Shimmering golden light pulsed under the shadows, spreading over the ruin like the touch of Midas. For a moment ghostly images of the past connected with the present, seeming interposed over the wreckage.

Adrenaline searing her veins, Callie lunged to her feet. Her mouth dropped open, her words scarcely more than a choking gasp. "Holy Jesus, Mary, and Joseph." For ten, maybe twenty seconds she considered running as the room clouded, thickening with the swirling lines of an oppressive force. Nothing in her training had prepared her to deal with supernatural phenomena.

The shimmering force spread out around her with blinding speed, eating up the rubble with incredible efficiency. She felt a touch then, something striking out like a blinding mental and physical blow. She faltered, felt the shove of a great strength slice straight through to her very bones. There was no time to run, no time to get out of the way.

Callie threw up an arm in front of her eyes, shielding her face from the oncoming rush of pure pulsing power.

A wash of illuminated sparks pummeled her back into the wall. She went perfectly still as a whirling vortex of images lit up around her. The force of an alien energy invaded her body, cutting through her like thousands of tiny sharp blades, unpleasant and invasive.

Callie felt the floor shift beneath her feet, felt ripped apart to the tiniest of atoms and reassembled, all in the space of seconds. Her breath caught in her throat, the sudden lack of oxygen threatening to strangle her. Too shocked to think clearly, she felt her knees give under her weight.

Unable to stay on her feet, she plopped down flat on her ass. Moaning in shock, she closed her eyes and tried to block the dizzying sensations flowing through every nerve ending.

Time slid away. Slowly, her agony receded.

Callie cracked open aching, swollen eyes and blinked. The splendor had returned, bright, beautiful, flawless. Trying to center herself and settle the acute nausea, she gazed around.

"This ain't no wild tripping hallucination," she muttered.

A shadowy movement caught the corner of her eye. Stiffening, she turned her head in time to see several shadows go streaking across the room. Apprehension flooded through her.

She wasn't alone.

Chills scraped up her spine. She had the feeling she was being watched, felt the weight of many eyes boring down on her like laser beams. Yet every time she turned where she believed the stares were coming from, she saw little more than the shift of light displacing.

She swallowed, knotting her hands. "Iollan?"

No answer.

Shivering, Callie climbed to her feet. Rubbing her hands over her arms to still the rising goose bumps, she took a cautious step forward, then a few more. She swayed where she stood, bracing herself to keep from falling. The change from trash to treasure sure packed one hell of a physical wallop. Trying to shake the disorienting vertigo hampering her wits, she cautiously progressed. Uneasiness nagged.

The shadow shifted in front of her. The curtains veiling the canopied bed undulated as if touched by invisible hands. Shifting the curtains aside, she saw a white satin comforter and matching pillow shams. Sinful. And alluring.

Gaze settling on the bed, she felt hollowness trickle through her gut. It had nothing to do with fear and everything to do with desire. Wetness pooled between her thighs, the beginning of a throbbing ache of emptiness.

Without knowing why, she stroked her hand across the cool smoothness of the comforter. Waltzing in her mind's eye the way flames might dance in the nearby hearth, a forbidden fantasy hovered on the horizon in her mind.

Her eyelids fluttered shut. A soft moan escaped her lips. She pictured herself lying on the bed, naked, waiting for the lover who would part the drapes.

A powerful arm banded her waist, tugging her into a male body even harder and more powerful. Legs and hips collided. A muscular chest pressed against her back. Warmth whispered across her nape. "You should have care when walking with shadows."

A strange sense of familiarity flooded through her. Callie's breath caught in her throat. Her body sparked in acute awareness of his frame pressing into hers. She knew Iollan's touch, welcomed it. He felt like a rock wall, sturdy and powerful. She automatically adjusted herself to his contours, fitting their bodies together.

Salacious vibrations crackled along her nerve endings. She inhaled slowly, remembering his intimate touch, his passionate lovemaking. She felt the desire between them, untamed and fierce.

Closing her eyes, she sank into him. One of her hands slipped behind her, fingers digging into tight denim to urge him closer. Anticipation coiled around her heart, working its way to her most intimate warmth. Her breasts tingled, nipples tightening into little peaks.

She needed him. Wanted him, damn it. Her body was more than ready, suddenly aching for fulfillment. At the moment she didn't give a damn about anything other than his hot body on those cool sheets.

Head tilting slightly, Callie offered the vulnerable softness of her neck. "I don't know what you're doing to me, but it's driving me crazy."

His arm was an iron band, preventing her from moving. Instead of a hungry mouth ravaging her skin, something cold and solid pressed against her temple. "Forgive me, Calista."

Callie's eyes snapped open. Dark metal glinted near the corner of her eye. Realizing his intent, fear jetted through her veins. She writhed, scratching at the arm locked around her waist.

Iollan released her.

Trapped by the bed, she tumbled face forward onto the mattress. She whipped over onto her back, raising her weight up on her elbows. Her mouth dropped open.

Iollan stood a few feet away, overwhelming her with his presence. His big frame filled her vision. The power he radiated was that of pure malice. The gun in his hand was pointed straight at her forehead. His stern lips held the shadow of disdain.

Every fiber in Callie's body tightened like a wound spring. She quelled the instinct to try and get away. Run, and he would overtake her. Run, and he would shoot her down like a rabid dog. Iollan Drake had killed before. And, she realized, he intended to kill again.

Mesmerized, obsessed, and terrified all at the same time, she gulped to catch her breath, steady the hammering of her heart. Her blood pounded so fiercely behind her temples that she found it impossible to think straight. She'd known it was possible he'd take her down. Some part of her had hoped that wouldn't be the case. That part was, apparently, mistaken.

Eyes chilling to a subzero temperature, he leveled his gaze. The gun in his hand didn't waver. "Surprised?"

Damn. How did this happen?

Just crazy.

And definitely not any drug this time.

Forcing herself to focus, she glared. Unfortunately visual daggers weren't deadly. "Surprise isn't the emotion I'm feeling right now," she grated. "Nice to know you were going to fuck me over without giving me a kiss this time."

He eyed her from head to foot, sprawled across the bed in a position normally very pleasant for a man to see. His look was intimate, probing. Hungry. His lips curled with a sly sensuality. "Fuck you? I thought about doing that first. I love humans. You're so gullible and so easy to manipulate when your hormones are skipping around."

Callie immediately clamped her knees shut. "Fat chance."

Iollan shrugged. "My loss. Though I'll admit it was clever of your people to send in a woman this time. I almost didn't guess you were an agent. You should have had the sense to stay away."

Icy fingers wrapped around her spine. She licked dry lips, but didn't argue. No sense in denying it, trying to keep the game going. "How long have you known?"

Eyes chilling to a subzero temperature, he said, "I wasn't

sure at first. But blood doesn't lie. The moment I tasted you, I knew you were dangerous."

She bristled. She wasn't the one posing any danger at the moment. "So why the gun? Why not just rip out my throat with your big bad teeth?"

He shook his head wryly. "It's the twenty-first century, love. Trust mankind to make killing easy and efficient. Besides, ripping out your throat would be too messy. "And—he bared his teeth, seemingly perfectly normal—"it's awkward on the fangs." A sly grin escaped him. "You do remember those, don't you?"

Callie didn't move. She barely dared to breathe. "Freak." Her voice was a smothered monosyllable.

He clearly heard her. "Oh, please. I enjoyed fucking with your mind almost as much as I enjoyed taking that beautiful body of yours." His eyes raked her in an obscene manner. "Most pleasurable. Alas, the party has to come to its end."

Their eyes locked. Every cell in her body expanded. Just looking at him made her break out in a sweat all over again. And not because of the gun in his hand. Slow horror crept up her spine as fear channeled straight into her libido. She couldn't possibly be turned on. How could shivers so easily turn into quakes of excitement? Sexual yearning coupled with knowing the man intended to kill her just wasn't normal.

Feeling the pressures of a body craving satisfaction, Callie shivered. All the blood in her body migrated to her groin. Coils of desire tightened through her, nervous energy crackling in the air. The idea of having sex with a dangerous man made her melt all over again.

She pushed out a breath, really annoyed at herself for still wanting him. Somehow she had to summon the will to deny her desire for him, pry her mind off the image of making love with him. "No fair," she murmured.

His jaw clenched. "What?"

She swallowed the knot of panic blocking her windpipe. "I still want you, damn it," she grated. "You've got a fucking gun stuck in my face and all I can think about is having sex with you again." Her voice rasped, unrecognizable to her own ears.

As if she'd struck a nerve, his brows drew down. His expression thawed a little. The gun in his hand wavered. "I wanted you, too." He muttered a curse through gritted teeth. "More than I've wanted any woman in a long time."

Callie swore there was a glimmer of need under all the mistrust in his eyes. Total irrational relief swept through her. A chance. All she wanted was a chance. She had no business talking this way, just because she found a man who filled the emptiness in her heart. Her eyes met his and she let out a long breath. "There's something between us, you and me."

She didn't get any further.

Iollan shook his head reluctantly, lips pressing into a tight thin line. "There's nothing, Calista." He levered a bullet into the chamber. "We are at war, and I can't let personal feelings get in the way of protecting my people."

His words hit like a fist. Shaken by fine tremors, cold to her very core, she forced herself to swallow her fear. If he wanted her to beg, plead for her life, he had another think coming. Losing her life meant nothing. People were born. Lived. And died. Simple. She knew how she'd gotten into this world. Knowing how she left it wouldn't matter in a few more minutes.

Callie lifted her chin, meeting his gaze directly. "So back up your mouth with a bullet then. Go ahead." She wet parched lips with the tip of her tongue. "Pull the damn trigger."

15

A bullet to the head. Maybe even two. That's what she was going to get. Christ. For a vampire, he wasn't very imaginative when it came to the methods of delivering death. Still a bullet was effective. No fuss. No muss. No pain.

A bead of sweat trickled down her spine. As an agent working in the field she'd known her luck might run out at any time. Once again a man had fucked her over, and done it most excellently.

Once she'd made the decision to take the bullet, there was no hesitation or doubt. She'd chosen the path her life would take. Now that she'd chosen her death, she was eager to get on with it.

The wait was excruciating.

Callie's thoughts darkened. She bared her teeth and snapped, "What are you waiting for? Let's get this fucking show on the road." She kicked out in anger, foot swiping empty air. Let him get close enough and she'd be glad to punt those balls of his straight up between his shoulder blades. If she had to die, he might as well hurt. A lot.

She closed her eyes, expecting to hear a shot ring out momentarily. *Oh, please, let it be quick.*

Seconds ticked off.

Nothing.

The soft brush of his footsteps approached the bed. Something heavy dropped with a muffled thud. The mattress sank under his knee.

Squeezing her eyes tighter, Callie felt his weight shift closer. A hand came down near her shoulder. His leg bumped hers. Fingers brushed along her jaw, sliding into her hair.

She instinctively lifted herself, tilting her head back. She smelled the dark musky scent of his duster. She smelled his skin, heated with the scent of an aroused male. Her limbs turned liquid. She smelled her own arousal, felt the dampness between her thighs.

She didn't dare open her eyes, didn't dare hope.

Searching lips brushed the curve of her throat. "Calista," he murmured. "Forgive me."

She looked up, tears welling in her eyes. Relief pierced her daze. Instinctively she jerked into a sitting position, blinking up at him. "There's nothing to forgive." Her words came out, a thin whisper of relief.

"I feel it," he said, low, tormented. "I want you too much to watch you die."

Before Callie said a word, he closed the brief distance between them. Suddenly his mouth was on hers, burning hot straight into her core. His lips were hungry, tongue thrusting deep with demand that she open up, submit. Desire was like steel, immovable and overpowering.

Helpless against the needs of her own traitorous body, Callie surrendered. The intensity in him seemed to enfold and engulf her. A wave of electric shock zinged through her body. Exciting, wicked warmth filled her. She was afraid she would dissolve into a sticky puddle.

He was so close. Aroused.

Arms winding around his neck, a yearning, needy sound rose from her throat. His mouth was relentless, filled with desperation and longing. She'd never been so torn in her life. Her thighs opened. She wanted to be taken completely with the same anxiety driving his kiss.

Everything came in a rush.

Callie wasn't prepared for the mix of excitement, wonder, and anticipation filling her—all sensations she wasn't ready to acknowledge. She hadn't predicted this. Hadn't expected anything like it. Things like this, feelings like this, didn't blossom overnight. She wanted him more than life, more than the oxygen driving her lungs or the blood pounding in her temples. She wanted . . .

Oh.

Strong hands gripped her shoulders, pushing her back. "This can't work." His voice was taut, ragged as his breathing. "We can't do this."

Fighting to catch her breath, and steady the aching emptiness of his withdrawal, Callie swallowed.

Hovering just inches away, Iollan looked fabulous. Heart-stealing fabulous. Whatever he was, he wasn't hard on the eyes. Rested, he looked bright, vital, and very much alive. His clothes were still the same from head to foot, even down to the knee-brushing duster. His thick dark hair gleamed, the unruly layers enhancing the line of his strong jaw. And his eyes. Like living flames, so clear and bright they couldn't possibly be a natural color.

Her internal temperature ratcheted up a few more notches. "It's all right. I want to."

Averting his gaze, Iollan slowly shook his head. A sigh shuddered out. "I can't. If I take you again, I won't be able to let you go."

Her heart twisted. "Me either."

Iollan leaned back, putting some distance between them. "You should go."

She looked up briefly puzzled. Was that it? Just get up and leave? Definitely not on her agenda. Her whole body yearned for the next sweet touch of his hands on her naked skin, his lips on hers.

Their gazes tangled, his avoiding, hers questioning. "Why?"

Fleeting wariness crossed his face. He glanced toward the windows, toward the night that beckoned him. "I have to feed," he said slowly. "Soon." His final word hammered.

The skin on her scalp crawled when he reminded her of that simple fact. No matter what she might feel for him, Iollan Drake was a vampire. *Is*, she corrected herself.

Callie pursed her lips, making a quick decision. She didn't suppose donating a little of her blood would hurt her. Her skin heated as she remembered the previous withdrawals he'd made. She didn't recall that she'd minded a bit. "You can take mine," she started to offer.

He gazed at her, his eyes lighting with fresh desolation. He reached out, brushing her lips with the tips of his fingers. "Just walk away from this place, and don't look back."

Callie felt her heart lodge in her throat. Common sense told her to go, but too many emotions competed inside her. Not to mention that his immediate proximity continued to wreak havoc on her hormones. She blinked, fighting for control. "I'm not leaving."

Iollan closed his eyes briefly. "It's not safe for you to stay." His admission failed to disguise the yearning in his voice.

Callie refused to accept that. Something inside tugged at her. Her attraction to Iollan Drake was one thing; she'd dismiss that as purely hormonal. But the seeming gentleness of his spirit collided with his image as cold-blooded killer.

A cold-blooded killer didn't let a federal agent walk free.

She reached out, touching his arm. "I'm just trying to understand what's going on."

A shudder passed through him. Anguish shimmered across his face before a slow smile of regret tugged at his lips. He withdrew from her reach. "Sometimes I think there is no understanding."

Seeing him so resigned and hopeless shook her to the core. Steeling herself against his withdrawal, her fingers curled into anxious fists. She gave him a beseeching look. "I'm willing to listen."

"You should go." Sliding off the bed, he walked toward the bay windows at the rear of the room. Unlatching one, he pushed it open. A breeze winnowed in, bringing with it the sounds and smells of the city at night. He leaned into the frame, head cocked as if listening to invisible voices.

Her concentration on him was so complete that Callie almost didn't notice the shriveling and sinking of the bed beneath her weight. She glanced down, eyes catching the pale glimmering light of heatless flames. A strange gray film seethed around the edges of the walls. She saw flames licking at the furniture, smelled acrid smoke singeing her nostrils and lungs.

Mind reeling, she felt her feet scrape the floor. She stumbled, almost falling. The contortions around her continued, closer now, dizzying her with a whirlpool of intense action. Everything was beginning to melt and fade around her, withering and receding back to its original state.

The end came within seconds.

Darkness flowed around her like a thick boiling cloud, sapping the very marrow from her bones. She felt fear, an almost anguished longing for a place she'd never known as a whole. A minute more and it would be forever beyond her reach, forever beyond her touch. Once it was gone, once Iollan was gone, it would never come back.

Neither would he.

And then there was darkness, all around and all consuming.

Callie stood, lost in its center. Her head felt tight, like her skull was in a vise. She drew a shaky breath, lifting a hand to her forehead. For a moment the darkness thinned and she saw the windows, little more than gaping holes in the walls now. Iollan stood, a silhouette posed in shadows. He seemed ghostly, unreal.

She took a tentative step forward, trying not to trip. The debris was almost an obstacle course. More steps. Her nerves were taut, wanting to get out of this place. But she wasn't leaving. Not willingly and, God forbid, not alone. She stopped, standing just behind him. She reached out. Her hand hovered, but didn't touch.

For the longest time, Iollan didn't respond. When he did, it was to glance over his shoulder. His hand closed into a fist. "Now you see what I really am," he said in a low voice. "Nothing more than shadow and ruin."

"It all seems real to me. You seem real."

He glanced over his shoulder again. His face, starkly austere in the pallid moonlight, brooded with a distant, inhuman calm. The night suited him. He looked more stunning than ever. "A minor manipulation in energy, just an illusion, nothing more. Come the day, I won't even exist."

Not impossible to guess why. "Daylight."

He nodded. "The sun saps our energy. Daylight incapacitates us to an almost fatal degree." A hollow tone haunted his words.

Two and two connected. Her heart missed a beat. "Energy you replace through blood."

A painful hesitation. "We are *psi-sangre*."

The term meant nothing to her. "I don't understand."

His laugh was low, intimate in its amusement. "We draw our strength and vitality from consuming blood energized by sexual energy. In return we try to give much pleasure."

Callie stood motionless, lulled by the remembrance of his powerful hands on her body. Trying to block her reactions to his words would be futile. He was close enough to ignite any number of erotic fantasies, every one arriving with a clarity that made her cheeks flame and sent molten lava through her core. Even the dull ache in her head from having the splendor sucked away around her didn't detract from the humming in the rest of her body.

"You did give me pleasure." Goose bumps prickled over her. "A lot of pleasure."

Slowly, Iollan turned. His gaze sought hers, somehow connecting through the dim light filtering in. "It's strange not to belong anymore, to stand on the outside looking in. We keep to the shadows because we must to survive. But we also know human passions and human needs because that part of us never truly died when we crossed. We are still people with emotions, though many call us monsters."

The low, intimate timbre of his voice made her legs tremble. Somehow she was able to remain standing. His words, spoken so simply and with such sincerity, almost made her cry. She wanted to soothe his pain and assuage her own need to touch him at the same time. He hovered like a moth at the window, seeming to know that physical contact would probably sink them both.

I should let him go.

She shook her head. She couldn't.

Callie squeezed her eyes shut. The heart she'd thought mended ripped a little more. The tear was tiny, but telling. "I know what it's like to stand on the outside. I've spent my whole life there."

Her words seemed to draw him in.

Stepping away from his perch, he reached out and tenderly cupped her face. His fingers were cool against her too-hot skin.

"Then you know why I can't ask you to join me. I won't condemn your beauty to the night alone."

Relishing his touch, she pressed her hand to his. "I'd shun the light to have you just one more time."

Iollan pulled her close, his forehead connecting with hers. A jolt of electricity went all the way to her toes.

"You and I are natural enemies," he murmured. "I could kill you now and no one would be the wiser."

His dark, serious voice drew her in with its power. She pressed her hands against his chest, fingers clutching his shirt to draw him closer. "You won't," she breathed. "You can't."

His hands circled her hips. "We attempt to do no harm. That has always been our way." His warm breath brushed her cheeks, her lips. "I want you to know I didn't choose to become a murderer." He was grasping at a redemption she had no authority to offer.

Heart swelling painfully, she felt her pulse rocket. Feeling as if she'd tremble into tiny pieces if he didn't kiss her soon, she shook her head. She didn't want to know the details, didn't need to. "Please, don't tell me," she breathed. "I don't want to know."

He pulled back a little.

Callie tightened her hold, pressing her body into his. Her breasts were against his chest, and her hips vibrated with delicious anticipation. He was tall, so tall her gaze barely grazed his shoulder. If he wanted to, he could pick her up and break her in half like a twig. She didn't have to think long to know that as a nonhuman, he'd be stronger and faster.

One of his hands slid into her hair. Claiming a mass of her thick locks, he gently tugged her head back. "Tomorrow, you'll belong to them. And tomorrow I would have to kill you."

Body held captive by his powerful hands, she gasped at the sheer primitive male power he exuded. Her whole body trembled and she completely forgot she was supposed to be afraid.

"I don't want to think about tomorrow." A wedge of air stuck in her throat, forcing her voice to hoarseness. "I want you tonight."

Silence.

She sensed the hesitation in him.

"I never wanted to hurt you," he murmured.

"I know."

"It won't happen again." He traced his lips over her cheek to her mouth. "I'll die first."

His mouth sealed his words with a kiss. His palm anchored her head as his mouth gave her the connection they both so desperately sought. They came together, at first tentatively, then with more force as passion flooded through them. Long and hot, yet also sweet and warm. Through the vibrations passing between them, Callie felt his hunger and yearning.

She wanted him like crazy. Even up against the wall in a burned-out building would do. She didn't care. "I need you," she whispered into his mouth, almost frantic to feel him inside her.

"I need you, too. Desperately."

Her fingers tangled in his thick hair, pulling him toward her neck. "More than blood?" she breathed.

He groaned against the soft pulse in her throat. "More than my life."

Pushing her jacket off, he tugged her T-shirt out of her jeans, lifting it up over her breasts. The fabric of her bra did little to conceal her swollen nipples, aching for the slow sweet torment of a male mouth. Heat pooled between her thighs, cream wetting the crotch of her panties.

With a smooth, confident move he pushed her sports bra up halfway over her breasts so her nipples were exposed, protruding prominently from the binding of tight material around her body. "I've missed these." He lowered his mouth to taste her, exploring one tight peak with his eager tongue.

The gesture obliterated all sanity in Callie's head. He suckled gently, then harder until ripples of pleasure left her breathless and quivering.

She reveled in the sensation he ignited in her body. "Feels wonderful." Her breath rasped softly but urgently over her tender lips.

He tweaked one rosy tip. "I know what you crave." He kissed her again, his mouth lingering over her lips, tongue caressing their soft outline. "Tell me you missed my cock."

She smiled. "I missed your cock."

"Good." He plundered her mouth, ravishing her lips until they were swollen from his licks and suckling. Pleasure, undiluted and pure, coursed through her.

Her hands explored the durable ridges of his body, finding him, rubbing him through his tight jeans. The soft moan of pleasure he gave drowned out all the little voices in her head, voices that cautioned her to stop, put her hands on his chest and push him away.

She couldn't.

The alarm in the back of her mind went blissfully silent. Everything came to a standstill. They exchanged a silent, intimate look. How this might end, what would come of it, she didn't care. There were no yesterdays, no tomorrows, no grief. Now was the only time that mattered, the heat of the moment.

She raked her lip with her bottom teeth as she unbuttoned his shirt. Her hands shook with nerves. Her only awareness was the intense pleasure of sliding her hands over his bare chest. His hands were on her hips, holding her against his erection. She felt the tension in his fingers as he gripped her, and then he was caressing her, tracing her narrow waist, cupping her breasts.

He surrounded each nipple with five adept fingers, teasing them expertly. The fire of lust lit his penetrating gaze. "I can't stand the thought of another man's hands on your body."

Callie moaned as his fingers and thumbs came together, the

dusky tips locked between them. "Even though you shared me with your brothers."

"They had their taste, but no more." He squeezed the stiff nubs. Darts shot through her, striking crucial nerve endings. Need overcame reason. All her defenses crashed down around her feet. "I won't share you again." He started kissing down her neck, lazily running his tongue against her skin.

Callie reveled in the feel of his lips on her anxious skin. Her breath caught in her throat, but she didn't care. She needed him more than she needed oxygen, more than she needed life itself.

Somehow her clothes melted away, leaving her deliciously naked to his skimming hands. His clothes, too, vanished, revealing the length of his magnificent male body, all solid planes and eager flesh. He was inflexible, thick and throbbing with need.

He pressed her back into darkness, as cool and soft as silk. Looking up at him, she saw his eyes glowing with an unearthly splendor. His hands drifted over her body, touching, exploring, going lower until he found the hot, slick junction between her thighs. His fingers rubbed her clit before he slid between her creamy folds, stroking back and forth until she ached for total completion.

Swaying as if in a trance, her vision blurred. From a faraway distance, she imagined she heard a low rhythmic chanting. The flow of blood through her veins sounded strongly in her ears, a muffled throbbing seeming to entwine with the mystical words of an ancient race filling the air.

For a moment she felt as though she were rising, expanding toward the ceiling above her head, passing through it to touch far-flung moons. Her soul fluttered in an invisible breeze, a wraith of energy shimmering. Stars glimmered around her, a million candles flickering in an endless eternity where time and space ceased to exist.

Suddenly, her senses shifted and light and sound seemed to

fuse, twisting and contorting into an indescribable blending of her pulse and the hot darkness of the vampire's heart.

His for the taking.

Basking in the glow of his dazzling gaze, she felt like a goddess, the holy mother of all that was beautiful, lush, and fertile.

Iollan's mouth covered hers even as his cock pressed for entry between her spread thighs. She opened wider, angling her hips to encourage his entry. Her moans increased in demand and urgency.

He didn't disappoint, gliding deep inside with a solid thrust. His cock stretched every inch until there was no more to offer. Their bodies melded into one, fitting together perfectly. They were one, at last.

Her breath came quick and shallow. "God, that's perfect." Her fingers dug deeper into his shoulders as he plunged and plundered. They moved together, her hips rocking in response to the press of his. The feel of his body skewering hers was heaven.

Iollan's eyes glowed like an ocean under moonlight. "We're close, love." He raised her hips, pulled her slightly up, then impaled her again. "Don't fight it. Just let it come."

Callie's fingernails scratched up and down his bare back as he ground his hips almost savagely against hers. Her sex grew slicker with every thrust.

Hunger was his master now.

She didn't see the change in his face, the emergence of his fangs to know what was going to happen next. She just accepted it the way she would accept the pain he'd inflict. With joy and welcome. She wanted him, wanted the pain. That was enough.

Callie cried out as his teeth tore into her skin. Her body shuddered deliciously, even as warm blood trickled down her neck. She sucked in a breath on a soft moan of pleasure and her body bucked beneath his. She climaxed. Hard, so hard, yet barely aware it had happened.

Callie's eyes slowly opened and focused on his face. Iollan's luminous gaze locked with hers. Slowly, oh so slowly, he leaned forward and they came together. He covered her mouth with his. She tasted her blood still clinging to his lips. The taste wasn't unpleasant, but rich and feral.

A growl broke from her throat. "I want more."

16

Callie awoke to darkness, a blank void of nothingness. She knew she was awake, felt the press of a blindfold across her eyes. She opened her eyes, staring into the blankness. A hint of light filtered through the material.

Get that thing off my eyes.

Nothing. Her arms wouldn't answer her commands to move. Something held her hands immobile. Instinctively she tried to jerk into a sitting position. The resulting explosion of pain sent her straight back down. A sluggish groan rose to her ears, feeble and without objective, extended by the wheeze emanating from her mouth. She couldn't control her limbs, couldn't rise to her feet.

Callie writhed, her wrists twisting against soft restraints. She flexed her fingers. Ouch! Something poked the back of her hand, sending a painful jolt shooting up her arm. The skin on her scalp crawled.

Invisible claws clutched at her, threatening to yank her back into the chasm of unconsciousness. She resisted, fighting to remain aware. As usual her memory seemed to be one big jigsaw puzzle, one scattered all over the floor. At this point there seemed little hope of finding all the pertinent pieces.

Callie had just enough presence of mind not to panic. Doing that would probably hurt her more than it would hurt her captors. Staying calm would be the safest bet right now.

Taking a deep breath, she concentrated on dragging her mind out of the dense fog gripping her senses. Her whole body was one big jumble of aches and pains. She felt like she'd been kicked to pieces and put back inside out and upside down. Her mouth was so desert dry it might as well have been glued shut. God, she was thirsty. So thirsty she would cut off her right leg to get a drink of water.

She eased back against the pillow. The pillowcase under her head was clean. The scent of Lysol and bleach used to clean the linens assailed her nostrils. Someone was taking care of her. Good sign. That unburdened her tension a bit, lifting a great weight from her shoulders.

Stilling her breath, she concentrated on listening to her surroundings. The low buzz of a monitor and the soft hush of faraway voices clued her into her whereabouts.

Hospital.

She heard them before she saw them.

Someone watched her. Callie felt it in the back of her neck and the incessant drone in the back of her skull.

"Who's there?"

An unfamiliar female voice answered. "Just a minute." The sounds of a body shifting, footsteps closing the distance between chair and bed. Sounds of breathing as someone bent over her. "I'm going to take this off your eyes. Are you sure this is what you want?"

Licking parched lips with an equally parched tongue, Callie nodded. "I don't understand why I was blindfolded to begin with."

A soft chuckle. "You came in complaining the light hurt your eyes. We were just trying to make you feel better. You said you needed the dark . . . that sunlight would burn you up."

I did?

Callie considered. "Will it?"

"Hasn't so far." Another chuckle from the mystery woman. "Would you like me to draw the blinds first?"

Callie didn't think things were so fucking funny, but managed to bite her tongue. "No. I want to see."

The mask slid off.

Callie's eyes snapped open. She blinked, once, twice. Blurry images cleared, then sharpened. Eyes adjusting the wash of light, an unfamiliar face swam into view. White uniform and concerned expression. A nurse.

She cast a hurried glance around the room. Typical hospital room, bed, monitors, a single window covered by slatted blinds. Gray skies outside, rain pattering against the glass. Everything seemed to be in place. Except the window had bars. Meant to keep people who wanted to get outside, inside.

Callie's gaze settled on her restrained wrists. The effort delivered a wave of nausea. An IV ran from her left arm to some mysterious substance in the bottle hung above her bed. Oh shit. Waking up in a hospital was one thing. Waking up in a place with bars on the windows and bound to the bed didn't bode well.

"What the fuck is going on?" Rising fury emanated from every pore. Hysteria vibrated in her voice.

The nurse placed a reassuring hand on her shoulder. "Don't panic. Your hands had to be restrained to keep you from tearing out your IV."

Callie glared at the suspicious bottle. The back of her hand was bruised with multiple needle marks. Apparently someone had mistaken her for a pincushion. "What are you people poisoning me with?"

A second voice answered. "Nothing more than a saline solution to replace the fluids in your body. You were dangerously dehydrated when you came in."

Callie looked at the new intruder. The woman who'd walked into her room commanded instant respect. She wasn't young—late fifties, maybe early sixties. Beautiful face, a cap of brown hair, highlighted in a chic youthful way and perfectly arranged. Slender, she wore a gray suit under her white lab coat. Gold earrings and a touch of lipstick were her only adornment. Back ramrod straight, she carried a clipboard in one hand, a cell phone in the other. Her glasses were plain black frames, perched halfway down her nose. She looked like she talked no nonsense and took no shit.

Flipping her cell shut, the woman stepped up to the bed. "I'm Doctor Collins," she said as an introduction. "I've been your attending physician during your therapy sessions and recovery."

Callie ignored her. "I don't know you. Where are my people?"

"We are your people, Agent Whitten," the doctor returned smoothly. "Rest assured that Agent Reinke has been notified you're awake. He'll be here shortly."

Relief. Someone knew where she was.

Lying the clipboard on a nearby bed table, Doctor Collins began to loosen a cuff around Callie's wrist. "I think these can come off. You seem sane enough now." The nurse rounded the bed, quickly helping to remove the second cuff.

Callie gingerly lifted her abused hand, moving it to rest across her stomach. "Therapy sessions?" she gritted out in stunned confusion. "While I was—" Her words stalled. "Unconscious?" The question came out as a reedy whisper. *Oh, shit,* she cursed silently.

Doctor Collins nodded. "Yes."

Throat working painfully, Callie leveled her gaze. "How long have I been out of it?"

Honesty compelled an answer. "Two days."

Her tongue swiped over parched lips. "I don't remember anything."

Seeing Callie's discomfort, the nurse poured water from a carafe at her bedside. Unwrapping a fresh straw, she guided the straw to Callie's mouth.

Shooting her a grateful look, Callie sucked. Cool blessed water trickled over her tongue and down her throat. She swallowed in long grateful gulps, drinking until the cup was empty. The slight ache in her skull instantly diminished. She felt better, human. Hunger rumbled deep in her gut, a sure sign she'd survive.

The nurse smiled as she refilled the cup and offered more water. "Think you can handle some juice?"

Callie sipped the water, wishing it was darker, richer, and hotter. "Coffee, please. I need caffeine and sugar. A major infusion."

The nurse looked askance to the good doctor.

Doctor Collins shrugged. "I don't see why not."

"Something to eat?" the nurse asked.

Callie leaned back against her pillow and sighed. "Food would be wonderful. I'm so damn hungry I'd eat a shoe."

The nurse smiled. "Shoes, we don't serve. Though I suppose our cafeteria's food isn't much better than leather most days."

"Get her something light," Doctor Collins suggested. "Soup and crackers would be good."

The nurse hustled out just as Roger Reinke shot in at top speed. Paul Norton scurried hot on his heels. Norton hovered in the background, a silent wraith. By the look on his face, he wasn't happy.

Roger hurried to her bedside. He reached for her hand. Slack jawed, uncertain, skin as pale as a corpse, genuine concern creased his features. "Thank God. You had me worried." He looked a little grayer around the temples, a little older and a lot more tired than she remembered. His eyes were filled with the vulnerability of concern and remembrance of things passed.

Callie felt her hand in his, but remained curiously distant from the press of his skin against hers. She pursed her lips. She realized it no longer *hurt* to see him. No twinge in her heart, no pang from the time they'd shared together. He was just someone she used to see naked, someone she now didn't see naked. The old wounds in her heart seemed to have healed, didn't feel so fatal now.

A shudder wracked her. Damn it. Roger was the one who'd made the decision to end their affair. He had no right to hover like a worried lover. He didn't deserve the place at her bedside. Not for one minute. He'd forfeited the keys to her heart.

She squelched further thought. Apparently the part of her brain storing Roger Reinke mementoes was perfectly intact. Too fucking bad. She wouldn't have minded a memory wipe of that section. Time to toss the mental box into the fire. The moment had finally come when she could look at him and not fall to pieces inside.

Passion, elation. *Dead.*

Grinding mental gears into reverse, Callie gently withdrew her hand from his. No reason to let sorrow and ugliness squeeze the life out of her. Resentment was the wrong emotion to be throwing at him right now. Concern for a fellow human being's welfare should be allowable. And welcome.

She drew a calming breath. No time to dwell on the past. More immediate concerns loomed. "I'm fine. Really."

Reinke clamped his jaw, nodding solemnly. His wall of self-control reasserted itself. Nothing between them but work. "You had us all worried there." He took a step away from the bed as if to emphasize the distance.

Callie rubbed a hand over her face. "I suppose I'd be worried, too, if I remembered what happened." She swallowed heavily and forced herself to go on. "According to Doctor Collins, we've been in therapy for two days—and I have no idea it ever happened."

Doctor Collins spoke up. "A form of hypnotherapy was employed. Under sodium pentothal, we were able to take you back through the day you disappeared. We had to move fast, pull the memories out before they dissipated entirely. I tried to restore as many as possible."

Callie shot the doctor a narrow glance. "Just what exactly did these sessions entail? And why don't I remember them?"

Collins answered again. "During our sessions, we decided you wouldn't remember until you asked to. This was implemented primarily to allow you to rest and get your strength back."

Callie eyed the three warily. "I don't like the idea of you people fucking with my head."

Roger started to put a hand on her arm. He aborted the instinctive move midair. Callie's look said she wouldn't welcome his touch.

"Entirely necessary, Agent Whitten," he said, putting on his sternest face. "What we are dealing with touches on a matter of the most confidential nature. Your involvement in the investigation changes your status as an agent."

Callie shivered as if a chill wind had swept through the room. By the look on Roger's face and the sound of his voice, this didn't bode well at all. What the hell had she stumbled into?

She shot a look at Norton. A frown wrinkled his forehead. Saying nothing, he studied her like she'd somehow grown a third eye in the center of her forehead.

"You're going to have to explain that one, Roger," she said, bristling. "I'm not following everything here, and I have a feeling there's a reason why. It's not a good feeling either. I don't like having my mind messed with by Doctor Frankenstein there."

Roger nodded. "I understand. But this comes from higher

up than me. I need to make it clear that if you choose to re-member, you'll be automatically transferring into a top-secret area most people in our own fucking government don't know exists. This is hush-hush, touching on national security mat-ters."

There was a pause while she considered that.

Trying not to let her ambivalence ruin the business at hand, she turned matters over in her mind. Burning with curiosity, she wondered if knowing would be the wisest move. A nagging feeling came over her. Sometimes not knowing was the safest course to take.

Walking the safe path had never been her forte.

"Tell me."

Doctor Collins glanced to Roger Reinke, who in turn got the nod from Paul Norton. "You still going in, Norton?"

"I'm going in, too," Norton said.

Norton's words caught her by surprise. "You're in this, too, Paulie?"

Shifting nervously, Norton nodded. "Yeah, Callie. I'm in. We're partners, you know? We've been working this thing to-gether." He did not look excited. He did not look thrilled. He looked terrified.

That look should have warned her to say no. Whatever was lost in her head could stay lost.

Not good enough and not an option.

Deluged by unexpected emotions, Callie lay there, feeling like a deer caught in the headlights of an oncoming truck. Sud-denly everything was all mixed up. She didn't know what to think anymore.

Or whom to trust.

She considered a moment. There was an old saying that good judgment came from experience. And experience came from bad judgment. She'd never been known for having good judg-ment. She did, however, have a hell of a lot of experience.

"Tell me."

Roger turned to Doctor Collins. "Do it."

Collins considered for a second. She took off her heavy framed glasses. Serious dark eyes drew Callie in with their intense power. "This is going to be tough to accept."

Fighting to keep patience and sanity, Callie searched her abused mind. No easy answers appeared. Her brain just wouldn't function fast enough to answer the questions.

Callie's jaw tightened. "It's pretty tough waking up blindfolded and tied to a bed with a needle in your fucking arm. I see bars on my windows and I don't know where the hell I am or where I've been." A harsh laugh escaped her. "I feel like shit. And on top of that I have you three nattering nitwits telling me I can't handle what's in my own fucking head. So please, stuff your concern up your tight asses and give me back my memories."

Collins's eyebrows rose above her frames, but she gave no rebuttal. "Perfectly understandable, Agent Whitten." She cleared her throat. "If you would follow my instructions, we can do exactly as you've asked."

"Thanks," she said and met the doctor's gaze. "Let's do this."

A pause. "Close your eyes and relax, please."

Callie settled back against her pillow. "Okay."

"Now, take three deep breaths," Collins instructed, her tone soothing and firm. "As you take these breaths you will feel very calm and relaxed."

Callie closed her eyes, acutely aware of each slow breath expanding her lungs.

"Imagine yourself standing on the top of a staircase and as you go down from the top step you are getting more and more relaxed," Collins said. "Count backwards from ten, very slowly. As you reach the last step you will be deeply relaxed, so relaxed that you cannot move the muscles of your body even if you want to."

Callie counted, mentally picturing and descending the imaginary staircase.

"At the bottom of the stairs is a door," Doctor Collins said. "When you open it, you will know what you have forgotten." A pause. "Is your hand on the doorknob?"

Her hand rose, reaching for the imaginary door. "Yes."

"Do you want to hear your word, Callie?"

Her throat tightened. "Yes."

One word.

"Drake."

Slowly, a slew of images began to take shape in her mind. A tremor went through her whole body. She shut her eyes. Painful longing stabbed through her as memories of Iollan Drake solidified and fell into place.

She squeezed her eyelids tighter. "Oh. God."

"Do you remember now?" Doctor Collins asked.

Callie whimpered. What she remembered couldn't possibly be believed. God, his touch. Those strong steady hands exploring her naked flesh, the fullness of her breasts, the soft valley between her thighs. The press of his solid male body against the yielding softness of hers. Then the bites, the exquisite feel of sharp teeth penetrating her neck.

No.

She drew a shuddering breath, wanting—no, needing—to deny everything she remembered in a rush of sights, sounds, and sensations.

Impossible.

Memories poured in like water through a sieve, filtering into her harried brain from all sides, giving no peace and offering no respite. More than filled, more than tasted, she'd been possessed body and soul by a man whose unique hunger would forever haunt her memory. She'd been so thoroughly conquered she didn't think she'd fully recover.

The flood of emotions turned her limbs liquid. Her psyche took a blow. "He's not human."

The words tore from her lips, half disbelief, half anger. Bitter acid rose in the back of her throat as conflicting feelings raged through her. Every emotion she'd ever experienced over a lifetime now came to center and focus around a man she'd found darkly alluring, and perilously deadly.

Doctor Collins laid a gentle hand on her shoulder. "I tried to ease you into the idea during our sessions. It's difficult to take, I know."

An understatement.

17

Heart beating a mile a minute, Callie walked between Roger Reinke and Paul Norton. Her head turned every which way as they progressed down a wide corridor. On the outside, the facilities looked like an ordinary seven-story office building.

Inside was a far different story.

The building sat on a four-mile circle of government property, perfectly landscaped, pristine, as still as a fly trapped in amber. Property restricted to civilian personnel. Property fenced and patrolled by armed security guards.

Callie fingered the badge clipped at her waist. Her security clearances were written into the small piece of plastic that now granted her access into the government's most secret of inner sanctums. They'd only made it inside after enduring innumerable security checks. All movement through the complex was accomplished through badges and codes. When she'd slid her newly minted ID badge into the scanner, she'd held her breath, expecting the red light to remain red. To her relief, it switched to green and she was allowed to punch in her code and proceed along with Norton and Reinke.

Where they had proceeded to boggled the mind.

A new guide led the way through the maze. A tall cadaverous man who rather reminded Callie of the actor who'd played Lurch in the *Addams Family* television show in the sixties. He lumbered, a giant of commanding presence and booming voice. The blind and dead couldn't fail to see him coming. Those who did steered a quick path out of his for fear of being run over. He, too, wore the all-telling white lab coat.

In Callie's mind, white coats didn't exactly bode well. She was noticing a lot of white coats. Those troubling coats below unsmiling and serious faces meant business. Bad business. Under the seeming serenity, a more sinister note vibrated. Maleficent and corrupt forces were in power. The strings of fear they pulled taut sought to restrain free thought and independent action. Those who had control wouldn't easily relinquish it.

The good professor's name was Terrence Forque, pronounced like the eating utensil. The grand tour of a captive audience was his forte and he took ample advantage to remind them several times that only the best of the best walked these hallowed hallways.

Officially, the building was known under the code of A-51 ASD. What it meant, few knew.

Now Callie knew.

Area 51, Alien Sciences Division. Location, just outside Belmonde, Virginia. The U.S. government didn't explicitly acknowledge the existence of the A-51 ASD facility, nor did it deny it. The area surrounding the facility was permanently off-limits both to civilians and normal air traffic, and protected by radar stations. Uninvited guests were met by armed guards. Deadly force was authorized if violators attempting to breach the secured area failed to heed warnings of security to halt.

"The project dates back to nineteen forty-seven, with the advent of the crash in Roswell, New Mexico," Forque explained. "At that time we encountered conclusive proof of aliens and their existence among us. This in turn prompted then-president Truman and J. Edgar Hoover to implement a program geared toward the study of alien species and technologies as they were discovered. Needless to say, we have uncovered evidence of many types of aliens among us. Most, I am glad to say, are benign."

An unpleasant weight settled in the center of Callie's chest. She'd learned from her career in the bureau there were times when an agent wasn't told every detail about an assignment. The know-how and determination were usually all the government felt it necessary to arm agents with. Sometimes having the knowledge was more of a burden than knowing nothing.

Callie almost wished to go back to blissful ignorance. Any feelings she'd foolishly allowed to develop for Iollan Drake needed to be squashed, something easier said than done. She needed her work. And the focus of climbing the ladder in the area of national security was certainly a goal to reach for. She had to keep that goal in sight and stop permitting memories of a hot man and hotter sex from overriding her good sense.

"Is Drake one of these Roswell aliens?" she asked.

Forque shook his head. "Not of the species found that day. They call themselves the *Niviane Idesha*, which we have determined to mean *shifting spirit*. From the history we've gathered, these are interdimensional travelers. Their universe of origin is not known, nor do we know exactly how long they've been among humankind. Our estimates date back to the time of Christ, give or take a BC or an AD, though we've only been aware of them through the last few decades. They've integrated well into human society—almost to the point of invisibility."

"Makes sense," Paul Norton piped up.

Lumbering along at top speed, Forque nodded amiably. "They're notoriously slippery and require very delicate handling once in captivity. We've lost several nice specimens. They don't seem capable of surviving long in an artificial environment. Overall I find them to be an entirely unique and fascinating species, very intelligent and crafty."

"And dangerous," Roger Reinke said, frowning. "Not only can they change their physical form, they can shift energy, as well as erase memory. One talent would be bad enough. Given all three, plus a hunger for blood, and this is nothing we need running around unmonitored."

Callie glanced at Reinke. "You knew all along what he was and you let me fuck him. Thanks, Roger. I appreciate your putting my ass in the sling and my neck on the line."

Reinke gave a good-natured grin. "If we didn't think you could handle it, you wouldn't have gotten into the game to begin with." He shrugged. "Besides, you'd already fucked him. Or did you think we didn't know that when Faber gave you a free pass?"

Scowling, she pushed out a breath. "Christ. You knew?"

The corner of Reinke's mouth lifted at the irony. "We're the FBI, honey. We know who, what, where, when, why, and how."

It occurred to Callie that the country was truly becoming a surveillance society, where CCTV cameras and listening devices were used to track people minute by minute. "Nice to know the government screws its own." The words leapt out before she checked them.

Politeness flew out the window. "The government reams everyone. You knew the risks when you came onto the job. From what I heard, it seemed to me you enjoyed yourself quite nicely." A single eyebrow rose in mischief. "As for that bastard comment . . ."

She stared at him, scandalized. "Stuff it, Roger," she growled. "You might have warned me he'd be drinking my blood. I didn't sign up to be a donor."

"Seems to me that you didn't discourage him," Reinke said. "Anyway, you earned your badge to the ASD."

That career triumph seemed bitter and empty now. Instead

of feeling proud of herself, regret and remorse filled her. And she didn't even know why. She just felt hollow inside. When she wasn't feeling bloated and queasy.

Stress.

Professor Forque ignored them all, bestowing a patient smile on what he considered a slower and lesser species than himself. "This is your new headquarters now," he reminded with a slight hint of impatience. "One of the United States' most sensitive areas of research."

Norton just looked miserable. If his chin dropped any lower to the floor, he'd trip over it. Clearly he wasn't happy with his new adventure in the land of science fiction turned science fact.

Leading them into an elevator, Forque pushed the DOWN button. Callie caught her breath when the car plunged straight down, passing several floors by the look of the digital readout on the wall. "We actually go a quarter of a mile underground."

Callie pressed a hand against her queasy stomach. The urge to vomit had never been stronger. "I feel every inch of it, too."

She clamped her teeth together, wondering if her breakfast of eggs, sausage, and hotcakes was going to come back on her. At the time, she'd been starved, shoving food into her mouth like a refugee who hadn't seen a decent meal in months. No amount of food seemed hearty enough to fill the hole in her middle.

Two uniformed guards manned the desk. They flipped open a log, once again checked IDs, and entered the names into record.

Callie scanned the floor. Her stomach did another backflip. This place had a curiously familiar feel.

Forque outpaced them. He navigated them down the hall, pointing and saying. "I've prepared a short visual lecture on the Niviane Idesha—their biology and how we are faring in the area of weaponry to combat their spread among the general population. I believe you will find this very interesting."

"No doubt," Callie muttered under her breath. At this moment all she was feeling was surreal, as if she'd stepped into a funhouse that had no way out. Less than a month ago, she was manning a desk in the Siberia of cold cases, unhappy in her exile from the coveted inner circle of fieldwork. Now she was smack in the middle of a nice fat government conspiracy.

Never believe anything until it has been officially denied. For the good of the public, the government would marginalize, intimidate, and silence the truth.

In this case, maybe that wasn't such a bad idea.

Time would tell.

Professor Forque briskly led them into a morgue.

This one was no different than so many others she'd seen before. Even the body stretched out on the gurney looked familiar. Too familiar.

Fuck.

Callie wasn't in any mood or frame of mind to be viewing yet another corpse.

A tiny Asian woman with beautiful almond-shaped eyes and a sleek fall of blue-black hair greeted them. Wearing a pair of green scrubs, she was in the process of sliding on a pair of rubber gloves.

"Agents, meet Doctor Akemi Yuan, head of our pathology department," Forque said. "She's been leading and developing our knowledge of the Niviane Idesha."

Doctor Yuan didn't offer a hand, holding up her gloved ones. "Just getting this one ready for you," she said by way of an apology.

"Please proceed," Forque urged, eager to show off the specimen.

Akemi Yuan countered with an easy grin. "It's not like he's going anywhere, Terrence." She nodded to her assistant, who tugged the white sheet off.

The body was a naked male, early twenties. Lank hair, staring eyes, jaw locked in a painful scream. Hands and arms were contorted, back slightly arched.

Norton winced. "Jesus, he didn't die easily, did he?"

Doctor Yuan shook her head. "Unfortunately most of them don't survive the extraction."

Eyebrows shot up.

"Extraction?" Callie asked, swallowing to keep the rise of vomit at bay.

Yuan nodded toward a nearby glass jar. "Agents, meet one of the Niviane Idesha."

All eyes turned. A sickening sight greeted them. A snake-shaped squiggly mass having the transparency of a jellyfish floated in formaldehyde. Wide eyes, big jaws, a set of fangs to die for. Bristly ridges along its spine gave it the appearance of a porcupine mated with a reptile.

Everyone moved in for a closer look. It looked nothing like anyone would ever imagine an alien would: dwarflike, erect, vaguely human-shaped, gray-skinned aliens with large craniums, large egg-shaped eyes, small mouths and noses, and long, nimble fingers. No. This thing was entirely different.

Norton wrinkled his nose and said, "It's all fucking fangs."

The spectacle of the creature in the jar made Callie's skin crawl. A wave of dizziness left her swaying. She moved away from it. Oddly enough she wasn't disgusted by the idea of what the opaque lifeless thing represented. She was repulsed that scientists wanted to cut it out and put it on display.

"Holy shit." Norton looked horrified. "Is this for real?"

"Very real," Yuan said crisply, eyes taking on an emerald gleam, that of the scientist in her element. "The symbionts are alien life-forms inhabiting the base of the neck of the human host. When a host and a symbiont are joined, the resulting individual is an entirely new being. When the symbiont dies, the host also dies. This is our first successful extraction of a symbiont. Unfortunately, their cellular structure begins to deteriorate almost immediately upon death. To date we've not extracted one usable strand of DNA."

The feeling that something wasn't right was strangely, weirdly strong. "How does the symbiont merge with its human host?"

Doctor Yuan shook her head. "We don't quite understand the complete process yet. What we do know is that the guest is fully capable of rewriting the cellular DNA of the host, altering the human biochemistry into an entirely new structure. Once the merging is complete, symbiont and host are essentially a single being. A being, I might add, with some dangerous abilities."

That word again. Dangerous.

The uneasiness in the pit of her gut was impossible to ignore. "How come we consider these things antagonistic toward humans when they are still an entity unknown to most of the public?"

That got everyone's attention. Roger Reinke's lips pressed into a thin line. Norton's gaze remained riveted on the jar and its gross content. Forque crossed his arms and looked pissed. Yuan looked insulted.

"We're food to them," Yuan said, speaking as if she were addressing a small and rather dim child. "Their diet consists of a single element: blood."

Electricity rippled through the room.

An uncomfortable silence followed, the agents holding their collective breath at the sideshow freak in the jar.

Bile rushed up again, burning the back of Callie's throat. The room around her felt unbearably hot even though the temperature hovered around a cool sixty. She swallowed it down. The thought that something like this lived inside Iollan Drake made her throat, and heart, ache. And her body. The steely planes and solid muscle sending her into the throes of rapture didn't belong to a human being. Thinking of the way he'd touched her, claimed her, made her throb all over.

Knowing what she knew now, would she sleep with him again?

In a heartbeat.

The feeling of doubt kept nagging.

Callie glanced at the tiny Asian woman. "Having been in the position of donating a few pints, I have to admit I don't remember the experience as unpleasant or threatening."

Yuan swooped in with her hammer, determined to nail down the facts. "Most likely because they have the ability to alter memory. Think about it, agent. Would you like the idea of one of these things invading our political leaders? These things spread as easily as a virus, invisible and almost undetectable."

"Everything has an agenda, and we feel this species is no different," Forque added in the authoritative manner of the expert. His expression turned grave as he went on. "For them it's at a primal level: survival. And at what cost to human lives? We suspect the clans we've detected are only the tip of the iceberg. These things are spreading worldwide even as we speak."

As if looking at the victim of an accident, Norton couldn't seem to tear his gaze away. "This is getting spooky," he mumbled, visibly shaken. "I mean, if these fuckers look like us and act like us, how the hell do we tell them from us?"

Doctor Yuan beamed at the brighter pupil. "We've identified a couple of telling traits of symbiotic possession inside the human body. One is a prominent ridge of scarring at the base of the neck—the entry of the symbiote into the body."

"So we just go around asking to see people's necks?" Norton asked sarcastically. "That ought to simplify things."

Callie suppressed a snicker. Norton had a habit of shifting into asshole mode when displeased with the answers he received. In Norton's mind, things had to make sense. Things like this most definitely didn't make sense to a Jew from Brooklyn.

Doctor Yuan lost her spark. "Another thing we've identified in hosts is an unusual amount of scarring on the neck and shoulder area. These things have a distinctive bite and leave an equally distinctive scar. Agent Whitten, I am sure, can show you hers if you have any doubts."

Callie blushed, feeling every bit the sore thumb. She'd offered her neck more than once. Willingly.

"A host—or *bloodmate*—is usually chosen from the pool of former victims," Doctor Yuan continued.

"Like anyone would volunteer to be fucked over by that thing."

Callie frowned daggers.

Norton caught her displeasure and shrugged, giving a weak smile. "Sorry. Present company excluded."

Callie decided to gather her own information. Norton could taste his own shoe leather later. "I've seen three of these things up close. In all three instances I noticed the eyes to be a brilliant coppery shade with an almost oval, nearly animalistic, iris."

"That's the most telling trait we've identified so far," Doctor Yuan confirmed. "Another is their extreme sensitivity to sunlight. They can't take it, at any level."

Professor Forque broke in, speaking with a certain grim amusement. "Put them in the sun and they fry like eggs."

Callie grimaced. Empty hands opened and closed. She had no doubt that Forque hadn't tested the theory on more than one specimen. Gruesome thought. "Sounds horrible."

Forque shrugged as if she'd commented on nothing more than the day's weather. "Another way we can identify their clusters is through electromagnetic spectrum. In their shifting of energy, the Niviane Idesha produce nonfatal levels of electromagnetic radiation due to accelerated electrons."

Callie went still as a thought occurred to her. "So shouldn't these things be of more interest to the military?"

Doctor Yuan reassumed control. "If it flies, they get it. If it's ground bound, we get it," she explained dryly. "Our main area of interest lies in their longevity and ability to shift. If we can rework their DNA to suppress the blood hunger, imagine what a boon that would be to humankind."

Sounded more like a curse to Callie. More along the lines of the splitting of the atom than the fountain of youth. Abilities like that in the hands of humankind didn't bode well. People were stupid, destructive, and irresponsible. Scientists with a God complex in particular.

Norton's frown returned. Damned if he wasn't going to start up again. Callie didn't blame him.

Roger Reinke's gray eyes narrowed. A scowl hardened his features into something sadistic. "We've developed weapons that take care of these things just fine." He pressed his agents with a look conveying a great deal more than mere words. "We're going to do whatever it takes to stop these things. We have to stop their invasion into the population if at all possible. If we have to use deadly force, then so be it."

Oh, no.

Hearing his words, Callie felt the sick clenching nausea seeping into her guts turned into sharp shards of ice. The hair on her arms stood up. She turned away from the thing in the jar. Straight into the body on the gurney. A face filled with fear met her gaze. The fear looked familiar. Too familiar.

She froze. A frisson of something cold and acidic spread through her. Her gaze immediately whipped toward the corpse's neck. Recognizing the dotted line of shallow punctures circling his neck, her heart leapt inside her rib cage. The only difference between this body and that of the woman she'd viewed less than a week ago were the eyes. Where the female's had been a natural color, the pupils of the male's eyes looked as stony and white as pure marble.

The girl had been seen with Drake. Agents were tracking both. Two and two came together as to why the mutilated body would be dumped back on the streets.

The girl was human. Wholly human.

Petrified by her discovery, breath deserted her.

This isn't right. It can't be.

Needing to confirm her suspicion, Callie looked at the wrist of the corpse. Sure enough, there it was. That small dotted line of punctures. Ditto, the opposite wrist. Identical in every way. Except the eyes. That gave them away. The eye color. The girl's were brown.

Her pulse shot into hyperspace. The whole scene was strangely surreal. This corpse bore identical damages to other corpses she'd viewed, the most recent purported to be a victim of Drake's.

A lie.

She knew that as surely as she knew her own name.

A jolt arrived as the realization penetrated her skull, from inside her own body. This time the chill going down Callie's spine penetrated clear to the core. The blood drained from her head so quickly she was positive she'd faint.

Her guts curled into knots. There was a strange buzzing in her ears. Callie prayed for strength. And she prayed even harder she was mistaken about the suspicious conclusions suddenly gripping her like pit bulls that wouldn't let go.

Praying didn't change the facts and she knew it.

Callie had to step away, close her eyes, and try to erase the visions lingering in her mind. Having the truth dumped in her lap without warning was disturbing. She didn't want to look at the mangled corpse anymore. Especially when the victims in question had been hunted—and slaughtered—by her own government.

Definitely trouble with a capital *T.*

18

Callie sat in the back of a crowded van, crammed between Paul Norton to her left and Roger Reinke to her right. Dressed in tactical combat gear and the vest, she hardly believed the day's events had progressed to this point.

Hunting vampires.

Capturing, she mentally corrected herself.

Their orders were clear: Do not kill the subjects. That honor was reserved for people like Doctor Yuan and Professor Forque. Such decisions were made above her head. She had her orders. Personal feelings had no place beyond her duty.

They hit a bump. Shoulders jostled.

Paul Norton elbowed her. Hair neatly cut and beard shaved off, he no longer looked like the junkie he'd portrayed for months. "Fucking unreal, huh?"

Holding her gun in her lap, Callie glanced down. The legendary items of vampire hunting were different in the real world of the twenty-first century. Instead of stakes, crosses, and holy water, the agents were outfitted with guns, infrared goggles, and Geiger counters.

"Yeah, really wild." Tension arced through her. Grip pressed against her palm, this new weapon felt strange in her hand. Better get used to it. She'd be using it a lot, if what Professor Forque said was anywhere near truth. From now on, she'd be part of the first response team. Where these things were found, she'd be sent. The pace in her career had just stepped up.

Callie drew a breath. *I can do this.* Maybe it was better she'd made the choice she had. The weaker emotions, the ones she'd struggled to keep in check, likely needed to be put in their place. Personal feelings would no longer be allowed to get in the way of doing her job. It wasn't as if she didn't understand or comprehend the threat such a species as the Niviane Idesha posed to humankind.

All she had to do was her job—like it or not.

She considered her weapon with detachment. Undesirable but necessary. "Who'd have thought we'd be shooting the fuckers with silver."

About the size of a standard .38, the gun fired small dartlike ampoules primed with pure liquid silver. As explained by Doctor Yuan, colloidal silver inhibited the symbiont's ability to draw oxygen when introduced into the system of the host. That in turn rendered its supernatural abilities useless.

The van screeched to a stop. Double doors opened, spilling a bunch of caffeine-wired, bleary-eyed federal agents out into the street.

Callie hurried out of the van. Her forehead was cold and clammy despite the warmth of the day. Sliding on a pair of sunglasses, she surveyed the area. As a lead agent, she'd be one of the first to go in. At this point she had the most experience in dealing with the things.

She glanced at Roger. His mouth was a thin tight line, his gaze flinty and merciless. He'd scarcely said ten words to her.

The efficiency of the bureau never failed to amaze her. It was awesome to see agents fan out and take their places, moving like clockwork and never missing a beat. Dark vans blocked off the street on both sides; police cars rerouted traffic away from the area. A literal wall of moving metal formed a ring around the target area. Nothing would be getting in. Nothing on two legs would be getting out, either.

When the FBI took control of an area, they took control of every last inch. Held at bay by extra police officers called in to assist in crowd control, the locals gawked like kids at a circus seeing pink elephants for the first time. Everyone wanted to see and know what the hell was going on.

Tight-faced feds were equally tightfisted with information. The word out on the street was that it was a drug raid. Given the area and accessibility of the building in question, that sounded plausible and logical. Dealers made a quick backtrack, hustling off to check their own supplies.

Callie glanced up and down the street, so familiar in a creepy sort of way. She'd pointed the way to this location, giving investigators their first solid leads into how the creatures managed to hide so efficiently and be virtually unseen. During daylight hours the Niviane Idesha needed to be out of the sun's light, a thing fatal to their species. Abandoned and condemned buildings were more than perfect. They were everywhere.

The sun tilted lower, reminding everyone the time to get moving had arrived.

Callie checked her watch. Another hour before night descended. The raid had to be timed with perfect synchronicity, when the creatures would just be beginning to rouse from their state of *daysleep*, unfed and at their weakest.

Roger Reinke stepped up beside her. A cadre of special agents equipped and trained in handling the aliens joined them. Aside from Reinke and Norton, Callie knew none of them. They obviously knew Roger. All eyes turned toward him.

"I don't have to remind you guys not to use excessive force unless necessary," Reinke said, his tone allowing no discussion.

"These things move fast, but they're sluggish this time of day, weak. Hit them with one, maybe two shots. Any more than that and we'll be dragging bodies out of there."

The men all nodded in agreement.

"We'll take 'em down easy," one agent smirked.

"They'll never know what hit them," another said.

"Good. Let's do this right, then." Roger Reinke glanced over at Callie. "You sure you can handle this?"

Drawing in a deep breath, Callie nodded once. If they knew how bad she shook inside, they'd send her packing. She felt hopelessly out of her depth. More than afraid, she was fucking terrified. "I've been in there, seen what these things can do," she heard herself say flatly. She flicked the safety off her weapon. "Time for a little payback."

The agents went inside, spreading out through the first-floor lobby. A couple carried Geiger counters, checking the readings.

"Well?" Reinke asked. "Any activity?"

"Through the fucking roof," the agent answered. "There's definitely been a concentration of heavy activity here."

Roger considered the plan of action. "Spread out through the floors. Be careful of structural damage. If it looks like it isn't safe, don't go in. Force as many as you can into shifting. We want Drake, but we'll take as many as we can round up."

"Yes, sir." Infrared goggles went on.

Reinke turned to Callie. "You want to lead the way to where Drake took you?"

Heart rate bumping up a beat, she nodded. "Third floor."

"You know what to look for?" Reinke asked as they ascended the stairs.

Puffing slightly, Callie frowned. "I've seen them in action," she reminded him. "They move like shadows."

He tapped the infrared goggles perched on the top of his head. "You can see more of them through these." He laughed a little. "Actually look like a big Frisbee."

Midstep, she paused, cocking an eyebrow at him. "You've done this before, I take it."

He shrugged. "A few times. When you see one, fire. The silver will force an almost immediate shift."

She nodded. "This I have to see."

Reinke flicked a glance at her. "I hope you do."

"So, tell me. How did you even get in on this?"

Reinke scowled. "I wondered when you'd ask that," he mumbled.

"Don't lie," she insisted point-blank.

Roger's mouth quirked up. "About six months."

She threw him a suspicious look. "The bureau broke us up, didn't it?"

His mouth twisted bitterly. "Yes."

Callie swallowed, sorted through myriad questions and came up with the answers on her own. Surprisingly the conclusions arrived with little anxiety. At least their abrupt parting made sense. "I see."

Roger glanced away. "I had to make a choice and I chose my career. I didn't want to, but I had to if I wanted to take the step up."

She nodded. Who the hell wouldn't? The bureau had to make sure that an agent working a top-level security position was solid and stable in all areas of his life. An affair, even with a fellow agent, wouldn't be sanctioned. "Given the same ultimatum, I'd have probably done the same thing."

He snorted in that old familiar way that she'd once found so endearing. "So I'm not an entire bastard?"

The muscles in her cheeks involuntarily bunched. A smile sneaked out. "Half a bastard then," she conceded. "Somehow I have a feeling I'm here because some strings were pulled."

Roger looked at her, his handsome face grave. "I wanted my best agents. Not many women could've walked into this the way you did and made it a success. I knew you would."

Standing a few steps above him, Callie looked down. Her heart no longer slammed against the wall of her chest when she recalled their affair. Over. Not even in a painful way now, but definitely a conclusive one.

"Thanks, Agent Reinke." All she needed to say.

"You're welcome." A pause as his mouth quirked up slightly. "Agent Whitten."

With an unspoken agreement, they started walking again. They reached the third level. Where Callie remembered a door, a gaping space where a door had once stood ruled. Only the crappy faded carpet looked the same.

"He might not be here anymore."

Reinke lowered his goggles. "We'll see. There were three apartments on this floor. Lots of crevasses, places to hide. These things don't need much space. I'll check out the place over there. It'll be dark soon. Better get a move on."

"Okay." Callie headed toward the one she knew.

Pushing the door open, she stepped gingerly over the threshold. She looked around, wincing a little at the devastation. Such a beautiful place. Now nothing more than a vague memory to be manipulated by an alien species.

Callie slipped on her goggles. Everything looked different, disorienting her until she got used to the change in her eyesight. Once her vision adjusted she saw everything fairly well. As she picked her way through the debris, her boots creaked with every step she took. She felt a chill creep into her bones and a long shiver ripped through her. The atmosphere around her was spooky, eerie even.

A swell of claustrophobia cut through her, a smothering shroud of foreboding, guilt, and regret. She felt a tightening in her chest, a strange emptiness in her mind. Suddenly she wanted to get out, get away from the place where her induction into things not of this world had taken place.

Callie quickened her pace. Her strides carried her swiftly

through the first room and into the second. In a swift, half-conscious thought it occurred to her that he'd probably abandoned it. In fact, she hoped he had. Why would he risk staying?

For her? Of course not. Sleeping with a man three times didn't mean she was in love with him, no matter how much she'd enjoyed the experience. As for the *L* word. Better to stay emotionally unattached. Less risk to the heart.

Not ready to take another blow yet.

"If he had any sense," she muttered, "he got the hell out of here." Callie laughed, but there was only self-condemnation inside the sound. The late-afternoon sun filtered through the remnants of bay windows, flooding a good portion of the multi-room apartment in sunlight.

A shot of movement in one dark corner near the sunken area where the Jacuzzi had been stopped her.

What the fuck?

She peered through her goggles, disbelieving her eyes.

A shape, blazing hot, darted across the floor. Zipping down one wall, it abruptly stopped, hovering.

"Shit!" Lifting her weapon, Callie rushed up, almost stumbling in the process. "I actually can see the fucker."

The silhouette went into motion.

Adrenaline seared her veins. Sweat trickled down her temples. She ignored it. As long as it didn't fog up her goggles she'd be fine. Her forefinger instinctively curled around the trigger, feeling but not pressing. For a few seconds her hands trembled.

Movement. A quick flash.

Callie's whole being focused on the shape revealed by her goggles. A sense of familiarity filled her and she knew, *just knew*, the thing's identity. Drawing a breath to steady her nerves, she tracked it. She had the target clearly in her sights.

Any minute now.

The thing zigged to her right.

The barrel of Callie's gun expertly followed. Her attention

stayed fixed on the shape, but she didn't fire. Not yet. A twinge in her neck warned of trouble with her aim. She relaxed her muscles. Tense muscles made for jerky reactions. Her mouth was dust dry. Her heart pounded against her rib cage as if she'd just done a hundred yard dash.

Focus. Concentrate.

Callie swore and adjusted her stance. Adrenaline kicked in, giving her an extra and much-needed jolt of energy. No telling head from tail, ass from elbow. She'd just have to fire and hope she hit something.

Getting it in her sights, a smile curled up one corner of her mouth. "You didn't run far enough, motherfucker." She pulled the trigger. Instead of a loud bang, a soft puff filled the air as the dart released.

The dart struck its target.

Something hissed, scrambling back as if in pain. The shift from small shadow to a man-sized shape took place almost instantaneously.

Callie stood there, stunned. Mouth dropping open, she ripped off her goggles.

Iollan Drake's tall frame loomed in front of her. Fangs bared in pain and anger, he looked like nothing belonging to planet Earth. His eyes glowed like phosphorescent coals, and a furious snarl poured over his lips.

Stunned disbelief coursed through her body all over again. Callie felt sick, dizzy. The silver had forced a shift, just as promised. Aside from that it didn't seem to be slowing him down. He stood within half a dozen feet of her, his tall frame overwhelming her vision. The power he emitted swathed her.

The creature that had emerged from inside Iollan looked scary. And ready to fight. The low, feral growl of the angry beast emanated from his throat.

Sudden insight is like a flash of lightning. It comes and goes without warning. Six foot four of towering angry vampire didn't match five foot ten of a trembling-in-her-boots woman. A woman about to get her ass kicked. An understatement.

She was shaking so hard that she nearly lost her grip on her weapon, and confusion swirled through her mind. Suddenly she wasn't prepared for this moment. Icy fingers wrapped around her heart with incredible force. Her head reeled from the unexpected sight. Seeing him in his true form, she felt her spine vibrate with acute sensitivity. He'd filled his hands with her flesh, filled his mouth with her blood.

Oh, shit. Talk about waking the sleeping beast.

The dart had struck Iollan in the shoulder. Brushing it away like lint, he snarled softly. "It'll take more than a little of your poison to put me down."

Callie quelled the instinct to run. Run, and he would overtake her. Run, and he'd kill her. Every fiber in her body tightened like a wound spring. Nervous energy crackled in the air around her.

Fear tightening her chest, she hefted her gun back into firing position. "Don't move. I don't want to hurt you any more than necessary," she said through the dry roar in her ears. She had no doubt he would rip her to pieces if given the chance.

Iollan Drake's glowing gaze moved from the weapon in her hand to her face. Bittersweet recognition warred with the pain of betrayal. "I gave you your chance to walk away, Calista." Low and rough, his words were guttural, menacing. "I see you repay my gift with betrayal."

"You knew what I was when you made the decision to let me live," Callie countered. Her voice was shaky but determined.

Jaw clenching, Drake's eyes narrowed. His hands tensed into fists at his sides. "Wrong decision."

"Tough shit," Callie snarled. "You've been fucking with humans a long time. About time you got fucked back." Finger poised above the trigger, she didn't fire a second time. Shooting the man she'd made passionate love to—fanged or not—definitely wasn't on her list of top ten things to do in her life.

Iollan's gaze cut to the gathering darkness outside. He seemed nervous, a wildcat fighting the cage; he quivered, as if anticipating escape. "The only one who's going to get fucked is you." Without warning, he swooped forward. Suddenly he seemed to be everywhere. And then he struck with a clothesline blow, knocking her flat.

She landed on her back, the blow forcing the breath out of Callie's lungs. A pile of arms and legs, she fought with every ounce of her strength to escape. Her sharp fingernails scored several deep scratches across his left cheek. Bigger and stronger, he quickly gained the upper hand. Ducking her flying hands, he wrestled her down. His body straddled hers. Fingers like iron bands pinned her wrists down.

Her adrenaline-driven frenzied human strength didn't come close to matching his. "Goddamn you, let me go!"

Iollan's strong jaw locked, stubborn and determined. "Be still and be quiet," he hissed, panting from the effort of keeping her pinned.

Glaring up at him, Callie kicked and writhed. Her hands were locked in place. *Damn, he's strong.*

His control over her body made her quiver, breath coming quick and shallow. Pressed beneath his weight, she easily recalled the times they'd made love. The warmth of his body pressing against hers felt so familiar. So right.

Not the thing to be thinking about now!

She stilled, glaring up at him. Pushing her chin out, she bit out defiantly. "You bastard! I should have pumped you full of that shit."

Iollan held on to her like Super Glue. "I should have ripped out your throat when I had the chance. Maybe now is that time." He bared his fanged mouth and dipped his head toward her vulnerable exposed throat. The pinch of sharp points pushed into her skin.

Callie immediately stilled. Squeezing her eyes shut, she refused to scream, refused to beg. She wouldn't plead, Goddamn it. The hot demand of tears pressed at the back of her eyes. She blinked them away, ignoring the tug of emotion at her heart. *Don't be stupid.* She'd made her choice. Now she had to live with the consequences.

The sharp pressure at her neck vanished. Surprised, she opened her eyes. Iollan hovered above her. The anger in his eyes had morphed into something else.

He drew a deep breath and let it out slowly. The cold in his face dissipated, and his expression softened. Beads of perspiration dotted his brow and upper lip. "I don't want to kill you, Calista." He turned his head, just a little. When he looked back at her, his fangs had vanished, retracted.

Head still spinning, Callie wasn't sure she'd heard him correctly. "What did you say?"

Lowering himself, he briefly touched his lips to hers. "I don't want to hurt you." His words were spoken as a whisper against her lips.

An immediate shudder went through her. "Y-you don't?" she stammered back stupidly.

Shaking his head, Iollan drew his hands away. The delicious curve of his lips made her feel as though the room was doing a half spin. "No, I don't."

Her gaze strayed to his face. His eyes twisted her insides. No hate. No anger. Only regret. "Why?"

Iollan traced one finger across her full lips. "I told you. I made a mistake," he whispered through a ragged sigh. "And fell in love with my enemy."

Callie gazed into his eyes, lost in what blazed there. Fluttery feelings spread through her like warm honey. "No, don't say that," she mumbled, her response barely audible.

A slow smile turned up Iollan's lips. "I wanted you enough to risk staying." He leaned forward, brushing a soft kiss against her lips. "I wanted to taste you one more time."

Shaking her head, Callie swallowed the lump building in her throat. A pent-up breath rushed from her lungs. "We can't."

Iollan's gaze caught hers, digging, probing. "One more time is all I ask."

Callie started to protest. Sexually, he was the aggressor. A woman he made love to was engulfed by sheer lust, swept away in the erotic whirlwind he evoked in the female body. He went from tender to rough, from pleasure to pain, in the blink of an eye. "There's no time."

Iollan ignored her. The savagery of his desire spurred him on. His hold tightened. Instantly a blaze of desire ignited between them, as though it had been simmering below his surface composure for too long, waiting only for a spark from her to burst into full flame.

Callie felt his mental strike. She stiffened, trying to fight the pressure building inside her skull, and failing. The force pushing inside her brain was relentless, refusing to stop until all access was granted.

Her world blurred as two different sets of images from two different minds—hers and his—mingled and merged. At the same instant an electric sensation smacked her right in the center of her forehead. Iollan's will cut through her consciousness and she lost all control.

Time slowed to a standstill, reality slipping into a dimension filled with funhouse mirrors. Darkness crept in.

Callie's mind hazed. Something had definitely settled inside her skull. Drake had tasted her blood more than once. He knew her down to the very last cell in her body, down to the very last thought in her head. The pressure branched out like a spider's web, traveling with unnerving speed through her brain.

For a moment it seemed as if the entity inside looked out through her eyes. Then it turned inward again and she remembered lying in a damp naked sprawl under Iollan's muscular body.

Then, his bite. His deliciously painful bite, driven into her skin by unnaturally sharp teeth. Instead of rejecting the pain he delivered, she'd reveled in it, sunk into it. The discovery had been sweet and drugging.

Iollan Drake didn't blink. His intense stare lanced her. He mentally pushed. Harder.

Callie gasped. Her chest heaved one, twice. She braced herself. Self-control wasn't lost or adrift. It was drowning. She floundered in the confusion of two conflicting viewpoints. Images kept intruding inside her brain, raw and vivid fragments of their bodies pressed together. She shivered, remembering the feel of his lips crushing her mouth, exploring her breasts.

The knot tightened inside her belly. The pulse between her legs grew stronger, more insistent. Incredible sensations shimmered through her.

The unexpected buck of climax surprised her, slamming her into a hot burst of carnal pleasure. A shudder went through her. Her body silently screamed, every muscle tightening with need. Whirling thoughts danced with the pulse pounding in her throat. Even now, seeing him in his true form, she still wanted him.

Desperately, and without doubt.

The illusion of pleasure suddenly melted. Unwelcome reality swiftly intruded. She felt as though hours had passed, but only seconds had ticked by.

Jarred from the fantasy, Callie locked her jaw. Her head felt as if a stick of dynamite had been lodged between her ears. She shook her head, swallowing against the nausea. "Get out of my mind," she grated between gritted teeth.

Iollan's invasion receded a little.

Grateful, she gasped. Her tongue traced dry lips, wetting them. Aware his body still controlled hers, she wriggled out from under him. He let her go.

Callie sat up, grasping her head. "Thanks for a nice fuck, but this isn't the time for those kind of thoughts. You should be thinking about getting the hell out of here."

The hand Iollan lifted to rub his eyes trembled. The silver was beginning to infiltrate his system, weakening him. "Maybe I'm tired of running, of being driven into hiding time and time again," he snarled, but the hateful tone in his voice fell well short of the emotion. The intensity of his voice told her all she needed to know.

Guilt twisted her inside. As tough as she wanted to appear, she was shaken up pretty badly. Not because of what he was, but because she'd be responsible for his capture. "Seems to me running might be a good way to stay alive." How ironic. The captor wishing for a way to get him the hell away from this place before the rest of the agents caught up.

He gave a fatalistic shrug. "Maybe it doesn't matter anymore."

Terrific. A suicidal vampire.

Callie glanced toward the windows, the burnt frames offering a glimpse of sun as it sank lower, dipping behind the faraway horizon. Shadows gathered, thickening. Her gaze locked with Iollan's across the narrow expanse separating them.

"It matters to me." She started to touch him. Climbing to his feet, he backed away from her reach. She stopped. "Can you get the hell out of here without being seen?"

Eyes intense and focused, Iollan nodded. "I just need the darkness, Calista. I can be gone."

Emotion tightened her throat. Remembering the corpse on the table, the mutated thing in the jar, Callie gazed toward the gaping windows. No matter what Iollan might be, she couldn't do that to another sentient being. Conscience wouldn't allow it.

Time to make a decision. The hunt for the vampires wasn't going to stop, but she could prevent the capture of at least one. If he just happened to get away, well, would that be her fault?

She blew out an anxious breath. Fuck the job. Plans had just changed. She'd deal with the fallout when the time came.

"Just get the hell out," she hissed under her breath. "Get away from this place."

A voice behind and to her left cut her off. "Take one fucking step in any direction, Drake, and I'll pump you full of this shit." Charging in like a general leading the troops, Roger Reinke activated his communications link. "We have an agent down. Get your asses in here, double time."

Head twisting around, Callie cursed under her breath. God-damn it. Roger had his weapon up and sighted. No way he'd miss at this distance.

Caught like a rat in a trap, Iollan Drake reacted like a feral animal, purely instinctive and self-preserving: snarling, his lips curled up, revealing deadly fangs.

Caught between the two men, Callie held up a hand. Keep your head, she warned herself. Don't lose it now. Helping Iollan was her first and only thought.

"I'm okay, Roger," she called. "He didn't hurt me."

Looking past her as if she hadn't spoken, Reinke glared a stream of pure wicked hate. "Just move," he warned Drake. "And I'll gladly send you back to the hell that spawned you."

Callie took a deep breath, hoping to clear her head a bit more. She needed to convince Roger that Iollan Drake wasn't a threat. If they let him go, he'd disappear. Somehow she'd find him again, or he'd find her. She just knew it.

And then it happened. Precious time ran out.

Voices shouted, moving closer and closer. More agents burst in, weapons drawn, giving the familiar warning to freeze. Seconds later, the entire place seemed to be swarming with jacketed bodies.

Callie's guts knotted as agents rushed forward. Several men surrounded him at once, backing him into a corner with their weapons. They came too fast, from too many sides. The night had, for once, failed him. The shadows no longer gave sanctuary.

A couple of agents shoved Iollan to his knees, twisting his arms up behind his back. Seconds later, solid metal cuffs ratcheted around his wrists.

The sight barely registered because strong hands grasped her arms and hauled her to her feet. When they stood her up, she struggled to jerk out of their grasp. Her knees wobbled, refusing to hold her weight. No such luck. She wasn't going anywhere her legs didn't want to.

Callie groaned. She'd tried to free Iollan and failed. Guilt swooped in on crimson-tipped wings, wrapping her in a dark mantle of shame. "Fuck."

She watched Iollan's captors grasp his elbows and bodily haul him across the room. They were none too gentle; there was no guarantee the prisoner would make it downstairs intact. Agents believed one of their own had almost fallen in the line of duty. A few looked more than eager to play catch-up.

Callie briefly closed her eyes, silently praying they wouldn't kill him. A hand on her shoulder forced her eyelids open. Her gaze automatically trekked toward Roger Reinke.

Concern creased Reinke's face. "Did he hurt you, Agent Whitten?"

Callie shook her head. "No, I'm fine. Really."

She wasn't.

19

Cold and inhospitable. That's what Callie thought of the prison block. No way she'd want to be a prisoner in this place. White ceramic tile floors and walls gave the block a sterile and impersonal atmosphere. Sinister even. Thick steel doors dominated.

Doctor Yuan, Professor Forque, and a couple of lab assistants led the way through the forbidding maze of halls. Like a man on his way to his execution, Iollan Drake walked between Roger Reinke and another agent. Since his capture Iollan had mantled himself in silence. He wouldn't respond to the questions the scientists had peppered him with, choosing instead a show of fangs. Just the way a wild animal would. This wasn't earning him any brownie points, nor did it prove the more evolved species to be more intelligent.

Callie didn't blame him. Put in his position, she supposed she'd give a show of fangs, too. Right now she didn't think it was the right tactic for him to employ. Might be better to show he was more human than the humans. The way he was being treated and regarded would probably improve a lot.

Callie was hailed as the conquering hero, the agent responsi-ble for capturing the *most wanted* of the species. Her success had come at a price, one she realized she hadn't been prepared to pay.

Callie felt horrible for betraying him.

The claustrophobia of the whole situation overwhelmed her. As an agent of the government, she was also government prop-erty. Refuse to cooperate and she'd probably be sitting in one of these cells herself. No way they'd let her run free, memory or not. At least Toryn and Cadyn had escaped, most likely in hiding. Iollan must be grateful for that small mercy. Not that he had much to feel grateful about.

A cell was chosen, a door unlocked. Everyone went inside, most of them willingly. Two not so willingly.

A small square cell, maybe twelve by twelve. Not much to it. In fact, except for the floors and walls and a strip of phos-phorescent light glaring down from above, there wasn't even a bunk.

Callie stiffened. What the fuck was going on?

She soon found out.

Doctor Yuan produced a syringe out of one pocket of her white lab coat. "Hold him still," she ordered the agents.

Callie frowned. The sight of any syringe automatically set her nerves on edge. "What the hell is that?"

Doctor Yuan approached Iollan. "Just something to keep him calm while we cuff him." Uncapping the needle, she nod-ded to the men. "Hold him, please."

Drake's lip curled back, showing the full length of his upper and lower fangs. A low growl emanated from his throat. Mus-cles bunching, cords thickening in his neck, his pale eyes blazed as he struggled between the agents.

Roger Reinke and his partner moved into action. They pressed Iollan back against the wall, anchoring him with their weight. "Better hurry up, doc," Reinke wheezed. "Holding this fucker back is like trying to hold back the ocean."

Yuan didn't blink an eye. She calmly stepped up on the tip of her toes and slid the needle into the vampire's jugular. Under the plunge of her finger the syringe emptied into his veins.

Iollan's growl turned into the low rumble of a moan deep in his throat. Stubbornly, he wouldn't let it out.

Yuan stepped back. Satisfaction glinted in her dark almond eyes. "That'll keep him quiet a while."

Iollan's eyelids fluttered, but he forced himself to keep his eyes open. His hair was limp, and dark circles ringed his eyes. Unusually pale in the filtered light, he seemed to have skin with the transparency of paper. His flesh looked cold, with no sign of a pulse. His gaze had dulled, the vibrant color of his irises nonexistent, sapped away by the poison Doctor Yuan had introduced into his veins.

Callie gritted her teeth, forcing back the emotions rising in the back of her mind. The sight of this magnificent man reduced to little more than a lab rat caused tears to sting the backs of her eyes. She quickly blinked them away. Right now she felt the lowest of the low, as if she'd slain the last living example of an extinct species.

Focus, she ordered herself. She had to find a way to get Iollan out of this evil place. She didn't know how yet, but she vowed that she'd move heaven and earth to find a way. Twice he'd had the chance to kill her and twice he'd drawn back. He wasn't a killer, except in self-defense. He'd have been right to take her life and she knew it.

Tucked into her shoulder holster she had a weapon that would fire real bullets. A mad fantasy flashed through her mind. She could pull her gun and drop the agents, then get Iollan the hell out of this place. Then she'd get him somewhere safe, where no one hunted vampires.

Fat chance.

Her fantasy shattered when Iollan slumped against the wall, then slid to the floor in a semiconscious heap. His head lolled to one side.

Callie winced. So much for that idea. Iollan wasn't in any shape to walk across the room now, much less make a mad dash for escape.

Doctor Yuan pointed to a far wall. "Put him there."

Roger and his partner dragged Iollan to the wall. Metal rings had been fixed into the concrete. One of the agents removed the cuffs holding Iollan's hands behind his back and pushed him into a sitting position. At the same time, Doctor Yuan's assistant produced another pair: thick leather cuffs and a leather collar.

Callie gasped at the sight. As the assistant opened the collar, she saw a row of short silver spikes inside. The device went around Iollan's neck. He winced as the restraint bit into his skin. Cinched tight enough for the spikes to penetrate vulnerable flesh, the restraint device was locked and then attached to the ring in the wall by a short chain.

Her brow wrinkled in fierce disapproval. "What the hell is that?"

Doctor Yuan didn't blink. "We can't feed too much liquid silver into their systems or we'll poison them. We've found that the penetration of solid silver works much better; keeps them unable to shift."

The sound of tearing material told Callie the other two cuffs were being applied. Her gaze swung back toward Iollan, watching as his wrists were securely cuffed and attached to the rings.

Iollan hissed when the cuffs went on, hands weakly flexing open and shut. The spikes penetrated the soft skin of his inner wrists, releasing tiny rivulets of blood before the pressure of the spikes resealed the wounds. By the look on his face he'd like to tear everyone a new asshole.

Callie pointed. "Christ, he's bleeding." Arms slightly spread, Iollan's cuffs were attached to the corresponding rings on either side of his body. His hands hung at the level of his head. All in all it looked very medieval and extremely uncomfortable.

"It'll stop," Professor Forque said, speaking for the first time since they'd entered the cell. "These things have an amazing capacity to heal." He was dead serious.

Callie shifted, planting her hands on her hips. She leveled him with a withering look. "You guys must get this stuff from the de Sade school of research. This is fucking inhumane. Isn't this kind of treatment against the Geneva Convention?" She hadn't intended for the words to come out laced with disgust.

"He isn't a prisoner of war," Roger Reinke pointed out. "Doesn't apply here."

"Oh? Then what is a prisoner of our government called if held against his will and tossed into a tiny cell without any facilities except for torture?"

"Calm down, Agent Whitten," Roger Reinke warned quietly. "This isn't torture. It's the way we handle them. A few days of solitary and he'll change his mind about how he wants to be treated."

Anger rising like a hot flash of red inside her skull, Callie's eyes narrowed. "It's wrong. It's degrading. You're collaring him like an animal and chaining him to a wall. If that isn't a clear violation of basic rights, human or not, I don't know what is. No wonder they consider us at war against their species."

Roger Reinke refused to be baited. "Drop it, Whitten. Insubordination won't be tolerated."

She didn't have much choice, it seemed. Close to putting her ass on a very narrow line, she fought to rein in her fury. Hard to do, but necessary.

Professor Forque stepped between them. "Don't you think right now he'd tear your throat out if given the chance? At the base level, they are no more than animals, and we must treat them as such."

Feeling like dirt, Callie lobbed a nasty scowl. "No. I don't think he'd tear my throat out." Her breath rushed out and her knees felt wobbly. "He's had plenty of chances and didn't. He could have killed me tonight, and he didn't."

Forque offered a thin smile. "Given your level of intimacy with the subject, I can understand your emotional attachment, Agent Whitten. Let me assure you we're taking that into consideration. In fact, we're expecting you to act as a liaison toward convincing him to cooperate with us during his testing."

Callie's first reaction was to refuse. Then she rethought her strategy. Agreeing to cooperate would keep her near Iollan. She silently cursed herself for showing her anger. Getting pissed off would get her kicked behind a desk again.

Not a good strategy at all. She didn't trust Yuan or Forque a bit. *Keep your friends close and your enemies closer*, she counseled herself.

She nodded stiffly. Given the government she worked for, she didn't have many choices. "Of course. Having come this far, I'd expect nothing less."

Forque nodded. "I want to assure you, Agent Whitten, we intend to treat this specimen very carefully. Though we've caught others of the species, this is the first time we've gotten hold of a sire. That will make all the difference in our research. The rest have been drones, and fairly useless in the area and reproduction of the species."

The floor opened up under her feet. "Sire?" The single word tripped stupidly off her tongue.

Forque referred the answer back to Doctor Yuan.

"We've determined the Niviane Idesha have a very structured reproductive cycle," Yuan explained. "Most symbionts are asexual, unable to replicate themselves. However, like a hive has a queen bee, this species has a hermaphroditic symbiont capable of reproduction. When another sire is birthed, it in turn branches out in a new area to begin its own clan. Drake is a sire."

Callie's guts turned to liquid ice. She glanced at Iollan and blanched. Reproduction of the species? Oh shit. Speaking of reproduction. She counted back, searching her mind. The first time they'd made love, he'd been very careful to use a condom. But the second time, no, he'd taken her without one. Though she'd also been with Cadyn and Toryn, they hadn't taken her vaginally. The third time she'd been with Iollan, again no condom.

She imagined slapping her hand to her forehead, something she'd soon be doing in private. Since she'd gone undercover she hadn't been regular in taking her birth control pills either. Talk about stupid. She bit back a groan, trying not to remember how beautifully their bodies fit together and how incredible sex between them had been. When he'd entered her, she'd welcomed him. And when he'd climaxed, her womb had retained his ejaculate. Alien sperm.

Oh, God, what if I'm . . . No! An automatic refusal rose in her mind. Remembering her bouts with a queasy stomach, she swallowed, trying not to choke over the lump simultaneously rising in her throat. *If* she were carrying a baby, the pregnancy could be ended with no one the wiser except herself and her doctor.

Some protective female instinct kicked in. She realized the idea of carrying Iollan's child wasn't exactly repulsive. Handsome, charming, and alluring, he was an easy man to fall in love with. She didn't have to examine her heart to know she was already halfway there.

Standing there, Callie suddenly felt so alone. Shivering, she considered Forque and Yuan. If they found out, there'd be no way she'd be allowed to abort. She couldn't imagine any child of hers chained up like a dog because it wasn't . . . human. She was a fool to have walked herself straight into an unplanned pregnancy.

Possible pregnancy, she reminded herself. Nothing's solid yet. Just to be sure, she'd be making a trip to the drugstore as soon as time allowed. She didn't know how long a woman was supposed to wait before testing, but she wasn't taking any chances. She wanted to know ASAP.

Callie slipped on a blank expression. No time to think about herself. Looking at Iollan, she saw his breathing appeared to be uneven and his movements, limited as they were, seemed restless. His sharp teeth gnashed in pain. The effects of the silver were beginning to fully manifest in his system.

Enough of this. Callie started to rush toward him.

Roger Reinke caught her arm. "Leave him alone, Callie. You don't know what you're doing."

Refusing to be deterred, Callie shook off his hand. "He needs help." Going to Iollan's side, she dropped to her knees beside him. Her gaze sought his. "Calm down," she whispered. "I'm here. I want to help you."

Iollan shook his head as if to warn her away. A wry smile twisted his lips. "I need no help from your kind."

Stung by his words, Callie blinked back tears. Just being close to him, seeing him in such torment set her on edge. "I'm sorry," she murmured. "I didn't mean for them to do this to you. I swear I didn't know it'd be like this."

Iollan's pale gaze slid toward his captors. Seeing them, his entire body tensed in recognition. A low growl rose in his throat. "As Tacitus said of Rome, 'They made a desert and call it peace.' " An ironic laugh escaped him. His pained expression grew worse. "These humans slaughter my kind and call us hostile."

Professor Forque laughed outright. "Please, spare us the history lesson. You're alien. Your *kind* doesn't even belong on planet Earth. Exterminating you to keep humans safe isn't genocide. It's self-preservation."

Iollan closed his eyes and grimaced. He turned his head as much as the collar would allow. His fangs retracted, shrinking back into the shape of normal teeth in the blink of an eye. "We came in peace and only to survive," he gasped. "No one is taken without consent."

Yuan hurried to break in. "We want to understand your kind. Work with us so we can know the species better."

Iollan slowly shook his head. "Your science is slaughter."

Callie froze. One hand strayed to her stomach. She pressed a hand against the flat plane of her belly as though she'd been kicked in the gut. The memory of the mutilated thing floating in a jar of formaldehyde caused her teeth to grit in frustration and pain.

Iollan's words were too true and she knew it. The only ones who'd benefit from these so-called explorations were humans. Once science had extracted the traits they wanted, the source would most likely be exterminated.

Completely.

Callie silently determined that wasn't going to happen, come hell or high water.

For the rest of the people listening, Iollan Drake's words didn't go over well at all.

Doctor Yuan crossed to her captive. Kneeling to his level, she gave him a narrow look. Dark almond eyes sparked. Her smooth hair had broken free of its bun, falling like the wings of a raven around her face. She looked like an insane little ninja, something no one wanted to mess with.

"We do what's necessary to get the answers we need," Yuan warned. "If I have to take your kind apart layer by layer, I will. You want to live, cooperate. If not, I'll put you on my table and dissect you alive and awake."

Iollan braced himself against her onslaught, visibly forcing himself to remain alert. He bared his teeth, no threat to anyone right now. "Watch your back, dangerous lady. Lose sight of me once and you'll never see me coming."

Yuan frowned, clucking her tongue. "Guess we're going to be doing things the hard way."

Close to stepping in with her own threat, Callie was relieved when one of Doctor Yuan's assistants rolled a small cart into the cell.

Yuan stood up, looking over the cart. "Not that he deserves to eat." She picked up a unit of blood. "You going to drink this or do I have to put an IV in you?" She was obviously more accustomed to working with corpses; her bedside manner left a lot to be desired.

Iollan blanched. "It's dead."

Yuan looked like she wanted to smack Iollan upside the head with the bag. "It's blood. Food, you idiot. You're a vampire. It's what you eat."

Iollan's brows drew together and his lips firmed. His piercing glare turned to amusement. "Apparently your knowledge of the Niviane Idesha is lacking when it comes to our care and feeding," he said sarcastically. "I need blood. Directly from its source." He eyed the bag in Yuan's hand. "If you've mainlined others with that shit, you've fed them the equivalent of a diet soda."

All faces in the room looked thunderstruck.

"We are psi-sangre," Iollan said. "We need living blood." He paused and took a deep breath. "The blood has to be energized," he finished. "Sexually charged."

Professor Forque's face lit up as if he'd been handed the secrets to the Holy Grail. "So that's one of the keys we've been missing. My God, how simple—and how logical. Of course they'd need blood from a living source. They are an energy-driven species."

"That makes us no more than a Duracell battery," Doctor Yuan commented sourly. "So how do you propose feeding him, Terrence?"

Callie stood up. "I'll do it. He's accustomed to me, has tasted me."

Roger Reinke stepped in. "That part of your assignment is over, Agent. Too dangerous."

Pinning her ex-lover under a glare, she gave a bitter half smile. "It wasn't too dangerous when I didn't know what he was, Roger. It's my neck—and my ass—on the line. I think I'll make the decision when to stick them out from now on."

Roger glared. "I don't like the idea of you continuing intimate contact with this—" He pointed in frustration toward Iollan Drake. His face took on the cast of hot pink neon. The idea of consensual sexual activity between a human and vampire clearly disturbed him. "This thing . . . It's not even human. It's disgusting you'd even want to save it. All of them should be marked for termination."

The depth of his hatred rippled over Callie's skin like a bad rash. She ignored his last words as if he hadn't said them.

"I'll keep that in mind, Roger." Rubbing her arms with her hands, Callie broke eye contact and turned away from Reinke. To see him so deeply prejudiced against another being—human or not—disturbed her.

"Mandatory quarantine for twenty-four hours," Yuan snapped crisply. "He'll have to stay here."

"And cuffed," Roger Reinke put in. "I don't want those restraints removed."

Callie gritted her teeth. "That's fine. I'll make do. Tomorrow, though, I'd like to see him in more comfortable surroundings. A lot more comfortable."

Forque stepped into the fray. "It'll be done. However, I agree that he'll have to remain bound."

"I also want someone posted outside this door," Roger

Reinke said. His tone brooked no argument. "If you have problems, someone will be nearby."

More gritting. "Fine."

"Anything else you need, Agent Whitten?" Doctor Yuan asked.

Callie started to negate that, then thought better of it. She'd made a lot of demands. Best to give these Nazis a little leeway if she wanted to keep them cooperating. She glanced toward the door. Solid steel, there was a narrow mesh window of thick glass. Not exactly privacy, but enough for now.

"I want you people to get the hell out."

20

The cell emptied, leaving only herself and Iollan Drake. Thank God, they were alone.

Callie glanced over her shoulder. Sure enough a cadre of anxious eyes peered through the glass window. Gawking like kids looking for a peek at the sideshow freak. Sad. In their eyes, the Niviane Idesha weren't human and therefore didn't deserve the simple human consideration of decent treatment.

Or privacy.

Oh, well. Given his position and predicament, there wasn't a whole hell of a lot Iollan Drake could contribute to the situation. Pumped full of poison, he probably wasn't going to be that damn responsive. She'd have to do all the work.

Not exactly an unpleasant idea. Everything she needed to do, she could manage without shedding one stitch of clothing. The only thing anyone would see was her back.

Callie walked over to him. Her gaze slid to his powerful thighs, bringing her more intimate knowledge of him vividly to mind. She remembered how he'd touched her, lead her into the sexual act with an exhilarating power that would leave her breathless and trembling. She wanted him, no holds barred.

Stepping over his outstretched legs, she dropped to her knees. Her body straddled his. Settled against his lean body, she felt him stiffen.

Iollan made a move to unseat her, but she stayed firmly planted. He made a face, gently shaking his head as if to warn her away. "Don't do this to me, Calista."

She reached out, brushing strands of dark hair off his pale forehead. "I want to help you."

She saw his throat work. "Kill me then," he muttered through his teeth. "Take your weapon and kill me."

Callie shot him a look of profound disbelief. Without thinking, she glanced down at the gun holstered under her left arm. A few minutes ago she'd been tempted to use it on the humans. Now Iollan had asked her to use it on him. "I won't," she started to say.

Iollan persisted, his voice a harsh whisper. "A headshot will kill. Once the brain is damaged, the symbiont inside will also die. They won't keep me for breeding."

"Don't ask me that." She shook her head. "I can't. I won't."

His jaw tightened. "You are just like the rest of them. Taking everything, giving nothing."

His words hit like a knife to the heart, sharp and cutting to the quick. "That's not true," she said, voice dropping to a whisper. "I've seen the man beneath the vampire. I know you're more human than they are. I want that man, the man I fell in love with."

Iollan sighed with obvious frustration. "It's too late for love, Calista. It's too late for us—"

Her guts clenched painfully. Not wanting to hear anymore, Callie decided to shut him up. Capturing his face between her hands, she kissed him.

Iollan's lips parted under the sweep of her invading tongue.

Callie pressed deeper. Their kiss intensified, each drawing from the other. She moved her pelvis against his, fitting her body to his in a move guaranteed to raise even the deadest of men. Following the length of his outstretched arms, her hands found his. Their fingers linked.

The need for air forced her to pull back.

Callie tightened her hold on his hands. "I'll get you out of here," she breathed. "Somehow, I will. Just don't give up on me."

A slow smoldering fire came to light in the depths of his eyes. "You have something in mind to get me out of here?" The curve of his lips made her feel as though the room was doing a half spin.

She shook her head. "Not yet. But I'll think of something. Just give me a little time."

"They won't let me go alive," he warned. "Granted by your hand, death would be a mercy."

A faint alarm sounded in her mind. "I'm not going to kill you."

Iollan's lips stretched into a sad smile. "If I don't feed, it'll only take a few days for my symbiont to turn on me." He grimaced. "A painful way to die, but preferable to what your people have in mind for me."

Callie stared at his face, not really seeing it. "You're not going to kill yourself, either," she said, her voice steady with resolution. She reflected on how easily she'd fallen in love, so quickly that she hadn't realized her heart had been stolen until after the lock on the strongbox had been broken. "If you love me, I'm just asking you to trust me."

Iollan watched her closely, the fine lines at the corners of his eyes creasing slightly. "Are you, Callie?" he asked, very soft and very low.

Her mind suddenly blanked. "What?"

"In love with me?"

A shuddering breath rushed out. "Yes."

Hands still pressed together, his strong fingers tightened around hers. "Good. That is enough then."

Her hands trailed down the sides of his face, settling on his broad shoulders. She'd totally lost control of her good sense, and didn't care. "God, you're making me so crazy."

A slow smile turned up one corner of his mouth. He shifted his hips beneath her weight, reminding her how closely their bodies were pressed together. "If I could get my damn hands on you, I'd do that and more, love."

Callie was suddenly conscious that her legs were spread apart over him. "We'll just have to improvise." She tugged at the front of his shirt, working the material out of his jeans. Unbuttoning his shirt, she slipped her hands around his waist, enjoying the feel of solid muscle under her palms.

A shudder of need went through him as her hands explored the planes of his broad chest, fingers circling his dusky male nipples. "You are the only woman I've desired in a long time," he marveled in a low murmur. "I wanted you the day I saw you."

Callie leaned forward, pressing her lips to the corner of his full mouth. "Less talk, more action." Her mouth claimed his in a fervent kiss, deeper and more intense than the first. She'd have sworn she felt his heart beating against her breasts, or perhaps it was her own. She couldn't really be sure; their bodies suddenly felt melded together. She reached down and deftly undid the top buttons of his jeans.

A soft groan escaped him.

Callie drew back. "Am I hurting you?"

Iollan sucked in an angry hiss. "Not you," he grated. "Damn this fucking silver they've pumped into me. I don't think you're going to get much out of me tonight."

"Guess we'll have to improvise, then."

His hands flexed. "Not that I want to." He sighed with obvious frustration.

Callie pretended to think. "I'll just have to take matters into my own hands then." A wicked smile crooked up her lips. "You like to watch, don't you?"

He eyed her with delight. "I'm still human enough to enjoy watching a woman get herself off."

She laughed and licked her lips. "Dinner and a show. Can the night get any better?"

Iollan almost strangled himself trying to shake his head. Eager hunger gleamed in the depths of his eyes. "I can think of other places I'd rather be."

Sliding off her tactical assault vest jacket, Callie dropped it to one side. "We'll just have to make do." Her shoulder holster and weapon followed, landing on the pile with a soft thud. Fixing her gaze on his, she started with the top button of her blouse. Slowly, one at a time, she undid the front of her navy uniform shirt. The soft cups of her bra hugged her full breasts.

Using just the tips of her fingers, she traced the path of the lacy white material. "Mmm, I seem to have a little too much on." She unsnapped the front clasp, letting the cups fall away. Her nipples protruded, front and center.

Iollan moaned softly. His breathing grew deeper, more ragged. "You have beautiful breasts."

Callie traced the tips. Tiny electrical shocks sparked through her body. Her nipples puckered, then hardened, as she gave each a gentle twist. "Want a taste?"

He raked his bottom lip with eager teeth. His arms strained against the cuffs holding him, muscles cording from the effort to free his hands. "Definitely."

"Glad to oblige." Hands shifting to his shoulders, she lifted her body, guiding one nipple toward his waiting mouth.

Instead of immediately claiming the morsel, he traced the

protruding tip with his tongue. His teeth scraped the sensitive skin.

Closing her eyes, Callie's head dropped forward, her face just inches from his head. Her free hand cupped and caressed her left breast. "Oh God." Pulling in a breath she inhaled the musky scent of heated, sweaty male flesh, an intoxicating scent. A low moan built at the back of her throat.

"Touch yourself," he whispered against her breast.

Callie drew back. Sliding her hand down her bare belly, her fingers stopped just short of the dark blue fatigues she'd worn in the raid. "I'm so wet," she murmured.

His tongue traced his lips. "Let me taste you."

Undoing the single button, she eased the zipper down. White cotton panties peeked out. Hooking a thumb in the elastic, she eased the front down, revealing the curve of her shaved mound.

Iollan almost choked. Voice hoarse with desire, he whispered. "What are you thinking about?"

Callie slid her free hand between her legs. "I'm thinking about your cock." The thought sent a rush of pleasure through all her nerve endings. She stroked her clit with the tip of her finger, with light, soft pressure. She briefly caught her bottom lip between her teeth, dying to relieve the terrible ache between her legs.

Iollan shifted restlessly. One of his legs came up against her back, pressing into her. "Inside you," he pleaded.

Pushing her ass back against his muscular thigh, she spread her legs wider. Feeling wonderfully wanton and fierce, she traced the lips of her labia, rolling the tender flesh between her fingers.

Heat enveloped her fingers when she slid into her slick sex. Quivering with tension, she burned with desire. Nearing climax, she delved two fingers deep, pressing them into the center of her passion, meeting each slow, delicious wave by grinding her ass against his leg. The first shivers of her orgasm washed over her.

Iollan shuddered, perfectly echoing the quakes ripping through her body. "Magnificent," he murmured. A fine flush had risen up on his skin, heightening the spark in his luminous eyes.

Closing her eyes, Callie fell back into her new favorite fantasy, the one where three men were making love to her. Her fantasy had her on her knees, sucking Cadyn's cock as Iollan lay beneath her body, claiming her cunt. Toryn stood over them, taking her from behind. She imagined the feel of Iollan's cock sliding deep into her as Cadyn fucked her warm mouth. She'd had a taste of three men and had been entranced by the thought of three cocks to tease and please her. All the men would reassure her with soft whispers and softer kisses.

Iollan pressed his thigh against her ass, bucking his hips at the most critical time, slamming her fingers deep.

His move sent Callie over the edge. Silken muscles gripped her fingers, rippling with prolonged power. Incandescent pleasure of the purest sort exploded through her. Inner fever shattering, she moaned loud and long, the last coherent sound she was capable of making.

Rocketing into the stratosphere, her orgasm went on and on, each pulse hotter and wilder than the last.

Breath hissing inward, Callie gasped, running her tongue over her dry lips. Her throat was parched and her lips were rasped raw by her heavy breath. She floated back to earth on the softest of wings. Her fingers slid slowly out of her tight sheath.

Iollan relaxed beneath her, sighing in contentment. "Beautiful," he murmured. "I've never seen a woman enjoy orgasm more than you do."

Callie smiled and pressed into him, her abused hand seeking his lips. Fingers tracing a sexy path, she spread her cream over his mouth. She followed with her own mouth, eager to taste her female spice on him. Tongues met and waltzed with the fire burning inside them both.

"Think I'm hot enough?" she asked when their kiss had broken. The question rippled from her throat like a purr.

Iollan gasped. "More than enough and then some."

Callie tipped her head, offering the softness of her neck. She moved until she felt the burn of his hot breath on her tender skin. "Do it." Her hands circled his narrow hips, fingers digging into his skin.

Iollan savored her neck. His tongue traced a moist hot trail across her jugular.

She closed her eyes. Her pulse beat frantically against his mouth. The tips of her nipples pressed into his chest, slick with the perspiration of his own intense arousal. "Give me the pain that's so delicious."

Sharp teeth scraped. Penetration came swiftly and without hesitation. Iollan's fangs sank in as deeply and surely as if he'd impaled her with his cock. A small sound of satisfaction escaped her throat when he bit.

Warm lips pressed against her skin, suckling hungrily.

Blood flowed from Callie's veins, driven by the intense beating of her heart. Sheer undiluted pleasure coursed through her as he suckled.

Mind clouding, that familiar hazy sensation followed. Blackness loomed.

Callie's breath caught in her throat. She felt herself teetering at the brink of consciousness as Iollan fed from her throat. She didn't care if he took every last drop.

21

When Callie woke, she found Doctor Yuan's anxious face hovering above her. Drawing a sharp breath, she immediately glanced around. As her vision adjusted, she realized she'd been moved. No longer in Iollan's cell, she seemed to be in some sort of an examination room, stark white walls and floors, a padded surface under her back.

How long have I been unconscious? She didn't remember passing out.

She tried to sit up. To her relief they were alone. Good. She didn't exactly feel like seeing any men after . . . Cheeks heating from the memory, she glanced down. Her clothing had, thankfully, been shifted back into place.

Doctor Yuan pressed her back. "Lie still. It's normal to feel a little dizzy after giving blood."

A weak smile creased Callie's lips. She tried to swallow. It hurt. Her chest seized as she sucked in a lungful of air almost too antiseptic to breathe. No germ would escape unscathed.

Her neck felt swollen, a bit numb. A low ache throbbed behind her eyes, but otherwise she felt intact. "Is that what I'm doing?"

Doctor Yuan nodded. "That's what it looked like to me." Producing a thermometer, she popped it into Callie's mouth. "Your demonstration was the first time we've ever witnessed an actual feeding. Very illuminating as to the behavior of the species."

Considering that she'd been on display in the most intimate of circumstances, Callie didn't feel any compunction to accept her praise. Marshalling all her strength, she pushed herself up on her elbows. "How is Iollan?" she mumbled around the glass sticking out of her mouth.

"Unhappy, but stable."

Hard not to bite the thermometer in half. "You'd be pissed if you were chained up."

Yuan spared her a glance. "We'll move him to more suitable quarters tomorrow. He'll have the basic amenities."

Well, that answered that, without telling her anything at all. Callie hoped her words were more than lip service. Bad enough Iollan had to endure captivity with handling most people wouldn't inflict on a mongrel dog. She'd damn sure follow up to make sure he got better treatment. No wonder his kind didn't trust hers. Hand it to ham-fisted humans to rush in with the deadliest of force. She wondered if it had occurred to anyone to just *talk* to the Niviane Idesha in a diplomatic and reasonable manner.

Yuan retrieved the thermometer. "Low-grade fever, but nothing to get excited about." She probed the area around Callie's neck. "The bite doesn't seem to be infected. These creatures seem to have an antiseptic in their saliva to arrest bleeding and begin healing after they've fed. The punctures are a little ragged, but clean. You'll heal."

Resisting the urge to toss back something irreverent, Callie swallowed and kept her humor to herself. "Glad you think so."

Putting the thermometer away, Yuan reached for a syringe and uncapped its sterile needle. "I've taken a few smears to look at, but I'd also like to get some blood and urine from you. We're interested to know if continual feedings are affecting you in any biological way. We're still not clear about the Niviane Idesha's reproductive capabilities. Obviously, the sire somehow *seeds* the victim with the symbiont, but the process is unknown. We're sure they are a 'recruit, not reproduce' species. Anything we can learn will help us better understand them."

Callie stayed still and tried to keep her calm. Her blood and urine might reveal more than she wanted Doctor Yuan to know. She stiffened. "Is that a request or an order?"

Yuan immediately frowned. "Given the circumstances and the nature of our research and your, ah, closer than normal involvement with our subject, I suppose I could pull rank and make it an order."

Callie felt her patience thin. "Figures," she mumbled irritably, not exactly pleased that the whole of the government had somehow become involved in her sex life. If she was—or wasn't—pregnant, well, that would be obvious soon enough. She held out her arm. "Take what the hell you think you've got to have. I've been a fucking pincushion—or fang cushion—since this whole thing began." Unbuttoning her cuff, she rolled up her sleeve. "If I'd known he was an alien, I'd have definitely thought twice about the sex thing."

Yuan slid the needle into a vein at the crook of Callie's elbow, deftly drawing a rush of crimson liquid into the syringe. Her touch was amazingly light, given that most of her patients weren't normally among the living. "I see you have some scarring."

Callie stiffened, cursing silently under her breath. It didn't take the blind to see the scars. There were plenty. She shouldn't be surprised Yuan had noticed. Her job was to explore every inch of a body, inside and out. Explaining her history as a cutter would be awkward. She'd managed to dodge it in psych testing when she'd joined the bureau by telling her old tried-and-true lie. Those side lectures in college had paid off nicely. Most days, she could out-normal the truly normal.

"Childhood accident," she said, keeping her tone casual. "I fell through a plate-glass window."

"Ah." A bit of blissful silence followed, then an unexpected question. "Do you find him attractive?" Yuan asked conversationally.

Whoa, whoa! What was this? The question came totally out of left field. She didn't dare try to dodge the subject. She was, she realized, intimately involved with the subject. Of course they'd want to know all about the sex.

Quickly debating a way to answer, Callie decided truth would be best. Then she wouldn't have to remember what she lied about. "Sure. What woman wouldn't?"

"Is he . . . ?" Yuan's gaze darted away.

Delicious tension grew. Callie had an idea what the next question would be. Inappropriate as it might be, she should mind the intrusion. She didn't. "Is he what?"

A minute passed. Embarrassed tension grew. Obviously curious, the good doctor who should be well versed in the ways of human anatomy and its workings fumbled like a schoolgirl. "You know, his male equipment. Is he . . . built?"

Callie used the most scientific description that came to mind. "Like a brick shithouse," she said without embarrassment.

That seemed to please Yuan. "Good?" Loaded question.

Callie had to answer honestly. "He fucks like a stallion," she replied with a grin. "I've never had such intense orgasms. You want the absolute best sex of your life, honey, get a man who sucks."

The stoic Yuan blushed. She didn't look much older than Callie; Yuan was maybe her senior by a few years. Yuan was certainly young and pretty enough to have a very active love life if she so desired.

Trying to build a rapport with the woman, make her understand Iollan wasn't exactly much different from the human he'd once been, Callie looked her straight in the eye. "You ever meet a man and that spark's right there? An instant attraction that just makes your body tingle and all you want is to get the guy naked and horizontal? That's how it was when I saw him. Instant lightning. Everything about him attracted me."

Yuan briefly worried her lower lip. "I've met one or two in my time," she admitted behind a shy grin.

"And?"

Yuan laughed, but it was a nervous laugh. She quickly backtracked from inquisitive woman into scientist. Confidences over, the conversation went back to business. "Unfortunately romance took a dive when I started working here. Seems like this place devours my life, in more ways than one. Most times I sleep in my office because it's too late to go home."

Understandable. "Lonely life."

Yuan filled three vials with Callie's blood, labeling each as she spoke. "Lonely, yes. But my work has its rewards. The cutting edge of science, discovering new life-forms."

Callie conceded. Her own studies had once consumed her in such a way. "I can see where it'd be hard to go home."

Yuan set the syringe aside, pressing a cotton pad laced with alcohol to the prick left in Callie's skin. "If you correlate the history of vampire legends among primitive peoples with the now proven existence of the Niviane Idesha, you see how closely legend and fact compare, even giving us their possible date of arrival on our planet."

Callie held the pad in place until the blood ceased to seep from her arm. "But do you really consider them hostiles? They seem to be fairly benign. I mean, humans aren't cowering in fear they'll be attacked by vampires. A few people I know would even volunteer for the honor."

"They might be perfectly peaceful," Yuan countered. "But when might that change, and for what reason might it change? Examine our own human history, if you will. Think of the wars mankind has fought against his own species. No matter the conflict, whether for religious, moral, or political reasons, every war has come at great cost to human life. It's always for the advancement of civilization. Eventually, they will want to advance."

Yuan's words brought to mind Iollan's comment. The Niviane Idesha, he'd said, were tired of hiding in the shadows.

Could it be true, Callie thought, that they'd someday want out of their cloak of anonymity? As much as she hated to admit it, Yuan's words made sense. Even Rome, mighty Rome, had fallen. Battle lines were being drawn. Which side to choose? Her own species or the man who'd gotten under her skin in more ways than one?

Logic told her head not to let her heart rule.

Short fight.

Callie's heart quickly sliced logic to the quick before she'd even realized which side she'd chosen. She was completely smitten, and there wasn't a damn thing to do but try and keep her cool.

Unpleasant tension grew. She shifted to put some space between them, not easy to do when lying flat on an examination table. "I can't deny that might happen someday."

Yuan's expression grew unyielding and stubborn. "If we'll inflict such damages on ourselves, how might we react toward another species? Hate and prejudice are powerful motivators. Imagine a war between us and them. Pure chaos. What's more, despite their weaknesses, Niviane Idesha are stronger and faster than humans, certainly more evolved biologically. As much as I hate to say it, I'd rather see them exterminated than the other way around."

Callie forced her chin up. "And I'd rather they'd never have been found if all you're going to do is wipe them out." Her words came out sharply.

Yuan's lips pressed into a thin line. A nerve had been struck and she wasn't pleased with her patient. "I think you're too close to the subjects to keep an objective perspective, Agent Whitten. Once you've worked with them longer, you may change your mind."

Callie wasn't in the mood to be placated. "Is that the purpose of this study, to find out a way to exterminate the Niviane Idesha completely?"

Yuan offered a narrow smile and a plastic cup for urine. "That, Agent Whitten, is classified information. As it is, you're strictly on *need-to-know*. Could you fill this, please?"

Callie didn't argue the point. Yuan was right. Grimacing at the telltale cup, she gave herself a good swift mental kick. Having an alien's baby hadn't been part of her plans. Not by a damned long shot.

Taking the cup, she considered tossing it back in Yuan's face and getting the hell out. That would probably be the wrong thing to do.

Sliding her legs over the edge of the examination table, she looked around. "Which way to the bathroom?"

Yuan pointed to a nearby door. "As much as you can spare, please."

Feeling the pressure in her bladder, Callie imagined she'd be able to spare quite a bit. She hopped off the table, and her head swam a bit with wooziness. Clenching her teeth, she refused to waver. Marching toward the bathroom, she shut the door behind her.

She locked the door, grateful to have a moment's privacy.

Since this whole assignment had begun, it seemed like she'd had eyes on her twenty-four hours a day, seven days a week. No mirror, but the reflection in the silver-plated face of the paper towel dispenser looked terrible, like death warmed over. Eyes lined with fatigue, cheeks paler than twin moons in the sky, and hair a nasty tangle, she certainly wouldn't call herself beautiful at the moment. She looked and felt like a thousand-year-old hag.

Setting the cup down on the edge of the sink, she lowered the lid of the toilet and sat down. She collapsed, leaning forward until her forehead rested on her knees. Her hands locked around her head, a parody of a woman expecting a head-on collision.

Close to tears, she sucked in a ragged breath. "I . . . oh, God, I wasn't prepared for this. Pregnant . . . What the hell am I going to do if I am?"

She nibbled her lower lip, torn between fear of the tragedy in her past and the uncertainty of her future. A quick bio ran through her mind. Thirty, unmarried, unstable, fucking an alien—a real alien, no less!—and enemy of the state. Shit. That couldn't be written in a fucking book.

She slipped her hands between legs and abdomen, pressing them to her stomach. What would it be like to feel her belly large and round? She didn't know. She'd never been pregnant, but the idea wasn't an unpleasant one.

Letting her gut lead, Callie made a spur-of-the-moment decision. Pregnancy was too big a risk. She wasn't in any shape, emotionally, to carry and raise a child. Hell, she didn't even have enough stamina to commit to owning a goldfish. Nightmares of her rootless childhood kept her from sleep most of the time, and even her own people were keeping a close watch on her. Sane, respectable federal agents didn't get knocked up with alien babies. "I don't want his baby."

The acid in her stomach called her a liar. She grimaced. She did. Suddenly she'd had enough of hiding behind the emotional walls she'd built to keep life at bay. God help her, she loved Iollan, and carrying his child would be a privilege.

She didn't know yet if she was even pregnant, but if she was, well, she'd deal with it. Goddamn it, she would. When down to the wire, she'd always looked out for herself. That's the way it was. That's the way it always would be.

Trust no one.

Her mouth quirked up at the thought.

Releasing a tremulous sigh, she lifted herself with a jerky heave. Her entire body trembled with the effort. Nevertheless, she drew back her shoulders and called on all her inner willpower to appear calm. Her stomach churned acid.

Standing up, she raised the lid, unzipped her pants, sat, and reached for the plastic cup. She hated testing of any sort. An invasion of privacy. But no one working for the government ever truly had a private life. Roger had confirmed that.

Not even my piss is my own.

Ten minutes later, she handed over the cup. "It's late and I'm tired," she told Yuan. "Any chance I can go home?"

Claiming her latest specimen, Yuan nodded. "Agent Reinke's waiting outside for you. He'll take you home."

Callie headed toward the door. Just as her hand hit the doorknob, the image of a tall, broad-shouldered man wriggled its way into her brain. Remembering the way Iollan had touched, kissed her, she shivered as a rush of heat filled her. Her body automatically responded to the slightest thought of his overwhelming maleness. Not impossible to do, given that she'd memorized every muscular conture. The rhythm of her heart was disrupted every time she thought about him.

Not good.

But inevitable. Head over ass, she'd tumbled into love without even seeing it coming.

She paused, turning back to Doctor Yuan. Her gaze rested

on the woman she was sure intended the Niviane Idesha to become an extinct species. "His name is Iollan Drake. Don't forget, he was a human being once. He still has feelings and needs—just like the rest of us. I'd appreciate it if you'd keep that in mind."

Yuan's mouth opened as if she intended to say something to the contrary. Then a thought seemed to strike her. Eyes softening, she nodded her understanding. "Of course."

22

Roger drove a discrete Saturn sedan, just the sort of car the mysterious G-men would be expected to travel in. The highway separating the government facilities from the city was long and dark, almost deserted at such a late hour.

Hands bunched nervously in her lap, Callie looked out over a gently rolling landscape lined with various hardwood trees. This part of Virginia was scenic, absolutely beautiful, part of what she'd like about living in the area. Accepting her position with the ASD would mean relocation. She still hadn't had time to stop and think about moving. Uncle Sam would foot the hotel bill for the agents until relocation was completed. Eventually, she'd have to take some well-deserved time off and move. Leaving the Richmond field office would be bittersweet. The old would be behind her. The future stretched ahead, wide open.

At least she hoped it did.

Part of the old she'd be leaving behind was her ex-lover. Roger Reinke would not be moving. His climb up the ladder in the ASD would be higher than hers, his role to coordinate and lead future searches for new clans of the Niviane Idesha. As for her own role . . .

Callie's brow wrinkled in thought. For some reason this still hadn't been clarified or confirmed. She'd believed she'd be working with Roger, but that had been quickly negated. Though she'd still be partnered with Paul Norton, their base of operations would be inside the ASD. For the time being, the only thing she'd be stalking was a desk and a computer terminal.

It occurred to her this might be because of her involvement with their newly caught prize.

A sire.

Who can make more of his kind. Capable of reproduction.

Callie shivered. Something she definitely didn't want to think about just this second. She'd think about it later, when necessary, such as when she'd missed her period.

Since they'd entered the car, Roger had been unusually quiet, saying barely two words since Yuan had released her from the examination room. Since Roger wouldn't tolerate any unnecessary sounds when he drove, the radio hadn't been turned on. Drawn out by the steady hum of the engine, the silence grew, unbearable and entirely too long.

Unable to take it anymore, Callie glanced his way. Lit by the glow of the dashboard, his face, half in shadow and half in light, looked angry. "You okay, Roger?"

Roger hedged. His jaw flexed. He kept his full attention riveted on the highway. "Fine," he answered tersely.

They say you never know someone until you live with them. Callie had never lived with Roger. But she had slept with him, and had gotten a bird's-eye view of his moods and storms. His actions were the quiet in the eye of the hurricane. Something was due to break. Soon.

Might as well get it over with.

She cleared her throat. "Something bothering you?"

Roger didn't look at her. "No."

Not true. Unspoken resentment emanated from him like sonar signals. "Really?"

He bristled. "Nothing."

"Anything I did?"

"I don't want to talk about it. Drop it, okay?"

"If I fucked up, tell me."

Roger drew a deep breath. He glanced over at her, his expression freezing even more. "The raid," he said finally. "Drake got you down pretty easily."

Callie let out a long breath. Ah, so that's what was on his mind. Couldn't blame him. On her mind, too. Like anyone could forget it. Not. "Drake's a big man—strong—and he isn't exactly human."

A narrow look. "You seem to like that."

Her defensive wall shot up. "Like what?"

Roger kept his hands on the wheel, gaze returning to the road. "Fucking Drake." His words came out in a snarl.

Gritting her teeth, Callie narrowed her eyes. She recognized the emotion in his words, dripping with unspoken jealousy. Oh, Christ! What was it about men that made them go all primitive and primal when the subject of a new lover came up?

She'd been crushed when Roger had left her. Regardless of how much it hurt, she had healed. Had survived.

"Is that what's got your goat?" she asked in annoyance. "That I slept with another man?"

"He isn't a man. He isn't anything that belongs on this planet."

"Felt like a man to me in every way that counts." Callie's smart-ass remark leapt out before she curbed her tongue.

A scowl froze Roger's face, and his breath rushed out between clenched teeth. "I saw what happened between you and Drake during the raid. I heard everything."

Callie's heart clutched painfully. The fine hairs rose at the back of her neck. Ah, shit. She felt herself go cold inside, all the way to the tips of her fingers. She didn't know what to do, what to say. Deny it? What would be the use? If she lied, he'd resent it even more when the truth came out. She had her honor, too. Lose that and she'd compromise everything.

Swallowing heavily, Callie decided to try to explain, and hope he'd understand. "I can't tell you what happened," she admitted through quivering lips. "When he got me down, something strange happened. Weird. He made a connection—"

Roger snorted. "I saw your connection. Looked like he was fucking you, to my eyes." He turned his narrow gaze her way. "And it looked like you were enjoying it. A lot."

Stiffening into stone, she tried to defend herself. "My God, Roger! You didn't see it all." Her hand rose to her bruised throat. "He had those fucking fangs of his right at my throat; he could've ripped me a new asshole. I knew it and he knew it."

Her words sounded unconvincing, even to her own ears. Spluttering and gasping, she sounded like the classic liar. She'd been fingered and rightly so. She'd practically committed treason.

Not good. Especially when one got caught.

She'd never be trusted again.

"I'm sorry," she said softly. "I fucked up."

Shooting her an ugly look, Roger suddenly swerved the car off onto a dark side road. The car slammed to a halt. Had she not been wearing a seat belt, Callie would've gone flying through the windshield.

"I might have forgiven that," he said in a voice gravelly with anger. "But after tonight, I don't think so. My God, you practically fucked him right before my eyes."

Callie stiffened. "That's unfair and you know it," she said quietly. "If I might remind you, you guys put my ass on the line without warning me what I'd be up against. I've been doing the best I can."

Roger's hand shot out. A hot flash of pain sizzled. Sparklers shot across her eyes. "*Doing* Drake in front of everyone wasn't part of the job description," he hissed. "Acting like a fucking whore, getting yourself off."

Hand flying to her mouth, Callie felt wetness trickle over her bottom lip. She drew her hand away. By the low illumination in the car, a bluish fluid covered her fingers.

Damn! Shocked by the blow, she lost the ability to think. Roger's outburst of irrational fury had caught her totally by surprise. She didn't hit back. She'd only make the bastard madder. And a mad Roger Reinke was a force to be reckoned with.

Without a word, she pointedly unlatched her seat belt and opened the door. Gravel crunched under her boots. Stumbling around to the front of the car, she leaned against the hood, fighting to catch her breath.

She heard Roger open his door. Slamming it, he stepped heavily, the rasp of rocks sounding ominous. Illuminated by the twin beams, he loomed in front of her.

Callie glanced toward the highway. Eerily quiet. Deserted.

"Get back in the car." Roger's voice snapped with impatience.

She gave him a narrow look. "No." She sucked in her fat lip, tasting her blood. "Not until I get an apology."

He laughed. "Apologize for what? Calling a whore a whore? Give me a break."

Callie snorted. "You sound a little jealous, Roger. What's the matter? Not getting enough?"

Wrong thing to say. Another hot branding iron slammed into her face.

Slamming back against the car, Callie raised her right arm to ward off his next blow. She dodged around his body, intending to run like hell. She wasn't fast enough.

Roger expertly blocked her, his leg knocking hers out from under her body. Holding out her arms to break her fall, she skidded on dozens of tiny rocks, palms scraped raw. She scrabbled forward on her knees, struggling to get away from this bizarre nightmare come to life.

A boot caught her in the side, flipping her neatly over onto her back. Her head struck bare ground. "Not so fast, babe," he panted. "I'm not finished with you."

Air vanishing from her lungs, Callie spluttered, gasping for breath. Fierce agony ripped through her. Blackness swam in front of her eyes. Fuck! Just what she didn't need. A jealous ex-lover on her ass. Roger seemed to have tossed sanity out with his brains. Right now he was thinking with his balls.

And his balls said she'd taken things with Drake one step too far.

Clutching her head, Callie tried to sit up. She blindly reached for the gun holstered under her left arm. Her grasping fingers grabbed nothing. She'd given up her gun to feed Iollan Drake and hadn't reclaimed her flak jacket and weapon before leaving the facility. Totally unarmed, she'd have to rely on her training to fight hand to hand.

It didn't get her very far.

A hand pushed her back. Two booted feet came down on either side of her body.

Callie gulped and looked up, trying to focus fuzzy vision on the giant. The fear in her stomach exploded and shivers swept over her in waves.

Hands on his hips, Roger looked down on her with a sneer backed up by a lot of angry male muscles and testosterone. "You always were a hot bitch, babe. I always said you'd fuck a snake if someone would hold its head."

Callie looked up between his muscular thighs. She clenched her fists, striking out at his crotch. Vision skewed, she missed. "Better to fuck a snake than you, asshole."

A chuckle slid from the back of Roger's throat. "Maybe we should test that theory right now." He bent and powerful fingers circled her arms. Hefting her to her feet, he planted her against the hood of the car.

Callie dug her heels into the fender and bucked to throw his heavy weight off. The car bounced from their combined weight. Roger's heavier body, greater length, and unyielding physical strength gave the older agent every advantage. Mix in a black belt in karate and hand-to-hand combat training in the military, and an efficient killing machine emerged.

Though she fought like hell, her limited strength wasn't getting her far. Outclassed and outmaneuvered, she had to admit defeat. "Let go, you big ape!"

Stubbornly holding his place, Roger easily pinned her arms behind her back. "I think the correct word is Neanderthal."

She spat at him. "Bastard."

Roger lifted a leg between hers, jabbing his knee up between her legs. The pressure of his thigh was right against her crotch. The uncomfortable friction verged on painful. He chuckled. "You're about to find out how true that is." His vicious tone sizzled across her ears, burning straight into her soul.

Silence.

Callie forced herself not to wince. A violent shiver shook her, leaving her muscles quivering like jelly. Apprehension constricted her throat, but just barely. Roger's jealousy was like a rabid animal, raging and ready to devour.

You'll survive this. You know you will.

An acid smile twisted Roger's mouth. He ignored her pointed silence. "Look at you. Legs spread open, just the way I remember. Instead of letting that freak poke you, why don't you come back to where you got it so good to begin with?" Knee pressing, his heavy-lidded gaze smoldered.

Feeling the pressure to the center of her chest, Callie glared back. Impossible not to be baited. "You're the one who gave it up," she sneered. "Remember? Right now, there isn't a piece of you I know, remember, or want." Talk much braver than she felt.

Roger Reinke gave her a brutal stare. One of his hands left her wrists. He groped between her legs. Thick fingers pressed against her clit, rubbing. "In a few minutes you'll remember everything—and then some."

Callie's mouth went bone dry. The ultimate control a man had over a woman. She forced down another surge of panic. Not a bluff. "Raping me isn't the way to make me remember."

Skewering her with a leer, he rubbed with painful friction. "You can't rape the willing, babe." He said slyly, "I bet if I dipped into you right now, you'd be dripping."

Willing? Her left foot!

Callie tried to wiggle away. No go. He held like Super Glue. She glared at her tormentor. "You want to bet?"

He snorted and rolled his eyes. The flat of his hand slammed into her cheek. "I'd win, honey." Hand leaving her crotch, he rubbed roughly over her belly, and then her breast. Finding one full mound, he squeezed. "If you want to keep your job and stay near that freak you like fucking, you'll keep your mouth shut and take whatever I give you." Insistent hands pulled at the waistband of her pants, working the button open, the zipper down. "Otherwise, you'll be right in there with him. In a cold dark cell where no one will ever see or hear from you again."

Callie glared at him through narrowed eyes. "If you have to get your fucking rocks off, Roger, hurry up. I'm cold."

Snorting a chuckle, Roger grabbed her by the shoulders and spun her around. Fingers digging into the back of her neck like iron bands, he pushed her face against the hood. "That's my girl. I know what you like. The more painful it is, the better you like it."

Not when it comes with getting the shit beaten out of me.

Roger tugged her pants down. "Ready to be fucked right,

honey?" His zipper came down and he aligned his hips with hers. A hot pulsing cock pressed intently against her ass.

She braced her palms against the hood. "Go head and knock off a piece if it'll make you feel like a man."

Roger chuckled evilly. His legs pressed against hers. "That and more, baby."

The blood emptied from Callie's head, rushing straight to her clit with a mind-spinning speed. The small organ pulsed with new sensitivity. A lover of rough sex, she moaned raggedly.

A knowing chuckle. "I know how you like it." Roger's stance shifted, the thick round head of his cock brushing through her labia.

Callie fought to pull her scattered thoughts together. "Then do it," she snarled back.

"With pleasure." Roger jammed his cock in deep, one long and painful stroke of pure invasion, forcing himself as deep as physically possible.

Nipples tightening, Callie felt every thought in her skull evaporate. Jaw muscles straining against the fire ripping through her insides, she breathed heavily, sizzling from the top of her spine to the tip of her toes.

"Are you enjoying this, babe?" he managed to grate out.

Choking past the pulse beating in her throat, she spat. "I'll live, but you'll always be an asshole."

Jerking his hips even more forcefully against hers, Roger slapped her across the ass. More heat blazed. "Still like the pain, baby?"

Blood running hot, she sucked in a harsh breath. "Better than I like you."

Unrelenting, Roger slid his cock out of her and thrust it up her rectum. He sprawled on top of her, pinning her writhing body under his larger girth. Pressing his chin into her shoulder, he breathed across her ear. "Just a little reminder of who was there first."

Every nerve ending below Callie's waist burst anew into painful life. The pain scorched. Humiliation scalded like acid. Nostrils flaring, she panted through her mouth to lessen the ache. She was afraid, but angry.

Refusing to let her mind linger on the sensations, she began to tremble, fingers digging into the metal hood under her hands. "That hurts, you bastard!"

Roger's fingers dug deeper into her hips. His cock speared again and again. "Too bad, bitch."

Driven by jealousy and rage, Roger Reinke was out of control. He grabbed a handful of her hair, wrenching back her head, brutally driving his erection as deeply as physically possible.

Callie groaned in violent protest and squirmed beneath him. Her legs shook and her anal muscles involuntarily gripped his cock. Unwanted heat stabbed her bowels, coiling between her legs. She whimpered in defiance, and desire. The darker half of her soul liked the pain, damn it!

Roger held her tighter and jabbed.

Callie gasped. Pressing her knees against the fender, she arched up against Roger's broad chest. Her moans increased with the demands of a body spinning out of control. Forced or not, denying her need for physical satisfaction was impossible. Helping Iollan had only served to whet her desire for full penetration.

Aching with the sheer intensity of her secret shame, Callie gave in to his intense possession. Climax roared in, primitive and raw, a fireball of sensation erupting between her thighs. A ferocious scream broke from deep inside her throat as she came apart in fierce surrender.

Panting, slicked in the sweat of the aroused male, Roger came, filling her with hot semen, gripping her hips so forcefully he bruised her skin. A moment later he released her. Stepping back, he zipped his pants as if nothing had happened.

The prick.

Callie slid down the hood and fell face forward onto the ground in a limp heap. Spatters of red, white, and blue exploded like fireworks behind her eyes. Feeling as though she was drowning in a murky pool, she realized the brutality of his actions made her sick.

Roger coldly prodded her with a boot as if nothing had happened. "Get up." A cruel laugh escaped him. "It's not like you haven't had it like that before." Turning away, his boots crunched heavily on the gravel.

Head bowed, tears pricking her eyes, Callie bit back an expletive. Her whole mind, her whole soul, ached with acute revulsion. Deep within her psyche, something sounded. Her initial shock was fading, but what was left in its place was even worse, a sick kind of anxiety, coupled with something more, something she dared not analyze.

Revolted at how eager her body had been to find pleasure in the pain, Callie curled her fingers into angry claws.

Because she'd enjoyed what he'd done.

She refused to think about it. Some truths were too unbearable. Loathing herself, spasms in her guts seemed to shake her entire being. *No. No. No.* Brutality and force were unacceptable, under any circumstance.

Callie looked up at him through sparking eyes. "Is this what you did to the other women, Roger? Have a little fun before you killed them and dumped the bodies?"

That stopped him dead in his tracks.

Whirling furiously, Roger glared down. "Who told you that?"

She knew then she'd hit a sore spot. Guilty as charged.

Her lips twisted. "I have two fucking eyes. How many people have you mistaken for *them*, only to find out they're still one of *us*?"

Roger's answer came, chillingly precise. "Collateral damage." He made a disgusted noise. "You hang with the enemy, you die with the enemy."

Her heart pounded with long, jarring beats. "Easier to keep blaming Drake, isn't it? How convenient for your conscience."

With a few quick strides, Roger Reinke came within kicking distance. Dropping onto his haunches, he struck her backhanded. "If you are a wise woman, you will keep your eyes closed and your mouth shut."

A burning sensation raked her face. Bastard! she wanted to scream. Shaking off the blow, she spat at him. "Why should I?"

Roger reached out and caught her under the chin. He wrenched back her head. "What's going on here is bigger than you think. And anyone who jeopardizes that will be considered expendable." He tightened his grip, fingers digging painfully into soft skin. "Do I make myself clear?"

Unable to move her head even a fraction of an inch, Callie silently indicated her compliance. She comprehended fully the change in him then, and it chilled her to the bone.

Callie understood. Perfectly. No choice but to agree. Didn't mean she had to like it. Didn't mean she had to play by their rules. It did mean she'd have to tread carefully. And never get caught without her gun again. Next time, she'd kill him. And there would be a *next time*.

Guaranteed.

23

Callie came tripping into work at ten AM, an hour later than scheduled. Given the prior night, she'd thought about calling in sick and spending the day in bed. Roger had used a pretty heavy hand on her, giving her a couple of nice bruises on her face and a fat lip. Then she remembered Iollan Drake. Held in the cells below ground in solitary confinement, chained like an animal. No way she'd let him go through that alone.

Suck it up and move on.

She had covered the bruises with heavy foundation, and a lot of luminous lipstick had made her fat lip look Angelina Jolie sexy. Add dark glasses and she looked like any woman who'd had the shit kicked out of her by an ex-lover. Everyone noticed, but no one dared say a word.

Above ground the ASD offices, simply called the International Division of Scientific Research or IDSR on the outside, boasted a nice architectural design with plenty of light and space. Aside from the fanatically high level of security, it seemed like any other government building. Though the offices she'd share with Paul Norton weren't corner prime with a terrific view, they were serviceable.

Already at work by the time she walked in, Norton hunched over his desk, which was piled high with folders, coffee cups, Post-it Notes, and tablets filled with scribbles that would be totally useless to anyone else. Norton operated in total chaos and knew in a second which pile he needed something from.

Callie, on the other hand, usually couldn't find shit, even when at a desk as neat as a pin. Her habit of plastering everything with Post-its didn't help. She invariably lost them, no matter how carefully she applied them to her bulletin board, monitor, and whatever surface might be handy for sticking.

She schlepped over to her desk and collapsed into her chair with a heavy sigh. She needed to be filling out her paperwork, writing up the many reports required of an agent. *Piss on that.* Coffee and cigarettes at hand, she planned on taking it easy for a few days. She doubted Roger Reinke would say a word to her. Passing her in the hallway on her way in, he'd averted his eyes and passed her without acknowledgment.

Callie had smiled her sweetest, said "Good morning," and breezed on her way. Revenge is a dish best eaten cold, she reminded herself. Just a matter of time.

She glanced at her partner. Shaved and shorn of his beard and moustache, Paul Norton had put on his good glasses and his best suit, which wasn't saying much. A street rat, Norton worked better undercover than he did in the requisite suit and tie. His suit was rumpled, tie undone, and his glasses were perched half-crookedly on his nose. With his short stature and owlish appearance he looked more like a harried businessman than a hard-nosed government agent.

Norton looked up, doing a double take when she slid off her dark glasses. "What the fuck happened to you?"

Callie sipped her coffee, a double mocha latte, extra dark

and strong. She lit up a cigarette, also a no-no in the nonsmoking building. She'd stolen an ashtray from the hotel. Let Uncle Sam pick it up. "I ran into the bathroom door last night."

Norton clearly didn't believe her. "Twice?"

Callie wasn't in a mood to be honest at the moment. "Yeah, twice." She shrugged. "No big deal." She sucked on her cigarette, relishing the burn on the back of her throat. The nicotine and caffeine weren't helping her woozy stomach, promoting those pesky thoughts of pregnancy. *I am not knocked up.*

Norton didn't look convinced by her lie. "If you say so."

She puffed some more. "I say so."

He adjusted his glasses, straightening the frames. "Just more shit we have to cover up, I suppose," he muttered.

Callie nodded in agreement. "That and then some." She eyed her glum partner. "What's the matter? You look like someone ran over your dog."

Norton shook his head in dismissal. "Nothing." Sitting up straight, he busied himself with a couple of files spread across his desk.

Curiosity grabbed her. "What are you working on?" Knowing Norton, he'd finished his reports, in triplicate. The little fucker typed ninety words a minute without looking at the keyboard. Callie managed fifty on a good day.

Norton shifted, uncomfortably clearing his throat. "You ever get the feeling you're in over your head?" The question came out of nowhere.

Callie flicked the ash off her cigarette, leaning back in her chair. Comfortable thing, too. Nice place to rest an ass all day. Maybe getting out of fieldwork would be the best thing, especially since Professor Forque had indicated she'd be working closely with Drake—the sole reason she'd decided to take this transfer. Conscience wouldn't let her refuse.

She winced. Her heart wouldn't allow it either.

236 / *Devyn Quinn*

A frown tugged her lips down. "Truthfully? I've felt like that since the day I woke up with a needle in my arm and someone else walking around in my head."

Norton gave her a tight grin. "It was shitty of them not to tell you what you were up against."

Callie arched a brow. "You knew?"

A slight nod. Guilt dripped. "I was told about a week before they brought you in. Nobody managed to get near Drake, so they tossed your ass out there as bait."

Stomach twisting, Callie snuffed out her cigarette. Suddenly the damn thing didn't taste so good. In fact, there was a bad taste in her mouth, acidic and bitter. "So I've since figured out."

Norton picked up a pen, fiddling nervously. For the first time, Callie noticed how alarmingly pale and wrung out he looked. Like a man who hadn't slept in weeks. "You want to know what's bad about this?"

His question flooded her mind and set her bowels to knotting. "That they're cutting those fuckers up alive and awake?" Sarcasm dripped.

Taking off his glasses and briefly pinching the bridge of his nose, Norton shook his head. "That's already bad enough. But no. What bothers me is we don't know what they plan to do with them."

Callie's stomach roiled. "Medical advances for the human race is what I've gathered they're looking at. I'm no scientist, but the DNA of the Niviane Idesha seems to merge very well with human DNA. I'm going to assume those they've captured were one hundred percent human at one time."

Norton's throat worked. He glanced over his shoulder as if afraid other eyes watched. Very possible. Every action, from e-mail to internal reports, was logged and examined by superiors. You couldn't take a piss or grab a cup of coffee without passing security.

"That's the trouble." Norton's voice dropped to the level of a whisper. "They're not treating them like anything human, just test subjects without feelings or any sort of intelligence. They've got their hands on living aliens—aliens with abilities we can only dream about. Abilities I don't believe just any man was meant to have. The Niviane Idesha cull and choose among us for a reason. You've been chosen. You know that."

Scary words. Provocative words.

A prickle of alarm rushed up her spine. In the back of her mind, she'd been thinking the same thing, and wondering: what exactly did the scientists intend to do with the species?

Norton opened one of the folders on his desk. "I've been studying the history of the ASD and its objectives—that is, what bits they'll let me see. Most of it's classified."

Callie snorted. "Like that's a surprise. Don't forget, we're working on a need-to-know basis."

Norton made a sour face. "I hate that." Turning to his monitor, he logged into the system via a GUI that took users into the main ASD application, if their level of access allowed it. Both Callie and Norton were still at level one, pretty basic stuff. Cases, basic history, resources. Nothing fancy. "Which is why I was working to get full access. I want to see Yuan's e-mails."

Her astonishment was huge, but quickly absorbed. Rising from her chair, she walked around to his desk. She bent over his shoulder, close to his ear. "You're not thinking of doing what I think you are?"

Norton nodded. "You bet your ass. I got Professor Forque to give me his user ID and password."

"Willingly?" she asked.

"More or less." Norton gave a sheepish grin. "I can be very persuasive when motivated."

Callie's breath hitched in surprise. Hearing his words, her fingers dug into his shoulder. "And you think Forque can be trusted."

"I made sure he could." Norton looked away. "I also made sure he'd keep his mouth shut."

Callie knew better than to ask what he'd done. "If Forque spills, you'll lose more than your career. They'd fire your ass and shove you in a place so dark no one would ever find you." Moreover, telling her his plans had just placed her own feet on very thin ice.

A sigh shuddered out of him. "Do I look like I fucking care? Every time I shut my eyes, I keep seeing that poor bastard Doctor Yuan so proudly displayed." He sucked in a breath, not waiting for an answer. "What they are doing is evil. Pure evil."

"You think you can stop it?" she asked, her voice low.

Norton nodded at his monitor. "I'm taking this directly over Roger's head, to Sam Faber. If he won't listen, I'll go to a friend in Congress, or even the media."

The coffee Callie had drank felt like lead in her stomach now. "That's crazy, Paul."

Norton paused, as if mulling her words. "I have a conscience, Callie. This can't continue." Gaze hard as rocks, he frowned more deeply. "Fucking career be damned, I won't be a part of any kind of genocide."

Logic tried to step in. Her partner was about to throw his career—hell, his life—away. She had to do something to prevent Norton from making a fatal mistake. "They're not human. The only way to know about them is to study them. A few may have to—" Her eyes pinched closed as her vision wavered, and her throat tightened. Though her words seemed to make sense, she no more believed them than she believed in the tooth fairy.

Norton turned in his chair and put a hand on her arm. "They may not be human, but they aren't animals, either. You know that more than any of us."

She flushed hot all over. She locked gazes with Norton. His eyes glittered with righteous anger. Mind warring with her heart, she had to make a decision. She imagined herself pregnant. Imagined herself as the mother of Iollan Drake's child. Of losing custody of that hybrid child because it wasn't entirely human. Whether boy or girl, that child would be taken from her, poked and prodded—dissected—in the name of scientific discovery. Her greatest fear, losing her family, would again be realized. Such a fate for her child was a terrifying prospect, and something she couldn't let happen.

Turn Norton in or help him reveal the truth.

The answer was a no-brainer.

She straightened her shoulders. Things were about to get interesting. "Let me help you. I can get in without compromising you or Forque."

Norton looked at his monitor and then back up at her. "You sure?"

Callie nodded, making her decision firm. "Yes, I am."

"Do it," Norton said, eyes flashing.

She nodded. "Scoot over then and let me go to work."

They traded places.

"What are you going to do?" he asked.

Her lips worked as she raked them with her teeth. "You know the military trained me to hack enemy computers. Well, I never forgot how, my friend." Thinking fast, she set her fingers in motion. She immediately disabled the keystroking program that recorded a user's every action. "Never thought I'd be doing this to one of ours. The network's tight, but you had the right idea. We just have to make it look like we belong there."

Callie logged into an underground hacker's resource via the Internet. "There are ways around everything, as long as you know where to find the information."

Norton gave a lopsided grin. "And you know how to do that?"

Callie quickly found what she was looking for. She grinned at the ease.

After a number of clicks, she was connected to the network, logged on as JForrester, a name she made up. With administrator rights, she could do anything and go anywhere she wanted.

Norton whistled under his breath. "How the hell did you do that?"

Callie shrugged. "It's what happens when you know how to use your power for evil."

"Remind me not to piss you off."

Her fingers hovered over the keys. *No big thing*, she assured herself. *Yeah, right.* Breaking into the database that housed highly classified material wasn't exactly something she attempted every day of the week. Not only would her career be toast if she was caught, she'd be serving a long stretch behind iron bars.

Conscience niggled. As an agent who'd sworn an oath to protect her country she had no right to do this. But as a human being, she had the moral obligation to find out the truth. Standing by while another race was destroyed for being different wasn't ethical or right.

And if she got caught? *Without justice, there is just us*, she reminded herself. *And the unjust.*

"Shall we?" she asked. If at all possible, she had to find out what the ASD had planned for the Niviane Idesha.

Her partner nodded. "Let's go."

Snorting a chuckle, Callie opened the file and began to read. A second later, she stopped and pointed. "Look at this."

Norton bent close to the screen, his eyes tracing Callie's finger. He read, "Project Shadow-Wing."

The tips of her fingers tingled. "Who thinks up these funky names for missions anyway?"

A look passed between them, a shared signal only partners knew and understood from each other. This look said they were both about to be hip deep in a lot of secret shit.

And neither wanted to back down.

Norton shook his head. "Don't know. But it sounds ominous."

Callie scanned the screen, her pulse thrumming. "Guess we'll find out." She continued to scan the information. They'd hit gold, but didn't know it yet. The data she'd pulled up was massive and complicated. She didn't understand a lot of it. What she did understand chilled her to the bone.

Silence thickened as they came across the same thing.

Norton stared at Callie as if he was unable to believe his eyes. "Am I reading this right?" He shook his head in awe. "Are they planning to structure a breed of alien-human hybrids?" He ran his hands through his hair, clearly upset.

Scrolling down, Callie caught Iollan Drake's name. "*Breed purity.*" "*Implementation of desired traits.*"

She gave herself a second to process what she'd read, then cleared her throat. "Not hybrids, Norton. Full-blooded. They're planning to harvest stem cells from fertilized embryos and use them to reconfigure human traits with those of the Niviane Idesha. They've got their sire now. The rest weren't useful; that's why they were so focused on Iollan." She pressed a hand against her stomach, which slowly did a somersault. Her voice wavered. "If they have their way, they're going to try and create a new race of superhumans."

"Selective breeding to create a new race," Norton muttered. That's—" He stumbled, at a loss for words.

A frisson of tension mingling with excitement raced up Callie's spine. It didn't seem possible. "Playing God."

Wanting to dig deeper, she came to an entry made by Doctor Yuan. Her observations were almost giddy. Yuan had tied her whole life up in studying the Niviane Idesha. Clearly she respected them as a species, but held little regard for them as individuals, as beings with needs or feelings.

Because he was such a prize, a first, Iollan would be safe. Guarded like Fort Knox, but he wouldn't be grievously mishandled. He'd soon be moved from solitary confinement to a quarantine cell, more hospitable and, she hoped, more comfortable. No more drugs were to be administered, either. Plans for testing of his full abilities as a shifter would soon commence.

One thing became glaringly clear as she read through the Shadow-Wing file. Through the use of stem cells, Doctor Yuan was confident once they found and destroyed the blood-hunger gene in the vampires, an alien-human hybrid would be the improved species, one that should prevail through future generations. Given time, lines between the two would begin to blur until only a single master race existed.

The implications hit her square in the stomach. Though still only a projection of science in the planning stages, Project Shadow-Wing provided a chilling glimpse of what the project's team believed themselves capable of.

A frown marred Paul Norton's imperfect features. His silence told her he was disturbed. Deeply disturbed. His breath huffed out. "Do they really think they can pull this off?"

Norton's words registered somewhere inside Callie's brain. She tried to shake off her fear and failed.

The research behind the program was an active and ongoing thing. The bits and pieces she understood seemed to chart remarkable progress. The two species, human and alien, appeared to merge seamlessly. Too much so for comfort. "They're not thinking about it. They're doing it. Stem cell study and exploration is already making leaps and bounds."

Norton shuddered. "God help us all, then."

Callie's body felt rigid, every tendon locked into place in front of the computer she worked at. "That might not be enough," she grated tightly. "It's said history is doomed to repeat itself." A short laugh escaped her, the precursor to hysteria. She quickly nipped panic in the bud. No time to make mistakes. "This isn't the first time someone's tried to create a master race."

A huge weight rolled onto her conscience. Without knowing it at the time, she'd given them the key to opening the forbidden box when she'd helped capture Iollan Drake.

Fingers shaking, she closed that file and opened another, not really knowing where she was heading. A subdirectory of the ASD agents' files came up, her own among them.

Norton pointed. "Personnel files? Mine's got my badge number beside it."

Callie noted her own. "So does mine." Beside it was another set of numbers, looking oddly like a date. Two weeks into the future. Curiosity told her to press on.

Seconds later, her complete profile lit up the screen. Childhood, education, military service and training, college transcripts, and bureau service record. There was an eerie pause as she found out what the date meant.

Listed across from the birth date was the same date, only it was listed under *date of death*. Under that, for cause of death, a single word has been typed in: TERMINATED.

Callie stopped reading. A cold shock of fear washed through her body. She hesitated, momentarily paralyzed by what she'd read. A rush of panic caused her heart to miss a beat. She blinked, hoping her mind wasn't playing tricks. It wasn't.

Her palms were suddenly wet enough to leave prints on the desktop. Her psyche immediately veered into panic. Roger Reinke's prophetic warning rose in the forefront of her brain, echoing soundlessly in her ears. "Everyone is expendable," she murmured.

Norton pressed a hand to her shoulder. "This isn't good."

No time to freeze.

Callie quickly yanked her thoughts back in line and checked Norton's file. Thankfully blank. She breathed a sigh of relief for her partner. "No shit."

Lips compressing into a line, Norton gave her a look burning with disgust. "They've marked you for assassination."

Gooseflesh rose on her arms. Her mind whirled. Tendrils of

fear crawled in her stomach, coiling into spirals that seemed to rope around her lungs and heart. "Why? What the fuck did I—" Clarity hit her before the words finished leaving her mouth.

She'd gotten too close to Iollan Drake. Making love to Iollan had reverted from being strictly for the job to a personal thing. She'd lost contact with her objectivity, with the purpose of the mission. She'd become intimately involved—something the bureau clearly wasn't going to allow.

Face losing all color, Norton smiled a grimace full of acid. "Copy it," he hissed. "All of it. Now. We need every bit of this."

Barely able to think straight, Callie slid a blank CD into the burner. She squinted as the drive went into motion, mentally willing it to burn the disk faster.

Her thoughts turned dark. She didn't want to believe science fiction had turned into science fact. Mankind always seemed to be determined to meddle with things best left unexplored. Humans were dominance crazed to the point of insanity. No amount of suffering and destruction would stop the march toward the future.

She snapped out of her reverie. "At least you're safe."

A harsh laugh escaped him. "Not for fucking long, I bet."

She forced her attention back to the screen, memorizing as much as humanly possible. A few minutes later, the copied disk popped out.

Callie handed it to Norton. She quickly logged off. "Can you get it out of here?"

Norton tossed her a look that wasn't exactly brimming with confidence. Making things disappear was his specialty, but in this case he'd be lucky if he made it outside to the parking lot. "I think so." He tucked the disk into an inner pocket of his jacket.

Muscles tensing, Callie shuddered. "Don't think it, know it,

Paul. Having that disk puts you right on my level. Both of us
have grass for asses now."

As though carrying a heavy burden, Norton pulled his
shoulders back slightly. "I'll make today the day I vanish. I suggest you do the same." He reached for her hand, giving it a
squeeze. "When you walk out of here today, don't look back."

"I won't."

Right then the phone on her desk rang. Their gazes locked.
"This ain't no coincidence," Norton said.

Callie got up and walked to her desk. The phone bleated, a
second and third time. "Should I?"

Norton advised. "Act normal."

She answered. "Whitten."

Forque's voice filled her ear. "We need to meet," he said by
way of a greeting.

Her eyebrows shot up. "Oh?"

"We have a problem," Forque started to explain.

Callie didn't need to hear any more. She knew what the
problem was.

Iollan.

"I'm on my way."

24

Callie walked beside Professor Forque. As they passed the guard's station, the sliding glass door in front of them made a whooshing sound when it slid open to admit them to the cell block. They quickly stepped through. A sucking sound commenced when the door slid shut again.

Hearing the door slide back into place went across her senses like fingernails across a chalkboard. Panic clawed at her throat. She swallowed, feeling nauseated. Her stomach churned. It dimly occurred to her that she might be walking into a trap—that there would be no going back to a free civilization. The jail cell she might be looking at could be her own if her computer-hacking intrusion had been detected.

That seemed not to be the case. For now.

"Very secure," she commented of the facilities. The floor felt like glue under her feet. The farther she progressed, the more she felt oppressed and hopeless.

Forque nodded, pleased. "We've had it specially designed for holding the Niviane Idesha. Every inch of this area is hermetically sealed. We want to encourage them to use their shifting abilities—all within a controlled environment, of course."

Callie gave a tight smile. "Of course," she said, trying to inject some conviction into her voice. She failed. Right now she wasn't very interested in the ASD facilities. She already knew getting out was damn near impossible.

The bureau had become like the tip of a sword in her back. According to the file she'd read, her death would take place in two weeks. There were so many ways for murder to be delivered. One thing was certain, though. However the fatal blow was dealt, she'd probably have never seen it coming.

Forewarned was forearmed.

She drew a deep breath, fighting to keep calm. Showing her fear would be the worst thing to do. Weapon holstered at her side, she'd already made the decision to defend herself if necessary. Make a move on her and she'd pull her gun and take as many men with her as possible. She might crash and burn, but she wasn't going alone.

Forque ignored her lackluster tone, lumbering along in high gear. He led her down a hallway punctuated with more ominous-looking doors. If he'd noticed her obviously bruised face, it didn't register on his face. Other concerns harried him.

"We've moved Drake into more comfortable surroundings this morning," the professor began to explain. "Unfortunately, he's responding poorly to his surroundings."

Hardly a surprise. The previous night's memory leapt into her mind. Remembering the evil way they'd cuffed Iollan, she shivered. "Oh?"

Readjusting his glasses, Forque frowned. The lines in his face looked taut. "Although they appear to be a perfectly intelligent species, in captivity they seem to revert to a level of low primitive intelligence. Their actions are animalistic, not something you'd expect in such an evolved species."

She frowned. Despite her general disgust for the scientific research of the center, she felt that Forque at least took a human interest in the Niviane Idesha. He seemed to want to understand and communicate with them. Yuan, on the other hand, only seemed to want them on her table for dissection.

Callie barely stomached the sight of Akemi Yuan. Every time she thought about Yuan, she pictured the proverbial mad scientist locked away in some lightning-lit stone tower, waiting for the right strike to raise the beast.

She snapped out of her thoughts and focused on the discussion at hand. "I doubt I'd be feeling very friendly if someone had slapped the cuffs on and thrown me into an empty cell," she said. "Of course they feel threatened. Anyone who wants to survive would. That only makes sense."

Serious-faced, the older man sailed ahead, his massive steps threatening to leave Callie in the dust. "Perfectly understandable," he said. "I doubt I'd feel very friendly if the situation was reversed. Putting them in these glorified cages is ridiculous. I've argued for a more diplomatic approach, but it's fallen on deaf ears."

She quickened her steps. A light shiver shimmied down her spine. "Then why don't you try that?" she suggested.

Forque gave her a grim smile. "In military minds, anything that doesn't look or act human is considered a threat," he returned with evident sarcasm, unintentionally revealing the thorn in his side. "We're going to stomp until the Niviane Idesha are as extinct as saber-toothed tigers."

A chill trickled down Callie's spine. She tucked that bit of information away in her mental file, and alarm tightened her chest.

God proposes, man disposes. A vivid memory of Iollan holding her, kissing her, caused her throat to tighten. She swallowed, unable to imagine losing him.

Callie knew then she was in too deep, and over her head.

Her palms started to sweat. What to say after such a remark? Nothing useful.

Their walk down the hall ended abruptly, relieving her of the necessity of a rejoinder.

Wringing his hands in obvious frustration, Forque stopped. "Here we are."

Like other cell doors Callie had seen on this level, it had a face of glass with wire mesh pressed between its layers. A keypad on the wall beside it controlled the locking mechanisms.

The fact that she still had full security clearance proved that her little intrusion into the system hadn't been detected. Norton had the disk. Norton's terminal had been used. If push came to shove, she'd plead innocent.

Callie slammed the door in her skull on that idea. No way she'd let Norton take the fall alone. They'd gone into the plan to expose the project together. No backing out now. Somehow, she'd have to make Iollan understand she wasn't planning to abandon him.

Forque stepped aside to allow her access to the narrow window. "Take a look."

She stepped up to the window. Inside she saw a sort of apartment, a combination living and kitchen area. Narrow cabinets over an even narrower counter allowed for the storage of personal items. A neatly made bed occupied one section. A table with bench seats was attached to an opposite wall, and a tiny fold-down desk and chair served as the only other furniture. Walls and ceilings were stark white. In the open arrangement there was nowhere to hide except in the bathroom. At least some basic privacy was granted.

The cell—and it was just that—appeared empty.

Forque tapped her on the shoulder and directed her attention toward the farthest corner. "There." His voice was an unnecessary whisper. "He won't move."

Callie's gaze settled on Iollan Drake. Professor Forque didn't

250 / Devyn Quinn

have to say anything else. She saw the problem for herself. Her thumping heart leapt into her throat, threatening to cut off her air.

Crouched in a corner, Iollan Drake sat, his back to the wall. Wrists and neck still cruelly cuffed, he stared straight ahead, unblinking and ominously immobile. Open but unfocused, his eyes were dull, pale, and flat. The brilliant copper sheen of them had faded to a dull amber shade. Through the torn material of his shirt, his forearms and neck were a mass of deep, vicious scratches. He'd clearly tried to tear off his restraints, to the point of self-mutilation.

Iollan didn't appear human. His brow thickly ridged, he bared his canines in a snarl, half-pain, half-despair. His skin was ashen, gray with the poison of the silver spikes seeping into his system. God, he looked . . . fragile.

Seeing him, Callie felt her heart twist in pity and shame. She couldn't speak. Tears threatened. She successfully blinked them back. It was a shame that people who called themselves rational and intelligent would needlessly inflict pain on another living entity, alien or not. It upset her to think this beautiful, magnificent man had been reduced to little more than a shell of his former self because of what he wasn't. Human.

Fury hit. "Jesus Christ, can't you see you're killing him with those things?" She looked again, wincing. "It's almost like he's going into shock. Catatonic."

Antsy, Forque searched her face. "We tried to get the restraints off. He won't let us near him."

Callie wanted to throttle the living shit out of him. She had to suck in a breath to calm herself. "Try harder."

Forque, face white as milk, countered, "We've noticed he's more responsive when you're with him."

Her glare withered. Her palm just ached for a strike at his stupid face. "Maybe that's because I treat him like a man instead of a circus freak," she shot back between gritted teeth.

Pale and pensive, the professor acquiesced. "The bond you've developed with him is undeniable. We'd like you to continue working with the subject on an exclusive basis."

Callie winced as soon as the words were out of his mouth. She should have expected this, known exactly what Forque wanted when he'd summoned her to his office for a meeting. Listening in on the call, Paul Norton had shaken his head and mouthed a silent "No!" The actions of the bureau had been too volatile for his comfort zone.

Exclusive basis automatically implied a long-term commitment. Given that she and Norton were scheming to expose the project and its inhumane practices, lingering unnecessarily wouldn't be possible much longer. Her own life hovered on the line. If she didn't get out now, she never would.

An excruciating decision.

Walking away from the bureau might be the only way to save his life, but where would that leave him in the meantime? Alone.

Her conscience prodded in protest. Hands flexing at her sides, Callie looked back into the cell, hating the sight. Christ. Could she leave Iollan without even saying good-bye or trying to explain what she had planned?

Her feelings chimed in with a volume and intensity difficult to ignore. Walk away and she'd surely be signing his death warrant. A cold, damp sweat rose on her skin. In captivity, Iollan wouldn't survive. She knew that as surely as she knew her own life wouldn't be worth a shit if she didn't try to help him before she skipped out.

Damn it. She hadn't expected to fall in love.

The thought jolted. How unbelievable. But how wonderful, in a strange and bizarre kind of way.

Torn between honoring the greater cause and duty to a single cause, Callie had a decision to make. A no-going-back decision. Step into that cell with Iollan and she might never step out again. There might never be another chance for her to walk away from the federal compound a free woman.

It was a risk she had to take. Leave now and Iollan probably wouldn't survive the night.

Callie trembled, barely able to stop her words. She shouldn't be feeling this way, shouldn't let her desire for Iollan override her own instincts for self-preservation. "I'll do what I can."

Forque looked relieved. "Thank you." He started to punch a series of numbers in the keypad.

She pointedly cleared her throat. Her mouth felt parched. "Those cuffs are going to have to come off. No telling what damage that shit Yuan pumped into him last night is doing to his system."

Extracting a key ring from his coat pocket, Forque selected a key and handed it over. "I warned her not to go so heavily with the sedatives. We don't fully understand this species' biology yet. If the damages are irreversible, he'll be useless for study." He sighed. "If he's even able, he'll need to feed. Now that we know they need their sustenance straight from the source . . ." A slight rush of red blotted his already ruddy cheeks.

Fingers curling around the precious key, Callie trembled, unable to stop her reaction to the thought of Iollan's lips on her pulse. Blood rushed through her veins, flooding her with an erotic warmth. The attraction she felt for Iollan was both powerful and absolutely tangible. Keeping an objective distance had ceased to be possible.

Watery blue eyes searched every feature of her face. "Are you all right, Agent Whitten?"

Nipples tingling, Callie almost trembled into pieces. She and Iollan had forged a bond, an unbreakable connection between—dare she think it?—mates. He'd entered more than her body. He'd crossed the threshold into her mind. What they shared went beyond explanation or mere words.

Fear cooled the warmth trickling between her thighs. "I'm fine," she bit out.

The professor's gaze searched her face. "If this is something you can't do, perhaps we can find a surrogate donor."

The words went all over her like a dash of ice water. Surrogate donor. The fuck they would! Didn't Forque understand the connection the Niviane Idesha developed with their lovers (victims?) was more than a matter of sharing bodily fluids? It was a symbiosis, a joining going past the physical and into the metaphysical.

She shook her head. Determination and resolve turned her spine into a steel rod. She'd do what she had to, no matter the consequence. "He trusts me. Take that away now and you'll lose him. He'll will himself to die."

The muscles in Forque's jaw tightened and jumped. "That's what I'm afraid of." Unexpectedly, he took her arm, squeezing. He bent close, keeping his voice low. "I don't agree with the direction our research is taking us in. I'm doing my best to get Yuan off the project now. She's getting . . . unstable."

The conspiracy thickened.

Callie bit her tongue. No way she'd jeopardize a potential ally. "I hope you're able to do that," is all she allowed.

Abruptly, Forque seemed to sense his confession was out of order, or had perhaps left him too exposed to an untrustworthy source. Inward searching eyes cooled. He straightened and his hand fell away. "We do what we must."

Callie nodded, but said nothing. She ached to press him for more details, but he'd obviously discarded the subject. She took a moment to rethink her decision and knew she'd decided on the correct course of action. *Somehow* she'd bring this facility down, brick by brick if she had to.

One wrong step and she'd blow everything. "I'm ready," she said simply.

Concern creased his face. "Do you want a guard?"

She negated that immediately. "No. Just me."

Forque cleared his throat.

Her look wasn't friendly. "What?"

"I can't let you take in a weapon," he said in a half-apologetic manner.

"Oh." Callie drew her gun. "Right." Surrender it and she'd be unarmed and wide open—without immediate backup. Not from Iollan. In his condition he couldn't harm a fly. Reluctantly she surrendered her service weapon.

Securing the weapon in a nearby bin, Forque punched a series of numbers into the keypad by the door. It slid open, a giant mouth eager to consume.

Callie drew a breath, and stepped over the threshold. The door slid shut, lock clicking into place behind her back like an unspoken threat. Her pulse thrummed in her throat, and her mind jammed.

Too late to turn back now.

25

Copper eyes tracked Callie's progress across the room. As she closed the distance separating her from Iollan, a low growl of warning emanated from his throat. No recognition lit his narrow gaze.

Callie took another few steps. Closer.

Iollan's lips curled away from his fangs. A strange look of intense cunning settled across his pale face. The beast inside him watched, and planned. His eyes were slits, twin pools of hostility. His long growl deepened, primal. A warning. In his eyes she was prey. Nothing more. Nothing less.

The sound delivered an unpleasant jolt to her nerves. She hesitated, wondering if she'd be able to get close enough to get those cuffs off. *He's hurting.*

Callie forced her fear away. Behind the mask of the angry vampire, she believed the gentle side of this man still survived.

The lights glared down, an illumination keyed up to an almost unbearable degree. No wonder he was listless. He normally rested during daylight hours. Not only had he been thrown into an artificial environment, he was being denied a basic element every living thing seemed to need: sleep.

A panel on the wall controlled light and temperature for the occupant's comfort, though a master board outside overrode the internal one. Callie doubted Iollan knew or cared.

She keyed down the lighting, turning off the overhead tracts and activating the strips running along the lower edges of the walls, the kind of unobtrusive lighting theaters use to guide patrons in dark arenas. Tinted in a soothing shade of peach, the lights were restful on the eyes. Swathed in a veil of pastel illumination the cell felt more habitable, less of a threat.

Callie tried approaching him again.

Pulling her shoulders back, she held out a hand. Her fingers uncurled. Palm up, the key to the cuffs rested in the center of her hand. "I can help you," she said slowly. "Just let me come a little closer."

Iollan shifted so that he looked directly at her. Gaze glittering like the blade of a knife, he glared with savage intensity. "Closer hurts." His accented voice was guttural, forced, as if he'd just learned to speak her language. Gaze flicking over her, he snapped his teeth, a gesture of disdain and contempt.

Shock and sympathy made her hands tremble. Her fragile wall of self-control threatened to crack and shatter entirely. The key nearly slid off her hand. "I'll help the pain go away. I promise."

A shudder wracked him as he fought to shake off his stupor. He eyed her warily. A laugh escaped him, sharp and fractured. "Every time humans get close, we suffer."

Callie felt as if her heart twisted and broke in half. "God, no—" she started to say. A sad sigh murmured deep in her core. "I never meant for this to happen."

Iollan's gaze slowly lifted and focused for the first time in definite recognition. Growl subsiding to silence, his snarl dropped away. "My mistake was not killing you first, Calista."

Absolutely numb, she rubbed a hand over her face. Her whole body felt weightless, insolvent. "You should have." She swallowed heavily, forcing herself to go on. "I wish you had."

Turning his head just a bit, Iollan closed his lips over his fangs. His long canines shrank away, vanishing. "I couldn't— Better to lose my life." A grim expression settled on his face. He swallowed heavily, forcing himself to go on. "My kind has no value, no right to live. Humans hunt us to slaughter us." Nails gory from clawing at his own flesh, he flexed his fingers. "If I take my own life, at least I'll die my own way."

Hearing his words, a tremor went through Callie's whole body. She drew a shuddering breath, wanting to deny it all. The flood of emotions threatened to turn her limbs to liquid. *No.* A fierce inner protectiveness rose. He wasn't going to kill himself. "That's not going to happen."

The barest trace of a smile crossed his arid lips. "It's happening, love," he murmured softly.

Looking at him, she imagined how painful such a death would be.

Reaching deep down into her resolve, Callie somehow found the strength to go to Iollan's side. His damn legs were so long she had to step over them to get close to him. Moving in a slow and easy way, she knelt, and paused. "It doesn't have to."

Iollan didn't stir. Limp, heavy, he breathed with forced endurance. There was a long and faintly uneasy silence. Then he slowly shook his head. "Might as well." Voice faltering, he slipped back into silence. He was tired, his nerves frayed.

She reached out and stroked her hand down a cheek rough with stubble. "You don't have to die." His skin was cold, frightfully so. All warmth had abandoned him, leaving an arctic chill in its wake as his strength ebbed away. Wishing the warmth from her body could somehow be transferred to his, she tried for a smile. None arrived. "Let me help you."

A sad look haunted his gaze. "I can't live in this cage they've got me in. I've always needed the wind at my back."

Callie's heart beat wildly. Even in pain, he was so damn striking it made her throat ache to look at him. Her fingers itched to sift over his skin, to feel the rippling planes of his body against hers. "It'll be that way again," she promised.

Silence.

He doesn't care anymore.

She'd have to convince him otherwise. Would he ever forgive her? Who cared? Alive he'd have the luxury of anger. Dead, he'd be nothing. And she'd be alone.

Callie's hand dropped to his neck, to the collar cinched tight. "This is coming off." Fingers shaking, she guided the key into the lock. Somehow she got it open. "You don't have to wear it anymore." Loosening the straps, she peeled the leather away from his abused flesh. A row of shallow punctures ringed his throat.

Pushing out a breath, Iollan raised his hand, tracing the damages in his neck with the tips of his fingers. "I'm sorry you had to see me this way."

Callie wanted to kiss him so badly that she ached. Feel his lips on hers, taste him. "No need to apologize." A harsh laugh escaped her. "We both got fucked in this one."

His gaze searched for and found hers. In the depths of his eyes she saw past the pain and anger to the hunger. Not physical hunger, but emotional hunger. He touched the corner of her left eye, tracing the bruise there. "Your people?"

Need jolted through her like lightning striking. Knowing hidden cameras probably monitored every move, she quickly shook her head. "It's nothing."

The growling beast threatened to return. "If they've hurt you, it's something to me."

Callie shivered. If only he knew. But no, he must never . . .

Catching his hand in hers, she gave the lightest of squeezes. "I'm fine."

His eyes narrowed. "You're not a very convincing liar."

Forcing herself to focus, she turned Iollan's hand over, revealing the deep trenches he'd scored around the hateful cuff binding his wrist. She unlocked it, then worked the buckle open and peeled it away. The second one quickly followed. "Seems we're right back where we started." Letting the cuff drop, she traced the punctures in his wrist.

Iollan reacted instantly. Trembling, he closed his eyes. "Damn it, when you touch me it's like fire through my veins." A yearning sound tumbled from his mouth, not of pain, but of pleasure.

Exactly how she felt.

Callie put a little more pressure on his sensitive skin. His body wasn't the only one responding. "Do you remember the first night we made love?"

Uncertainty flickered. Then he slowly nodded. "Yes."

She leaned in, closing the distance between them, so that only he heard what other ears shouldn't. Knowing if he died, it would be the end of her, she must convince him his life still had meaning.

"You said you knew the darkness inside me," she whispered, low, tormented. "I know your darkness now. What you are doesn't scare me." Her words caught on a sob, but she swallowed and forced herself to keep speaking. "Please, I need you to be strong."

Iollan's gaze fell to their hands, fingers entwined as their bodies had once been. A desolate look clouded his eyes. "What you ask of me, I can't give you." He glanced around the cell. However comfortable his captors had tried to make it, it would never serve an adequate purpose. "Surviving here, like this. I'm not an animal, Calista. I can't be kept. Not even for you."

Guilt descended, grinding her under strong jaws. Callie's

260 / Devyn Quinn

soul compressed at the despair in his eyes. A wave of bitter torment rose at the back of her throat. Heart close to pounding through her chest, she bent closer. "Please . . . I've done something."

He didn't seem to understand. "Don't," he said through a resigned sigh.

She persisted. Untangling their fingers, she slipped her fingers around the back of his neck, persisting until his gaze met hers again. "My job, my ass, my life is on the line here," she grated through clenched teeth. "I can't say how, but I'm going to get you out of here."

As if shaken by the intensity in her voice, he lifted his brows in a silent question. She'd caught his attention.

Relief crashed over her. Callie recognized in his eyes the plain unspoken truth. He didn't want to die. Not in this place.

"Trust me, please. That's all I can say." To seal her words, she leaned into him. Her lips met his, soft as the brush of a butterfly's wings. Now that the cuffs were off, his skin was warming.

Iollan stiffened for a fraction of a second, then accepted her kiss. Hope sparked in her soul and caught hold. Telling him what she and Norton planned would put him in more danger, something she dared not risk. She just needed time.

Precious time.

And he needed strength.

To get it, he'd have to feed.

Callie's grip on the back of his neck tightened, fingers digging in. Iollan stifled a moan when her tongue brushed against his, a sweet hot tangle of craving and desire. The feel and taste of him zinged through her, bringing to mind every angle of his cock, the memory of his full length sliding into her waiting sex. A soft pulse warmed between her thighs. Just like the first night she'd encountered him. She'd wanted him then.

And she wanted him now.

When their kiss broke, the warmth inside her skittered away, taking its pleasure back to the darkest corners of her mind. The fine hair rose at the nape of her neck. Scary how right it felt between them. She'd never felt like this when she'd been with Roger.

"No fair," Iollan breathed.

"What?" she asked, unable to tear her eyes away from his, from the rippling swirl of gold waltzing within the coppery depths. Despite the symbiont inside him, she believed his soul to be a human one.

His fingers brushed her breast, nudging the nipple so obviously peaking under her blouse and bra. "A kiss like that is guaranteed to bring the life back into a man."

Callie chuckled softly, enjoying the curl of desire tightening in her chest. "That's exactly what I intended to do." Beg, plead, cajole, seduce. She'd do whatever it took to keep him alive.

He glanced over her shoulder. His eyes narrowed in suspicion, stormy and dangerous. His lips started to peel back. "Others watch us," he warned her.

She placed her fingers gently against his mouth. "Not much longer. I promise."

A tremor passed through him. He tensed, muscles tightening. A momentary anger locked his jaw. "I need—" Pained hesitation swept over him as a fierce inner struggle began to rage across his face. His lips pressed shut in a tight grimace of frustration.

She nodded. "I know." She reached for the top button of his shirt, unsnapping it. Then another, and a third. She pushed open his shirt, baring his skin to her touch.

Half a gasp escaped his lips. His trembling lessened. "Damn you, Calista." Body tensing, he sighed when her warm fingers skimmed his naked skin. He moved restlessly, her touch weakening his fiercely held self-control. His copper eyes burned with simmering, potent appetite. "I'll have to feed soon. You know that." His instinct to survive was stronger than his will to die. Stronger still was the need to replenish his strength.

Callie closed her eyes in supplication. "Why don't you get out of those clothes and we'll talk about it?" For a moment his defenses dropped, and their minds touched. Her nearness, her touch, was drawing him out, leading him toward the inevitable resolution.

Iollan caught her slender waist, drawing her closer. His hands slid up her back, an intimate and accepting gesture. "That could be rushing things." His trembling hands and ragged breathing revealed he had the same thing on his mind.

26

The bathing area attached to Iollan's cell held a sink, toilet, and shower unit, a decent and comfortable size.

Callie watched him strip off the remnants of his shirt and toss it aside. Her gaze lingered on his bare chest, his sculpted biceps. He was lean and trim, with not a spare ounce of fat to trouble his body. Abdomen tightly drawn, as if etched in stone, he was filled out in all the right places. Scars, too, marred his pale skin, a long one tearing across his abdomen. Smaller, less prominent ones dotted his neck and shoulders. He, too, had once fed the hunger of a vampire.

A tingle of attraction warmed her insides. Close to drooling, she jerked her gaze away. Excitement simmered beneath the relief of seeing him back on his feet.

Lust teemed, coiling in her womb. "Oh, God."

Bending to pull off his boots, he glanced up. "What?"

Callie realized she was holding her breath and let it out. He seemed to be coming back to a normal semblance of his self. He was uncomfortable, but trying to stay calm—for her sake as much as his own.

"You. Just looking at you makes me ache inside."

Iollan raised his brows, but didn't respond right away. Setting his boots aside, he ran his hands through his hair, the long, raven-shaded strands falling back in messy layers perfectly framing his strong jaw. "In a good way, I hope." Wry humor briefly touched his voice.

Callie lifted her chin, smiling. She knew he was uncomfortable, trying to make the best of a terrible situation. He'd calmed down since the cuffs had come off, and seemed more rational, more settled.

Her gaze traveled down his body, snagging on his narrow waist, the low-slung jeans hugging his hips like a second skin. Need delivered a potent kick between her legs. "A very good way."

Giving a sulky smile, Iollan's hands settled at the top of his jeans, undoing only the single top button. Coppery eyes smoldered, a sultry hue. His zipper crunched down. He watched her reaction steadily, heat radiating in his gaze. His own expression made his thoughts crystal clear.

Callie's mouth went dry at the peek of dark curls. Her heart immediately skipped a beat. The animalistic male power he exuded overwhelmed her like a gigantic wave. Desire burst over her in a flood of moist warmth. A wedge of air blocked her throat. All she heard was the sudden rush of blood in her ears, echoing the pulse of need rising in her gut.

Somehow she grabbed hold of her wits before they flew off and left her a drooling, sex-crazed idiot. She made a choked sound, a groan maybe. She wasn't sure. All she wanted was to reach for him, to touch him. "Looks to me like you're getting your strength back."

He didn't have to ask what she meant. He knew.

Iollan showed her his wrists. The thin lines of the punctures had faded, almost gone. The deep scratches he'd inflicted clawing at the cuffs had closed into red puffy scars. "It doesn't take long to heal once the silver leaves my system."

His eyes looked brighter than they'd been a few minutes ago. Electricity jolted through her. She trembled, feeling the shiver all the way to the tips of her toes. "Is it selfish to say I want you?"

Iollan reached for her, pulling her close. The feel of his hands settling on her hips drew another pulse of her twitchy energy closer to the surface. "No more selfish than I was." His voice was very soft. "I wanted you, too." His intimate touch surprised as much as his words.

Tears pressing behind her eyes, Callie squeezed her lids shut. "I didn't want to tell them where you were," she confessed in a rush. "They invaded my mind, used drugs. I had no choice."

Iollan's hand slid under her chin, tipping her head back. "Don't blame yourself," he gently chided.

Exhaling heavily, Callie reluctantly opened her eyes. "I do, because you trusted me." She tried to smile, and failed. "You showed me what you were, and I betrayed that."

Gazing into her eyes, he tenderly stroked his thumb across her lips. Her skin tingled as desire whispered up her spine. His gaze was so calm, so gentle. He had no anger toward her, blamed her for nothing. She held her breath, waiting.

"Against your own will." Iollan's stroke grew heated, more insistent. The firm pressure of his thumb stroking her lips ushered in a whole new rush of pure liquid pleasure. "If I'm going to lose my life, at least I got my wish of one more day with you."

Heat ripped through her. Her body yearned to feel his hands touch her in all the ways she knew he could, exploring all her hidden places until she cried out with pleasure. "This isn't our last time."

Silent for a moment, Iollan's throat worked. "Don't make

promises." He sighed without bitterness. "Just let me enjoy having you here, now."

He kissed her, mouth thoroughly plundering. His tongue skimmed across her lips, the nip of his teeth scraped.

Callie stiffened a fraction of a second, then melted into his arms, need tearing through her like a racer burning rubber on the track. The nerves in her belly eased as other sensations replaced them, a sharp tug of pure pleasure. Moaning her need into his mouth, her hands worked inside his jeans, sliding them down his hips and over his ass.

Breaking their kiss, Iollan stepped out of his jeans. Gloriously naked, his grin held no shame. "Seems to me someone is overdressed."

A blush turned her cheeks hot. "Then do something about it," she dared in a low, breathy voice.

He did. Experienced fingers unbuttoned her blouse, exposing her creamy breasts in their lacy bra. Impatiently, he unsnapped the catch. He cupped her breasts, thumbs lightly brushing her erect nipples.

She closed her eyes, concentrating on the sensations he evoked. "That feels so good."

Iollan's hands slid down to her waist. "I try to please." His accented voice rumbled, sultry and teasing. His eyes locked with hers, and a slow smile turned up his lips. "But it wouldn't be fitting to make love to such a lovely lady when I stink like a hog."

The vision of suds slipping over his smooth skin caused her to shiver. If nothing else, the man was civilized. She'd have taken him without benefit of a bath.

Opening the shower door, he turned on the taps. Hot water flowed out, a steaming cloud filling the air around him. His gaze caught hers, beckoning. "You can join me, if you like."

Stepping under the water, he closed his eyes and ran his

hands through his hair, clearly enjoying the silky water as it eased the tension in his neck and shoulders.

Callie stood, entranced by the sight of the water sluicing across his shoulders and down his back. The flex of muscles in his arms and shoulders was poetry in motion as he commenced to wash himself. Round and firm, his ass was peach ripe, perfect for biting.

And she wanted a taste.

Kicking off her shoes, the rest of her clothing quickly followed. She stepped in behind him, rubbing her hands across his broad shoulders. "Need a little help with your back?"

He glanced behind him and waggled a brow. "Any time." He handed over the soap. "At your leisure." The low intimate timbre of his voice caused her legs to tremble.

Slicking her hands with suds, Callie kneaded the soap into his shoulders, tracing along the blades and down his spine. Her palms roamed.

Shifting his legs apart, Iollan flexed his shoulders. His breath hitched. "Umm . . . feels good."

"You feel good." Callie stroked her hands over his hips, briefly cupping his ass with soapy hands. "Turn around."

Iollan obediently turned.

She continued washing, working over his chest, down his arms, washing away the dried blood flecking his pale skin. Holding one of his hands in hers, she worked each finger. Iollan had big hands, strong hands. His fingernails were longish, square tipped. His wide palms were heavily calloused.

A thought occurred. "Can I ask you something?"

A tic twitched at the corner of his mouth. "I suppose."

She smiled tentatively. All her nerves came rushing back. "Who were you? I mean, before, when you were human?"

Iollan studied her face a moment. "Nobody, I suppose. Just a poor working man."

"Your accent," she started to say.

"Is Irish," he murmured. "I was born there, in 1813."

Surprise curled in the pit of her stomach. Her eyes widened in surprise. "That makes you . . ." She tried to do a mental calculation and failed. A hot, naked male and hot steamy water clouded her mind.

He made a face. "One hundred and ninety-four years old." A pause. "Not too old for you, am I?"

Her throat thickened. She swallowed. "How did you become, ah, one of them."

A soft laugh escaped. "Quite by accident." His gaze blanked with memory. "I was thirty-two when the blight hit, bringing the famine that would kill so many of us. My wife, my daughters, the land . . . When you're poor, no amount of prayer or hope can help you. I was born and raised Catholic, but I gave up on God then."

His words struck with more force than a bullet ripping through fragile flesh. Her throat worked, fighting off the rise of sick torment. "I'm sorry I asked."

He smiled, and her heart tightened at the trace of unhappiness haunting his eyes. He looked a million miles away, as the horror of the memories replayed in his mind. "I hated being human, and I hated being weak. Nothing I could do but keep myself together, no matter how much I didn't want to."

Callie had no response. Never in a thousand years would she have guessed him to be nearly two centuries old. "I'm glad you did," she said, striving to keep emotion out of her voice.

A shudder wracked him. He quickly mastered it. "I didn't leave Ireland intending to live. I just left to find my death somewhere else. In England, I found work, keeping the gardens of a lady who loved her flowers. She only came out at night, though, walking the paths along the grounds. So pale . . . And her eyes. I loved her eyes."

Callie reached up, touching the tip of her finger to the softness under his left eye. "Like yours are now," she whispered, shuddering delicately. "Pure liquid fire."

His breath sighed out with his nod. "Yes. We soon became lovers and she showed me her world, asked me to join her." His throat worked as he recalled the memory of the time. "Everything she was, I wanted to be."

Callie hung on his every word, entranced. "And so you became one of them?"

"I had nothing to lose," Iollan admitted. "And everything to gain. The night she gave me my symbiont, I became a man reborn. It became a part of me, and I became a part of it."

Breath jerky and shallow, she had to ask a final question. "Are you sorry you became one of *them*?"

Iollan shook his head. "My symbiont and I are one, and I have no regret of that. No one's forced to take that step into their world. That isn't their way." He reached out caressing her cheek. Though he spoke steadily, he watched her with an intensity that delved deep. "When the Niviane Idesha found our world, they only wanted to settle and survive, something we all want in life."

Trembling, Callie pressed his palm to her face. His words, so sincerely spoken, touched her. Her soul silently cried out, craving the passion and love of this incredible man. "I want that, too."

Iollan's arms circled her, his tall frame melding with hers. "I wanted to give you the gift." Large masculine hands searched for and then stroked her nipples. "Many times." His head came down. A hungry mouth nibbled lightly at her lips. The erotic nibbles felt like small electrical charges on her skin. His eagerness thrilled her to the bone.

Callie whispered against his mouth. "I would have accepted." She longed to be kissing him, having him hold her. She wanted him to spread her legs and penetrate her, go deep inside her, feel his taut abdomen against her belly, hear his breath in her ear, and match the pounding of her heart with the pounding of his cock.

Head tilted down, Iollan parted his fine lips. His arresting eyes sparkled with pleasure. The gleam of anticipation was unmistakable. "Maybe someday you will." Never flickering, his gaze was liquid heat. With that one scorching look, he owned her. Body and soul. The unmistakable urgency of sex radiated from him, laced with a deeper need to make more than a physical connection.

Callie's arms circled his neck. "Why wait for someday?" she murmured softly. She couldn't let him go. She'd never let him go.

He kissed her again.

She accepted his kiss, her tongue darting out to tangle with his. His hands roamed her body, which was slender and strong under his touch. She quivered with tension, a fine flush rising up over her throat. With water beating down on her skin, she felt as though her brain had melted. A delicious lassitude crept over her, dulling her wits. She felt as if she'd been drugged, but she didn't care. All she pictured was her body writhing beneath his. Impossible not to imagine how her legs would feel wrapped around him.

"Touch me," she murmured.

Iollan nibbled the tip of her upturned chin. "Gladly." He skimmed his hands down her back, finding the round curve of her ass. He lightly slid his fingers between her crack, gently caressing.

Callie grasped the rail of the shower and leaned back. "All over my body."

Iollan's mouth covered a nipple. Sucking hungrily, he massaged her free breast, teasing the nipple by rolling it between thumb and forefinger. "I want to please you." He kissed the softness between her breasts. "Taste you . . ."

A shiver ran through her body. "Yes," she moaned, running

her fingers over his shoulders, pushing him lower. He knelt and her hands moved to the back of his head, guiding him. A low lusty growl of want and desire followed. "I need to feel your mouth on me."

Iollan lifted one leg over his shoulder to give him better access to her sex. Letting her guide him, he moved forward. His mouth claimed her, molten passion atop her throbbing clit.

She splintered, hovering on the edge of climax.

He moved his hands under her ass. Moving his tongue up and down between her swollen lips, he licked in a steady stroke.

"Oh, God," she panted, one hand holding the rail, the other pulling at his hair.

Iollan slipped his tongue into her opening. The tip of his tongue curled around her slit, then pushed deeper into her.

Callie's thighs quivered, tightening around his head. His hands squeezed her ass cheeks. He tongued her, orally fucking her. Her hips rocked back and forth in a rhythmic motion. Climax came without warning.

Her back arched. A torrent of pleasure grabbed and refused to let go. "That's it!" Body roaring in pleasure, she felt her innards convulse, then shatter around her. The water shimmered like a million tiny rainbows

It went on and on.

Cock throbbing, Iollan stood up and turned her around to face the wall. He ran his hands over her ass, squeezing then parting her firm cheeks as he pressed his hips to hers and rubbed his cock against her puckered anus.

Callie growled deep in her throat and pushed back against him. A seismic quake began inside, rippling inside her in a way threatening to tear her asunder.

He leaned forward, kissing the back of her neck, nibbling at the soft hollow between her head and shoulder. "I need you," he whispered, his voice gruff with desire. He gripped and lifted her up, positioning his legs between hers. Using one hand, he guided his penis to her slit, aligning the engorged head against her warm nether lips. Hips pressing forward, his cock slid smoothly inside.

They both moaned.

Callie closed her eyes as he began to thrust, slowly at first, then faster. His tempo grew as he began a rocking motion guaranteed to give her every last inch. The movements of his hips ground their bodies together until they weren't just joined, they were a single entity. With each gliding motion, his cock penetrated more fully and deeply inside her sex, each thrust creating a friction all but unbearable in its intensity.

Lust took over. Want exploded into need all over again.

Iollan slid one arm under hers, clamping it between her breasts, fingers digging deep into her shoulder. His other arm wrapped around her waist, lifting her onto the tips of her toes. His stroke pummeled, sure and strong, letting her know he belonged there. "I can't hold off much longer, love."

Callie's moans filled the air. She wanted this, wanted him more than she'd ever wanted anything in her entire life. Melding into him, she matched his rhythm, prodding his excitement. One hand dug into his hip, fingernails pressed into his flesh.

Rocking and rolling with the sensations, her body bucked. "Now, please," she ordered breathlessly. The exquisite pain of delight filled her like wildfire across a dry prairie. No stopping its force or hunger to devour.

Iollan throttled faster, going deeper. Sinking his teeth into the soft flesh of her shoulder, he marked her as his own. Tremors rumbled through him. His cock pulsed thickly as he shot his semen deep inside her.

Coming down from his high, he clung to her, body slowly adjusting as his breathing returned to normal.

As the last of Callie's own tremors eased away, Iollan turned off the taps. The water around them had grown cold, but it might as well have been scalding hot for all the heat their bodies generated.

Stepping out of the shower, Iollan snagged a towel off the rack and wrapped it around his waist. He grabbed a second one for her and held it open.

Bundling into his arms, Callie felt the quick shudder that went through him as his arms tightened around her. But she hardly needed air. She needed his body, his urgency, the slide of his cock filling her with his intense and demanding desire.

Iollan dried her, kissing every inch as he rubbed the soft cloth into her skin. She ached to be his again. She needed him with a fierce burning desire, a thing she had never felt for any other man in her life. He was a breath of fresh air in her stale, dank world.

Finished, he let the towel drop and pulled her close. Their bodies were separated only by the towel precariously tucked around his hips. He touched her cheek, then traced the curve of one ear. "This isn't finished." Anticipation dilating his gaze, lust roughened his voice.

"I know." Going up on the tips of her toes, Callie cupped the back of his head and pulled his mouth down to meet hers. The wall of his chest was solid, brushing against her bare nipples. The sensitive tips beaded in response. The moment of truth had arrived. Her heart was pounding, not entirely from desire. "If you can shift, can you get out of here?" she murmured against his lips.

Iollan's mouth tested, retreated, returned. "There's a chance. They've got every inch of this place sealed, down to the last crack. Even in shifted form, I have physical limitations." His lips turned up at one corner, taking on a wicked cast. "But I have other tricks they've not yet seen."

The delight of hope blossomed in her chest. All sorts of feelings fluttered in her veins. "Anything I can do to help?"

Hands circling her waist, he stroked the tender skin at the

center of her back. His hands were warm. Her skin tingled under his intimate touch. "Seeing you naked definitely helps."

She shivered. Seeing him naked did wonders for her well-being, too. In ways he couldn't imagine. Or maybe he could. "You'll need to feed," she started to say.

Iollan hushed her. "Yes." His gaze strayed toward the adjoining room of his cell, to the bed that waited. He swept her into his arms, muscles flexing as he balanced her weight.

Callie's hands gripped his broad shoulders. Not that she feared he'd drop her, but damn! He was so freaking tall. "Iollan, they'll see us!"

He carried her toward the waiting bed, kissing her cheek, her shoulder, whatever inch of skin he could reach. "Your people want to know what we can do. Fine. They'll see what the Niviane Idesha are about—in every way."

27

Iollan hit the narrow bed with his knee, tumbling Callie onto its firm surface. At least the mattress beneath her back was thick and comfortable, for what sliver of bed there was.

Callie tried to sit up. "They can watch us here," she warned again.

Tossing his towel aside, Iollan tumbled down next to her. His hand stroked her smooth hip. "I don't care." Pulling her close, he smoothed damp tendrils of hair away from her face, then traced her full lips with the tips of his fingers. His lips brushed hers and his hand drifted lower, touching her breast, circling her areola. "Maybe your people need to see we are not so unlike themselves."

Callie trembled. She moved her hips against his thigh. His physique was a powerful one, and she felt very soft and womanly against it. "How would it happen?" she asked. "Becoming."

In the low light of the cell, his eyes were bright, the glow deep within their depth coiling and snapping with his arousal. "I can give you a rough idea."

Without giving her time to consider the consequences, he rolled her onto her stomach, then stretched out on top of her. His body connected with hers. His penis, half-flaccid, half-taut, pressed against her buttocks. Supporting his weight on outstretched arms, he lowered his body until his mouth was barely an inch from her ear. Every inch of her skin tingled.

Callie held her breath, waiting.

Grinding his hips sensuously into hers, he nipped the curl of her ear. "First, I'd make you so damn hot, building your energies to their highest peak."

"And?"

Iollan nuzzled the hair from the back of her neck. Hungry lips scraped the softness at the base of her skull. His mouth teased and taunted with long slow licks and nips. "Then, I'd bite. Deep. And you'd feel a pressure crawling under your skin."

Half delight, half fright shivered through her. Longing rose in her. "What next?"

Iollan abruptly broke the spell, rolling off her. "The only way to know is to go through the change."

Disappointed, Callie rolled over on her back. They were lying so close she felt the rise and fall of his chest as he breathed, his pulse pounding under his skin, and lower. Getting bigger, she noticed. "Tease."

His smile flickered, serious and without humor. "The gift from one to another is a sacred thing. Mates are chosen carefully because the gift is so awesome." He glanced toward the hateful door of his cell. "Even if they strip me down to just atoms, they'll never be able to capture or understand the essence of our power."

A sad and solemn pain knifed her. *It isn't Iollan they'll dissect.* He was too valuable to lose. Scientists wanted his children, the DNA he'd pass to his offspring.

Callie slid her arms around him and held him, just held him.

Damp hair hanging in loose curls, he smelled fresh and clean. Pure. He hadn't shaved yet and a light layer of dark stubble covered his cheeks, giving another clue of just how human he still was. "Have I told you that you're awesome?"

A slow smile eased across his full mouth. His eyes sizzled under heavy lids. "Am I?"

She bit her lip, nodding. "More than you have any right to be."

His smile lingered. Deliberately, he leaned down. The tip of his tongue came out, tracing her lower lip. One of his hands drifted down to cup the soft round curve of her breast. He stroked her, hands easily finding her most sensitive places. "So are you." Suddenly, he was erect.

Sizzling heat rose between them as Callie's conscious awareness of her surroundings faded. There was only her man, holding her, kissing her. His hands caressed, sampling her body as if he couldn't get enough, couldn't get close enough.

Pressing her down, Iollan shifted on top of her. His legs took command of her, parting her thighs, cock nesting against her belly when he came down on top of her. A hot rush of breath brushed her cheeks, then her mouth, right before he kissed her.

Callie surrendered utterly to the whirlwind of passion. Her tongue traced his lips, gently biting down on his lower lip. He growled low in the back of his throat, muttering something incomprehensible in Gaelic.

Fingers flexing against the tight muscles of his back, Callie felt him move lower. Softly, gently, he nipped her neck, licking, kissing, tasting her. Lower still, finding the valley between her breasts before moving to one swollen nipple.

Heady with feminine power, she gently caught his hair. "Don't try to get out of feeding."

He nodded, grinning. "I'm going for a triple espresso."

Wriggling out from under him, Callie lay half over him, her

breasts pressing against his chest, legs tangled with his. She felt the ache between them, felt herself grow moist. She ran her fingers along his chest, teasing one dusky nipple.

"Is that all I am to you? An espresso?"

Iollan quirked a wry smile at her. "A triple mocha latte." He tweaked a nipple. "With whipped cream." His exploring hand moved lower, finding her pulsing center. His hand slid between her legs, stroking gently.

Callie moaned and reached to thread her fingers through his thick hair. "You touch me in all the right ways," she moaned, voice husky.

Smiling wickedly, he touched his mouth to hers. "I try to."

Snug against him, she gave her fingers free rein. She had only a moment to tease him before his arms came around her and he took control again. His thighs pushed between hers.

"No fair!" she giggled, but let him have his way. It felt so right to be under his weight.

"All is fair when pleasure is concerned."

Pinning her securely, he moved his mouth from her lips to her neck to the sweet hollow between her breasts. This time it was her turn to whimper as he kissed the swell of her right breast, his tongue whirling closer and closer to an engorged nipple. Pleasure flooded her when he began teasing the nubbin. Against the sensitive peak, his tongue felt smooth as silk.

Fighting his grip, Callie arched higher. The movement of his mouth, the pressure of his cock pressing between her legs inflamed her fierce craving to have him inside her. She was ablaze, and she wanted him all over again.

But Iollan was in no hurry, moving to her left breast and repeating slow, sensual circles around the pink bud. His mouth was driving her insane. Dragging her hands free, she dug her nails deep into his muscular shoulder, shifting her body and spreading her thighs. Slowly, she rotated her hips, begging him to relieve her.

"Please," she managed between ragged, husky breaths.

Iollan flashed a sinful smile and dipped lower, passing his palm across the smooth plane of her belly, then following with a dozen small nips and kisses. He ran his hands up the insides of her thighs, then kissed her just above her shaved mound.

Callie felt dizzy when he slid his fingers along her labia. She gripped the blanket under her body, nearly ripping it. His touch sent a hot rush to all her nerve endings. His fingertips felt like feathers, stroking her with the familiarity of a lover who knew where her every sensitive spot lay. He was careful and gentle, doing to her exactly what he wished as he eased two fingers inside her. Nothing to do but hold on as a whole new tidal wave of pleasure inundated her.

Gasping from the intensity, she cried out. "Iollan, don't tease. Fuck me, damn it. Fuck me."

While she was still pulsing, he added the soft pressure of his mouth.

Callie's senses shattered. Quivering with tension, aflame with desire, she gave herself to a delicious orgasm, meeting each slow thrust of his fingers. She wanted him more than she wanted the sun to rise in the morning sky. The world might end now, and she would not care.

He pulled away, leaving a sudden cold void, but not for long. He shifted his body, folding her in his arms.

She pushed up. "Let me please you . . ."

"Later." His mouth silenced her, and she tasted the spice of her female musk.

Lifting his body, he slid his cock deep. His glide in was smooth and easy. Warm and slick, her sex welcomed him. Clearly, he had been holding himself back, waiting for the right moment to join their bodies in a union that was almost holy.

Fluttery feelings spread through her like warm honey. "I'm a fool for wanting you."

Satisfaction lit his face. "There are worse things to be a fool about." Iollan's lips claimed hers again.

When their kiss ended, Callie let out a slow, pent-up breath, wrapping her legs around his waist to draw him deeper. Her senses were attuned to his breathing, his strength, and his strong body. Every beat of her heart, the blood they shared pulsing through her veins, made her that much more aware of his intense male domination. The power he radiated enveloped her. He controlled his every move, thrusting slowly in, pulling out, then thrusting again.

Suddenly, he stiffened. Fingers tangling in her hair, his head lowered, warm mouth searching her neck. Sharp teeth grazed.

An involuntary shiver tickled the base of her spine. Soon.

Eyes ablaze, the beast emerged. Lips curling back, fangs appeared, his teeth grew long and sharp within seconds. A low growl emanated from his throat. "Don't fight me."

Callie's muscles contracted in a spasm of fear. Strong hands locked around her wrists, a grip tight and unrelenting. No way she'd escape him now. Not that she wanted to.

Shifting her hips to take him more fully, she groaned. Her skin tingled under his demanding touch.

Iollan nuzzled. "I won't hurt you." Hunger, physical hunger, roughened his voice. His tongue traced a burning path along her soft skin. His teeth punctured near the vulnerable vein in her neck, bringing forth a rush of warm blood.

A quick shudder went through her. His bite was sweet and drugging, delivering a pain she welcomed. Held on to, savored. The feral male scent of him filled her senses. The pulse between her legs grew stronger, more insistent. Knots of need tightened in her belly. She was coming to the edge, so close she ached for completion.

Iollan feasted, drinking deeply. As he fed, his hips leisurely ground into hers. He licked and sucked while his cock ferried in and out, pleasing himself . . . and her. His bite deepened. He sucked deeply. Control breaking, he thrust into her depth.

And the world shattered.

Breath lost in a gasp, Callie arched beneath him as a white-hot burst of pleasure picked her up and tossed her into an abyss seeming to go on forever and ever. Her mind hazed, she lay in a naked sprawl, damp with sweat, panting. Time was lost in a liquid rush of pleasure.

His kiss chased away her drowsy fog.

When his mouth settled on hers, it felt so right that Callie unhesitatingly claimed his lips. With a quavering sigh, she tasted her own blood, a strange nectar to be savored. There was only the taste of him painted across her lips, and the weight of him pressed between her thighs.

Glaring lights flicked up. Blinding.

"What did I tell you, Doctor? She can't get enough sex."

An amused chuckle followed.

Roger. *Oh, God.*

28

Roger Reinke stood in the doorway. Holding a syringe in her hand, Doctor Yuan hovered beside him. Two other men were with them, heavily armed guards.

Callie struggled to sit up, pushing herself in front of Iollan, intent on protecting him. With what? Naked as jaybirds, both of them were vulnerable, exposed. Not a great position to be in at this precise moment.

She forced herself to sit straighter, staring the group down, determined to show no fear. She considered crossing her arms across her breasts, then decided not to. She had nothing to hide. "What the hell do you people want?"

Gray eyes flinty, features more rigid than stone, Roger was colder than an arctic winter. "You're under arrest, Agent Whitten."

Callie's blood pressure immediately dropped. Shit! They had somehow found out she'd hacked the system. Not wanting to jeopardize Iollan's safety because of her stupidity, she made a quick decision. She'd go quietly if they wouldn't punish him.

She started to slide off the bed. "I'm going to get my clothes," she said calmly. "Then I'll come with you."

Iollan grabbed her arms, fingers digging in painfully. "It's me they'll want."

Roger laughed. "Oh, we've got you." He gestured at the agents. Both drew their weapons. "One move and they'll fill you back up with silver." The detachment in his voice chilled.

He speared Callie with hate through narrowed eyes.

A perverse desire to slap that grin off his face rose inside Callie. "They'll do it," she warned Iollan in a near whisper. She gently shook off his hold. "Let me go. They won't hurt me."

Iollan's grip gentled.

Callie eased off the bed, careful to keep her body between her lover and their weapons. Still weak from blood loss, her head swam and her knees trembled. As long as she kept Iollan blocked, they wouldn't be able to get off a clean shot. Once she was out of the way . . . She shivered at the vision of Iollan again writhing in pain, poisoned by the hateful silver.

"Be careful," Doctor Yuan demanded the moment Callie stepped away from the bed. Her eyes settled on Callie's middle. "Don't hurt her," she said, grinning like a feral cat over a prime kill. "She's a valuable specimen now."

A what?

Callie remembered the blood and urine Yuan had collected. Oh, shit. Shock filled her.

No time to question Yuan's remark. Strong hands grasped her arms, dragging her to one side. Her arms were wrenched up behind her back. Her hands flexed behind her back, aching to break free. She shuddered at the prospect of Yuan gaining control of her child.

If there was a child.

Yuan gestured toward Iollan. "Now that we have a viable sample, get the cuffs back on him."

Callie's head swiveled. "Viable sample of *what*?"

Doctor Yuan smiled sweetly. "Semen."

Callie swore viciously under her breath. Fury rising, she jerked, trying to break free of her captors. That examination wasn't going to happen. No way she'd go up on a table and have her legs spread open. The pieces clicked together in her mind. Now she knew why they'd wanted her to seduce Iollan so badly. They needed a receptacle for his sperm donation. She snarled. "Like hell."

"Be still," Roger barked.

Grips tightened. She might have been almost as tall as the men, but she wasn't as strong. In the back of her mind she pictured breaking free and kicking them all in the balls, punting the useless things right over their shoulders.

Thumb on the plunger, Yuan raised the syringe in her hand. She gestured coldly toward Iollan. "Get those cuffs back on him."

Baring his fangs, Iollan slipped off the bed. "That won't happen again." Hands flexing at his sides, he stood straight, naked and magnificent.

Gaze burning, he seemed to be enveloped by a blur. Thick tendrils began to crawl around his body, forming and knitting into clothing. Before an eye blinked he stood, fully dressed—and ready to fight. Eyes flashing dangerous signals, he lifted his chin in a gesture of defiance.

Unable to believe her eyes, Callie took a deep breath. She snapped her lax jaw back into place. She'd seen him shift things before, but never like that. Slick. She loved it.

Roger Reinke drew his weapon. "Nice trick." Looking grim, more than a little worried, he leveled the gun, pointing it squarely at Iollan Drake's chest. "Bet I can put a stop to that right away." He fired.

Iollan's hand rose to the level of his heart, and he seemed to pluck something out of the air. Slowly he lowered his hand. Clenched fingers uncurled. Still intact, the ampoule rested on his palm.

Lips curling back, he flicked the useless thing aside. "Easy to catch us during daysleep, fill us with your poison." A mocking brow quirked. "Not so easy when we're strong and freshly fed."

"Damn it!" Roger squeezed off another round, and then a third.

Callie closed her eyes, praying. *Go*, she silently urged Iollan. *Get out of here.* Her lids fluttered open.

Iollan shifted. A small apparition streaked through the cell at lightning speed, and vanished. Where it went, nobody knew.

Her breath rushed out in relief. The ampoules hit the wall where he'd been standing, thunking hollowly as they exploded. Thank God. He'd gotten away.

Trouble beckoned, though. She was on her own now.

Yuan cursed in disbelief. "He's gotten out."

Roger's jaw tightened. "He won't get far. This place is sealed tighter than a fucking drum." He shot a glance at Callie. "Take care of what you have to do with her."

Callie's captors pushed her out of the cell. Large hands half-forced her down the hall, past the security station that would take them out of the prisoner's holding area. Professor Forque was nowhere in sight. She could almost hear the wheels turning in Yuan's head as they moved along.

An open elevator waited. She was pushed in, and the doors closed with an ominous whisper. The levels whizzed by, un-counted.

Another floor. The lab straight ahead.

An examination room. Sterile, as if for operations. Shelves held beakers, racks, test tubes, microscopes, and other equipment. A slew of white-coated people waited. If anyone thought it unusual to see a naked struggling woman locked between two men, nobody said a word. Considering the heinous experiments taking place here, that was probably a common sight.

An examination table stood in the center of the room. It wasn't the normal flat kind in most doctors' offices. A lump rose in Callie's throat. This was the kind of table made for female examinations—and for birthing.

The hackles on the back of her neck rose. They'd have to kill her to get her up on that table, her legs up in the stirrups. She'd fight tooth and nail.

"Shit." Her gaze collided with the doctor's. "What the fuck are you going to do?" She didn't care if she sounded hysterical. She didn't feel very reasonable at the moment.

Doctor Yuan looked at her. Her gaze drifted from Callie to the syringe she'd carried into Iollan's cell. "Originally, Agent Whitten, you were marked for termination, as a jeopardy to our research. I'd felt your involvement with the subject would serve no useful purpose."

The words struck like a blow to the chest. A violent shiver shook Callie. Stark naked, with two men holding her, her underarms were damp, her fisted hands burning hot. She leveled a disdainful glare at the twitching doctor. "Thanks a whole hell of a lot."

Yuan snorted. "You should be proud of yourself, Agent Whitten. After seeing you with the subject last night, I changed my mind about your value. Quite by accident, you've turned my research to a whole new arena."

The coils of fear that had been twisting in her bowels turned into shards of glass grinding up her insides. "Hybrids." She bit out the single word as an obscenity.

Yuan stared pointedly at her belly, then lower, to the space between her legs. "Exactly. Not only will I be able to obtain what I hope are viable sperm samples from your recent sexual activity with the subject, I'm hoping you test positive for pregnancy."

A body-shaking wave of revulsion swamped Callie's entire being.

Yuan chuckled. "You've saved your life by being a promiscuous tramp. Instead of a corpse, your body will serve as an incubation chamber." She lifted her syringe, cruelly clucking her tongue. "But that's all you'll be. From now on your classification will be EVE-A1, mother of an entirely new race."

Callie strained against the hands holding her. Panic flashed up and crested. Yuan seemed to be looking forward to turning her into a brainless vegetable. "You're fucking insane."

Yuan shrugged. "That's just the way science works. We have to have test subjects."

Callie refused to roll over and give up. "I'm not a fucking lab rat."

Yuan ignored her. "Get her up on the table and strap her down." Her lips curved in a sick smile.

The ball in Callie's stomach exploded. Her body went rigid, every tendon locking into place. She shook silently, but wouldn't let it show.

Swearing, laboring to keep her under control, the agents lugged her toward the table. Curses and vile threats punctuated the men's efforts. Assistants waited, ready to lift her off her feet, spread her legs into those evil stirrups.

Not going to happen.

She had to do whatever it took to get loose. Her plan was simple. She didn't have one. But she had to try.

Callie spun between the men, kicking and writhing, surprising them with the fresh intensity of her struggle. She broke free, running. Something tripped her. She sprawled, catching a glimpse of Doctor Yuan, foot sticking out. The bitch.

Rolling over onto her back, ready to kick out, she saw a

wraith dart pass her, stop and hover. Seconds later, Iollan's big body appeared out of nowhere. He positioned his body between her and the men surrounding them. She heard the gears in his head grinding as he shifted into the mind-set of defending them.

"Get ready," he grated under his breath.

"To what?" No time to be confused. Callie gathered her wits, geared up to act upon his slightest signal. "What the hell are you going to do?"

Iollan glanced back. A smile that rivaled the devil's for wicked intent turned up one corner of his mouth. "Don't worry about that. I'm getting us out of here. Both of us." He was serious.

All at once Iollan frightened, awed, daunted, and fascinated her.

The agents rushed at them, guns drawn.

Everything sped up, almost too fast to visually comprehend.

Before Callie knew what was happening, Iollan struck the first blow. His arm shot up in a defensive stance, palm out, fingers splayed. Raw energy radiated around him.

The agent leading the pack began to quiver violently, twisting in pain as his blood commenced boiling in his veins. He screamed and beat one-handed at his chest, writhing as his internal temperature rose. His eyeballs rolled to the whites, melting in the sockets and running down his face in gruesome tears. Without warning his body burst into flames. His gun dropped from lax fingers, striking the floor.

Chaos ruled. The white-coated assistants shrank away, scattering to safety.

Doctor Yuan ducked behind the examination table. No way she'd leave. Not when her prime specimen stood just a few feet away.

Callie watched Iollan jerk his left hand toward his body. The agent's gun flew to him, settling securely in his grip. In a smooth counter turn, he whirled on his heel and fired the weapon at the second agent. These guns weren't loaded with silver. They were loaded with bullets. Deadly to humans.

Struck squarely, the agent dropped to the floor. Grabbing his chest, he screamed in pain.

Callie scrambled sideways, grabbing the pistol that had slid from the agent's hand. "I didn't know you could do that." In less than a minute, two men were felled. The count was going down. *We just might get out of this with our asses intact.*

Iollan gave her a quick smile. "It's a power we're sworn never to use against humans."

Callie's grip tightened on her weapon. "There's an exception for every rule." She gestured at her own nudity. "Any chance you can help me out here?"

A smart-ass grin. "I prefer you naked."

Sheesh. Men.

"I'd like to be dressed right now," Callie grated back. "Not very practical when you're trying to take names and kick ass."

Iollan obliged.

A tingle. A tickle. Clothes melting on. T-shirt forming around her shoulders, tight jeans hugging her ass. Boots. Heavy boots. A jacket, leather. Nice.

She glanced down. "Perfect."

And just in time.

29

The lab doors burst open. Heavily armed security personnel immediately swarmed in. Roger Reinke led the charge.

Callie's thoughts reversed. Maybe not.

Harsh voices yelled for Iollan to drop his weapon. He ignored them. Instead, he lifted the gun in a mock salute, a move meant to taunt, annoy, and humiliate.

Going up on her knees, Callie grabbed for his arm. Panic thrust chilly spikes through her breast. "You're pushing it too far," she warned. "Just get the hell out. I'll be okay."

Copper eyes alight with the thrill of the fight, Iollan was the typical Irishman, in his element when buried up to his ass in trouble. He didn't even stop to consider the fact he might be on the losing side.

The expression in Iollan's eyes changed subtly as his gaze settled on her. She'd never seen that look before, and it produced a shiver of fear to her core. Mental gears were shifting, a strange look swept over his face. In an unguarded moment, a play of intense emotions colored his features; hatred, and, yes, deep unadulterated fury. Something was going on inside his skull and it wasn't good. "I won't leave without you."

She tried to warn him. "There are too many."

Too late.

On the move, Iollan swung into action, attacking two of the closest agents. Ducking a slashing fist, he bodily tackled the nearest man.

Sprawled flat, the agent barely had time to react before Iollan crushed his wrist with a knee. Without even looking back, he simultaneously lifted his arm above his head, parrying the attack of the second agent. Iollan viciously responded by bringing his body up, simultaneously striking with a blow of his gun across the man's leg.

The agent screamed and fell back, but not before Iollan pressed the barrel to his groin and fired. The agent fell away, sprawling flat.

Giving a killer flash of predatory teeth, Iollan savagely brought his heel down on the man's breastbone. The shattering crack of bone filled the air, crushing the sacs around the man's heart. Crimson rivulets gushed from the agent's nose and mouth. He died instantly.

No time to watch her man playing hero. He wasn't their only target. She considered her options and made a decision. The insanity needed to end. Now. Come hell or high water, there'd be no way she'd be taken alive. If they carried her out of this place in a body bag, so be it. Death was better than what Doctor Yuan had in mind.

Callie took a wild shot at one of the advancing agents. The man yelled and scrambled out of sight, ducking behind one of the counters. The glass-faced cabinet behind him shattered, sending a spray of glass over his hunched body.

A return spray of shots pelted. Ping. Ping. Ping.

A fresh rush of fear spiraled through her. Diving at the floor,

Callie lunged for cover, feeling heat sting across her thigh. Clutching her leg, she shot a glance downward. Material split, a hot red tear scorched her skin. Thankfully, the bullet hadn't penetrated, but just grazed.

Close call. Too damn close for her liking.

Head down, she skittered across the glass-covered floor, feeling sharp pieces bite into her palms. She wanted to stay near Iollan.

Callie scrambled to her feet. The back exit loomed just a few feet away. Her mouth almost watered. Freedom. "Let's just get the hell out."

Propelled by the action, Iollan didn't seem to hear her. Like a demon possessed, he tore his way through the onslaught, challenging every man who stood in his path. The men around him were falling like flies.

Rising like an evil omen through the chaos, Roger Reinke launched forward. Raising his weapon, he screamed. "Drake!" His cry was harsh and fearless. Eyes absolutely flat and cold, he fueled his actions with pure hatred. Profile indurate, his jaw locked with determination, he made his intent frighteningly clear. He had a goal to accomplish. Nothing would get in his way.

Irritation writhed inside her, and Callie's heart rate simultaneously sped into overdrive. "Iollan, look out! He's got a gun!"

Fangs bared in menace, Iollan Drake whirled. The move was a fatal one. He turned right into the path of Roger's aim.

Face twisting cruelly, Roger Reinke fired. Again, and again.

Body coiled spring tight, Callie struggled to think clearly. *Do something!* Muscles bunching, she launched herself from her position, trying to throw herself in front of Iollan. She didn't make it, falling a few feet short. The bullets slammed in squarely and solidly, riddling his chest.

The vampire's body jerked. Struck multiple times, he was slammed against the wall by the force of the bullets. As if in slow motion, he slid to the floor. Eyes wide and glazed with pain, he bled from the wounds. Dark stains spread through his shirt, soaking it.

Lips trembling before she pressed them together, Callie felt sick to her stomach. She was responsible for this. Her senses reeled, but her mind remained amazingly clear in the eye of the storm.

Shock morphed into anger. Her response came automatically. She didn't stop to consider the consequences.

Callie reared back on her haunches. Aware of the weapon in her hand, she raised the gun, pointing it Roger's way. Revenge was within her grasp. Adrenaline searing through her veins, she seized it with both hands. She'd been trained for a moment like this, but to use deadly force against her own people would be paramount to treason.

No more thinking. Just do.

Bracing to take the bastard down, Callie slammed her finger into the trigger with vicious force. She didn't hear the blast, barely felt the recoil.

Firing, she mentally clicked off the shots. One, in passion. Two, in premeditation. Three, death penalty. Four, she didn't care anymore.

Her aim was true.

Gurgling frantically, flinging his arms out as if to stop the spray of ammo, Roger Reinke staggered. Ten, maybe twenty seconds later, he dropped like a stone. Landing with a dead thud, he shuddered like a fish out of water. His jaw flapped, but no real words came out. Only a low, streaming groan.

The crackle of voices over a walkie-talkie screeched. Answering the call, one of the agents held up his hands. "Cease fire, cease fire," he commanded. "All agents stand down immediately."

Guns were lowered. Everything went dead still. Everyone looked dazed.

The ongoing silence pumped up the tension to an unbearable degree. The silence telegraphed how badly everything had gone awry in the space of a few minutes.

The sound of death is silence . . . a terrible nothingness . . .

Nostrils flaring, Callie wiped her nose on her sleeve and drew in a ragged breath. The smothering atmosphere reeked with the stench of gunpowder, torn flesh, and blood.

She gagged, panting to keep from passing out. A thick layer of sweat drenched her, trickling down between her breasts, chilling her to the bone. Pulse racing, she exuded the scent of unadulterated fear. Disoriented by the carnage surrounding her, she began to tremble uncontrollably, barely capable of understanding the severe trauma overwhelming her senses.

Fighting to keep panic at bay, Callie drew herself up. Though their weapons were drawn, none of the other agents fired. Like her, they seemed stunned, in shock. Even Doctor Yuan stood motionless, surveying the ruin around her like the survivor of a terrible storm.

The chills were subsiding, and strength was returning to her numb limbs. So much had occurred in the space of a few minutes that her bewildered mind barely took in the many separate events.

Only one thought came through loud and clear. Iollan needed help. Fast.

Scrambling to her downed lover, Callie sank to her knees beside him. Putting her weapon aside, she tore open his bloody shirt. Her eyes searched every inch of his chest, zeroing in on the damages. Seven small round holes pierced his pale skin.

Shit. This was bad. Very bad.

Callie swore under her breath. "Christ." No way he'd survive such a massive dose to his system. She pressed her hands to the wounds, trying to staunch the flow of his life from his body. The muscles in her arms barely worked. Sticky blood covered her hands. His skin was cold, ice cold. His usually bright eyes were dark, alarmingly dulled. She began to shake.

A tear tracked down her cheek, then another. She clutched one of his hands and silently willed her strength into his battered body. "Don't die, damn you." Prayers, pleas, and promises tumbled together in her skull. If only he'd live, she'd never leave him.

Iollan's eyes flickered open. He blinked several times, as if fighting to regain his focus on her face. His dull gaze collided with hers. Icy fingers tightened on hers. "What makes you think I'm going to die, love?"

She flinched, jaw clenching in a tight spasm of surprise. "What?"

Struggling into a sitting position, Iollan closed his eyes, then opened them again, pulling in a deep breath. He lifted a shaking hand to his chest. "The fucker loaded me with lead." A weak laugh escaped him. He grimaced, fangs retracting back into normal teeth. He actually made a face, winking. "Painful, but survivable."

Her heart slowed to a normal beat. Relief jazzed along her nerve endings, then had her shaking her head in admiration. Unable to argue, Callie gazed at her own weapon, the one she'd used on Roger. Not that standard issue service weapon at all, but the specially modified version that fired the special ampoules of liquid silver.

More agents burst in, weapons drawn.

As they rushed toward her, Callie snatched her weapon, now useless. In her confusion she wasn't sure what she'd do. Hit them with it maybe.

She didn't have to.

As the men neared, she recognized familiar faces advancing through the ruins of the lab. Samuel Faber, Mitch Reeve, and Charlie Grayson. Professor Forque followed in their wake. And, thank the gods above, Paul Norton.

Seeing Doctor Yuan, Reeve and Grayson went into immediate action. Handcuffs were produced, snugly applied. The good doctor was taken away.

Pressing past the men, Norton rushed to Callie's side. "It's over," he breathed. "Project Shadow-Wing is no more."

Callie felt the tension in her body drain away. All her prayers had been answered. *Thank you, God.* "You got the disk out?"

Behind him, Samuel Faber seconded the news with a grave nod. "We had no idea what was really going on. Now that we do, this division of the ASD is shutting down." He glanced at Doctor Yuan's unhappy figure. "Permanently."

Faber's words registered inside Callie's brain, but she couldn't move a muscle. She felt as if she'd been worked over from head to toe with a steel rod.

It's over.

Callie made no comment. Too busy trying to process it all, she glanced at Iollan. He met her gaze and held it fast. Hand searching for and finding hers, he smiled slowly and seductively. She hadn't lost him.

With their fingers locked together, Callie couldn't look away. Her world went wet and blurry. A single tear rolled down her cheek. On the surface nothing made sense. In her heart, everything did.

And that was all that mattered.

30

Callie gathered her heavy coat around her shoulders and stepped out into the night. It was chilly outside, the late night wind frosted with the hint of the coming winter.

She looked around. At close to midnight, the streets were nearly empty, deserted at such a late hour. Clouds, thick and purplish, hung low to the ground. A light fog misted the air, perfectly suiting her chilly mood.

Outside the building where she'd spent the last three months giving her testimony, the city seemed like a wasteland. In the wake of the meltdown with the ASD, a commission had been appointed to investigate its operations. Not a lot of good had emerged from the inquiry either.

Roger Reinke still had his job. *Damn it.* She wished she'd had more than silver to pump the bastard with. Given the chance again, she wouldn't hesitate.

Neither would Roger.

Without any real purpose or destination in mind, Callie started to walk, passing her car in the otherwise empty parking lot. She didn't know where she was going. She just wanted to walk, feel the mist on her face, the tug of the night's breeze through her hair. She didn't suppose it mattered where she went now, or if she ever arrived at any specific destination. Nobody would miss her if she didn't.

Technically, she was out of a job. But she hadn't been fired. She'd quit, too emotionally wounded to care that her career had slipped through her fingers. Tomorrow was Friday. At least she'd have the weekend to think about her future. Monday loomed ahead, empty. She had no place to be. No place she belonged to anymore. Her career was over. Finito.

Digging in her coat pocket, Callie paused to fish out a cigarette. Her lighter seemed to be missing. Damn. She dug deeper.

Footsteps sounded behind her.

She froze. Her heart quickened in her chest. Fatalistically, she fought the urge to turn around. If someone was going to walk up and put a bullet in the back of her head, now would be the time to do it. No one would see anything, nor hear the shot.

Anxiety knotted her gut. No use trying to run. She wasn't fast enough to outsprint a speeding bullet.

Callie placed her cigarette between her lips. The bastards. She wouldn't put it past the bureau to send an assassin. She knew a lot about the way they worked. Perhaps too much for her own good.

"Looks like the lady could use a light." The accented voice was familiar, too familiar.

Callie turned.

Iollan Drake stood behind her, cocky grin and all. All in black, his familiar duster flared, then settled around his legs like the wings of a raven coming to rest.

Her gaze swept him, so incredibly tall and solid. A tremble started deep in her loins. He looked good. Damn good. The night suited him. He belonged there.

Tucking away her blatant stare, she reminded herself to breathe. She wasn't sure what to expect. He'd vanished like smoke, somehow dodging through security in the melee that had followed the Project Shadow-Wing debacle. Apparently a chest full of bullets didn't prevent a vampire from shifting and getting his ass gone. The feds still wanted him. Badly. The commission's inquiry into the Niviane Idesha hadn't turned out well for his kind. Even though he'd been cleared of the fabricated charges against him for sex trafficking, the fact remained that he had killed a lot of agents. He'd also revealed abilities that, frankly, scared the living shit out of those who'd seen him in action. That kind of power had to be squelched. Permanently.

She managed to break free of the entrancing spell he wove, pulling her thoughts together. Heart flipping, she felt her knees shake. "Can't give it up," she croaked.

He leaned in close, snagging the cigarette from her lips. "You need to," came his husky whisper.

She ignored that. Too much stress to quit. "You came back. I didn't think I'd ever see you again."

Copper eyes alight, his jaw tightened. "I had to." His gaze searched her face. "There's one thing I had to find out."

"What?" She wanted to kiss him. Yearning threatened to burst every cell in her body. She'd give her soul to taste his lips just one more time before—

Iollan's question dragged her out of her thoughts. "Are you . . ." He stared at her expectantly, waiting.

Callie knew what he meant to ask. Maybe she should lie, to spare his feelings. A spurt of guilt negated that idea. "No." Her hand pressed to her middle. He had the right to know the truth. Suddenly she felt like she'd shatter into tiny little pieces. "I lost the baby, miscarried. No one ever knew . . ." Yuan had taken her samples too early. She'd tested negative, thank God.

Making love to him hadn't been the smartest move, and she hadn't managed to come out unscathed. Though her body showed no lingering aftereffect of their brief relationship, her heart still carried scars. Deep scars.

She didn't blame Iollan. His sudden desertion had been necessary for his own survival. The miscarriage was her fault. Smoking double, eating little, and stressing over the commission's investigation, the long months spent working late nights . . . Having the child just wouldn't have been possible, given the atmosphere of growing fear and paranoia.

She'd survive. She always had.

Iollan looked straight at her. The silvery mist reflected in the depths of his copper eyes, making them shine with an otherworldly brilliance. His hand rose, brushing her cheek. By the look on his face he also remembered their nights together. "I suspected you were," he said, words hitched as his throat worked. "It's why I had to come back. I needed to know."

His caress blazed like a torch on her chilled skin. She shook her head. Desolate tears sprang to her eyes. Foolish. "It's for the better, considering . . . the circumstances."

Silence stretched out.

Iollan's hand fell away. He leaned in close, scowling. His teeth flashed in the darkness, a brief hint of fangs, then none. "That we're still enemies?"

An image of her throat, torn, invaded her skull. Not a comfortable thought at all. A flood of goose bumps washed over her. Fear briefly chased alarm. "Technically, yes." Though the commission had shut down Project Shadow-Wing, behind closed doors the government's committee had also decided that the Niviane Idesha posed a threat to the public.

Though most of the agents and research staff involved had testified that the vampires were, for the most part, a benign race, other voices had vehemently argued the opposite. The commission decided that action must be immediately taken to contain the rogue species.

Callie squeezed her eyes shut, hating to deliver the news. Misery laced her conscience into tight psychic knots. "A new task force is being spearheaded. The hunt will continue for your kind. Complete termination of the species is the goal." Guilt stripped her raw, bare, and to the bone. She tried to wrap her mind around the commission's decision and failed. Stupid fucks. What they couldn't control, they feared. What they feared, they'd wipe out. Exterminate.

His somber expression communicated in a loud volume. "Even though they were killing us, they're still afraid." Quiet bitterness laced his words.

"What you did at the compound frightened a lot of people," she said.

Iollan drew a miserable breath. His face blanked, as if he was having trouble deciding what emotion to settle on. Anger, remorse, resignation. All nipped at his heels, making him a miserable man. "What I did was wrong. We were never to use our gifts to harm." Voice going low, he finished. "I've done that, broken the covenant."

Callie refused to let him punish himself. Enough of that had already happened. "You defended yourself." She paused, letting a brief silence load her words. "And you defended me."

Rubbing the back of his neck with an anxious hand, Iollan settled on anger. "And I would do it again, given the chance."

She took a step toward him, wanting to comfort him. Shaking his head, he backed stiffly away. Damn. He was going to bolt. She just knew it. Forcing herself to be still, make no sudden move, she shoved her hands into her pockets. "There's nothing wrong with what you did. Don't ever think it."

The corner of his mouth lifted in rueful irony. His face shadowed. "And in doing that, I've condemned all my kind to slaughter."

All true, damn it.

Iollan sighed. "For safety, we've all scattered again, each of us going our own way. Cadyn, Toryn, many others . . . Hopefully they will each find their place in a world that doesn't welcome our kind."

Nausea welled up inside her. There was more he needed to know. "I wasn't appointed to work with the new task force," she informed him quietly. "Because of what happened between us I'm considered"—her fingers rose, making quote marks in the air—"expendable."

Iollan looked away. For a moment he seemed to hover between fight or flight. "So that's how things stand?" His sigh barely reached her ears, so soft as to be one of resignation.

The breath stalled in her lungs. "Yes." She moistened her lips, sucking in a heavy breath. "But I don't give a shit. It's not my problem anymore."

He wasn't expecting good news. "Oh?" Bitterness edged the single word.

Callie's words came out in a rush. "I don't work for the bureau or the ASD anymore. I resigned. Just tonight before they got a chace to fire me—or commit me."

Iollan looked like she'd hit him with a sledgehammer. "Are you kidding?"

She tilted her head back, looking into his open, beautiful face. "No, I'm not." A scared laugh escaped her. "In fact, I'm scared shitless now. I know too much and people who know too much usually don't live very long."

Iollan took a step closer. His big hands wrapped around her arms, possessively claiming. He lowered his head. Callie thought he was going to kiss her. Hands slipping around her waist, he pressed his forehead to hers. "Then come with me."

Callie stood rigid, unable to move. Her pulse leapt. The weight of his hands on her hips, the smell of his skin, so fresh in the bracing crisp night, dizzied her. His touch never failed to make her all warm and gooey inside. Erotic thoughts were difficult to ignore. Just the thought of making love to him and she was toast with a capital *T.*

Heart pounding, her body tingled clear down to her fingertips. "I . . . I don't know."

He smiled and her blood heated all over again. "You do know," he murmured.

Iollan Drake was right. She did know. And she was scared to death.

Suddenly his mouth was on hers, sweet and burning hot. Pure, raw emotion filled her. When his tongue speared hers, she reveled in the primitive contact of mouth on mouth. A fireball of need exploded.

Her hips jerked and her thighs trembled. Groaning long and low, Callie pressed her body against his. She was already wet and hot, consumed inside with voracious lust.

Their kiss broke.

Reluctant to pull away, Iollan cupped her face and nuzzled her, nipping her bottom lip with his teeth. The tease was warm and sensual, sending her mind into an endless dizzy spiral. "I'll do anything to convince you." His hands slid lower. Cupping her rear, he guided her hips to his. His tight jeans barely contained his growing erection. He pressed harder, letting her feel his full length. "Anything."

He'd drawn her in, deep and fast. His words made her all hot and shivery. Invisible fingers wrapped around her soul, compressing with a powerful hold. "Mighty convincing."

The way he touched her never failed to arouse her. Just the thought of his cock made her want to toss off her clothes right then and there.

Iollan's mouth dipped toward her ear. "Come with me, Calista. Don't make me walk away alone."

Lost. Without him in her life these last few months, she'd been lost. Utterly lost. Now she had a chance to walk away clean, leave the past behind. To him, she was Calista, not Caroline. She never had to *be* Caroline again if she didn't want to. And why would she? Caroline knew only trouble and turmoil. Calista . . . well, she'd have a clean slate, start her life over. The idea was attractive. What did she have to lose?

Nothing.

The muscles in her stomach coiled, tight and anxious. Did they stand a chance? Or should she back away and let him go? The answer whipped into her mind with the speed of light. A little shiver wrung every drop of doubt from her cells. She sighed with contentment. "Never."

Iollan tightened his hold. "Don't you mean forever?"

About to answer, Callie never got the chance. His mouth covered hers before she could change her mind. Not that she would. She belonged to him now.

Embracing his destiny.

Embracing his midnight.

Turn the page for a preview of
RUNNNG WILD,
by Lucinda Betts!

On sale now!

1

Silence smothered the dunes as the officiating *klerin* held up his arms, his black sleeves rippling in the hot breeze. "We will begin," he said deliberately when all eyes were upon him. "We will greet the morning sun to initiate the marriage ceremony, joining the lands of the Sultan and the Raj through the beds of Raj ir Adham and Princess Shahrazad."

Shahrazad stifled a shiver. Haniyyah should have been wedding the Raj, but instead her head stared at her from the Pike Wall, her cousin's once lustrous skin now waxy and pale. Talking to the soldier had been enough to negate the engagement, but touching him . . . What had possessed Haniyyah to touch a man? Shahrazad would never emulate that behavior.

"Please, begin," the Sultan commanded the *klerin* from the opposite dune. "The sun awaits your salutation."

The *klerin* nodded, closed his hands together over his heart, then turned toward the sunrise. As the *klerin*'s salutation flowed from one asana to another, he took the warrior's stance, the same one he had used to behead her foolish cousin. God hold her in his eyes, she would miss her.

The hot sand burned through the soles of her slippers, but Shahrazad didn't move. She didn't lift her eyes. She had never spoken to an unrelated man. And by God's eyes, she never would touch one. Ever.

"Princess Shahrazad?" a man's voice asked from several steps behind her. She jumped, and the tiny golden bells on her wedding veil jangled in the desert's morning heat. The *klerin* glared at her interruption.

"Hush," her mother-in-law-to-be whispered to her. "Do not embarrass my son."

"I heard a man—" she started to whisper, but her nurse caught her eye and gently shook her head.

"There is no man in the women's tent," the old woman said, her lips barely moving. Her kohl-rimmed eyes didn't leave the *klerin* as she added, "How could there be?"

Despite the sun beating down on the silk canopy, the words chilled her—she had heard a man's voice.

"Princess, come to me," the intruder whispered again, his words sliding over her like a snake.

Who was he? Her husband-to-be stood below, his broad face impassive, his blond hair tucked neatly into his gold turban. She caught another glimpse of her cousin's head, Haniyyah's black hair floating around her lifeless face. Shahrazad felt faint, and the desert seemed to swim and ooze around her. Was she hallucinating?

"You will come to me," the stranger said, his words more insistent. Wasn't that his robe brushing the backs of her calves? She couldn't be imagining that. Why didn't her mother-in-law-to-be stop him? Why didn't her nurse?

"You'll not belong to the Raj ir Adham," the stranger said in her ear. Now she could feel the heat of his body through her silk *oraz*, smell his oddly feminine scent of gardenia blossoms. If he leaned forward . . .

If he leaned forward and touched her, her world would crash. If he touched her, she was ruined.

"You'll belong to me."

Something in her snapped. She jerked her chin hard, making her bells ring again, loudly this time.

The noise made the *klerin* stop in the middle of his sun salutation, and he glared into the women's tent. "Obey the rules," her mother-in-law-to-be said as Duha looked at her, worry etched in her ancient face.

"Look behind me," Shahrazad whispered. "Who is it?"

Ignoring the glowering *klerin*, her mother-in-law-to-be looked quickly where directed. With a tight expression, she shook her head. "There is no one," she hissed. "How could there be? What in God's eyes is wrong with you?"

"But—"

The woman hardened her features and pointedly looked away, and the *klerin* continued his chant.

She heard a shifting of robes behind her. "You'll be mine," the stranger said. "And you'll enjoy every heartbeat of it."

She froze absolutely, like a mouse hypnotized by a cobra's gaze.

And then he touched her. He actually ran his fingertips over the small of her back. He stroked her flesh. "I can grant your heart's desire," the stranger whispered in her ear, his breath heating her skin.

Before she could move, before she could draw in one more breath, shame enveloped her. She was spoilt—and she'd ruined her family's chance to survive the *shitani* invasion.

She could not bear this.

"Leave me alone!" she said, turning toward her assailant, her bells jangling even after her voice died. Below her the *klerin* stopped speaking, but more chilling, Shahrazad saw no man, only an empty spot where the man should be standing.

"I will take you from here," her mother-in-law-to-be hissed. "My son will wed a more stable woman."

Was she insane? Shahrazad's eyes fell on the Pike Wall and her cousin's dead eye seemed to wink at her. *You'll join me here*, she seemed to say. But Shahrazad couldn't let that happen. The *shitani* would lick up her land with their demonic tongues, tear it up with their demonic claws.

"I am sorry, mother-in-law-to-be," she said, keeping her eyes down. "I don't know what's come over me."

"I'll come all over you," the man breathed in her ear.

Channeling her rage, Shahrazad realized she needed to do something drastic. She was not crazy.

The heat of the man's body told her exactly where he stood, even if her eyes hadn't seen him. She knew where to strike. Lifting her foot so gracefully that not one of her bells rang, she kicked back with all her might, aiming for his groin.

Her face hit the woman standing in front of her, bruising her lip. Her mother-in-law-to-be fell into her neighbor as Shahrazad's elbow slammed into her chest. A masculine yelp started to come from the throat of her assailant, and then—silence.

She stumbled again as the body behind her unexpectedly vanished.

Duha sent her a worried glance, the wattles on her old neck shaking as she clutched Shahrazad's arm and refused to release it. Her aunts and cousins stared too, but her mother-in-law-to-be tightly shook her head, refusing to dignify the fiasco.

The invisible stranger hadn't doubled over in pain as she'd expected—he'd simply vanished.

And Shahrazad thought she might faint. The touch from this disappearing man could mean only one thing: a magician had cursed her, cursed her marriage.

And no one defeated a magician.

* * *